"WELL, WELL, IT'S MUD-FACE. SO YOU SQUIRMED YOUR WAY HERE."

Aleytys turned slowly, trying to control the surge of fear and anger that shook her when she heard that deep fluid voice, a voice she'd heard only one time waking, a thousand times since in nightmare.

"Mud," he said. "Look at that, all of you. Look at what you want to call Vryhh. I will not, I will not have that slime call itself Vryhh. I will NOT." Silence from all the Vrya in the dome. "To the death, Mud," Kell said into that silence. "I declare war between us. I declare that you and any who try to help you, Mud, will die at the hands of me and mine."

Mastering her own rage, Aleytys sucked in a breath, let it out. "To the death, cousin," she said at last. . . .

JO CLAYTON has written:

The DIADEM Saga

DIADEM FROM THE STARS
LAMARCHOS
IRSUD
MAEVE
STAR HUNTERS
THE NOWHERE HUNT
GHOSTHUNT
THE SNARES OF IBEX
QUESTER'S ENDGAME

The DUEL OF SORCERY Series

MOONGATHER
MOONSCATTER
CHANGER'S MOON

others

A BAIT OF DREAMS
DRINKER OF SOULS

QUESTER'S ENDGAME

A Novel of the Diadem

Jo Clayton

DAW BOOKS, INC.

DONALD A. WOLLHEIM, PUBLISHER

1633 Broadway, New York, NY 10019

DAW Collectors Book No. 677

First Printing, July 1986

3   4   5   6   7   8   9

PRINTED IN U.S.A.

WHO'S WHO AND WHAT'S WHAT

For old readers of the series who are obviously folk of
intelligence and taste but alas not Mento-the-Marvels capable
of memorizing telephone books and regurgitating the contents
on cue, for new readers who are courageously plunging into
the ninth (and last) book about Aleytys and the diadem, here's
a combination orientation and memory jogger.

ALEYTYS:
Born in a mountain valley called the vadi
Raqsidan on a world called Jaydugar,
raised in an agrarian, preindustrial culture. Psi-empath and translator, healer,
flamethrower and worrier. She's had
one child, a son, had him stolen from
her before he was a year old, gave him
up again when he was about four. She
acquired the diadem after she ran from
a barbecue where she was going to be
the roastee. In her travels from world
to world, while she was searching for
her mother, she was (among other
things) sold as a slave to provide meat
for a wasp queen's egg, then she rode
a smuggler's ship as his bedmate and
translator. Finally she got a steady job
with Hunters Inc on Wolff. In the bits
of time left over from her struggles to
survive and go on with her search for
her mother, she got to know more about
the diadem and the entities trapped

v

within it, acquiring three live-in friends and critics. Sometimes it got very crowded inside her skull.

DIADEM, the:

An artifact from an ancient extinct civilization. Both a trap and an instrument of great flexibility and power. A focus for psi-forces, a prison for the self-aware part of the wearer once the wearer's body is dead. Gold-wire lilies with jewel hearts set on a chain of flat gold links. Once it's on someone's head it can't be removed until that person's dead or until it's temporarily deactivated. It swims easily from reality to reality, invisible until its powers are called on. When Aleytys first acquired it, she had almost no control over it; as she learned to know those within it, her control increased but was never complete.

HARSKARI:

The first to be caught. Jealous of her skills, angry at the breakup of their relationship, an ex-lover constructed the diadem and gave it to Harskari saying it was a peace offering. As soon as she put it on, he killed her and threw her body into a volcano, where it burned to ash. The diadem with her consciousness trapped within was untouched. Her lover's revenge. In the course of time, the diadem was ejected from the volcano during an eruption, and lay sealed inside a clump of lava for eons until the working of wind and water eroded it loose. All this time Harskari was awake and aware of the nothing around her, hanging on to her sanity by the fingernails she didn't have. Civilizations rose and fell around her. The sun went nova and ashed the life off the world. And still she was awake, aware. More time passed. A wandering singer happened by, landed to do some repair work on the rusty cobbled-together wreck she was flying world to world. She found the diadem, dusted it off, was enchanted by its loveliness and set it on her head. And Harskari finally had some company.

SHADITH: Singer and poet, the last of her kind. The second trapped and the second freed. In the early days when Aleytys was still ignorant of any technology more complicated than a water mill, Shadith provided instruction and information and occasionally took control of Aleytys's body and talents to deal with things that were dangerous mysteries to the mountain girl. Shadith is now installed in the body of a young girl, a hawk rider killed in a skirmish on Ibex. Shadith prodded Aleytys into repairing the body and sliding her into it, stabilizing her in the emptied flesh. She looks about fourteen, a slight energetic girl with café-au-lait skin, chocolate eyes, brown-gold hair a riot of tiny curls. In her original body—different appearance, different species—she crashed on a primitive world and lay moldering in the ruins of her ship for several millennia until one of the natives happened on her ship and took the diadem from her crumbling skull.

SWARDHELD: The third of the trapped entities. Raised in his father's smithy, meant to follow his father's trade as swordsmith and armorer. Driven from that by his restless, rebellious nature (a repellent brat, he told Aleytys), he joined a mercenary band so he could eat, rose to be companion and war leader to a shrewd and devious man who managed to put together a small but thriving empire, had to flee when the man was poisoned, discovered the diadem, came back out of the mountains to avenge his friend and commander, became an emperor of sorts himself with the help of the diadem, was poisoned in his turn and joined the other trapped spirits. On a world called Nowhere he was sucked out of the diadem by a floating ghost (a creature that preyed on life force), but when the ghost was distracted by an attack from Aleytys, he broke free of it and slipped into the body of a man just stripped of life. Supported by Aleytys and the others, he managed to spark new life in the abandoned flesh and found himself embodied for the first time in millennia. This accident and its outcome showed Aleytys that it was possible for Harskari and Shadith to acquire bodies of their own if they wanted them and found suitable ones.

RMOAHL, the: The diadem lay in their treasure vault for generations until it was stolen by Miks Stavver. They are intelligent, unaggressive, communal, hierarchical, spiderish beings. And very very patient. They are fanatical about their treasures; what they have, they intend to keep. They will go to just about any lengths to regain what is lost, though they avoid causing pain or injury almost as fanatically; their fearsome appearance is to some degree deceptive; though they will fight effectively if driven to it.

STAVVER, MIKS: According to him, he's the best thief in known space. A compulsive gambler. Challenged by impossibilites. The only way to steal anything from the RMoahl and make a profit on it was to get rid of it very quickly indeed; the RMoahl hounds would go after the object and forget the thief. His plans went seriously awry, he crashed on Jaydugar, lost the diadem to a trio of local witches who passed it to Aleytys, collected Aleytys and got them both offworld. He was her lover for a while and later, after they parted, played surrogate father to her son when the boy ran away from home. Gambling fever eventually did him in when he wagered money he didn't have with beings who had no sense of humor.

SHAREEM: A Vryhh. Aleytys's mother. Caught in the delirium of a swamp fever, she crashed on Jaydugar; too sick to defend herself, she was enslaved and sold to the Azdar, Aleytys's father. She recovered from the fever to find herself pregnant. As soon as Aleytys was able to manage without her, she left a letter telling her daughter about her and how to find her, then wangled her way offworld, back to the life she was leading before the disastrous days on Jaydugar.

KELL:

A Vryhh. He loathes the thought of a half-breed Vryhh and has tried before to destroy Aleytys. He maneuvered reactionary, power-seeking Watukuu into secretly rebelling and trying to take over a colony world in order to use it as a base to attack the government of the homeworld; then he maneuvered that homeworld government into hiring Hunters Inc to deal with the rebellion. He played games with the mind of Canyli Heldeen, the director of Hunters Inc, so that she assigned Aleytys to the Hunt. He captured Aleytys and started to torment her, but with the backing of the Three, she defeated him, then let her need to heal dictate her actions, something she was sorry for almost as soon as it was done.

LINFYAR:

Aleytys went to Ibex to find Kenton Esgard; according to the instructions her mother left in that letter, he could put the two of them in touch. When Aleytys arrived, she found his daughter Hana in charge of his house and business while he was roaming over Ibex, driven by his need to extend his life, hunting a place called Sil Evareen where men were supposed to live forever. In her search for him, shortly after Shadith acquired her body, Aleytys came across a small boy running away from home and castration. He had an extraordinarily beautiful soprano voice and his owner wanted to keep it unchanged. He is about nine years old, covered head to toe with short, very soft mottled brown fur. He was born without eyes, only faint furry hollows where they would have been. His mobile pointed faun's ears can hear sounds far beyond the normal range of mammal ears; he has assorted proximity senses that serve him almost as well as sight, and echo location for more distant objects. He learned very early the arts of surviving in a place where children born visibly mutant were put outside the gates once they were weaned and left to the whims of weather and the hunger of predators. Aleytys means to send him to University where he can get an education and further training in music. He is not enthusiastic about this idea and keeps poking about for some ways to postpone (preferably forever) such a dreary outcome to his adventures.

WOLFF
warning bell
distance and direction obscure

Aleytys stepped from the cradle lift and shivered in the raw wind. She'd returned to spring mud and damp spring bluster, winter having come and gone while she walked across Ibex. Behind her she heard Linfyar's complaining chatter as he felt that wind in spite of his fur and the blanket he had wrapped about him, heard Shadith's impatient replies. Smiling a little, she started for the terminal building across the stained and cracking metacrete. Wolff's starport was kept deliberately crude and unwelcoming, only a rough field with a few battered cradles for ships and shuttles, a squat mud-colored terminal whose sole grace was a steep roof where dark red tiles rose to a peak; the Wolfflan wanted no outsiders tempted to stay and put pressure on scarce resources.

When she rounded the corner of the terminal, Aleytys saw Canyli and Tamris Heldeen standing beside a flitter, the icy wind blowing their coats and scarves into a shapeless flurry about them. Grey wasn't there. *Is he still furious with me?* She shortened her stride, excitement and anticipation beginning to drain out of her.

Head's smile was wide and warm. "There's a prance in your walk. You found what you wanted." She held the back door open, stood watching with quiet interest as Shadith herded Linfyar inside and settled beside him. Tamris followed them in and sat beside Shadith.

Aleytys slipped into the forward seat, wriggled around and sighed as Head took her place at the console. "I hope this doesn't mean you've got another Hunt I can't refuse," she

1

said, an amiable weariness in her voice. "I've got a visitor coming."

"No . . . um . . . not a Hunt . . ."

Aleytys turned to stare at Head, surprised by the hesitation and uncertainty in the words.

"You were gone longer than I expected."

"Ibex was complicated. Where's Grey?"

"Hunt."

Aleytys made a soft annoyed sound. "I thought he was done with all that."

"He was restless, needed a distraction. And Hagan was needling him. He thought he'd better get out before he lost his temper and made things worse for us."

"Hardheaded idiot." Aleytys moved restlessly. "When is he due back?"

"Seven months ago."

"What?"

"He's disappeared."

"Disappeared?" It came out scratchy. Her throat was suddenly dry.

"Wait till we get to your house. The reports are there."

"Right." She looked at her hands, expecting to see them tremble, surprised that they lay still on her thighs. She pressed down hard on the long muscles. "Is he dead?"

"I don't know."

Aleytys slid down in the seat. She couldn't comprehend it. *Seven months. Grey. . . .* She stirred restlessly. "What's doing with my home share?"

"Hanging fire." Head went silent as she edged the flier between two peaks of the angular and austerely beautiful mountains ringing the cup that held the port, mocking the mud and ugliness of the field. "We've just finished a fight over Dristig's seat in the Forsaemal. I wanted Grey on the Hunters board with me and Hagan knew it. He and his toadies started a nasty compaign against Grey. And you." Head chuckled. "Backfired on him. You weren't here." Another chuckle. "Maybe the best thing you ever did for me. Wolfflan don't like backbiting. He did drive Grey into taking the Hunt, thought he'd won, but we ran Sybille instead. He could handle Grey, make him explode and say things he wouldn't otherwise, but Sybille tied him in knots, made that snerp Lukkit he was pushing look like a halfwit, couldn't chew and walk at the same time. She took Dristig's seat in a sweep.'' She was almost cheerful now, talking with an ease missing at the beginning of the flight. ''Hagan's the next to go to the Wolfflan for confirmation.'' Her nose twitched. ''I'd appreciate it if you were on Hunt when that happens. It's going to be a bastard of a fight.''

''Grey?''

''If he's back by then. I know I promised not to push you, Lee. . . .'' She took the flitter up over a skim of clouds, shot a questioning half-smile at Aleytys, her thick pewter brows raised over rounded eyes. With a self-mocking shake of her head, she punched in the course for Aleytys's house. ''We'll have your home share put through by then. Sybille's working on it.''

''Thanks.'' Aleytys settled her head against the rest and stared up at the flitter's roof, seeing instead the leggy black orb of the RMoahl ship waiting out beyond Teegah's limit with that cursed patience, that not quite threat. Wanting their diadem. Stavver was luckier than he knew, getting rid of the thing. She wondered briefly what he and Sharl were doing, expecting to feel the familiar loss and longing as she thought of her son. Nothing. Still numb. She was as detached as if she were a ghost riding her own shoulders watching her body perform, pulling its strings.

The snow had melted around her house, though droppings of dirty white remained where shade was deepest under the trees. The gardens were mud slopping about struggling plants, and in the field by the stream her horses grazed at withered grass just pushing up new green shoots. Head set the flitter down in the paved patio on the south side of the house.

A fire crackled briskly, driving the unused chill from the sitting room; a pot of cha waited on a table beside a comfortable leather chair. Aleytys felt the numbness break inside her, pain at loss and pleasure at being home mixing uneasily in her. She dropped into the chair and stared into the flames,

quivering all over, fighting to keep control. Tamris poured
the tea and passed the cups around. She tapped Aleytys on
the shoulder. "Lee?"

Aleytys sucked in a breath, let it out in a ragged sigh.
"Please." She gulped at the cha, and the warmth spreading
through her eased some of the shaking. Tamris filled the cup
for her again, and she emptied it as quickly as she had the
first, then she set the cup aside and turned to face Canyli
Heldeen. "Tell me about it."

Head touched the fax sheets in her lap, lifted the top sheet,
put it back. "He left three weeks after you did. Told me he'd
been a fool, that his head was so scrambled he wasn't up to
dealing with Hagan, so he was going to clear out awhile. A
clutch of Pajunggs was here, looking for you, as usual, but
willing to settle for any Hunter they could get." She fingered
the fax sheets and sighed. "Simple Hunt, a find-and-snatch.
Should have taken Grey a couple of weeks, a month at the
outside." She cleared her throat, held out her cup for her
daughter to fill, using the time to examine Aleytys, her
shrewd light eyes flicking from face to hands and back.

Aleytys said nothing, sat gazing at the fire, waiting for her
to go on.

Head cleared her throat again, set the cup down. "I didn't
start worrying about him when he was gone a month—
sometimes the simple ones turn wild on you. After three
months, it wasn't a question of worrying. The Pajunggs were
getting nervous too; they wanted to know what was happening. I sent Ticutt over to Avosing to find out what Grey was
up to. First thing he reported was that Grey had got to Keama
Dusta—that's the only city; it's a colony planet, sparsely
settled, just a part of one continent. Anyway, Grey got that
far, spent a few days nosing about, then he vanished. Went
into the forest and didn't come out. You know Ticutt; Me-
thodical's his middle name. He set up a satellite drop, Grey's
ship, sent coded reports to it every night, and a squealer
pulsed them over to us. Then he went into the forest as Grey
had. And the reports stopped. That was three months ago.
Pajunggs been on my back. Very unhappy. But I waited

for you. Hagan's been exercising his tongue, or was until Sybille asked if he was volunteering.''

''Ah.'' Aleytys sat up. ''And you want me to do the volunteering.''

''If you will.''

A strained silence settled over the room. The fire crackled noisily, snapping and hissing; tendrils of adoradee vine tapped at the tall narrow windows, a jittery slithery noise. The leather creaked under Aleytys as she shifted position. ''He'd really hate it, you know. Me running after him like an overprotective mother after a half-wit child. Madar, Canyli!'' She slapped her hand down on the chair arm, the sound loud and abrupt. Linfyar spilled cha on his leg, yipped and began rubbing at his fur with a napkin Shadith pushed into his hand.

Shadith watched Aleytys, worried. She knew too much about the ups and downs of the relationship between Grey and Aleytys and too much about the bitter strength of the bond between them. She switched her gaze to Head and thought about what the woman had just said: *I waited for you.* TRAP. The word popped to the front of her mind and quivered there in big black letters. She bit her lip, wondering if she should wait or say something, but kept quiet when Aleytys spoke again.

''What a choice you give me,'' she said. ''In a few weeks my mother will be here to take me to Vrithian. You know how long I've waited for that.'' Absently she brushed at her hair. Her hand shook a little; she brought it quickly down and clasped it with the other. ''But what if I am the only one who can pull him out of that hole? Him and Ticutt? If they aren't dead already.'' She bent forward, her hair falling forward to hide her face. Shudders moved in waves through her body. Shadith got up from the floor where she was sitting beside Linfyar and went to kneel by Aleytys, cradling Lee's shaking hands in hers.

''I've thought of that,'' Head said softly. ''I've also thought about another time when someone came to us with a Hunt that was something else. Grey sucked in might be an accident; Ticutt makes it a habit. A habit we have to break, Lee. We're in the bind we kept putting you in—we can't afford to fail. Our reputation is only as good as its last manifestation. We'll have to send in another Hunter to finish the job, but we can't go on dropping drachs down that hole. Two of the top four left, Sybille and Taggert, but I don't think the outcome would be different. Eventually we have to come to you. Interesting, isn't it? We *have* to come to you.''

Shadith felt a jolt pass through Aleytys, nodded to herself. "Trap," she said, "because you're close to reaching Vrithian."

Aleytys freed her hands, pressed the heels of the palms against her eyes, pulled the hands down her face. "Kell."

"One of Ticutt's last reports." Head ruffled through the fax sheets, pulled one out, put it on the top. "He said he picked up a smell of an alien mixed up with the Sikin Ajin, a master designer who built some things for him that impressed the hell out of everyone around him. Just a wisp of a wisp, but after Sybille he's the best ferret we've got."

"Lee." Shadith caught hold of Aleytys's hand and shook it side to side. "Listen. Go to Vrithian. He'll come after you, he can't help it. Send me to Avosing. You know what I can do. And he won't be expecting anything like me, if he's hanging around there still. Linfy and me working together, we'll sniff out that trap and spring Grey loose before anyone knows what's happening. And Ticutt. You could probably do it better and faster, but look at it this way—you there on Vrithian, me on Avosing, we'll be coming at the same problem from different directions." She jumped to her feet. "You'll be facing Kell; you'll have the hard part. Linfy and me, well, it'll be a walk-over."

"Linfyar? No."

"Don't fuss, Lee. He's tough. Aren't you, imp?"

"Uh-huh." Linfyar flicked his pointed ears forward, then back. "I want to go, dama, I do. It's better than school." Vast contempt in the last word.

"No doubt, Linfy, but . . ."

"Lee." Shadith bent down and patted her arm. "Look, I'll take care of him. This is the best way, really it is." She straightened, turned to Head. "Want to bet Kell's had a long look at all the escrow flakes? Want to bet he's even found a way into Hunters records, knows everything about all your

Hunters, down to the way they breathe? Send Aleytys to Avosing and you maybe win, maybe lose. Send anyone else alone without backing and you lose for sure. Send a Hunter, Taggert maybe, and me, not together, working on our own, while Aleytys tackles the other end. You've got a better chance that way than any other." She spread her arms, then sketched a bow. "Aleytys isn't so good on the courtesies— she hasn't introduced me. I'm Shadith. Singer and poet. We've met but I was in another body then. Uh-huh, you got it."

Head put her hand over her mouth; her eyes danced with the laughter she couldn't quite suppress. After a minute she said, "You look about fourteen."

"So? The body is, I'm not." Shadith slanted a quick anxious glance at Aleytys, who sat stone-faced not looking at either of them, then fixed her eyes on Head. "I'm your wild card. Play me."

"You think a lot of yourself." Head's voice was dryly skeptical, the amusement gone from her eyes.

"Yeah."

"Aleytys?"

"Lee's going to Vrithian." Shadith stepped back so she could see both the women. "You have to, Lee, you know that. He wants to distract you, keep you and Shareem apart. Use that against him. Go with your mother, distract him with his own distraction, draw him off from Avosing so Taggert and I won't have to fight him, just what he's left behind." She started pacing back and forth along the hearth. "Listen to me. He knows you too well. Remember what happened the last time. He almost took you. If the three of us hadn't been there to back you, where'd you be now? He's had time to plan this. If you do what he expects, he's got you. Don't go after Grey. Shake Kell up, disappoint him, confuse him. Let me take care of the Avosing end. He'll come after you—he's got to. Vrithian is his ground, well, I know that, but it's not the ground he's got ready for you. Are you listening? Do you understand what I'm saying?"

"Is letting you get yourself killed the biggest favor I can do for you?"

"Hunh, I like your faith in me." Shadith clicked her tongue with disgust, then looked more closely at the woman sitting crouched in the big chair. "Stop trying to manipulate me. I know you, remember? I've lived in that head of yours far too long."

Aleytys sighed, straightened her back. "You don't have to beat the point to death, Shadow. I agree." She stretched her legs out, lay back in the chair, eyes closed, her face looking hollowed out. Her hands rested limp and motionless on the chair arms. "Give us everything you've got on this, will you, Canyli? Ticutt's reports, the Pajunggs' spiel. Anything else you can dig up." She lay still for several moments, then tightened her hands on the chair arms and got suddenly to her feet, a quick twisting movement so full of violence it was as if her body shouted, as if the grief, fear and fury she was holding under taut control were close to escaping her grip. "I'm going north to make a wild trek. It's something I have to do." She walked swiftly across the room, turned in the doorway. "Shadow, if Shareem comes . . . if she comes asking for me before I get back, you tell her . . . ask her . . . you know." She wheeled, knocked her shoulder against the doorframe, caught herself, then sped off down the hall, the click of her heels fading into silence.

"Ibex was difficult," Shadith said when Head turned to her, brows raised. "Painful."

Head smoothed a square hand over the short thick helmet of pewter-gray hair, the cabochon sapphire set in a heavy silver band catching light from the fire and gleaming suddenly bluer than the blue of her pale eyes. Those eyes were troubled. "She has only one of you left now."

"Yeah." Shadith rubbed her back against the edge of the fireplace. "But her mother's going to be with her. A full Vryhh. What about Taggert and me going to Avosing? Are you going to do it?"

"Have I a choice?"

"Sure. Sit on your hands. "It's me that's got no choice. To get Grey loose, it looks like I'll have to finish your Hunt for you." She sniffed with delicate disgust, then grinned at Head. "Don't you think you'd better tell me what the Hunt is?"

"It's in the data sheets." Head spoke absently, looking out one of the long narrow windows, seeing visions that disturbed her deeply. "No point in making mysteries. Avosing is a Pajungg colony, the Sikin Ajin is a Pajungg from the homeworld, was high up in the shadow government, what they call the criminal side, made enemies and skipped out, ended up on Avosing, where he stirred up a rebellion and has been a thorn in the official side. Grey was supposed to hand him over to the Colonial Authority." She rose from her chair, crossed the shadow-filled room and stood beside the window, looking out at the sunset reddening the glaciers on the mountain peaks. "They never spent much time together, one or the other off on a Hunt or testifying on Helvetia. And they had some spectacular fights. I never understood why they stayed together." She hitched a hip on the sill, leaned against the frame. "This hit her harder than I expected."

Shadith looked from Tamris to Linfyar and said nothing.

"The boy speaks interlingue quite well."

"He's a quick learner. And he sings like the angel he certainly isn't, and he has the appetite of a herd of caterpillars."

"I hear you. Tamris, take Linfyar into the kitchen and see what you can find to feed him."

Tamris wrinkled her nose, but left holding Linfyar's hand. The boy whistled a scornful trill but made no other protest about being shunted away; he was determined he was going with Shadith and didn't want to annoy her.

After the door shut behind them, Shadith said, "Some things I can't talk about, too private, but . . . The bond between them is, well, it's complicated, but it's not going away. She came out of Ibex determined to make peace with him, maybe start a baby—all that. She was excited and happy when we landed. It was a long way to fall." She wound a curl about her finger, frowned at the floor. With a sigh she raised her head. "You think he's dead."

"Why would any sane man keep him alive? Grey dead and Grey alive are equally good as bait. And Grey dead is easier to control."

"Kell's not exactly sane."

"I wouldn't count on him being as stupid as he is crazy."

"Not count on it exactly, but there's a sliver of possibility he's keeping Grey alive. Kell likes hurting things, and he knows what Grey means to Lee. I'm hoping Grey makes an acceptable substitute until he has Lee to play with." Shadith shuddered. "Weren't for Lee, I'd be hoping Grey is dead."

Head slid off the sill and began walking about the room, a sturdy squarish figure, solid as the furniture. "It's all guessing," she said. "Likely there's no trap, no devious plan, no mad plotter. Just Grey tripping over his feet." She stopped by the cha pot, lifted the lid, let it clink back down, moved on. "Just the Sikin Ajin being cleverer and more powerful than the reports make him." She stopped by the window again. "Clouding over. Be sleeting before morning. The Pajunggs lying their collective heads off, more or less normal for our clients. They all lie about something. Ticutt getting past his prime and careless for once." She stopped in front of Shadith. "It could be just that, a series of coincidences."

"Could be." Shadith traced a fingertip along the brand on her cheek, the acid-etched outline of a hawk's head. "Happens all the time. I don't believe it. Not a word. It's Kell."

"Yes." Head swung around to look at the door. "Vrithian. Will she come back?"

"Depends."

"On Grey?"

"Some. And Vrithian." Shadith stepped away from the bricks, stretched and patted a yawn. "Oh-ah, I'm tired. All this emotion. Look, Canyli, legends have a way of turning sour when you track them down. And this house, the land, the horses, they mean a lot to Lee. And she likes the work; forget how she bitches about it. And you're the best friend she's had in years. Pulling up is going to be harder than she thinks. Even if Grey *is* dead."

"I suppose it doesn't matter. We're committed whatever she decides. A matter of survival. You hungry?"

"I could eat a raving silvercoat." Shadith started for the door.

"Reminds me, you should talk Lee out of the trek. It's the worst time of the year." She opened the door and waved

Shadith through. "The silvercoats are coming out of their winter holes hungry and mean."

"Good." Shadith chuckled at the expression on Canyli's face. "She needs the toughening." They walked together in a companionable silence down the high-ceilinged hall with carved eiksjo panels and tapestries from a dozen worlds, boot heels clicking a double rhythm on the intricate parquet, heading for the stairs that led to the kitchen. "If you're worried it's a death wish, forget it. I've been with her the other times. She'll come out of it with a lot of rubbish cleared out of her system." A sigh, then a rueful short laugh. "I rather wish I were going with her."

"Why don't you?"

"No. Not this time."

Head was silent until they started down the stairs. She glanced several times at Shadith, amusement at her own hesitations and puzzlement on her face. Finally she said, "What does it feel like? Coming out after so long? I get the weirdest double impression when I look at you, ancient child." She shook her head, laughing a little. "I get the feeling I ought to mother you, and at the same time the thought appalls me."

"God! so it should."

"You had a kind of immortality. Now you could be dead and gone tomorrow."

"A short life, but a merry one." She sniffed the air. "Haa, that smells good." A flash of a grin at Head and Shadith was clattering down the last few stairs and pushing into the kitchen.

The Wildlands.
Mist and cold and fatigue.
Thicker than she remembered, the mist swirled around her, distorted what she could see of the ground so that footing was never certain, and would have disoriented her if the compass in her head hadn't kept her on the line she'd chosen. She ran through mud and slush, over ground still frozen, through patches of ghostly desiccated weeds, forcing herself on and on until she was stumbling along hardly able to lift her feet. She ran until the sun set and the darkness magnified the

sounds of stealthy movement thickening around her. She spent the night in the crude shelter the Wolfflan provided for the first night of a trek taken in this season.

In the morning she had the aches and uncertainties of her body to cope with along with the harshness of the land and the brutal cold. She began the struggle to relax into these things, to meld them into a smoothly articulated whole, knowing this would have to be done morning after morning when the night's disturbed sleep with its surges of fear and anger and grief would jar her out of that oneness of land and self. But, little by little, as the days passed and the outer world sloughed away, the days and nights would merge.

For a while her body and her memories distracted her, kept her from the center she was trying to find. Grey's ghost ran beside her in the fog, along with memories of the time she'd come here to set aside the dream of reclaiming her son. This time she came to Wolff with a dream that meant even more to her, a dream perhaps as illusory as the other.

By the fourth day she'd collected a following of silvercoats, gaunt shadows in the eternal mist, tagging her from cold camp to cold camp. There was no fuel left in this stony wilderness; whatever there had been was stripped out and used up by the first men and women coming to build the cairns and make the wild trek in pursuit of the oneness with the worldspirit that only exhaustion of mind and body would produce, that beating down of barriers between spirit and substance. Some came here driven by pride and fear and shame; most of those died, the rest of them came back empty, pride satisfied, shame and fear defeated for the moment. Nothing more. Other Wolfflan came out centered, filled, changed—enough to keep the Wild Trek from degenerating into a sterile game whose rules were only game rules that could be broken without recoil if the player chose to win no matter what. After a thousand years the Wild Trek was hammered into the flesh of the Wolfflan, into the mythology of this narrow hardy people. They seemed to know by instinct that if they gave up on this, they would start an inward spiral to destruction. Like the immortals of Ibex, she thought, and wondered if those feeble, trapped creatures had used her blood and cells to free themselves from their machines. Wondered if Kenton Esgard had begun to regret what he'd done to himself. Wondered if Hana had worked her way into the Vryhh data and got her hands on her father's business.

But those things touched her only fleetingly, phantoms in the mists, distractions from mind sores and body aches, from an anger so all-encompassing it had no focus, or rather many foci. Kell. Fate. Grey. Her own stupidities. Head. Hunters Inc. Harskari. Shadith. Shareem. Hagan. In turn and all together, she raged at them for forgetting what they were, what she was, raged at her powerlessness. No way to change the past. You could go over and over and over what had happened, what you'd done, what other people had done, you could see where you'd gone wrong, you could see what you might have done, by force of will you could make yourself believe for a few seconds that it had not happened, but you couldn't change any of it, not really, and if you lied to yourself, willfully blinded yourself, well, that was madness, a common enough madness and one that had its good points. Some things were too horrible to live with.

No fuel to fight the cold, no shelters after the first to keep off the silvercoats and that cold. After a long day's run she had to spend a racking time gathering stones and building a rough shelter so she could snatch a few hours of sleep with a degree of safety. Custom demanded that she scatter the stones, but she had to come back this way and she'd do the scattering then.

The first cairn.

She took a water-worn pebble from the pouch at her belt, stood holding it a moment. She wondered what she should say, then shrugged and tossed the pebble onto the cairn and went on loping through the fog.

Grey's ghost ran beside her through the long gray days. Neither spoke, but settled into the busy silences of snow and mist, hearing and not hearing the rhythmic body sounds, the grunts and hoarse breathing, the shish-shish of ghostly snowshoes on snow that wasn't there.

At least the snow is gone today, she thought. Grey's baby from his frozen sperm. Something to keep him alive, a part of him. No. Not now. If he was alive, if he'd be there to share the joys and irritations of raising a child, yes, oh yes, oh a hundred times yes. Without him—she'd had enough of fatherless children. No and no and no, the harsh explosive denials came with the thudding of her bootsoles. If Grey lived, if he lived, if Shadith brought him out of the trap, if he came out of Kell's torment not hating her, oh yes. Having Grey's baby now not knowing if he was alive or dead, that would be a sickly smarmy necrophilia. As she ran, she wept, slow tears that were as much grief for the child who might never be as for the man who was most likely dead.

Remembering that other run. The silence was deep between them. A shared silence. In the night camps that other time, they were sometimes lovers, sometimes just held each other. A good rich time.

Her mind was too busy. Her body had adjusted easily enough, but she was thinking and suffering, grieving and filled with anger.

The second cairn.

She stood a long time by the pile before she tossed the stone onto the sloping side, remembering all too vividly the bitter quarrel with Grey before she left for Ibex. She'd come back expecting to retrieve the relationship, to patch up once again the wounds they tore into each other. But there was no time, no chance to repair the damage. That sat like fire in her belly. No chance. Or if there was a chance, it depended on Kell's madness and his need to torment. She looked at the stone in the hollow of her gloved palm and wondered. Should she hope he was alive if it meant torment of a kind she couldn't begin to imagine? Was any life at all better than being dead? Shadith had deliberately opted for a finite life with death at the end of it, though she was guaranteed immortality. What did that say? She tossed the stone and started on.

Remembering the bad time after the second cairn, running with Grey . . . they moved in separate solitudes, turned in on themselves in the grim struggle to maintain sanity as they moved over endless white snow through endless white fog. An ice storm came suddenly on them and they were forced into

*shelter. The days passed dark and dreary. They grated on
each other until both were at the point of screaming. They
began treating each other with an exaggerated courtesy that
was bitter as the worst insult. When the storm passed over
and they emerged into the eternal mist, it was with such a
feeling of relief that the mere freedom of movement and the
explosion of space sparked a surge of joy in both.*

Rain began falling, a steady sluggish rain, not icy but cold
enough to soak in to the bone and steady enough to turn the
hard earth to a treacherous slop. Clay soil, fine-grained and a
good approximation of a frictionless material when saturated,
slowed her to a lurching walk. Strangely enough, though the
world wept drearily around her, though she was cold and
soaked, inhaling air thick with water, though her muscles
strained because walking in these conditions was a series of
controlled falls, in spite of all these things, the pain and rage
inside her grew paler and began to flow away.

The pack of silvercoats was bigger now, and bolder. She
could smell the rank odor streaming off them. She could hear
them clearly, that coughing, yipping call of theirs. Late that
afternoon she had to shoot two of them to back them off her.
Leaving the pack tearing hungrily at the bodies of their
mates, she ran on into the gray misery of the day.

The third cairn.

Gaunt and haggard, splattered with mud, she took out the
pebble, tossed it onto the smaller heap, then went wearily on.
Too much still needed working out. It wasn't time to turn
back yet.

Her long struggle was over; she was drifting, rudderless.
From the time she'd left her first home, she'd had the quest
for her mother to give a meaning to her life, something to
work toward even when she had to divert from the direct road
because something demanded immediate attention. But the
goal was always there in the back of her mind, not urgent,
not smothering anything else, her own pale pole star. The
quest was over. No more need to search. Over. *First deal
with my mother, then settle down with Grey, keep on Hunting, maybe raise a child or two, work my way into the*

ordinary life of Wolff. For a while, at least, for as long as I can manage.

That's what I planned. Madar knows what'll happen now. Though she couldn't extinguish a faint spark of hope, Grey was most likely dead. *And if he is, what keeps me here?* She brooded over the question as she ran, half her attention on the silvercoats slinking after her. She enjoyed being a Hunter. She even enjoyed having a name that meant something, though she found it irritating at times. Canyli Heldeen was a good friend. The best. Sybille was abrasive and a vicious infighter when her defenses were triggered, but after their bad beginning, she'd turned into a cranky and half-unwilling friend, defending Aleytys as much because she despised those who attacked her as from respect and liking. Most of that fractious collection of individualists assembled under the aegis of Hunters Inc. had grown into friends she valued. And there was Tamris. She had a tendency to stand in awe now; later she'd make a friend, much like her mother. Her life was what Aleytys had wanted for Sharl, cherished, with a warm haven to return to from her forays into life. Canyli had even managed to extend that carefully unsmothering care to her daughter's first Hunt, sending her with Aleytys, knowing Aleytys would let nothing harm her. Tamris was so unscarred by life, so . . . Aleytys shook her head, then regretted her absence of mind as she lost balance and slid into the muck, crashing onto hands and knees, bruising herself and bringing the silvercoats at her, feral snarling shapes flashing from the rain, their pads better adapted than her booted feet to the treacherous ground. No time for the darter, no time to get to her feet. She crouched in the mud and burned. She threw flame from her hands; her clothing ashed around her glowing body.

Silvercoats howled and died as the rain sizzled about them, leaving them soggy black corpses with chalk-white bones showing through brittle skin and burned flesh. Silvercoats fled howling into the rain, rushing in blind panic from the fire horror.

As the howling diminished, Aleytys scowled down at herself. Her clothing, her boots, her gear were smears of ash on her body, streaks of ash running out from her feet; the darter was a blob of plastic and ashy metal warped out of shape, half buried in the mud by her knee. She spat a few curses into the drearily falling rain, but broke off. All that did was take the edge off the fury that still churned in her. It did nothing at all for her embarrassment at her stupidity.

She got to her feet and stood letting the rain chill the heat out of her. Naked and shivering, she began to wonder if she would get out of the Wildlands or leave her bones and flesh to mingle with the bones of the ancient dead.

And discovered she had no intention of going back yet and even less intention of dying. She tapped her symbolic power river and brought her body heat to normal, healing her scrapes and bruises with an absent ease that startled her later when she thought of it. She lifted her arms as high as they would go, stretched her spine, rising onto her toes, letting her heels slam back into the mud, realizing suddenly that she felt very good indeed. Energized, vital, looking forward to the next day, looking forward to taking up Kell's challenge.

After a moment's thought she kicked about in the mud until she found the last pebble. She stood holding it a moment staring into the rain. It seemed to her Grey stood out there seen and unseen, hidden then revealed by the swaying curtains of rain. He lifted a hand in that way he had, amused and affectionate, the way he was in the best of times, then the ghost image faded into the rain.

Pebble in her mouth, she loped easily through the rain, her bare feet finding an easier purchase on the slick clay soil than her boots ever had. *Why didn't I think of this before? Hunh, tunnel vision, conditioned by other folks' expectations. Better watch that. Kell won't honor my blind spots.*

As the days passed she settled into the run, growing gaunter since she had to stop and hunt her food, but she didn't bother gathering rocks for shelters now, simply set out intangible alarms to wake her if danger came too near. Twice she woke to slice warning fire before the muzzles of hungry silvercoats. She killed no more of them; it seemed both unnecessary and somehow stupid, a distraction from the truth she was trying to find.

The fourth cairn.

Grey's cairn, a small heap of stones three spans high.

Remembering what he told her. At the foot of a thirty-meter cliff swept clean by icy winds, he built his cairn and carved his name into the cliffside. He stepped back, examined the crude letters and thought he should add something to tell the next one here what he'd learned in the silence of the shelter, then he shook his head. Grey. *It was enough. Whoever came here would have found his own peace. Anyway, there were no words for what he wanted to say.*

Aleytys flipped the pebble on the cairn and traced the letters still visible in the stone of the cliff after more than a dozen years of weathering. The rain had stopped and the mists were temporarily burned away. The day was clear and bright, deceptively warm where a bulge in the cliff shunted the wind aside. She sat in the quiet warmth, her back close to the hard gray granite but not touching it. She sat letting whatever would bubble through her mind, holding on to nothing, letting all go, the hardest of all disciplines, letting everything come and go as it would until the turmoil in her stilled, until the grief and rage and self-dislike flowed out of her, until even her joys stilled into quiet acceptance, until she was sitting in sunshine, then starshine, then rain, then eddying fog, emptied of all things, emptied of wanting and fear, until she was stone and wind and mist herself, her pulse slowed until her body beat with the great slow beat of Wolff.

She blinked. Moved a hand. Spat hair from her mouth. Rocked on her buttocks in a slow sway to break free of the trance she'd been caught in for . . . how long? She didn't know; her body clock said it was more than a day, and she accepted that. She was hungry. The problem of her future could wait. There was time for that, time for all the momentous decisions she had to make. Besides, experience had taught her long ago that most of those decisions would make themselves when the time was right.

She got stiffly to her feet, looked down at her gaunt naked body and chuckled at the thought of strolling into her house like that. Shake them up a bit. Then she sighed and shook her head. In the vadi Raqsidan, where she had been born and had lived for longer than the years she'd spent wandering, nakedness was reserved for sexual intimacies. Wolff was like that too. *I'll have to wander a lot longer before I shake that feeling.*

Certain and uncertain, centered yet drifting, she moved along the cliff and touched the letters of Grey's name. *If you live, my love, if you live, Shadith will find you. If you're dead . . . so stupidly dead, snuffed by a madman's whim . . . but what do you care if your dying had significance or not? Dead is dead. If you are dead, my love, nothing matters to you now. If I could be sure you lived, if I could be sure my presence wouldn't precipitate your death, if I could be sure, I would come for you forgetting everything else, my mother, Vrithian, everything, nothing Kell could do would keep me from you. I can't be sure of anything. Ay-Madar, for a clear-cut choice, something comfortably black and white. Doesn't work that way, does it, my love. . . . I want it to be me, but oh no it can't be me, she'll come for you, child out of my head born into a new body. Like Swardheld. I didn't tell you who and what Swardheld was, I was too angry at you, I never let you know that much of me, and oh my dear, oh my love, I'm sorry for that. Can't change it now, can't change any of it. . . .*

"Ahhh . . ." She brushed her fingers over the chill stone, then turned to begin the run back to the flitter.

WOLFF
getting set

Aleytys walked into the sitting room and found Shadith stretched out on her stomach on the rug in front of the fire, absorbed in the slide of her stylo across a sheet of paper laid on a book, the flying angular lines of her native script like bird tracks on the creamy white. Warmed by a surge of affection for that ancient child, she leaned against the doorjamb watching as Shadith stopped writing and began reading what she'd set on paper. With an exclamation of disgust she wadded it up and flipped it away to join similar wads scattered near the hearth.

Aleytys chuckled. Chuckled again as Shadith leaped up, twisting to face the sound as she moved, wary and lethal as one of the silvercoats. "Which is it? You bankrupt me paying for paper or you burn my house down?"

Shadith straightened, relaxed, ran inky fingers through her tangled thornbush of brown-gold curls. "You look better. When did you get in? I didn't hear anything."

"I wasn't noisy about it." She crossed the room, lowered herself into a chair, propped her feet on a hassock and sighed with the pleasure of being home again. "Anything interesting turn up?"

"Don't know how interesting." Shadith dropped into the other chair near the fire and brought her legs up. "I went through the stuff Head sent over, made some notes. Like to know what you think about them." She laced her fingers behind her head, gazed drowsily at Aleytys. "Unless you've changed your mind about sending me."

"No." Aleytys frowned at the fire. "If I want to draw Kell

20

off Grey, I go to Vrithian and stake myself out as bait. I hate that, Shadow, you don't know how much." A half-smile, a glance at Shadith. "Well, maybe you do."

"Mmm. What's Harskari doing?"

"Brooding, I suppose. I haven't heard from her since Ibex."

"She'll come out of that when she's ready."

"You said that before."

"Yeah, and got my head chewed off. By proxy. At least she can't do it in person anymore."

"More than time I found her a body. Maybe on Vrithian." She slid farther down in the chair, watched her bare toes wriggle. "Damn all screw-ups," she said. "I was settling in here."

"You can hang on."

"Think so?"

Silence stretched out, filled with small noises. The fire snapped, popped and hissed, threw out a fan of warmth invaded by wandering drafts. Wolfflan houses were built to minimize drafts, but during the in-between times, the short autumns and shorter springs when the houses were adjusting to rapidly changing temperatures, the chill crept about everywhere, touched everything. A whisper of air curled around Aleytys's legs, slid along her body and tickled at the short hairs at her forehead, passed on to rustle through the wadded papers on the hearth.

Aleytys stirred. "Kell! May his teeth fall out and his gut have holes like a colander and may all he have to eat be bone and gristle and hot pepper sauce. May everything he touches rot under his fingers. May he be a hissing and a bad smell to everyone who knows him." She sighed. "For all that's worth."

"Yeah. There are worse places than this to come home to. I always enjoyed getting back." Shadith slanted a glance at Aleytys, chocolate eyes curious and searching. "Don't scorch the earth behind you."

"I'm all right," Aleytys said, answering the look rather than the words. "I don't know. I'm still not used to having him gone. I don't know how I'll feel later. When I was flying back from the trek, I found myself thinking *when Grey gets back,* then pulling myself up reminding myself that it's too damn likely he won't be coming back ever. I've a feeling I'm going to keep doing that, and it's like getting kicked in the belly. But I've got good friends here." She closed her eyes. "Would you like living here, Shadow?"

"Never in winter. Nice to come and visit for a week or so—it's a cushy little world, this."

"Wolff?" Aleytys opened her eyes wide, stared at Shadith.

"Uh-huh. Everyone the same, lots of space, good living thanks to the home shares in Hunters. Tell you what I think, I like my worlds gaudier. Rougher. Full of life and anger and energy. Always something happening, a soup of species and races and cultures, boiling over. Wolff is too bland, people look alike, think alike. Live here all the time? No way."

Aleytys closed her eyes. "Still . . ."

"All right, all right, you need this. That's what I'm saying. Leave yourself a way back. You want a resting place." She pulled her hands down, let them lie limp on the chair's arms, grinned briefly at Aleytys. "Wolff's a great place for hibernating." She wriggled in the chair. "Your mum's running late."

"Said she'd be here." Aleytys brooded at the fire. "She will."

"Aleytys." The face in the comscreen was solemn and strained.

"Shareem." Aleytys felt a little strained herself.

"I'm stationary over the field. Come up for a while. I'll send a shuttle for you."

"Right. Will you be down?"

"We'll leave that for later if you don't mind."

"I hear you. Take about twenty minutes to get there." She hesitated, but there didn't seem to be anything else to say and she didn't know how to break off. She and Shareem stared at each other for a long moment, then each started to speak. Shareem grimaced, lifted a hand, let it fall; the screen went blank.

The doll-like android bowed with liquid grace and left. Aleytys stood in the middle of the oval room and looked

around. Grass and growing things, an impossible little water-
fall making impossible music in the heart of a starship. Light
coming from nowhere with the pearly tinge of a cloudy spring
morning. Smell of damp earth and green growing things,
elusive flower scents. Muted by distance, a bird singing
intermittently. Not quite familiar but haunting, suggesting a
dozen birds on a dozen worlds she'd visited. A room in her
mother's ship, thick with her mother's presence, though
Shareem was not there yet. Aleytys marveled at the quiet
charm of the place and felt exceedingly uncomfortable, as if
somehow, at this late date, she'd returned to her mother's
womb. Little prickles like the brush of electric hairs ran over
her body. *Come on*, she thought, *enough's enough. I'm as
unarmed as I'll ever be.*

"Aleytys."

The sound came from behind her. She turned slowly, her
stomach knotting, a tightness under her ribs that hurt when
she breathed. Her mother stood under the graceful arch of an
aphnyta limb, the dangling spear-head leaves fluttering about
her head and shoulders.

Shareem's green eyes widened; Aleytys felt alternating
snippets of fear and longing, quickly suppressed. Fear? Breath
caught in her throat as she remembered suddenly (she didn't
quite know why) leaning tensely toward the vidscreen in her
ship pleading with Stavver to let her see her son. And being
refused. Because her son hated her so intently he would not
even look at her. Something deep inside her broke, something
hard and cold she hadn't known was there. Her eyes blurred.
She held out her hands. "Mother?"

Shareem's hands closed on hers, strong and warm and
shaking more than a little, then they were hugging each other,
laughing and crying.

They lay stretched out on long comfortable chairs that
shaped themselves to the contours of their bodies, black
chairs in a small black room with one wall that seemed open
to space but was in truth a curved transparent substance that
magnified what lay outside. Meditation room, Shareem said,
for times when the years got too heavy. They lay in the chairs

with the flaccidity that comes after great tension is suddenly relaxed, not quite at ease with each other yet, groping toward an understanding of their likenesses and differences.

Someone floating invisible above the two women, looking for nonphysical signs of maturity (something rather different from age but too often confused with it), would have thought Aleytys the mother and Shareem the child. Shareem's emotions ran more facilely across her face, through her body, but there was more depth and passion in Aleytys. More confidence and self-esteem. She had been forced by circumstances and a comparative lack of mobility to live with the results of her actions, to pay (sometimes heavily) for unconsidered acts. With few exceptions, one of them being the series of events that led to Aleytys's birth and the struggle afterward, Shareem had been insulated from problems by Vryhh wealth and her Vryhh ship. If a situation became uncomfortable, she simply went away and forgot what happened as quickly as she could. It was a measure of her feeling for her daughter that she didn't do that, didn't dismiss the child as an unfortunate accident, but fought to guarantee Aleytys a place on Vrithian, took pains to make sure she wouldn't stay in the stifling culture of the Raqsidan. The outcome of that plotting, what Aleytys was now, she found rather disconcerting; she felt dominated by her daughter and didn't quite know how she liked that, yet she was filled with pride in her child and felt vindicated by her success.

Aleytys saw some of this. In spite of her wariness, she found herself unfolding under the warmth of her mother's aproval— Was startled by the ease and promptness of her capitulation.

"I'm glad you were a girl," Shareem said after a long silence. "Male Vryhh can be . . . difficult."

"Mmm." Aleytys turned to look at her. "How many Vrya are there?"

Shareem stirred, uncomfortable; the chair whispered as it changed to accommodate her change. "Not many," she said. The words were clipped as if she found them difficult to say. "Maybe three hundred." She stirred again. "There never were very many. We were an experiment that got out of hand." She tried a smile, gave up on it. "The eldest, they don't talk much about it. Ummm. About a thousand when Hyaroll found the way to Vrithian. Most we ever were was three thousand. We dwindle, Aleytys."

"Lee."

"Reem. That's why I was able to get you acknowledged. I suppose you're not going to like this. Three of the Tetrad wanted to know where you were, wanted you brought to Vrithian at once if not sooner. I squashed that idea fast; Hyaroll backed me up. We thought you should grow up in a healthier place than Vrithian."

Aleytys waited awhile before she tried to answer, filled first with anger, then resignation. A healthier place than Vrithian. Hard to swallow Shareem's easy passing off of those years of pain and struggle. "I hated you for leaving me," she said finally. "I hated you for a long time."

"Hated. Not hate. What changed your mind?"

"I found out how helpless a woman could be . . . lost my son before he could walk . . . lost him again, left him with his father because . . ." She closed her eyes, the pain with her again, unchanged, it never really changed. "That didn't work out—nothing I did for him worked out the way I wanted. I was going to be the mother you weren't, I was going to raise him with love and care and never leave him until he grew old enough to leave me." She lay silent for a moment, then rubbed her hand across her face, opened her eyes and turned her head so she could see Shareem. "Dwindle? Three thousand to three hundred, that's not a dwindle, it's extinction. Except . . . how long . . ." She chewed on her lip for a moment. "What about the longlife? Was that a lie? One man I . . . know believes in it."

More silence. A shuddering sigh from Shareem. "The day you were born, as far as I could figure it later, no way of being really sure, I passed into my nine hundredth year." She smiled. "Odd coincidence, whether it's exactly true or not, our sharing the same birthday. I had . . . small celebrations . . . for us each year." She cleared her throat. "I'm fourth generation on Vrithian. You're about *it* for the fifth. If we're a mistake, it's self-correcting. Taking a long time, but we're going to get there. No more Vrya. All Vrya males after Hyaroll's generation are sterile. Except for two or three, and they all fathered short-lived sports. Damaged. Distorted. And most Vryhh females are barren. Happened I wasn't one of them.''

Aleytys chuckled, apologized when she saw Shareem frown. "I wasn't laughing at what you said, but something else. Kell and his obsession with pure Vryhh blood. He one of the sterile ones?''

"Kell?" Shareem shuddered all over; the chair shuddered with her as it tried to accommodate her movement. "Where'd you come across *him*? He never said he knew you.''

"One of my Hunts and one of his projects crashed into each other a few years back. Reem, he implied damn hard he was my ancestor and yours.''

"Hunh! The only way would be cloning, and that doesn't work worth spit. What happened?''

Aleytys snuggled lower in the chair and sketched the events of the Hunt on Sunguralingu, the eerie hare-weapon, the battle with Kell. "That's it,'' she said. "I thought it was the disease warping him, so I healed him. I was really wrong that time, wasn't I?''

"You fought him, handicapped, you beat him flat, then had the gall to take pity on him? Lee, he might forgive you by the next big bang, but don't count on it.''

"Yes. I know.''

"What did he do?''

Aleytys pushed up, swung her legs off the chair, sat with shoulders hunched, hands curled over the rounded edge. She missed Grey with a deep misery, felt like crying but lacked the energy to press out tears. "He tried to destroy my son,'' she said, her voice muted. "He's going after Hunters now, attacking my friends, trying to trap me.''

Shareem moved uneasily but didn't sit up; instead she stared at the curve of Wolff hanging over them. "I wish I could say he's the exception, but it wouldn't be true. He's just an exaggeration of the ordinary Vryhh attitude toward the lesser species.''

"Lesser species?''

"His choice of words, not . . . ah, I can't say that." Her hands fluttered in small shapeless movements. "I might not say the words, but . . . I act . . . I treat people . . . oh, I suppose as carelessly, as thoughtlessly as he does. Not as meanly, I hope. I . . . I can't let myself get involved with them . . . they die so fast. Time, Lee, we've got so much, and it does funny things to us. The Eldest, a lot of them anyway, spent centuries in labs . . . well, not exactly . . . an umbrella word for all kinds of . . . of fiddling around with things . . . projects. Think about having ages and ages at your disposal to investigate anything at all that intrigues you . . . and a secret world to maul about . . . its natives . . . you can take from them anything you want, make them do anything you want . . . they're born and they die between one breath and the next. Think of it, Lee, even a single mind . . . working on a problem for centuries, turning it over and over . . . hidden away . . . coming out of hiding to see what other mayflies, other worlds, had done with it . . . stealing the best ideas . . . brooding over them. Think what that one mind could produce." More shapeless groping gestures. "But . . ."

"But?" It was a whispered sound, drawn out, a soft enticement to continue. Aleytys watched her mother struggling with an openness alien to her nature, a painful honesty that the child Leyta inside Aleytys thirsted to hear, evidence of something she'd desired without knowing it for all the years of her life, a need almost as deep as the need for food or breath, a need to know her mother really did love her. What Shareem was saying was interesting in itself, but the feeling behind the words was what Aleytys listened to.

"But they got bored, Lee, most of them. Bored! Sounds funny, doesn't it? The disease that kills us. Absurd, isn't it? One by one most of the Eldest took a dive into a sun somewhere. Or touched off the cores in their domes. Or died in boredom-related accidents, too tired to take care. A lot of the younger ones, we don't go back to Vrithian much. I wander and trade and amuse myself . . . do a project here and there . . . when I need something to make me feel like I'm . . . I'm not just a parasite sucking the life out of . . . I like the long ones . . . the ones that take generations . . .

they make the time go . . . but they're rare . . . mayfly folk don't have the patience. It's a long time yet before I hunt a sun . . . but it'll come. Everything wears out in time." Another gesture of her mother's hand; she did have lovely hands, slender and shapely, but she didn't take care of them. *She chews her nails*, Aleytys thought, and felt a surge of protective love for her mother; she wanted to scold her for neglecting herself, wanted to cuddle and comfort her as if she were the mother and Shareem her child. It was confusing and disturbing; she turned it over and over in her mind, almost missing her mother's next words.

"It's a mess, Lee. The Vrya who stay on Vrithian are . . . well, we're all dead ends, it's a failed experiment, but they . . . aah, it's a mess. You sure you want anything to do with it?" Shareem nodded at Wolff swimming serenely over them. "That seems a beautiful world in its chilly way."

"Come see my home." Aleytys stood, held out her hand.

"Why not?" Shareem took the hand, let Aleytys pull her up. "Any problems getting off the field? Wolff isn't a Company world, but I've heard they don't like visitors."

"They don't." Aleytys grinned. "But I've got pull." The grin became a chuckle. "Well, truth is I've got a couple friends with pull; all that fuss and red tape is taken care of, you don't have to bother with it, just hop in my flitter and come see my house." She followed Shareem from the room. "And my horses. Um . . . I've got a couple of people staying with me, but you don't need to see them if you don't want to, not to talk to anyway."

Shareem swung around. "What?"

"I'll explain on the way down. If you still want to come."

"Yes." Shareem looked wary, withdrawn, setting aside emotion and involvement with an abruptness that startled Aleytys and turned her wary too. "Yes, daughter, it's time you did a little explaining."

Shareem stood by a window in the sitting room, her back to the fire burning briskly on a huge open hearth; it made her a little nervous, for she wasn't accustomed to open fires inside living space. The whole house made her nervous. Her daughter's house. Even the ancient stone walls seemed to hold something of Aleytys. When she'd gotten out of the flitter and looked at it, she'd had the feeling it had grown in that spot like some gnarled old tree. A narrow structure at least four stories high, almost a lopped-off tower, plain, even ugly, massive. She felt the weight of it and wondered how Aleytys could endure that weight pressing down on her. A few steps out of the flitter, Aleytys stopped, closed her eyes, breathed in the rich soup of smells, raw green, wet dirt, horse manure, damp fur, something dead upwind of them, all carried undiluted on a wind that cut into Shareem like knives. She fidgeted, not so enchanted with all this nature; the smells were getting to her stomach and the wind was turning her into an icicle. Now, with the fire's heat licking at her back, with that wind kept firmly outside the double-paned windows, she could watch with appreciation and pleasure the spring foals chasing each other, the mares and stallion grazing in the greening pasture. Its yellow round flattening and flushing to red, the sun started to pass behind sawtooth peaks, their ancient massive glaciers chiseled by time and weather into intricate folds and falls. The air outside had a clarity that gave everything a luminous magical quality, hard-edged and immediate; the intensity of the colors scarcely seemed to diminish as the light began to die. Shareem wrinkled her nose at the display and thought, *I'm not going to get any fonder of this world than I am right now*. She sighed and turned to face her daughter. "What are you going to do?"

Aleytys was stretched out in one of the chairs near the fire, her ankles crossed, a heel sunk in the padded leather of a hassock. She held a long-stemmed glass about a third filled with a dark gold wine that had gone even richer and darker as the light outside faded. The room was filled with shadows; the only light inside came from the fire. "Vrithian," she said. "Shadith was right. Make him come after me." She lifted her head, sipped at the wine, let her head fall back. "Aschla skewer his liver, he couldn't have picked a worse time. Over two years since my last Hunt, I'm about cleaned out, enough credit left to pay the taxes on this place and maintain the power tap while I'm gone. If I'm not gone too long. And there's fuel and overhauling and maintenance on the ship. And Shadith. And Linfyar. No way around it, I'm going to have to borrow on the house and land." She took another sip of the wine, lay back and gloomed at the ceiling. "Damn. Damn. Damn. I just last year worked everything clear of debt."

Shareem moved her shoulders impatiently. She'd never bothered herself with such idiocies and didn't intend to start.

Aleytys felt her discomfort and let the subject drop; which didn't help all that much because every time she did something like that Shareem was forcibly reminded that her daughter was an empath and capable of sensing every fleeting feeling, and some of those feelings she'd rather keep to herself, nothing to be proud of, nothing she wanted anyone else to know about. *Empath. She didn't get that from me; who'd have thought that crazy clod who fathered her might have something so wild in his genes.*

Aleytys touched a sensor. The chair hummed around until she faced the windows; another sensor and a second chair moved up beside it. "Come sit down, Reem. We get spectacular sunsets this time of year."

Shareem settled into the empty chair, though she wasn't that interested in sunsets and had already seen as much as she cared to of this particular specimen. She watched her daughter instead. As the display continued outside, the faintly stern set of Aleytys's face softened, her eyes opened wider; she looked almost happy, absorbed in the play of light before her, accepting, vulnerable; she was responding to that miserable sunset with a passionate intensity that Shareem knew she could never share. She tried to laugh at herself—jealous of a sunset; what next?—but she could not bear to look at her daughter's face any longer.

When the colors had faded and the sky had darkened to indigo with a few silver spangles, Shareem glanced at her daughter and was startled to see tears silent and unforced sliding down her face. Aleytys wasn't trying to stop them or wipe them away. Her mouth was pressed into a thin line; she'd set the wineglass on the floor beside the chair and her hands were knotted together so hard her fingers were white about the knuckles and red at the ends.

Shareem must have made a sound, though she wasn't conscious of it, because Aleytys broke the grip of her hands, sat up, scrubbed at her eyes. "Sorry," she said. She groped beside the chair, found a bit of tissue and blew her nose, tossed the tissue at the fire. She took a few deep breaths. "Just as well I'm getting away from here. For a while, anyway." She drew the back of her hands across her eyes, managed a smile. "Grey and I used to sit here like this whenever our times home coincided." She groped for another tissue, blew her nose again. "It keeps catching me by surprise, that he might not . . . never mind."

She flipped up the top to the chair arm, danced her fingers over the panel there, then settled back as the chair switched around again to face the fire, a soft indirect lighing chased the shadows from the room, and exterior shields hummed quietly down over the windows. A hesitation, then she brought Shareem's chair back to where it had been; she raised her brows, then matched Shareem's smile with her own.

"I'm not asking you to help," she said. Shareem suppressed an appreciative chuckle at the care in the choice of those words. Aleytys was groping through a minefield that didn't exist, but she couldn't know that. "Just get me to Vrithian and—" the same uninsistent quiet tones, the same slightly hesitant speech—"and back off, and . . . keep silence." A lift and fall of her hand. "I don't want him more prepared for me than he is already. You know Kell, I don't. I don't know what your loyalties are, Reem. If you're against me in this, please tell me. I won't mind; after all, you've known him a lot longer than you've known me. All I ask is, don't get in my way. I don't want to have to go through you." She shook herself, made a groping helpless gesture. "I will, you know. He's left me no choice. I have . . . hostages, he'll strike against them, they can't fight him. I think . . . I think he'll put off facing me directly as long as he can keep me running . . . and hurting. Swardheld, Shadith, though they can take care of themselves better than most. Linfyar. Canyli Heldeen and the other Hunters. Grey . . . ah!" She looked down, then up, eyes shining with a film of tears. "I know I just said back off, Reem, but I can't . . . I need you, Reem. Will you help me?"

I need you. Simple words, but they cut deep and made Shareem feel like crying. Her arms ached to hold her daughter as they'd ached before. More than once she'd taken her ship cautiously into the mess around Jaydugar and hovered watching the world turn under her, had seen it frozen in the depths of winter, burning in the long, long summer, yet she'd never dared land and claim her daughter. So many reasons for not doing what she half wanted, half feared to do. And all of those reasons seemed empty now, as foolish as her urge to take a grown woman into her arms as if she were a hurting child, rock her, soothe her, tell her mother would make things right. Absurd, of course, and too painful to dwell on, so she pushed the thought aside.

"Help? Of course I'll help. When he knows we've met, which will be soon, I'll be a target too." She looked down at her hands, opened and closed them, ran her thumb over her wrist where scars would have been except for Kell's autodoc; her stomach knotted and her throat closed up as she brought up buried memories she'd never been able to wipe away, memories that surfaced in dreams though she'd never let them up in the daytime.

"Lee . . ." Her throat closed again; she swallowed and forced herself to a measure of calm—what else was time useful for but to teach you how to deal with your crises? "Lee, I don't know how much use I'd be if this thing gets sticky. He's got a—I don't know what to call it—if he gets close enough to me, I'll do just about anything he tells me no matter how I hate it. When I was very young, a child really . . . just out of basic training, ready to fight the world . . . you know—no, maybe you don't—I . . . he got hold of me and took me into his dome. He was young too, same generation, born about a hundred years before I was. And he'd just found out about the sterility thing. It was a shock; he should have learned it before when he was younger and more flexible, but the way chance turned, he didn't. Too bad. And too bad he learned it in the way he did, in bed with one of the more unstable Vryhh, a second-generation bitch named Nallis.

"Where was I? I was as foolish as I was young. He was healthy and handsome and had charm coming out his ears when he wanted to use it." She looked up, pushed the hair out of her eyes, a smile for her daughter, filled with wry recognition of the difference in their experience. "You wouldn't know about that—I don't blame you, Lee, if you don't believe me, but . . ." She spread her hands, clasped them together. "It's hard to tell you what I saw . . . all the things that make up what we call brilliance. He shone for me, glowed, burned, I can't find the right word, Lee . . . and a vulnerability, an agony inside I could make him forget; I didn't understand, and maybe that was what he needed. We played over the face of Vrithian, running with the sun, with the moons, seven-league boots on our feet, wings. . . . It could have been different if I'd known what was wrong with him, but if I had . . . I don't know . . . I didn't know how to help him later.

"My mother warned me not to go with him the time he came to take me to his dome, but I wouldn't listen. She said no one can help you there. I still wouldn't listen. Years had slid by while we were playing. I think you don't know what it's like, being young and knowing you have immense stretches of time ahead, there is no hurry for anything, you savor things, make them last, they have to last. Years slid by and he was changing but I didn't see it; there were long intervals when I didn't see him at all. Then he came for me." She dug around, found a crumpled old tissue and mopped at her face, sat tearing it into shreds as she went on.

"I found out what he was doing when he wasn't with me. Found out fast and hard. He had herds of women in that dome, Vrithli, even reptiloid females, though I don't know what he expected from them. Women of all sorts from outside the cloud, it was like a zoo in there, yes in more ways than one; he kept them in cages of a sort. Some he lay with, some he just used in experiments. I suppose he thought he might find some miraculous conjunction that would make him whole, yes, whole; he saw himself as maimed, deformed.

Nothing I said or did ever changed that, even after I finally understood what was happening to him. I tried to leave . . . wanted no part of that mess. He wouldn't let me go. He'd sired no children on any of the women there, blamed them, either they were barren or tricking him or sabotaging his experiments . . . how they could do that was something I never understood, because they were confined to those small cells, but he was beyond being rational about it by then.

"All the time I was there he watched me, had spy eyes on me when he was somewhere else, made me watch the tapes and tell him everything I was thinking. Sometimes he couldn't get it up with me, then he'd beat me . . . on the body where it wouldn't show. He was always careful before visitors . . . none of them saw the women . . . made me reassure my mother . . . pretend I was content . . . still in love with him, healthy, happy. More than once he almost killed me . . . ruptured spleen, internal bleeding, you name it . . . wouldn't let me die, though I'd have been glad to by then . . . shoved me in the autodoc . . . toward the end I was deliberately driving him into rages . . . either he'd kill me and I'd be free of his torment or he'd injure me enough he had to put in the autodoc . . . addicted me to that machine."

She passed her thumb over her wrist again, sighed. "Finally I looked so bad he wouldn't let anyone see me . . . told everyone I was pregnant . . . by him, of course . . . having a hard time . . . prone to miscarriage, so he didn't want me bothered. My mother didn't believe him, but she couldn't do anything until she figured a way into his dome past his defenses. She got Hyaroll to tease Kell away for a few hours . . . got to me . . . got me to open for her . . . got me out . . . she and Hyaroll, she told me he was my father, but he never said anything. They put my head together again . . . though the seams show if you know where to look . . . and when they were done with that, I started running. Been running ever since. I couldn't bring you to Vrithian . . . not a baby . . . you have to see that. I wish you'd killed him when you had the chance, Lee. You should have killed him."

Aleytys came out of her chair with an urgent suddenness that startled Shareem, knelt beside her, put a hand on her arm. "Forget what I said, Reem, just get me to Vrithian. Then you take off, scoot as far away as you can."

Shareem blinked. "Seven hundred years." She patted her daughter's hand with absentminded affection. "A long time to run. But I had a lot to run from. He didn't give up on me, not even then. I wouldn't go back to the dome, but . . . anything else, all he had to do was whistle and I'd come . . . nice little bitch, trained to heel. By that time he didn't really want me, just . . . he killed my mother, destroyed everything she was fond of . . . but me . . . lay back for years, apparently resigned to defeat . . . then he went to the Mesochthon, registered a death challenge . . . next day he . . . he meant to get us both, I think, but Hyaroll . . . he discovered something . . . I don't remember much about that time . . . something about collapsed matter, I think . . . I don't know . . . he wanted Mother to come and help him celebrate, she was always his favorite Vryhh, he was fond of me too . . . in his way . . . Mother . . . one of her damakin was about to foal, that was what she was playing with then, she liked working with animals, this one was so gentle and trusting it was near extinct on its homeworld, this damakin was about to foal and having a hard time so she wouldn't come . . . and I went instead of her . . . and Kell got a bomb through her defenses somehow, turned everything to slag."

She lifted Aleytys's hand, held it briefly against her cheek, put it with gentle precision on the chair arm. "How could he get away with something like that? We Vrya never acknowledged the right of anyone to judge our acts; we're all sovereign nations, Lee, with a population of one. Nations declare war on each other, don't they? We call our wars death duels. Kell did all the proper things, he issued a formal challenge at the Mesochthon, then killed my mother. Too bad, but she wasn't lucky or smart enough. Anyone who thought different could challenge him. But there was no one. Hyaroll wouldn't, and I'd rather have jumped into the sun naked. I think Hyaroll must have said something to him, though, because after that he more or less left me alone. Oh, he'd play . . . sick games with me, mock at me . . . after a while he got bored with baiting me and left me alone . . . until I came to

Vrithian with news of a daughter, something he took as a personal affront. Do you understand a bit more what's waiting for you? Lee, what I'm trying to say . . ."

"I know." Aleytys got to her feet, went to stand with her hands gripping the mantel, her eyes on the floor, her back to Shareem. "I think you underestimate yourself," she said quietly. "I think you're a lot tougher than you know. But what's the point trying to prove anything like that? Reem, I can't find Vrithian without you, there's no getting around that, but once I'm there . . . well, there's no real reason for you to stay."

"Lee . . ."

"I mean it."

"I know, but don't you think abandoning you once is enough?"

"You won't be abandoning me. Don't be absurd, Reem. I'm a grown woman; I've been taking care of myself for years in some very tricky situations."

"Yes, I hear you. Please hear me, daughter. Please, I'm done with rationalizing my failures. I can't do it anymore." She forced a chuckle that quickly turned real as her sense of the ridiculous woke from its coma. "Stop mothering me, Lee. Don't you feel a little silly trying to protect a nine-hundred-year-old baby from her better impulses?"

Aleytys swung around, set her shoulders against the bricks. "Habits. You make them without thought and spend years thinking how to break them." She closed her eyes. "I hate this, Reem. I loathe it. Hunting a man down, killing him. While he lies helpless looking up at you . . . me . . . eyes filled with terror and resignation. Ay-Madar, why can't I heal crooked minds? Oh yes, I've killed men and beasts before. With my hands, with my fire, with weapons of one kind and another. And felt them die. Felt their fear and pain and urgency and the nothing that's suddenly there. I can block some of that. When I'm fighting for my life, I'm too . . . concentrated . . . too busy . . . to feel—no, that's not quite right, feeling's shunted aside, I shut off the meaning of it. But slaughtering a helpless man . . . you said I should have killed him before . . . you were right in a way . . . I would

have saved a lot of misery . . . my baby . . . Grey . . .
Ticutt, who's my friend . . . you were right, I should have
killed him. I couldn't, Reem, I couldn't make myself do it. If
the same thing comes up again, I don't know. . . .''

"If you want an honest answer, Lee, I have to tell you
I don't understand a word of all that. Kell's not a man anymore, he's a thing; he should be grateful to you for ending
him.''

Aleytys drew the back of her hand across her eyes, pushed
at the hair by her face, tucked it behind her ears, looked at
her hand, let it fall. "A thing. "No." She slapped her hand
against the bricks. "No! I can't start thinking like that." Her
arms held straight out before her, she turned her palms up.
Her face went quiet and remote, but held no hint of effort, or
none Shareem could see. Tongues of flame hotter than the
fire behind her shot up from the hollows of her palms,
swayed and shimmered for a short time, then sank back into
her daughter's flesh. "If I start thinking like that, I'll soon be
no better or saner than Kell. No. I'll do this thing. He's left
me no choice. Better or saner than Kell. No. I'll do this
thing. He's left me no choice. But not gladly. And I won't let
myself forget that what I'm Hunting is a man, a wanting
feeling intelligence.'' She rubbed her hands along the bricks,
frowning at nothing, looking past Shareem at something only
she could see.

Shareem sat silent. There was nothing she could say. She
found her daughter's scruples absurd; as far as she could see
they were self-inflicted miseries Aleytys would do better
without. She'd made her mild protest; look what that had
brought. Anything more and she could drive her daughter
away.

Aleytys dropped her gaze, smiled suddenly. "You kept
truth at arm's length most of the time you were on Jaydugar,
didn't you? And that letter, ah, that lovely misleading letter.''

"You know my reasons." A small protest Shareem couldn't
help making.

"The truth shall make you free." Aleytys spoke softly,
sadly. "It doesn't always, does it?" She slid down until she
was sitting on the hearth, legs crossed, back against the warm

bricks. "But I prefer truth when it won't kill me outright. Makes life just a little simpler. And being able to tell the truth—with a small t, Reem, always a small t—that's so . . . so . . . I don't know . . . so comfortable. No straining the brain to pretend I am what I'm not, what you see is what you get, like it or no."

"No doubt."

Aleytys laughed, unfolded with a bounce, stretched her arms over her head, snapped them down. "I'm hungry. You want some Wolfflan food?"

"What's that?"

"Mostly meat and pastries, sweet glazes on the vegetables. But there's a place I know where the chef is accommodating and will spare the sauces and singe a steak to your taste. I'm not much on domesticity—Grey did all the cooking when he was home." She went still, her face blanked, then she shook herself and stepped away from the fireplace. "So you see, if you're hungry, it's eat out or go back to your ship, or, I don't know, not exactly polite to work a guest, but the kitchen's yours if you want."

"No autochef? Me in the kitchen on my own—that would be a disaster." Shareem tried for a light tone, something to lessen the squeeze on her heart as she saw her daughter grieving. "On Vrithian—and on my ship, I'll have you know—androids take care of that sort of thing. We'll try your accommodating chef. I'm sure I've eaten and enjoyed meals a lot stranger than his."

Aleytys nodded, started for the door. Over her shoulder she said, "You know where the fresher is if you want a wash or anything. I'll be rounding up Shadith and Linfyar." She saw Shareem's grimace and grinned. "He has private rooms, Reem—we won't be putting on a show for the public. What public there is." With a wave of her hand she vanished into the hall; Shareem listened to the diminishing clicks of her bootheels, leaned back in her chair and rubbed at her forehead. Exhausting, this meeting a daughter she knew only from record flakes and rumor. She had a feeling she was going to be worn to a nub before this thing was over.

*   *   *

Aleytys sat in Head's office in the chair where she'd been presented with so many reluctantly offered and accepted ultimatums. She smiled at Canyli Heldeen. "I expect to be back," she said. "This is only a leave of absence." She scrawled her signature on the sheet and passed it across to Head, took a sealed envelope from her shoulder bag, skimmed it after the leave agreement. "These are the papers leasing my ship to Shadith for three years, a drach a year. No use letting it sit around collecting dust and dock fees. At the end of three years, if I haven't returned to claim it, the ship's to be transferred to her name."

"There could be problems about that, Lee—she's a child."

"Hardly."

"Nonetheless, the way she looks is going to make trouble for her."

Aleytys rubbed at her eyes. "She'll just have to deal with that, Nyl. If it comes up. To tell you the truth, I wouldn't want to make anyone responsible for her actions—she's too likely to do something off the wall just for the holy hell of it and embarrass me and her guardian too." She shrugged. "If you run into problems with her looks, say her species matures . . . no, better let Shadow handle that and you just stare down anyone who objects." She settled back into the chair, sat with her hands resting lightly on the arms. "Deed to my house and land, that's in there too. If I don't come back in three years, or you don't hear from me, house and land are yours, your personal property."

"Lee."

"I said if." She chuckled. "Not a very big if, my friend. When are you sending Taggert off?"

"Three days after you leave."

"Good. Shadith's off tonight. She'll have time to worm herself into cover before he arrives. Is he going straight in like the others?"

"No."

"Ah. Clever man. I won't ask more." She got to her feet.

Canyli Heldeen came around the desk, hugged Aleytys vigorously, then walked with her through the outer offices and went down the lift shaft with her, all this in a companionable silence. She knew what Aleytys wouldn't say aloud—that at the end of those three years there was a very good chance she would own a house and horses, Shadith would own a ship. In the roofed flitter yard, Canyli put her hand on Aleytys's shoulder. "Take care," she said, then she turned and walked briskly toward the lift shaft, a square sturdy woman with her mind already turning to a dozen more urgent problems.

"Right," Aleytys said. She ran a hand through her hair, tried to push away the thought that she wasn't ready for anything, then she got into the flitter, eased it out of the yard and started home, going over everything that had to be done before she left, a very short list, half a dozen items; she tried to think of anything she'd forgotten, but couldn't dredge up a thing, everything turned off that had to be turned off, the girl who tended the livestock warned she'd be in charge starting tomorrow and she should call Head in any emergency, the loans finalized, credit in the bank with Canyli deputized to handle it, gear packed and waiting. She looked out at the empty landscape passing below her, bleak but with an austere beauty she appreciated more each year. "Tomorrow. The Dance begins tomorrow."

gameboard (first of two)

VRITHIAN IN THE MISTS
Second of five planets orbiting the star AVENAR which
exists in a slowly enlarging cavity within a cloud of faintly
glowing gases and dust
DAY: 28.003 hours-standard
YEAR: 585.001 days
Oblate spheroid, mean diameter 12,892 km
Density 5.72 times that of water
Rotational axis tilted 24°
Four major continents (GYNNOR, BREPHOR, SAKKOR,
ASKALOR)
Two large islands (LOPPEN, FOSPOR)
Two major island chains (SULING LALLER, FATTAHX-
EDRA)
Bodies of water:
   oceans: NORSTOR FISTAVEY, SUSTOR FISTAVEY,
          ISTENGER, VATACHAVAR, RABAHAR
   other: Seas of JUVELHAV, PAPUGAY
          Gulfs of MACADAO, PEFAXO
          Straits of TAVAKAY
          Lake SERZHAIR
Indigenes—two intelligent species with separate evolutionary
histories
ORPETZH: Warm-blooded reptiloids, tri-sexual (female,
          male, neuter; though the neuter does not partici-
          pate in sexual transactions, conception is possi-
          ble only when it is present; there is some indication
          that even copulation does not occur in the ab-

sence of a neuter), oviparous (only marginally
so; the infant is born inside a translucent flexible
shell, continues to grow and develop for another
thirty-five to forty days before hatching), average
adult height: female 160 cm, male 150 cm, neuter 120 cm, average life span 50 years standard
(approx. 31 years-local)

GALAPHORZE: Mammalian, bi-sexual, viviparous, average adult height: female 155 cm, male 175
cm, average life span roughly equal to that
of the ORPETZH

Moons:

MINHA: mean distance 154,000 km, mean diameter 1,775
km. MINACHRON: phase cycle full moon to full
moon, 12.04 days

ARAXOS: mean distance 244,020 km, mean diameter 3,
462 km. ARACHRON: phase cycle, full moon to
full moon, 26 days. A JUBILEE is called whenever an ARACHRON ends with the Vrithian year,
a minor festival occurs each time MINHA and
ARAXOS are full at the same time

VRITHIAN
THE CONTINENTS GYNNOR
AND BREPHOR

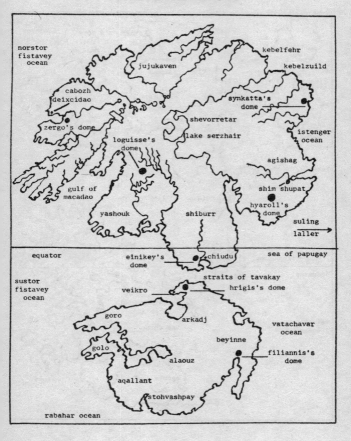

VRITHIAN
THE CONTINENTS SAKKOR
AND ASKALOR

norstor
fistavey
ocean

avagrunn's dome

beyilish

dromm

padje-lozel

loppen var

loppen
mesochthon

eshkhol

shareem's
dome

borbhal

guldafel

kell's dome

grasa dor
algozar's dome

the dak

istenger
ocean

bygga modig

gulf
of
pefaxo

juvelhav
sea

rosaro

nallis's dome

fospor

cobarzh

tropagora

equator

vatachavar
ocean

fattahxedra
islands

the sheng

ogomke

magoro

rabahar ocean

VRITHIAN
action on the periphery [1]

The Song of the Sorrows of Agishag

> sung to the children of Agishag as they are initiated
> into
> the rights and responsibilities of adulthood

the drums whisper
the hollow is dark
the torches wait for fire
listen
> (listen, listen, listen: the word goes round and round the
> drumroom, old ones hissing, hissing with anger and fear in
> the sibilant hot darkness, the manai listening, the tokon
> listening, the naidisa listening, all listening with fear and
> trembling)
once the Conoch'hi went where they willed
once the world was where the wind went and only that
touch the patterns of the line-Mother's life weave
feel the wind in the life-Mother's weave
> (the mana Amaiki touches the narrow strip of her own life
> weave, the knots and spaces that record the events she
> thinks worthy of memory and telling, the sun in her eyes
> when she burst the shell, the first bean sprout she coaxed
> from seed, little things and perhaps too many of them, her
> mother calls her hoarder, but her fingers slide over the
> story of her short life and bring her pleasure)
feel the pattern change
Hyaroll came

the Undying came and took the winds from the Conoch'hi
he set his hard hand on the Mother-of-All
the earth that feeds and sustains us
like a wild tedo he tamed her
like a herd of tedo he tamed us
the old he laid aside and would have slain
the life-Mother of the Conoch'hi rose up to him
the life-Mother sang him the worth of the old, the need of the
    young
he stayed his hand
for two hands of days and two more the old sang to him
by their song they bought their lives from him
but the sick and the crippled and the weak he took
the sick and the crippled he tormented, he changed
he sent them back to the Conoch'hi
strangeness came to the Conoch'hi
our ways were changed
our children were changed
we looked at them and could not understand them
through them came the dreams, the throwing of lots
through them came the ways of far-seeing, the knowing of
    tomorrow and tomorrow
three decrees he gave to the life-Mother of the Conoch'hi
to the Hundred Families he gave these decrees
I will give you peace, I will protect you from the zuilders and
    lallers
the shiburri, the shevorate, the stovasha and all others
I will heal the sick and send the rain and teach you what you
    need to know
in return you will do these things for me
five manai and five tokon and five naidisa you will send to
    my dome
to do my will and serve me in all ways
for five years they will serve within the dome
at the end of the five years they will return
at the end of the five years you shall choose five and five and
    five again
thus he decreed and thus it was done
this was the second decree

the Conoch'hi will cease to follow wind and water
the Conoch'hi will cease to follow the tedo herds
the Conoch'hi will live in villages and learn the heart of bulb
    and seed
of stone wood and iron
this was the third decree
the Conoch'hi will limit their numbers
for every six will seven only be born
any over that will be taken
any over will be sent away
then Hyaroll said
the Undying he said
live on the land as I have told you
live on the land within the borders I have set for you
live in peace and learn what you must
thus he decreed and thus it was done
    Conoch'hi heard
    Conoch'hi feared
    Conoch'hi sorrowed for the lost ways
    Conoch'hi obeyed
weep for your children, oh line-Mothers, life-Fathers, your
    children are gone
you have sent away your naidisa that the numbers might be
    kept
you have sent away your daughters that the numbers might be
    kept
you have sent your sons away that the numbers might be kept
weep, Conoch'hi, your children are taken
rejoice, Conoch'hi, they are taken not lost
of our flesh and our bone far-speakers were made
out of pity and play the undying he made them
the far-speakers give the taken back to us
none is lost
new families and old
none is lost
save only one line
hear the song of the lost
    (the singer's voice stills with a dying hiss, the drums keep
    beating; Amaiki trembles and strains to listen. To this point

all has been a repetition of things commonly known. What is coming is one of the secret things that adults know but never tell children. Amaiki straightens her back, touches her life weave another time, knowing she will not knot this song into it. This is too secret, too sacred, altogether too terrible)

these are the names of the lost
Children of Agishag must not bear these names
forget nothing
say nothing
hear the ancient anguish of the Conoch'hi
hear the sorrow of the Conoch'hi
hear the names of the lost

Tahere oc cuji
Oojitay oc cuji
Marai oc cuji
Mriize oc cuji
Yonikti oc cuji
Je-mawi oc cuji

line cuji is no more
line cuji cast off that name
weep for cuji who were, hayal who are
praise hayal who cast off their cions and their name
praise hayal and remember what they've seen
these are the names of the children of the lost
you will not name a child from these names
forget nothing
say nothing

Kurim, Kiraz, Shakati
Fonnim, Fanasi, Fukati
Misi, Miji, Achavai
Nunnin, Chacai, Alvanai
Shijun, Shaki, Nugavai

Hyaroll cast fire at them
you have seen the black ash of them
loom and lot, Hyaroll burned them
hatchling and dartling, Hyaroll burned them
the air stank of them
the earth stank of them

the stench of their burning lay on us for two hands of days
six days and six the smell lay on us
this is how that came to be
six and six they left cuji, adults and children they left
secretly they went out from cuji
Dum Cuji, the village of their line
in the night they went out
into the hills they went where the air smelled free to them
following a tedo herd they went
the summer passed.
they danced the tedo dance and waited the winter through
Hyaroll said nothing did nothing
nine hatched with the coming of the sun, six they had already
they danced the birth-blessing then they waited
Hyaroll said nothing did nothing
the summer passed
they followed the herd south through the hills,
north through the hills
they hunted and danced and mocked the not-free
the Conoch'hi waited and watched
desire and hope and fear sang in them
Conoch'hi not-free watched the free and hoped
the summer passed and with the cold of winter
came the voice of Hyaroll
cull your numbers said the voice of Hyaroll
cull your numbers and send the excess to me
the Conoch'hi waited
the Six did not listen
the free would not send their children away
Hyaroll spoke again
cull your numbers
cease following the herds
go back to your village and live as I bade you
the free laughed and danced and would not hear the voice
the Conoch'hi waited
three days they waited
five days they waited
on the sixth day, the day of the thumb, the day of power and
    blessing

on the sixth day Hyaroll spoke a last time
so be it, Hyaroll said
fire came from air and clothed the free
they burned, their children burned, manai and naidisa and
    tokon all burned
the hatchlings cried out and ran from the tents
fire leaped around them and they burned
when the Conoch'hi went to the hills
they found black ash and that only
the tedo had fled
the tents were ash
the free were ash
we showed you the black circle, Manai, Tokon, Naidisa
we showed you the circle of black rocks
no newa makes her nest there
no grass grows there
the water is bitter and no beasts come to drink
you have tasted the bitter water, the tears of the Conoch'hi
when you were children you were Conoshim'hi
the beloved of the earth
but you have tasted the bitter water, the tears of the earth
from this night you are children of sorrow
from this night you are Conoch'hi
    oh weh, weh, the bitter water
    oh weh, weh, the sorrow.
    (Amaiki mana-that-was caresses the strip of her own life
    weave, knots the sorrow knot into the cords, sings weh-
    weh with the others, but there is no sorrow in her heart,
    only a savoring of knots and spaces to come, the pattern of
    her life-to-be)

AGISHAG ON GYNNOR

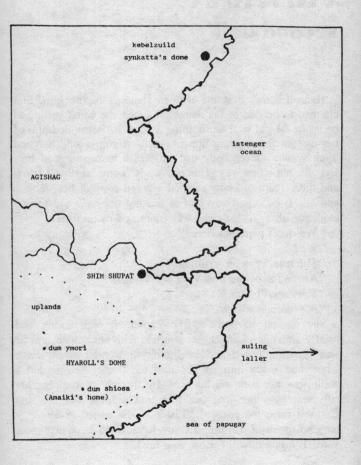

VRITHIAN
second bell

Hyaroll scowled at the woman standing before him. She claimed to be one of his daughters when she came yelling to be let in. Might well be, nothing against it. Reminded him of her mother, haranguing him like that. A stupid acid-tongued bitch with a clever body and little else to recommend her. Eybolli, her name was. This one whose name he didn't know and didn't care to know seemed a faded copy of her, tongue and all. If he'd had any part in making her he could see no evidence of it. At least she was running down a little.

"We don't want her here?"

"We?"

"The true Vrya on Vrithian."

"Ah. What of the true Vrya off Vrithian?"

"They aren't here."

"A profound insight."

She looked startled, then offended. It was faintly and briefly amusing to watch her struggle with her spleen, but he was growing bored and beginning to wonder what senile whim had made him let her into the dome. She forced a smile, put her hand on his arm. He thought of slapping her silly, pitching her into her flier and sending her off, but couldn't raise the energy. "Listen," she cooed at him, "it isn't so much of a thing, all you have to do is change your vote. The others will follow your lead."

"Oh?"

"So, maybe not Loguisse, but she doesn't count if the rest agree." She patted his arm. "Come on, Daddy dear, do it, hmmm? You don' even know what she's like. All you have to do is say nay instead of aye.''

''Go away.''

''What?''

''Go away.''

''I won't. I won't go until I have your answer.''

''You got it, same as it was the first time. The Tetrad will recognize Shareem's daughter as Vryhh.'' He shook off her hand, spoke to the android standing a pace behind him. ''Megathen, get her away from me.''

She glared into the abstract planes of the android's face. ''Don't touch me. I'll go.'' She switched the glare to Hyaroll. ''That dirty half-breed won't last a year. You wait. You'll see.''

VRITHIAN
players moving on
an oblique file [1]

Willow sat cross-legged, pricking blue lines into the skin of her thigh. Her head down, she pretended indifference to what was happening around her, but she was listening intently to Hyaroll and the female Vryhh.

He stood with his hands clasped behind his back, his feet apart, planted like a boulder in the grass of the small lawn. Old Stone Vryhh, he won't listen, you wasting you breath, woman. Old Stone Vryhh, stealer of life to fill the hollow in him. Go away, woman, leave him be. If that bitch stirred him up, chances are he'd dump his collection back in the stasis boxes before getting busy helping her or fighting her.

For several hundred years Willow had taken her life in small discrete bites as Hyaroll rotated his vast collection of life forms, giving them conscious existence until he grew bored with them. A few of them were always waked together for their brief hours of life, but others in the group came and vanished as ephemerally as mayflies. It was hard, this making friends and losing them to Hyaroll's whim; after the third waking she kept herself apart from most of them, spending her time with two beings who seemed linked to her, risking the hurt of losing them because she could not live without affection and touch; she would rather be dead, finally dead, dead with no hope of waking, than live like Hyaroll, unloving and unloved.

"Half-breed! A caricature. Pitiful. You voted against it at first. Say something, Har. Why did you change your mind? No, I won't believe you changed, you let her maul you into it." She went on with her rant, giving him no chance to speak. "Mongrel bitch. Knows nothing of our ways. Why should we have to . . ." The bitter voice went on and on, laying epithet on epithet, all washing against the stone of Hyaroll's indifference.

Bodri and Sunchild. Friends. The only bridge Willow had across the little deaths of the stasis box.

Bodri was grubbing about in the flower beds, singing his grumbling songs to the worms and bees and the good bugs, zapping the pests and parasites with stinging hairs that grew on several of his many fingers, trundling happily about the garden on his six short stubby legs. With his heavy high-domed carapace planted with vines and shrubs and flowering plants, feeding him sun-strength for the blood-strength they took from him, he looked like a many-times-enlarged beetle, but instead of mandibles and compound eyes, he had a leathery black face rather like that of a wise old sheep and luminous brown eyes that usually smiled with affectionate amusement at the world's absurdities. His snout was shorter and blunter than that of a sheep, his lips and tongue more flexible, able to shape with ease the words he loved almost as much as his plants. Four tentacles branched from his front shoulders, each of these split into six delicate fingers of surprising strength—Willow blinked and stared the first time she saw him at his most determined weeding, plucking diseased shrubs bigger than he was from the stubborn earth. Antennae like fern fronds sprouted behind little round ears; they extended his senses of hearing, smell and touch far beyond anything his ears, nose or fingers could tell him. They were lightly rolled now, curled up on themselves to escape the scratching of the Vryhh woman's shrill voice, but he was listening, Willow knew; he shared the anxiety growing in her.

He'd been here longer than any of the other beings, at least the ones Willow had met and spoken with; he was one of the first life forms Hyaroll had collected. The last of his kind and he knew it. One day when he was in a mood of gentle melancholy, he told Willow his folk were dying out even before Hyaroll took him; the species had gone on too long unchanged while their world changed about them. She squatted beside him, rubbing the tough supple skin of a tentacle, saying nothing, letting him ramble on. Around the fifth awakening, some four hundred years after his taking, he thought about joining them, dying with his dying folk. Settling down in a corner of the garden and stopping. Not eating, not sleeping, gradually shutting down mind and body. But Hyaroll had learned too much about him and wasn't ready to let him go; he wasn't sure just what the Vryhh had done to him, his memory was spotty about those events, but his body was turned against him, would not obey him if that obedience might put it in danger. After a short while he grew content with the bits of life he had and seldom yearned for more.

Sunchild drifted in slow circles overhead, a shifting golden shape invisible against the sun, hard to see even when he slipped down to brush against treetops or hover over the ornamental lake. He came and went, came and went, like Willow and Bodri pretending no interest in the two Vrya and what was happening between them. Like Willow and Bodri he listened carefully to what was said and not said, watched the woman move with angular energy about the sunny patch of lawn, back and forth before stolidly standing Hyaroll, her voice rising to a screech then disciplined back to calm, watched Hyaroll resisting her with his silence, his stone face.

Willow finished pricking in the design and set the needle aside. Sunchild came floating down to squat beside her, shaping as always into Otter's form. The first time that happened, she was furious and cursed him for mocking her grief, then listened skeptically as he explained he could not help it, he caught that image from her too strongly for him to resist it. She watched him trying to change and saw Otter's face melting like hot butter, reforming as soon as it melted. Go away, she said to him. I believe you, go away for a while. She put her hand across her eyes, dropped it to cover nose and mouth, then reached out to Sunchild's slippery shine. Are you ghost? she said. No, he said, nor demon. Just me. Yes, go away, she said, let me think on this, let me make a song. Let me sing it with you, he said, I am a child alone, let me sing with you. Not yet, she said, my mourning is not done, give me time to mourn my man, give me time to mourn my children, give me seven days, Sunchild, then I'll teach you to sing with me.

Now he squatted beside her and looked gravely down at the blue lines she'd pricked into her hide, the double spiral sunheart and the slanting wavelines, the water of mourning, the sun of joy. He pressed Otter's strong square hands on the reddened flesh (she felt only the lightest of tingles) and smiled Otter's lookatme smile as the redness went away.

Behind Sunchild the Vryhh woman changed her tactics, moved close to Hyaroll, patted his arm, spoke coaxingly cooingly to him. "Come on, Daddy dear, do it, hmmm? You don't even know what she's like. All you have to do is say nay instead of aye."

"Go away."

"What?"

"Go away."

"I won't. I won't go until I have your answer."

"You got it, same as it was the first time. The Tetrad will recognize Shareem's daughter as Vryhh."

During this last bit the iron man who served Hyaroll came out of the house to stand beside him. Willow rubbed at her thigh and wondered if Old Stone Vryhh had called him. Maybe he'd have that ironhead snatch up the woman and carry her off kicking and screaming and cursing; be a sight if he did and serve her right. *Make a song I will to set ol' Bodri giggling. If he does it. Come on, Old Vryhh, I'm tired o' her fussin.*

Hyaroll shook off the woman's hand, spoke to ironhead. "Megathen, get her away from me."

Willow leaned forward, biting back a grin, waiting.

The woman glared into the angles of ironhead's not-face. "Don't touch me. I'll go." She switched the glare to Hyaroll. "That dirty half-breed won't last a year. You wait. You'll see." She whipped around and stalked off toward the shaggy kadraesh trees and the wide white plates behind them where the fliers landed.

Willow grimaced and turned away so Sunchild wouldn't see the disappointment in her face and ask about it.

Hyaroll stumped off toward the house, followed by the

silent ironhead, who moved as if he were made of flesh, not stiff metal; the iron men that served the Vryhh fascinated and frightened and occasionally infuriated Willow. She had talked enough about them to Bodri and Sunchild to grasp that they were neither demons nor conjurations and she didn't need to be afraid of them, but sometimes she had the feeling that Old Vryhh was looking at her out of their eyes. She didn't like it and avoided them when she could.

"He looks *old*." Sunchild sounded surprised and shocked.

"Old Stone Vryhh, pretty soon he get so hard set he don't move no more." Willow wiped the needle on a bit of leather and put it in the case Hyaroll had given her a couple of wakenings ago. "He old like this dirt." She patted the ground beside her. "Always been old."

"Not like this." He turned the butter shimmer of his eyes on her, blank eyeshapes blind as those in the ancient statues moldering back into the dirt they came from that Hyaroll had set up in another part of the garden so long ago he'd forgotten he had them. How Sunchild really saw was something she didn't understand, though he'd explained it a dozen times or more. She passed her hand across her eyes, her mouth, ran the tip of her tongue along her upper lip and lower. He was a golden god sculpted from sunlight as he knelt beside her, his beauty hitting her like a blow. Every waking it did that at least once, astonishing her anew until she became accustomed to seeing him and forgot the form in the friend. He caught a bit of seed fluff floating past, watched it dance on his palm, then shook it off. "Have you thought what's going to happen to us if Hyaroll dies? Seeing how he was today, well, the fear sort of forced itself on me."

She stroked her forefinger lightly over the new design on her thigh, then clucked her tongue and slapped her thighs, beginning one rhythm, then another and another, and finding no hope in any of them, let her hands lie limply on her thighs. "I see this and that and it a burn in the belly, a bad smell in the nose. Can't make a song of a bellyache and a bad smell."

A rumbling chuckle and Bodri came trundling around, settling himself on grass beside Willow with flirt of his carapace and a rustling sigh. "Succinctly put, Whisper in my heart. Can't reason without data, try it and your brain rots, thus the bad smell."

Sunchild blurred a little, developing delicate antennae in response to Bodri's emanations; Willow was the stronger sender, so he kept Otter's form. "Then we'd better start gathering some, hadn't we?"

"Have." Bodri's antennae flared to full stretch, curled back into their resting mode. "And I've been thinking." He swung his big head back and forth between them, the laughter gone out of him. "Three things. Maybe he lets kephalos keep on running things after he's dead. If we're waking then, we live out our lives here and that's it. If we're in our boxes, well, we won't know anything about it, we'll just stay there till the power runs out and we rot. A throw of the dice which it is when the time comes. That's two possibilities. The third one puts kinks in my entrails. He doesn't like letting loose of anything that's his. What if he's arranged that when he dies, kephalos opens all the boxes and has one grand funeral fire with us for fuel? It would be quite like the man to make sure no one else enjoys his possessions." He looked around, lowered his voice to a whisper. "I have been thinking it is time we found a way out of being put back in the boxes."

Willow nodded, then she frowned and looked suspiciously about.

Sunchild watched her a moment, puzzled, then his mouth moved into the archaic smile that curled the lips and missed the eyes and hinted at mystery beyond mystery but right now only meant that he understood what was itching at her. He moved away until he could shed form, then he began flowing about the lawn, a flittering streak of light. He arced overhead and whipped about them, darted down, slid into the earth, came up under the stone bench were Hyaroll had been sitting before the woman came to destroy his peace, flowed through it, went soaring into the sky, extending his substance down and down and down until he was a faint gold stain on the air, one edge almost touching the grass, the other almost touching the dome web. He quivered there a moment, then snapped back together, came to squat beside Willow and Bodri, a meld of beetle and boy, Otter's face and body and Bodri's fern-frond antennae. "There are ears and eyes," he said, "but no one's listening; kephalos is busy with other things, and Hyaroll, he's sitting in a chair staring at nothing. For what it's worth, O source of all wisdom, I think you're right, I think our end is fire."

Willow stared at him. "Little burning won't do you much."

"Leave it to Hyaroll, Willow, he'll find a way."

"Hmmp." She pulled loose a blade of grass, chewed awhile on the tender end. Holding the green strip between her teeth, she looked at Sunchild, fluttered her hand like a bird in flight, moved it from near the ground to as high as she could reach, then let it drop onto her thigh. "No cage keepin you, Sunchild. How come you stay?"

"Is a cage. The dome. I can't pass the barrier shields. The forces that make it would tease me apart so thoroughly I'd never be coherent again." He laughed. "Like dropping an ice cube in that lake; it'd melt and you'd never ever get it back again."

"Hmmp. Is over everywhere? I walk five days that way and that and that"—forefinger pointing, she moved her hand in a wide sweep—"and I get to a wall. Over all that?"

"Like a lid on a pot."

She patted the ground beside her. "Go down."

"The pot's the same as the lid, Willow in my heart. Hyaroll likes to keep what he has."

"Hmmp." She turned to Bodri. "Eh Old Bug, you been thinkin maybe how we catch Old Stone Vryhh and thump him good so he let us loose?"

"I fear not, little Willow." Bodri curled his antennae tight against his bulging skull and settled himself more solidly on the grass until he seemed little more than a mound of rock and vegetation. He half-closed his eyes and sighed noisily, ruffling the grass in front of him. "My folk were never hunters, my Willow. Plants don't run away or chase you to eat you. I have tried to think of traps and ambushes and stratagems like that, but nothing works right. I'm back to theorizing without hard data, and it's a sorry ground to stand on when your life depends on standing."

Willow drew her legs up and wrapped her arms about
them, then sat glooming over all she knew about the dome
and what it contained.

Sunchild watched them awhile, then jumped to his feet and
began dancing about the grassy oval, playing with the butter-
flies, chasing seed fluff blown about by the erratic breeze.
Though considerably older in actual years than Willow and
Bodri, he was very young for his kind and easily bored with
sitting still. And it was a late spring day of surpassing perfec-
tion and life was strong and new about him. The smell of
death coming off Hyaroll had startled the what-if reflex in his
mind and he'd spoken the thought as naturally and easily as
he absorbed and stored energy from the sun. And with the
same ease, he set the problem aside. He did not hunker down
like Bodri and worry at problems until he understood every
facet and managed to tease out a number of solutions whose
choice depended on the effect desired. Nor did he find answers like Willow in the concerte patterning of song and
dance. He absorbed everything around him, then let his cells
rub up against each other until they produced a collection of
nonserial gestalts, an almost random flow of metaphor into
which he dipped a languid hand and came up with the answer
or image or poem or equation or whatever it might be that
something in him felt was needed, a zigzag sort of thinking
that had many strengths and nothing at all to do with rigorous
analysis of a problem or the development of a line of action
step by hard-won step. So while Bodri scratched at old
ground to see if he could find something he'd missed, while
Willow clicked her tongue and tapped her fingers and worked
her memory, Sunchild flowed from shape to shape to no-
shape and enjoyed the day.

"Sunchild talk to kephalos." Willow smoothed her thumbnail along a short thin eyebrow, drew it slowly down the side
of her face. "Hmmmp." She looked into her palms, closed
her hands into fists, opened them, rippled her fingers. "Maybe
he tickle kepha into openin a hole, we steal Old Vryhh's flier,
go." She flung one hand in an arc sweeping up. "Away-away."

Bodri grunted. Tentacle fingers wandered through the garden on his back, pinching and prodding, tending the plants

like a girl lost in the delight of brushing long thick hair. He wrinkled his black snout, yawned, showing broad chisel teeth and massive grinders. "What's the point of going out of the dome? Where would we go? What would the other Vrya do to us?" He opened his eyes wide. "And how long would it take for him to hunt us down? Day and a half maybe, probably less."

"Ummmp." Willow gazed through the transparent dome at the ancient hills, the worn-out old mountains reaching a few tough snaggles toward the sky, the sun glittering on glaciers as ancient as the stone. She sighed. "Can't kill Old Vryhh. Catch him?"

"How?"

"Ummp." She got to her feet, began wandering aimlessly about the patch of grass, feet and body shifting into a few seconds of one dance, then another and another, staying with nothing longer than a breath or two. Bodri closed his eyes again. She was making him dizzy.

Sunchild came sliding down shifting into the fronded boy, shimmering with excitement, losing his edges to no-shape. "Stasis box," he sang to them, his voice gone high and ethereal. "Push Old Vryhh in and forget him."

gameboard (second of two)

AVOSING
Third of seven planets circling the green star ADIL-BADU (Eye of the Jester) in the Pajungg constellation TAH BADU (God's Fool), fourth Pajungg-colonized world.

TAH BADU
(God's Fool): appears low on the horizon in early spring (point of observation being DJIVAKIL, the planetary capital) in the north temperate zone of Pajungg; it is a grouping of nine stars that the Pajunggs see as a dancer kicking his feet in an extravagant caper. The Tah Badu is an important figure in Pajungg myth, making an appearance in almost all the hero tales, sometimes only mentioned, sometimes as a major force. He is the disrupter, the trickster, the puncturer of pomposity; he can be very subversive to the established order, and songs featuring him tend to be both obscene and dangerous, the singer sometimes losing his tongue if not his head.

DAY: 32.111
hours-Pajungg The settlers could have produced clocks that eliminated the extra seconds but clung instead to the best of home. Every ninth day there is an extra hour added to keep the timing right, the AMUN-BAR. The nine-day cycle suited

them, the AMUN-BAR suited them. After several decades it took on a mystical quality for the Avosingers. Life seemed brighter, sharper, somehow more electric, more exhilarating than during the mundane hours. The AMUN-BAR became their intimate connection with this new world, something that separated them from homeworlders and outsiders. It was something that could not be explained, only experienced.

YEAR: 367.001 days
Oblate spheroid, mean diameter 14,312 km
Density 4.06 times that of water
Rotational axis tilted 16°
No moons
Two major continents

BADICHAYAL (Jester's Fantasy):	lightly explored, sparsely settled
ANGACHI (Nothing Much):	officially unexplored; known from orbital photographs to be mostly desert beyond the coastal fringes
Seventeen major island groups:	officially unexplored; positions known from orbital photographs
KEAMA DUSTA:	Sole settlement large enough to qualify as a city. Settlement and development of Avosing has been unusually slow for several reasons. Few heavy metals, those present hard to get at. Pajungg reluctance to disturb the homeworld and the Colonial Authority further by permitting more emigration. Pajungg refusal to grant permanent residence permits to non-Pajunggs. Avosinger reluctance to take in outsiders. And the POLLEN.

POLLEN: Avosing is a pollen-saturated world with few seasonal changes in the intensity of the phenomenon, though the mix of pollens does change; the heaviest saturation is in the forest area and around its fringes. These pollens are nontoxic but all are hallucinogenic to some degree; the coarser grains must be breathed in or absorbed by the blood through unprotected cuts to have any effect on an organism, but the finer grains can be absorbed through the skin. The effect varies with the individual and the particular mix of pollens he takes in. For most of the Avosingers, the most important effect seems to be visions of the dead; it is as if the spirits of the dead had migrated with the living to Avosing; it is not uncommon even in the heart of Keama Dusta to see someone conversing animatedly with scented air and shadows. This particular reaction is apparently determined by culture, since smugglers and other visitors interviewed don't share it. The Avosingers have developed ways of coping with the pollen effect and have incorporated these into their daily lives; they have become quite sensitive to their rhythms and make sure they aren't doing something vital when they're due to tune out the world. They have also developed several native counters to the pollens for use during emergencies. These are kept secret and are sold to traders and other outsiders for exorbitant prices, Avosingers being as practical as they are mystically inclined.

SWEETAMBER: Avosing's major resource
                       The resinous semifossilized substance
                       produced by a dying Kekar-Otar tree,
                       usually one with a girth approaching a
                       thousand meters, in conjunction with
                       colonies of jarbuatin, arthropods about
                       the size of a man's big toe. The
                       jarbuatin consume certain layers of
                       wood within the tree and excrete a
                       gelatinous substance that over a hand-
                       ful of centuries, under the proper con-
                       ditions, crystallizes into the substance
                       generally called SWEETAMBER. The
                       crystals are quite hard when they're
                       ripe, closely resemble black opal; when
                       warmed against bare skin they interact
                       with natural oils to produce a delicate
                       perfume that is attractive in all senses
                       of that word.

AMBERMINER: Any person, male or female, success-
                       ful at finding SWEETAMBER and
                       staying alive to bring it out.

AMBERJACKS: gangs of men who keep to the fringes
                       of the forest, preying on amberminers.
                       The forest usually gets them if the
                       miners don't.

INTELLIGENT
INDIGENOUS LIFE: None known.

THE INHABITED REGIONS
OF AVOSING

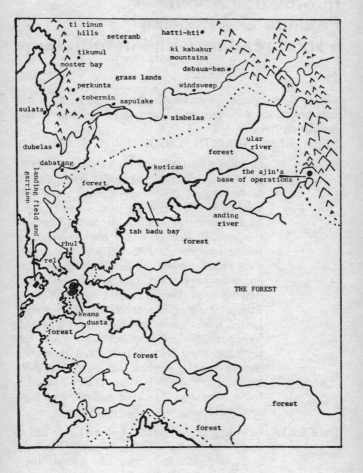

Conversation with More Information About Pajungg and Avosing
a short reading with interpolations

Aleytys's sitting room without Aleytys, late at night, a few days before the departure of Taggert and Shadith, eventual destination Avosing.
Present: HEAD, SHADITH, TAGGERT

HEAD: Ortizhao pulsed this over from University. Background on Pajunggs. (she ruffles through a pile of fax sheets, draws out a small stack held together with a paperclip, passes it to Taggert, locates another, gives that one to Shadith) You can read all that later. Let me give you the more interesting parts, then if you've got questions I can't answer, I'll toss them back to him and see what he says. (she lifts the top sheet, runs her eyes down it, begins reading phrases from it) Pajungg is a theocracy. Very stable. Lasted more than a thousand years standard. Very very slow progress in basic science. Every little thing had to be passed through a church board to see if it had the correct theological implications. Before Trader Madaskin found them, they'd reached midindustrial technology, inching into subatomic physics.

TAGGERT: (scowling at his bundle of sheets) I've had to deal with theocracies before. Touchy. You have to be born into something like that to know how to survive the traps. (pause, slow tapping of fingertips on the sheets) But we won't be operating on Pajungg, Luck be blessed. Hmm. Colonies. They can be more rigid than the homeworld, or looser, depending on who's doing the colonizing, fanatics or rebels.

HEAD: Breathe easier, Tag, you got the rebels. It's still going to be tricky. (looks at the sheet, reads) On Pajungg, the ordinary believer measures his favor with his god by how lucky he is. The hierarchy exploits this, rakes in a hefty percentage of most incomes; the churches are essentially gambling casinos. (she looks up, laughs) Curb yourself, Tag. Gambling's a religion with them. (she laughs again as Shadith grimaces at the half-pun, then reads some more) No taxes. Don't need them. And the richer you are, the holier. Closer to god. Chosen. More or less. Stealing is blasphemy; thieves can be killed by anyone who catches them. Doesn't rid Pajungg of thieves, just the stupid ones. With that sort of selection, what's left is very slick indeed. Thieves don't opt out of the system. Got their own government. The shadow side, as they call it, runs very much like the licit side. They're heretics, not unbelievers. The Ajin got too close too fast to the top men on the shadow side. Ajin. That's an earned honorific meaning something like the man with the nimblest of feet and fingers, or superthief. He left Pajungg for his health, but didn't leave his ambition behind. (she looks up) Slickest thief on Pajungg, that's your target.

TAGGERT: But we're hunting him on Avosing. Different place, different mix of people, different rules.

SHADITH: How'd they ever manage to get offworld? Like Taggert, I've seen a few theocracies. Stagnant is too mild a world.

HEAD: (switches sheets, glances at the new page, looks up) Dropped in their laps. (reads) A free trader

happened on them. (smiles) Poor dumb son
thought he'd found himself a rich new field to
plunder. (reads) The Grand Doawai wanted
new worlds to rule. He had Madaskin brought
before him and questioned about his ship: when
the Doawai wasn't satisfied with the answers
he got, he handed Madaskin over to the engiaja-
tah, the whips of god. (looks up, no laughter
this time, eyes move from Shadith to Taggert
and back) There are engiaja on Avosing too—do
your best to keep away from them. (a short
pause while she reads to the end of the page,
slips it onto the bottom of the pile; she reads
aloud from the new page) Can't get answers if
you don't know the right questions. The engiaja
are very good at getting answers, they have a
lot of experience in the field, but they didn't
know the right questions. He convinced them
he had only the dimmest notion how his ship
worked, that he knew how to fly it and that
was all he bothered to learn, why should he
stuff his head with more. They asked what was
left of him where they could get ships like his
and the training to fly them, the knowledge
how to build their own. He told them. Told
them how to summon another free-trader. Then
they let him die. (new page) Because they
knew too much about the malice of the dying,
they did not trust his information. Pajungg
lifespan averages three hundred years-standard.
They are patient. They waited for another trader
to show up. Took a hundred years, but one
came. Him they treated politely. He sold them
computers and software, stole programs for
them, kidnapped technicians and sold them as
slaves to teach the Pajunggs how to use the
technology. And when they'd got all he could
give them, the Grand Doawai gave him to the
engiaja with instructions to learn all they could

about the out-there. Then he sent ships scouting for suitable worlds. Kept starflight technology tight in the church fist. Only engiaja and fanatics fly the starships. (new page) Found four marginally useful worlds, set up colonies on these, then panicked. Pajunggs willing to leave comfortable familiar surroundings for danger and uncertainty were definitely not your ordinary citizen. And once they got settled into the new world, well, a world's a big place and they were a long long way from home. The problems were different on each world and pulled the colonists in different directions, but always away from the hard hand of the church. About fifty years-standard ago the Grand Doawai shut down all exploration and emigration and began sending out legions of enforcers to impose tight church control on the colonies. He did fairly well—even restless Pajunggs are a pretty calm bunch—then the Ajin showed up on Avosing and started aggravating the itches in the body politic. They couldn't catch him and they couldn't stop him; he wasn't about to sweep the Avosingers into kicking the home-worlders back home; they weren't going to get excited about any outsider, but they were willing to be amused by his antics and there was enough disaffection for him to collect a sizable following and keep the situation in a slow boil. Avosing's a peculiar world anyway. Lot of smuggling, the pollen, something fairly odd developing among the born-Avosingers. (she looks up, smiling) Ortizhao has several students there, observing. Smuggled them in, Pajunggs doesn't know about them, the Avosingers don't mind them, find their questions funny most of the time. He thinks the Avosingers will kick both the Colonial Authority

Jo Clayton

and the Ajin offworld when they're ready to act. That's the general situation you'll be dropping into Questions?

SHADITH: Yeah. Colonial Authority's a joke. Who really runs the place?

HEAD: Good question. Hard to answer. The grass-landers have developed a loose confederation between the villages, communal sort of thing, no one obviously in authority, but a few men and women who act as judges in disputes, settle questions of property value, act as advisers especially in deals with smugglers. Only consensus to back them, but everyone accepts their pronouncements. Why they're chosen, how they're chosen (a shrug), Ortizhao's students haven't been able to figure that out, everyone just seems to know who to ask for help. In the forest area—this includes Keama Dusta—amber miners, escpecially the retired ones, play the same role as the grassland judges. Just about everyone, whatever they do, if they live in or around the forest, they give lip service to the Colonial Authority but go to the nearest miner with their real problems. Ortizhao says he's beginning to get a glimmer of some organizing force behind all this but doesn't want to talk about it yet. And there's always the pollen. That complicates everything. There's some kind of potion the Avosingers make that's fairly safe to take in small quantities that seems to nullify some of the worst effects of the pollen, enough to let you move around without falling over your feet. The Pajunggs provided us with some when we insisted. University has been working on it, trying to duplicate it, but it's an enormously complicated organic. Partly from the liver of a fish the Avosingers won't identify, partly from an herb mix they say even less about. Doawai's engiaja have never managed to catch anyone who knew the ingredients, or they wouldn't talk if they did get caught. Anyway, right now we can't make it or analyze it, so we do what everyone else does and go by rule of thumb, one gram for every fifty kilos bodyweight every three days. And hope you aren't allergic to it.

SHADITH: Uh-huh. Given there's Kell's trap waiting for the next Hunter, the Ajin's probable paranoia about strangers, church enforcers looking for anything they can stomp, a population that doesn't care a whole helluva for either side and is leery of strangers, and that invisible government, I'd say we go in very carefully and very quietly. . . .

TAGGERT: And separately.

SHADITH: Right. And hope we meet in the middle with our hands around the Ajin's throat.

AVOSING
developing a second line of attack

Shadith brought the lander down about two hours before the local sunset; the globular little ship looked like a giant boulder and had some very sneaky shields. Swardheld was noncommittal about where and from whom he'd purchased that lander and even less forthcoming about why—though Shadith had some well-developed theories about that. When she finally located him, he groused about being left out of the game, but didn't complain all that much, let her have the flier and looked relieved when she left; he was nosing into something that interested him rather more than Aleytys's difficulties. *Is that what's coming to us,* Shadith wondered, *do we drift apart and finally have nothing to say to each other after so many years together?*

She landed on a tiny island, little more than a volcanic peak with touches of green, a few vines crawling up out of the sea, testing out the land, their roots still deep submerged. The pebbly shore was alive with small crustaceans that followed the vines out of the water, noisy with their cricks and clatters. With Linfyar helping her, she carried smaller stones and piled them haphazard about the lander until it looked as much a part of the island as they did, then she and Linfy juggled the shell and its bubble-seal across the groaning shifting vines, launched the shell and spent the straggles of daylight locking the plastic bubble in place, getting wet and battered, giggling and staggering about, beyond all expectation enjoying this misery perhaps because it was the beginning of danger and excitement, perhaps because they were young and healthy and simmering with unused energy.

74

Shadith pushed Linfy in through the hatch, tumbled in after him, checked to see the gear was properly tied down, then stretched out on the padded cot and started the motors driving the waterjets. As they eased away from the shore, Linfyar curled up on the other cot, more subdued inside the bubble: it shut off his major sense like a blindfold on a sighted boy. He dabbed at his arms and legs with a spongy towel, leaving for Shadith all worry about where they were going and how they were going to get there.

The shell ran low in the water, half the time almost submerged, the Lokattor holding them on course. It was a rough jolting ride, the shell tossed up by the wave it was mounting, slammed back down, over and over and over, without respite. The motor that powered the jets was nearly silent, any small sounds it made lost in the scramble of wind and water, but that silence cost them speed—the shell forged steadily ahead, swept up and slammed down, cutting across the long waves as it moved toward the mainland, but it moved no faster than a man's quick walk. A touch of insurance, perhaps not needed, but Shadith took chances only where there some possibility of payoff. Not far to the north was the large island that held the world's sole spaceport and most of the on-planet detection equipment, along with a garrison of church enforcers meant to discourage illegal landings such as the one she'd just made. According to Head's notes, the Pajunggs were dickering with several Companies for satellites and emission sniffers, hoping to cut into the hordes of smugglers hitting the surface of Avosing, drawn like flies by the sweetamber and the drugs distilled by the foresters from local plants, but they wanted the Avosingers to pay for the scanners. The colonists got a good portion of their income from dealing with those smugglers, and a lot of technology the church didn't want them to have; they weren't about to put themselves out of business, though they were too wary of the homeworld to be blunt about it; they just dragged their feet, studied the proposed systems with skeptical intensity, made reasonable objections and went on dealing with the smugglers, who had no more difficulty than Shadith evading the limited resources of the Authority. Up the Avosingers, she thought, may their shadows ever increase.

For four long hours the shell jolted across the ocean, then Shadith brought it nosing into an inlet about a day's march south of Keama Dusta, found a place where the land sloped to a flat sandy beach and drove the shell up onto the sand.

Standing in the hatch, she used a flamer on low power to sweep a section of the beach clean of vine and the scurrying life swarming there; with Linfyar perched on top of the bubble, ears twitching, pulsing out exploring whistles, she set up a tingler fence to keep the sand clean and discourage anything hungry that might come out of the forest tempted by the scent of warm meat. *I'll keep my meat on my bones, thank you.* She wrinkled her nose at the huge dark trees that came to the edge of the low wall of earth at the back of the beach, brooding in a silence filled with creaks, crackles, rustling leaves, long wavering cries. "Definitely not in the dark," she said.

"What?" Linfy slid off the bubble and came to stand beside her.

"We'll spend the rest of the night here."

"Sure. I'm hungry."

"Well, help me unload the shell and hide it. Then we'll eat."

Shadith spread her blanket close to the fence and sat looking out across the water. She felt extraordinarily alive. Free. On her own again, in her own body. Operating a scam of sorts, living by her wits and her talents. *Speaking of talents, wonder if mind-riding works on arthropods, the big ones making all that noise.* She reached into the forest and sought out the most organized mind, meaning to slip into it and see what she could learn. *Ah, here we go.* She started in, gulped in surprise, wrenched herself loose before she was controlled by something operating in that mind, a mind that was so close to true self-awareness, so close to true intelligence, she hadn't a hope of controlling it even without that other thing. Shaken

but fascinated—no hostility in that touch, just curiosity and a cheerful interest—she reached again, more cautiously. *Who?*
   Who you?
   A giggle tickled through her. *Singer, poet, friend.* Another giggle.
   Wanting?
   Knowing. Hunting. Lots and lots and lots of things.
   Patience, small voice.
   Why?
   Why not? The presence withdrew.
   "Now that's a thing." She pulled her legs up and clasped her arms about them. "Did that really happen or am I zonked in spite of that liver juice?" She giggled and dug at the wet sand with her bare toes. "Me with voices in my head. Funny, uh-huh."
   In a half-dream, deeply relaxed, she drifted for several hours until, toward dawn, mist rose from the waves and danced for her, silver streamers that shaped themselves into forms she remembered from so long ago she couldn't count the years, her six sisters, Weavers of Shayalin.
   She gazed at the graceful swaying images, black-and-silver similitudes of Naya, Zayalla, Annethi, Itsaya, Talitt and Sullan. Six sisters, weaving dreams and selling them to anyone who'd buy; from alien eyes, she gazed and could not quite believe in them. Weavers of Shayalin, dancing dreams.
   She watched the figures spin threads from themselves to shape shifting images, icons out of memory, dreams she'd learned too well in that long ago, that time long past.
   But the dance was silent, it lacked the play of the blended voices, was painful in that lack; when she could bear the silence no longer, she began to sing the ancient croon that mated with that dance, faltering at first because the human larynx could not produce all the overtones the Shayalin throat could hold; almost of their own volition her fingers sought out pebbles on the beach; she cupped them in a closed hand and clicked them together. Deep within her she was aware it was all illusion, a creation of her mind and the ambient pollen, but she was willing, more than willing, to accept the show and enjoy this projection of memory outside her head.

As she worked herself into the croon, shaking the three water-smoothed stones, the images of her sisters grew more detailed; eventually she thought she saw Itsaya wink at her, saw Naya smile, Zaya shake her hips and grin over her shoulder, saw each of the sisters acknowledging her with some characteristic gesture. She let herself sink into the experience, her whole body responding with both joy and sorrow.

Linfyar slept, hearing nothing.

The song went on. She moved in the dream dance with her sisters as she had before, odd one out, half the age of the others, the link to store the dance patterns, the shaping words, and pass them on to her children, her six and then one, six sterile daughters and one fertile hatchling that could be either male or female.

When the dawn was a faint red line on the horizon, when her voice had grown hoarse, her arm weary, she stopped her song and watched the similitudes dissolve into shapeless shreds of mist. As her concentration lapsed, she felt the presence behind her, listening and responding. Laughter and applause flooded over her. The presence retreated. She wondered again if it was just a twist of her imagination, then shook her head. Something different there, an alien quality she could almost taste, yes that was it, a different flavor on the tongue. She watched water and sky redden, then fade to an icy gray with the dawning.

When the sun was fully up, she woke a reluctant, grumbling Linfyar, handed him a meal pack and began rolling up the blankets, buckling them into the shoulder straps so Linfy could carry them. She collapsed the tingler fence and tucked it in her pack, smoothed her hand down the outside of the harp case, tapped her fingers on the leather, snapped it open, touched the loosened strings, sighed at the dull toneless tunks she produced. "Well, that can wait."

"What?"

"Bury that when you're finished with it."

"Sure."

"I mean it, imp."

"I hear you."

"Hunh." She tied the case onto the backpack, slid her arms into the straps of the packframe and rocked onto her feet. "We don't want anyone knowing where and when we came ashore."

He whistled a short sassy trill, modulated it into a breathy, cheery tune, kicked a groove in the sand, set the pack in it with exaggerated deliberation. In an almost dance, he used his feet to scrape sand over the pack, listening to the sounds the grains made so he'd know when the job was finished, squatted and patted the loose soil down with finicky little touches, smoothing it and smoothing it, passing his fingertips over the patch, smoothing it again.

She watched a minute, shook her head. "Stop fooling, imp. You've made your point. Here. Take this." She tapped the blanket roll against his arm. "I'm set. Let's go."

After she scrambled over the edge of the earth wall and pushed onto her feet, she eyed the great trees uneasily. Not so long ago a carnivorous collection of monsters very much like these had come close to sucking her dry. She moved cautiously after Linfyar, relieved when she passed through the margin of brush and fern to find no skirts of blood-drinking air roots on the trunks. She stayed wary. You never knew what trees could get up to, no matter how safe and rooted they looked.

The presence was suddenly there, laughing.

"It's all right for you," she said aloud, indignation quivering in her voice. "You know this place."

"What?" Linfyar turned his head, one ear quivering at her.

"Never mind." She caught up with him, glared at the trees around them, walked close beside him. Soft amused laughter sounded in her head. She ignored it, but after a tense sweaty kilometer or so, she saw the humor in the situation and grinned into the dappled shadow as she walked beneath the trees. After all those years as a voice in someone else's head, who was she to object to a voice walking through her own?

*   *   *

They walked north, keeping to the fringes of the forest. Now and then Linfyar would stumble, turn his head side to side, his pointed fawn's ears twitching. For the first time she thought to wonder what hallucination was like for someone born without eyes. Imagined sound? What kind? Memories from his old home? She started to ask, but changed her mind; she didn't want to be a part of the illusions, didn't know whether he would hear what she said or distort it into something else, perhaps something frightening. After several of these episodes, she saw him shake his head and then his whole body, grin and begin a lilting whistle, a raunchy trader's song she'd taught him on Ibex when Aleytys was off somewhere. She smiled. Aleytys fussed too much. Worried over things. In a way Ibex was good for her, all those dreary little enclaves obsessed with killing off everyone who was different and unless she wanted to spend a Vryhh lifetime there she couldn't change any of it; with all her power she couldn't boot them into righteousness. Still, just as well she grew up with that uncomfortable conscience firmly installed— what would she be like without it? Shadith shivered. *I should be glad she worries—I wouldn't be taking this walk otherwise.*

Halfway through the morning the presence came tickling back, didn't say anything, just hung around watching. She glanced at Linfyar to see if he felt anything. Neither she nor Aleytys knew much about the limits of his perceptions; he kept surprising them. He showed no signs of noticing anything strange floating about. He was whistling, more softly now, spaced bursts of sound, as if he were trying out his hallucinations, working on them, playing with the tricks his mind was throwing him. She laughed. He swung around and began to walk backward, grinning at her, his ears shivering and shifting about. "I think you like this crazy world," she said.

"Ay-yeh, Shadow." He waited for her, turned around and jigged along beside her. "Crazy-crazy." He liked the sound of the doubled word, said it again, "Crazy-crazy," began chanting it over and over under his breath. She worried for a moment about how he was going to find his way without his locator pulses, but his proximity sense and whatever else he

had was working well enough, because he negotiated the
tangle of roots more nimbly than she, avoided patches of
brush and low-hanging tree limbs, all the while continuing
the sotto-voce chant, changing words to try out different
combinations of sounds.

The world blurred suddenly, it warped and flowed into
strange shapes about her, images dripping down, melting into
each other, color melting into color, shapes ballooning, dissi-
pating like smoke, shapes doubling and redoubling. She stumbled to a stop, lost in this chaos, flung her hands out groping
for something solid. Anything. A small warm hand closed on
hers, held it with a strength that vaguely surprised her; she
heard a gush of words but understood none of them, their
sounds as distorted as the colors and shapes, understood only
that it was Linfyar who spoke. Trembling with relief, she
clung to those anchor points, Linfy's hand and Linfy's voice,
and let him lead her until the confusion faded.

When the sun was close to directly overhead, they stopped
to eat and rest awhile; in a thirty-two-hour day it was a long
time between dawn and noon. As they ate they talked about
things unconnected with this disconcerting world, things back
on Wolff, horses and colts, the vagaries of the house cats, the
song of birds that lived in the grove of trees behind the house,
the necessity or not for Linfyar to spend some years in
school; they tried out a few songs, blending their voices at
times, at times Shadith singing to Linfy's whistle, at times he
singing while she beat the rhythm with her palms on the
leather of her harp case. The listener in the forest drifted in
closer sometimes, sometimes retreated until Shadith almost
couldn't feel him, but never quite went away.

Shortly after they started on, Linfyar staggered, then began
running. Shadith ran after him, caught him before he could
hurt himself, hugged him tight against her, remembering how
much comfort she'd found in his touch when she suffered
chaos. Disoriented and frightened, he clung to her, whimpering and shuddering. She looked about, found a knot of roots
high enough to make a seat, lifted him into her lap and
rocked him like a baby, stifling her urge to sing to him; it
might make his horrors worse.

Finally she heard a long shuddering sigh and he relaxed against her. She risked a word. "Over?"

"Uh-huh, Shadow." For a moment longer he nestled against her, then he pushed away with nervous strength and stood on the bed of leaves with feet apart, his body a shout of defiance; whistling as loud as he could, he flung a scornful trill at the forest. "Hunh," he said. "Stupid trees."

Shadith laughed and rocked back onto her feet, the pack a weight that grew heavier with each hour. A lot of hours ahead before they got to the end of Linfy's stupid trees. She thought of making camp here and going on in the morning, then sighed and began walking. Might as well keep going. God knew what prowled here in the dark.

Episodes of confusion came steadily after that, none of them quite as bad as the first. Linfyar and she helped each other and kept moving; their metabolisms differed enough for one to be clear-headed when the other was muzzy. Irritated and a little afraid, she was tempted to take more of the counteractant, but Head had warned her against that. "We're running on guess and hope," she'd said, "and the fact that this glop has never killed anyone, though a lot of different types have taken it. Both you and the boy are mutated stock, no knowing what it'll do to you; the only reason for chancing it is that going in without it would probably be worse." Shadith endured and Linfyar endured and both kept moving. The exercise seemed to help. By midafternoon the severity of the hallucinations had diminished so much that for Shadith it was like looking at the world about her though a distorting screen. Shapes and colors changed, sometimes did the melting trick, but she knew where she was and what was around her no matter how wild the contortions got. Her mind and body were adjusting to the world, a wrenching experience but one that seemed about over. Linfyar was experimenting with sound, playing with what had terrified him just a short while before, so she knew he'd passed his crisis and was enjoying himself again; she watched him strutting along and chuckled softly. *I told Lee you were a tough little imp*, she thought, *and so you are, oh yes you are.*

*   *   *

When the sun was a hand's breadth above the horizon and shadows were swallowing the expanse of three-lobed ground-cover plant thick and soft as moss that stretched from the forest to the outskirts of the city, Shadith and Linfyar walked from under the trees and stopped after a few steps onto the clovermoss, enjoying the sudden sweep of a brisk cool wind.

Linfyar bounced on the springy growth, bent and broke off a stem, crushed the leaves and sniffed at them. "Walking on a mattress," he said. "Smells good." He rubbed the sap off his fingers, drooped all over, put on a pathetic little smile, turned himself into an image of extreme debility. "I'm tired, Shadow. I'm hungry. Let's stop."

"We're almost there, Linfy."

"You said that before." He dropped into a squat, looked stubborn. "You've been saying that for the longest."

"Well, it's really true now, we've got maybe half a kilometer to go. I can see it, Linfy, and if you listen, you can probably hear something. Besides, do you want to spend the night around the forest? Remember what we ran into on Ibex."

He crouched where he was without responding, his fingers wandering across the clovermoss, but his ears twitched, then swiveled in the direction of the city. A minute more and he got wearily to his feet, no play-acting this time. *He really is tired,* she thought. *Poor baby.* He sighed. "When can we stop?"

"Soon as we find a place to stay."

The inner city, the center of government on Avosing with its tall sealed buildings and covered ways, where the homeworlders of the Colonial Authority lived and worked, that city sat inside a high wall that was as unnecessary as it was massive, serving as a visual symbol of the distrust all of those inside it had for the world they were supposed to govern. The wall had only two gates—airlocks fitted with baffles and filters and everything else Pajunggs could think of to keep out Avosing air and the confusion it carried. One gate led to the great cathedral casino, the other into the city proper. Avosingers seldom used that one, for the city made them uncomfortable;

they went into it when they had unavoidable business with the Authority and otherwise stayed away. The rest of Keama Dusta, the greater part, was a vast sprawl of homes and businesses, huts and factories, taverns and warehouses, shops and showplaces, a clotted rambling conglomeration without apparent pattern to it.

Shadith walked into the fringes of the city, past crude shacks that could have been eyesores but weren't, structures thrown together from scrap wood, nothing painted, bits of this sort of wood and that fitted together into curving natural shapes, aged by time and weather into soft grays and umbers, vines of the blooming sort twisting about the timbers until the distinction between outside and in was lost. The strong slanting light from the setting sun intensified the textures, adding strong blacks and reddish highlights to the more muted colors. *I think I'm going to like these people, anyone with such a feeling for beauty.* She wrinkled her nose as the presence laughed in her head. *Giggling fool,* she thought at it. There were no streets, no straight lines anywhere, just the irregular spaces between the houses, some long and thin, some like roundish bulbs on a vine, all covered with the vigorous clovermoss. Spaces filled with a ferment of life, children running everywhere, food vendors with steaming everything on skewers over coals and under heat lights, taverns with clusters of tables out on the moss, with men and women sitting over beer and wine talking, laughing, men and women standing about talking with the air.

A lean woman with gray-streaked hair sat on the clovermoss in one of the nodes, legs crossed, back straight, hands resting on her knees, a vague smile lifting thin lips, lost in some ancient memory, watching it move before her, something cherished by the look on her lined leathery face. Playing shouting wrestling slapping at each other, children ran and tumbled about her, giving her a polite space to herself. When one of them dropped out of the game to stare at a patch of air, the others left that same sort of space about him or her and went on their games and he or she rejoined the action a little later without comment on either side.

All this was very interesting, but she was tired and Linfyar was stumbling along, clinging to her. She worked her way to one of the larger nodes, found an unoccupied patch of clovermoss, settled her pack beside her with Linfyar to guard it, unsnapped the harp case and sat tuning the harp until she had it right.

She didn't know what the local custom was for street performers—*don't even have streets here*—or what bureaucratic rites she was skipping, though Head had said the Authority rarely stuck its collective nose outside the walls; it was the invisible government she'd have to placate. Setting up and performing should bring quick action on that; street people, even without streets, protected their privileges. She got interested looks as she finished the tuning and began a ramble across the strings searching for something that felt right for the people and the place. More Avosingers drifted up and settled onto the clovermoss waiting for her to begin.

Perhaps because of the long dreamvision the night before, what finally felt right was the music of her people. She slid into the croon, using the harp to amplify her range and provide the sounds her voice could not. Almost at once her sisters were dancing again, frail ghosts swaying through the sundown shadows and the gathering crowd.

Beside her Linfyar straightened his narrow shoulders and began weaving his whistle into her wordless song, deepening and broadening the sound as if he tied into her memories as deeply as she did.

The Avosingers listened like ancient clients, eyes wide and dreaming.

And she was doing what she'd never thought to do, singing a dream for others. She was the link who learned and passed on but never performed except for her mother, her trainer, a link as she was. Before the Kanzedor raid that killed her mother and cast her aside, that took her sisters and her aunts, one of the many slave raids that stripped Shayalin of its weavers and destroyed a culture that had lasted for millennia, before she was wrenched from all she knew, sold as trash at the first bid, thrown on her own, her kin vanishing forever, her world irretrievably out of reach (by the time she worked herself loose, it had vanished as thoroughly as her family), before all that, her duty was to store in her brain what could not be recorded or written down, what her grandfather passed to her mother, her mother to her.

And as she made her music, it came to her that the weavers of Shayalin might be reborn—not as they were, there were no more Shallal, but something . . . something might be done. Maybe there were people she could teach, maybe a piece of that long-forgotten culture could live again. Hope throbbed in her voice, and joy. . . .

When the croon was finished, she settled the harp against her thigh and gave herself over to feeling good, smiling wearily as Linfyar jumped to his feet and began moving through the wakening crowd, shaking the collecting bowl, whistling a cheery coaxing tune, adding his charm to their appreciation to milk a handsome coinflow from the Avosingers.

One of her listeners got to his feet, shook his head and scuffed over to her, hands in the pockets of his shorts, a boy who couldn't be much older than Linfyar. "That's Sojohl's spot."

"Any objection to my using it when he's not around?"

The boy rubbed a bare foot over the clovermoss, wiggled his thick reddish brows, worked his mouth, stared vaguely over her head as he thought over his answer, scratched beside his nose, grinned suddenly, an electric beam as effective as any of Linfyar's. "Nah," he said. "But you got to move when he comes."

"How far?"

" 'Nother k'shun over."

K'shun, she thought. Emptiness. Right. This node is Sojohl's territory, whoever he is, and I move to the next empty node if he shows up. "Thanks," she said aloud. "I'm new here."

"Yeah, I thought."

She looked around. Linfyar was about finished; most of the crowd was drifting off. She turned back to the boy. "You know a place I can stay cheap? My friend and me, we need a roof and supper, been a long day, we're worn out."

He looked her over, turned to watch Linfyar. She didn't try rushing him, feeling no urge to rush, though the sun was beginning to play color tricks on the clouds overhead and the drifts of pollen that caught the light and glittered through the thick air, making round rainbows that shifted with the slow shift of the light.

"My mam," the boy said, startling her out of her drift. "She got a vacancy. You want, I could take you there."

"Yeah, why not?" She clamped her teeth together to shut in a yawn, snapped the harp back in its case. With a sigh of weariness and a feeling she was bruised to the bone by them, she slid her arms into the packframe straps, smiled her pleasure as the boy pulled her to her feet. "Mind if we wait till Linfy's finished? Your mother, however kind, will want to be paid."

"Yeah." He turned to watch Linfyar. His face was a little weasel's, all pointed, nose and mouth with almost no chin, close-clipped red hair like a weasel's fur; though he was as grubby as any boy would be at the end of an active day, it was only a single day's accumulation of dirt, no patina of neglect about him; she'd seen the signs often enough in her wanderings. He reached out, touched the harp case, pulled his hand back though she hadn't said anything. "You sing good."

"Thanks."

"That hard to learn?"

"Depends." She untied her belt pouch and watched Linfyar drifting back. "I'm Shadith," she said. "Friends call me Shadow. You can."

"Me, I'm Tjepa. Mam's Perolat."

"Well, Tjepa-si, I thank you."

Grinning again, he sketched a bow, pleased with her and with himself.

"How come you're the only one come to talk to me, Tjepa-si? Linfy's getting a good take, so they must have liked us."

"You sure don't know much."

"Tjepa, my friend, I have been here not so very long."

He jerked a thumb at the darkening sky. "Is it really so differnt up there?"

"All kinds of differnt."

He eyed her skeptically. "I bet you don't really know. I

bet you run away from home to here and don't know nothing about nothing."

"Hanh. Maybe you would, young Tjepa, and maybe you'd lose. Different kinds, different times. I'm a lot older'n I look to you. So why no talking?"

"Leavin it to me."

She raised her brows but said nothing as she opened the pouch and let Linfyar scoop the coins into it. After she tied the pouch back to the belt, she said, "Tjepa, this is Linfyar, my friend. Linfy, this is Tjepa. He says his mam can maybe rent us a room."

Tjepa stared at Linfyar, fascinated. "You got no eyes," he said. "How do you know where you're going?"

"Ears," Linfyar said and wriggled his. He pursed his lips and pulsed a rapid series of inaudible whistles at Tjepa. Shadith watched, amused. *Showing off,* she thought. *Wonder what other senses he's using and not saying.* "You 'bout this much taller'n me"—he measured off about an inch between thumb and forefinger—"and you're wearing shorts and a shirt made outta some slippery stuff, don't know what, and you got nothing on your feet and you got a gap in your front teeth that shows when you talk."

"Hey wild, Linfy, how you do that?"

Shadith tapped him on the shoulder. "Hey yourself, Tjepa-si. Let's go. It's getting dark and we're plenty hungry."

He nodded and started off one of the side spaces, a snake crawl that wriggled even deeper into the city, with Linfyar strutting beside him, forgetting his fatigue as he played his tricks for his new acquaintance, bouncing silent whistles off buildings around them or folk walking along, then describing what he learned. Shadith followed the two boys, amused by their antics and interest in each other. She worried briefly about Linfyar's chatter, wondering if he'd say too much about why they were here, but he'd learned survival in a hard school; playing a role was as natural to him as breathing. He was enjoying himself without giving Tjepa anything but the story they'd worked out. She relaxed and drifted along, the edges melting about her now and then but only small almost homey bits of disorientation. Rather pleasant, a floating bouncy

feeling. She came out of it with something like regret. A few
turns later she saw Linfy shiver and stop walking. Tjepa
quieted, led Linfyar on until he recovered, then plunged again
into animated exchange.

Tjepa led them to a large rambling inn built close to the
city wall, a ragged circle of small independent apartments
joined by a raised wooden walk with a vaulted roof resting on
irregular arches that looked grown in place rather than shaped
by any hand. Winding in and around the arches and over the
roofs of the apartment, luxuriant vines put out sprays of
crimson or saffron blooms or elaborate lacy leaves. The
apartment-cabins had tall thin windows with dark glass set in
graceful lead tracery; they were built of woods that had
weathered to a silver gray, roofed with rough-cut shingles of
the same silken gray. The inn had a graceful unstudied ease;
it sang to her of folk who liked to touch and stroke, who had
an eye for form and line, who had an aversion for symmetry
and repeating themselves, liking rather to take a theme through
subtly differing variations. It sang to her, *We are a proud and
independent folk, we prize harmony with earth and air and
each other*. She felt comfortable here; as she followed Tjepa
through one of the wider arches, she thought, *I'm coming
back here someday when I've got nothing on my mind but
enjoying myself*.

Inside the ring of cabins and the covered walks there were
neat kitchen gardens where vegetables and herbs native to this
world mixed with those from the homeworld, both sorts
growing with a vigor that reinforced the feeling of kinship
with earth and green growing things. She followed Tjepa and
Linfyar along the spoke-walk to the tower in the center.
Roughly circular, it looked like the lopped-off trunk of one of
the giant Kekar-Otar trees, rising three times as high as the
cabins, the same kind of long narrow windows scattered in a
haphazard way that made it difficult to tell how the inside
was arranged, but suggested it followed the freeform flow of
the covered walk. *I do like this place*, she thought once
again, and smiled at Tjepa's back.

Tjepa's mother, Perolat, was a tall lanky woman who
looked like a sister of the Avosinger in the meditative trance

in one of the outer k'saha, as much a kinship of spirit as it
was of form. She'd seen a number of men and women with
that calm competent look, that detachment, that lack of hurry,
seen them sitting at tables over glasses of wine, seen them
ambling along talking quietly together, seen them in the
crowd that gathered to listen to her. Perolat sat stretched out
in a comfortable chair with a glass of wine at her elbow,
watching pot lids bumping on the stove, wreathed in smells
that started Shadith's mouth watering and her stomach cramping, reminding her how hungry she was. Linfyar whistled a
lilting trill full of happy anticipation, but minded his manners
and waited for Perolat to speak.

Perolat's left leg was propped on a stool, metal and wood
and circuitry below her knee. She wore shorts and shirt like
her son, making no effort to conceal the prosthesis. She
looked lazy and contented and wholly unsurprised to see her
son dragging strangers into her kitchen. She sat up, smiled a
welcome, raised heavy pepper-and-salt eyebrows.

"Mam, this is Shadith and Linfyar. They new in Dusta and
needing a place to say. She says call her Shadow. She play
f-i-i-ine music."

Perolat pushed a strand of soft gray hair off her face.
"Musician?"

Shadith nodded, turned so Perolat could see the harp case
lashed to the pack.

"New here."

"Uh-huh. This morning."

"No ships down today."

Shadith smiled. "How interesting."

"Right. Your business. Hmm. Some rules we have here. I
don't know how you pay your way, girl, and don't get shook
by what I say. You a thief, that's all right long as you touch
nothing in the bebamp'n. That's us here outside the walls.
Authority and cathedral's fair game. Out here I don't care if
you see sweetamber heaped high, you don't touch. Not saying
you are a thief, you understand, but seems to me it takes
more'n a few songs to buy passage even on a smuggler's
ship, and you don't look old enough, or—forgive me—lush
enough to whore your way here, though there are some

clowns who like 'em young. Hmm. You plan to labor horizontal, do it outside the bebamp'n, don't mess in your nest. No offense meant."

"None taken. How much for a roof and meals?"

"Five piah silver the nineday, food extra."

Shadith frowned, then nodded; should have enough from the collection to handle that. "I'll take it a nineday at a time, if that's all right." She sniffed and smiled. "And supper when it's ready."

"Good enough. Tjee, take your friends over to Gourd." She turned to Shadith. "I named them for local plants. Supper's ten piah copper, pay when you get back here. You can give Tjee the rent once you get settled in. Supper will be ready in a half hour; come back here, I'll show you where we eat."

Tjepa led them away from the kitchen along a covered spoke. "Mam was the best amberminer on Avosing before she stepped into a senget nest and got stung so bad. Me, when I'm old enough, I'm gonna be better."

"Your mam, she had to quit because of her leg?"

"The leg she don't have, uh-huh. There some baad burks out there just waiting for you if you holdin amber. Got no nose, them, forest don't like 'em, they hang around the outside waitin for miners to come by. You got to be fast and tough for findin the lodes, then you got to be faster and tougher to get th' amber back. And the forest got to like you and you got to have a nose to find it in the first place."

"The amberjacks, they don't bother you here?"

"Better not." He waved a hand. "This part o' the bebamp'n, it's all miners and their fam'lies. Ol' jack he down to bones 'fore he get more'n two steps, and he know it. Like Mam said, what folk do outside is their business, here's home." He stopped before a cabin, slapped his hand against a metal plate set into the door. It slid swiftly, silently into the wall. Inside, lights came on. He crossed the room, stopped by metal panels etched and stained into a pleasant abstract of twisty vines, touched a sensor in one corner; one panel slid aside, uncovering a bank of sensor squares and a small viewscreen with a silver-blue shimmer. He ran a sequence on the squares, looked over his shoulder. "Shadow, you and Linfy put your hands flat on here, then it's you who can make things work. Door too." He waited until Shadith guided Linfyar's hands to the screen, then put her own there, then he said, "All right, you need anything else?"

Shadith looked around. A comfortable room, all earth colors, broad comfortable chairs, small tables, pleasant indirect lighting; a welcoming room and more for the money than she'd expected. She touched the border of the console. *Almost a gift. I wonder why.* She lifted her head, startled, as she felt a familiar tickling nudge from the presence in the forest. *Busy old ghost, aren't you?* She clicked her nail against the metal. "This isn't Pajungg make."

"For sure no. Mam got this stuff off a smuggler."

"Should you be talking like that to strangers?"

"Ahh, you're a right 'un. Mam knows."

"Hmmm. What will Linfy's whistles to do this equipment? He needs to find his way around but we can't afford to pay for replacements."

Tjepa frowned, shook his head. "Don't know; maybe he better hold off till I ask Mam." He scowled at the screen. "I can work it, that's about all. Mam wants to send me to school offworld so I can learn stuff like that." He wrinkled his nose, shoved his hands into his pockets. "I don't need to know all that brakka to mine amber."

"Maybe your mam doesn't want you losing a piece of your leg like her."

"Hunh, Mam don't worry about brakka like that; she just don't want to pay outsiders if she don't have to."

"See, Shadow"—Linfy's ears were flicking about, he was almost bouncing in place—"school's a waste of time for Tjee. He knows what he wants. Me too."

"Hunh, you! What do you know? Tjepa-si, ask your mam about up to ninety thousand per. About there. And before you go . . ." She settled herself in the nearest chair, pulled up a table. She scooped a handful of coins from her belt pouch, spread them on the table so she could get a look at them.

Copper and silver, no gold. Octagonal coins with milled edges.

Keeping his hands pushed down in his pockets Tjepa sauntered across to the table. "Hey, you did good, Shadow, that's not even half, is it?"

"No."

He glanced at her, turned very serious. "That big 'un, that's a ten-piah silver. Musta been a miner—more'n some folk make a whole week. The little silver ones, they're piahs, one silver each. You give me five o' those, you're set. Copper's same as silver. Big 'uns are ten-piah coppers, little 'uns are one-piahs. One hundred copper piahs make a silver."

She slid five of the silver piahs off the table into her hand, held them out. "Thanks, Tjee."

" 'S nothin, Shadow." He turned to go, turned back. "You think you could teach me, maybe a little bit, get me started like, playin something like . . . like your harp?" He cleared his throat. "I can pay. A little. I get an allowance, earn me a copper or two sometimes runnin for folk."

She heard the wistful longing he was trying to suppress and couldn't withstand its appeal. "A little maybe, but Linfy and me we don't stay anywhere very long. It wouldn't be much. Maybe a copper a nineday?"

He nodded. "I could go that."

"Well, if you find out you like it, maybe your mam could find you a real teacher. I have to tell you, Tjee, it's work."

" 'S all right." With a quick wave he trotted from the room.

Linfyar was silent; she could feel him sulking. She ignored him, emptied the pouch on the table and began sorting the coins out, counting them and slipping them back into the pouch. Half hidden in a pile of coppers she saw a small dark blob shaped like a teardrop. She held it to the light and watched blue and green and red fires play in its heart. Flawed but still sweetamber, and worth more than all the coins she'd collected. She closed her fingers over the drop, warmed it, then brought it close to her nose and smelled for the first time the fugitive sweet bite of amberscent.

"What's that?" Sulks forgotten, Linfyar knelt beside her, nose twitching.

"You cut deep enough, it's why we're here, Linfy." She held out her hand, let him take the drop. "Why everyone's here."

"Mmmmmh." A long blissful sigh.

"I see you like it." She chuckled, finished counting the coins and sliding them back in the pouch. "Forty-three piahs silver, plus the five I gave Tjepa makes forty-eight. Two hundred six piahs copper. Not bad for an unadvertised improvised effort. Lovely friendly place, isn't it, Linfy?"

"Mmmm."

She looked around, frowning. He was sniffing at the amber, his nose nudging at the drop, his ears laid back flat against his head, his mouth drooping open. "Getting high, are you?" She wrapped her hand around one thin wrist, doing nothing right then but letting him feel her hold. "This isn't going to be a problem, is it, imp?"

He said nothing, just shrugged and set the amber drop on the table. She took her hand away and got to her feet.

"We'd better start over for supper. I'm hungry enough to eat my way there."

Linfyar yawned and stretched, then got to his feet. He stretched again, wiggled all over, patted his stomach. "Me too. And tired enough to fall asleep in the soup." He giggled at the thought, mimed swimming motions as he followed her from the room.

The dining area was a long narrow room next to the kitchen, one wall a shallow curve with tall windows that let in the starlight. The air was scrubbed and just cool enough to milk an extra touch of pleasure from the fragrant steaming dishes marching down the center of a long table made from a dark glowing wood hand-rubbed to a high gloss. A dozen others looked up as Perolat ushered them in, seven women, five men, all of them spirit-kin to Perolat. *Step into my parlor*, Shadith thought. *Seems like the invisible government wants to look me over; is this luck or what?*

"This is Shadith called Shadow, maker of f-i-i-ine music

according to my son, and her companion Linfyar,'' Perolat
said, then led them to vacant chairs at the table.

The meal was a gentle but exhaustive inquisition. Perolat
saw to the serving while the others probed Shadith's past, her
attitudes, her plans for her time on this world. The food was
superb. Linfyar ate quickly, fastidiously, using his proximity
senses (mind fingers that didn't get greasy) to tell him where
the food was, his nose to tell him what it was. A few
questions came his way, but he handled them deftly enough;
the miners concentrated on Shadith, courteous but persistent.
She gave a thought now and then to blessing her misleading
appearance, something that otherwise was growing into an
irritating problem when she had to deal with strangers. Right
now, though, it was helping her. The miners were satisfied
with her answers, she could feel it, where they might have
dug deeper if she'd looked older.

RASHADA: (tall lanky woman with skin tanned so dark it
                was almost the color of the table, pale-yellow
                eyes, cool and assessing, not hostile, merely
                wary) That was a remarkable performance
                this afternoon. You are a gifted musician,
                young Shadith, but I think you were surprised
                by the effect you had on your listeners.

SHADITH: (chewing on a bit of meat, swallowing, taking
                her time) Surprised isn't quite the word. As-
                tonished. Staggered. Flabbergasted. Same thing
                was happening to me.

MARAH: (plumpish woman, shorter than the others,
                bland round face and deep-set eyes lost in
                shadows except for a glint now and then)
                Then that dream-effect is something new. It
                didn't happen on other worlds you've visited?

SHADITH: (tearing open a warm flaky roll and buttering
                it carefully, using the time to think about her
                answer) I have seen something similar, but
                not of my making. A long way from here. A
                long time ago.

HALAMO: (tall lanky man, like Rashada's twin, matching her feature for feature, the same cool yellow eyes, the same long rather bony fingers, almost the same voice when he spoke) A long time ago? You look like you've barely hit puberty. No offense. How old are you, Shadith?

SHADITH: Older than I look. Old enough I've touched a hundred worlds and brought away a little of each. Old enough to leave my home and people far behind. Actual years? I don't really know. Easy for travelers to lose track.

DIHANN: (a woman of stern and rather frightening beauty, exotic cheekbones and cat eyes, reddish tinge to her hair, wide full mouth, a way of moving, even sitting still and simply breathing, that made Shadith think of tigers and leopards lolling in the sun; her voice was deep and purring; she was the oldest of the women, lines in the velvety skin and the beginnings of collapse in her muscles, but she was still powerful and vividly attractive) Who are your people, ancient child, those folk you left behind?

SHADITH: You wouldn't know them. The Shallal of Shayalin, a world so poor and hard everyone left who could. My family is long dead. I escaped by chance, and I travel because one keeps on living and new places have new delights and there are always new places to see.

RANGAR: (oldest of the men, bald, hazel eyes, wide thin-lipped mouth, deep lines at the corners, corrugated forehead, heavy eyebrows) Shayalin. I don't know the name.

SHADITH: Why should you? It was dead before you were born. The last of the Shallal were exiles depending on their talents to survive. And it's a long long way from here.

GERADA: (a quiet, heavy-faced woman, thick dark hair
            lightly streaked with gray, smoothed into a
            meticulously neat knot at the back of her head;
            she ate with precise small movements, a deli-
            cacy almost absurd in the shift of large power-
            ful hands; she interested Shadith because she
            did not seem to belong among the more flam-
            boyant members of this inquisition; there had
            to be more to her than the silent uninteresting
            facade) What brought you here?

SHADITH: I could say chance, but who'd believe that? I
            came for my own reasons. I came for the
            sweetamber like everyone else. I came be-
            cause this is a wild world and a strange one
            and I collect strange worlds. I came because
            this is where the ship I was riding brought me.
            All of the above, or any, or none. Take your
            choice.

MELOHAN: (small, slight, hardly taller than Shadith, with
            fragile bones that looked as if they'd break in
            a high wind, perhaps the youngest of the
            twelve, hair black as tar worn in a long braid
            that draped gracefully forward over her left
            shoulder) What will you do here?

SHADITH: Sing, earn my way. Look about Keama Dusta
            for a while, visit other parts of the world,
            leave when I've seen all I care to.

KULIT: (tall lean woman with a short nose and short
            hair that curled tight to her narrow head, large,
            rather prominent quite lovely hazel eyes, eye-
            brows thin but strongly marked, flaring like
            wings so she looked permanently alert, a voice
            like kaffeh smelled, deep, dark, rich) We have
            a rebellion trying to gather force out there,
            guerrillas in the hills.

SHADITH: (giggle, flirt of her hand) Meaning, stay out of
            the back country?

BERGEN: (small neat man, hairline mustache rather un-
               fortunately emphasizing very full red lips that
               tended to pout, hairline brows to match, those
               wisps of hair dominating a soft-looking face)
               Unless you think you'd be amused by the
               Ajin's antics.

SHADITH: I don't get any fun out of pain. If your Ajin is
               like other rebels I've run into from time to
               time, he'll land hard on strangers in his terri-
               tory. Too bad.

PEROLAT: Quite like other rebels, young Shadith. You'd
               better stick to Keama Dusta until you leave
               us.

Perolat touched Shadith's arm. "Wait a little and share
some belas with a few of us, you and Linfy."

Shadith nodded, amused and a little irritated; she'd gone
beyond her second wind and was working on the third.
Seventeen hours since a sleepless night. But begging off
wasn't an option. What was coming, like the dinner inquisition, would be a test, she had no illusions about that. For
some reason, probably that enigmatic presence in the forest
and its unexpected interest in her, she had a lot more attention
focused on her than she wanted, maybe more interest than her
story could stand. As most of the miners strolled out, clumped
in small groups talking about minor events of the day, and a
number of quiet girls came in to clear off the table, Perolat
swept Shadith and Linfyar down a short hall and into a
high-ceilinged room where three others sat about a hooded
fire. The windows were cranked open to let in the cool night
air. *Trial by pollen,* she thought, wearily amused. The dining
room was air-conditioned so Perolat wouldn't waste her work
cooking for dreamers and the smells and flavors of her food
would be appreciated without distraction. Perolat took her to
a plump cushion, murmured welcome to Linfyar as he sank
down beside her. The rustle of the vine leaves outside the
windows, the stir of draperies, the crackle of the fire that was
the room's sole illumination, a snatch of music from a distant

inn blown in on the night wind, shut off abruptly with the closing of a door—these unobtrusive sounds gave the room a dreamy unreality that Shadith found disastrously enticing, combining with her body's more and more imperative demands for sleep to give the feeling that events were slipping rapidly out of control, even her own body was leaving her control. She tried to focus, but her mind felt like mush and the food she'd enjoyed so much so short a time before sat like a lump in her stomach, weighing down body and mind.

Perolat wheeled a serving table from one corner of the room, on it a large glass pitcher and big-bellied glasses whose flatly rounded bottoms fit comfortably in the hollow of a palm, a solid weight to them; good to sit by that fire holding those heavy elegant glasses. The belas she poured out for her guests was a lightly fermented fruit juice, heated and spiced with something local that was tart with a pleasant afterbite. Shadith sipped at hers and felt the fog draining from her head, some of the lethargy slipping out of her body. This part of the test was going to be harder than dinner. She'd had a lot of practice keeping her lies consistent. Now all she could do was be herself and hope they liked that self well enough to accept her as an amiable acquaintance so they'd leave her loose enough to go nosing after the Ajin. Her mind drifted to Taggert. *Wonder if he's made his way here yet . . . have to be in position to spring him if he hit the trap and tripped . . . wary, wily man . . . but so was Grey . . . Grey was angry, maybe that's what did him in . . . but it swallowed Ticutt, he wasn't blinded by anger . . . calm, deliberate, precise . . . cautious as a coyote around poison bait . . . Taggert coming in at some kind of slant . . . good luck to him. . . .* She sipped at the hot belas, watched Perolat finish passing out the glasses and take her own back to a chair, her mechanical leg making it difficult to get down to the floor.

The silence filled with night sounds stretched on and on. Linfyar fidgeted awhile, finished his drink, curled up beside Shadith, his head on her thigh, and went to sleep.

After a while Perolat stumped around refilling the glasses. She settled back in her chair, her half-leg propped on a small hassock. "Know any Pajungg music?"

Shadith yawned, blinked. "Never been to Pajungg."
"Ah."
More silence.

Ticha groped beside her pillow, brought up three curved, crooked pieces of hard wood like fossilized rib bones, began slapping them against her thigh.

Derek took up a long pipe made of a wood like Ticha's sticks. It had six holes cut into it and no valves. He tried a few notes, then began playing a simple tune, repeating it over and over, winding through the separate but related music from the sticks.

Awas left the room and came back with a huge gourd, strings stretched across a hole cut in the belly. She settled herself and began slapping a thrumming boom from the gourd, at the same time plucking the strings, producing a third tune, different from the other two but blending with them to produce a complex polyphonic music.

Shadith listened for a while, then began improvising a wordless song, like and not like her ancient croons, feeling her way into the music.

A flow passed around the circle, lapping her inside it. The music went on and on, expanding, developing, returning to earlier themes, the gourd player the leader if there was any real leader, the first to turn into new lines; Shadith was content to follow where she led, singing softly in her middle ranges most of the time, highs and lows when she was sure of herself.

Eventually Perolat began to sing, a rough untrained contralto that seemed to hold all the pain and wanting in the world, and joy, but a fleeting joy that touched a moment and went away, laughter in it too, the kind that celebrated but had a hint of pain in it like the drop of black that made white paint whiter.

Shadith stopped caring anymore if she passed the test, whatever it was; she forgot there was a test. Never mind age, culture, species; these were her kind.

Derek's pipe went up and up and up, ending in a high screech.

They collapsed in laughter, then sat up wiping eyes, while

Perolat went around again with the hot spiced juice, adding this time small saucers with cheese-filled pastries and candied fruits that Shadith found a bit too sweet. Startled out of sleep by the pipe's shriek and the jolting of Shadith's thigh, Linfyar sat up muttering, rubbed his nose. "What . . ." He sniffed, his ears pricked forward.

Shadith chuckled, handed him the saucer. "Here, I expect you'll like these."

Awas leaned forward, arms clasped loosely about the gourd. "I was there. At the k'shun this afternoon."

"Ummm?"

"You and Linfyar shaped our visions so we all shared the same one. Did you know that?"

Shadith straightened her back, rubbed at the nape of her neck, wishing she felt a bit more alert. "You saw the same thing?"

"No . . ." The word was a drawn out whisper. "That's not exactly what I said. Each person I talked to saw something that might be an interpretation of a single theme. As you intended?"

"I didn't know." She moved her shoulders impatiently, pressed the back of her hand against her mouth, pulled it down. The lie was harder to get out than she'd expected; she liked them too well, these Avosingers. Still, she hadn't much choice, and she wasn't working against them; from what Head said and the impressions she picked up at dinner they weren't that enthused about the Ajin and his cause. "Maybe it was a freak thing; maybe I can't do it again." She looked around at the quiet faces. "What dream would you like me to try?"

Perolat smiled. "Something simple, something you know as well as we do." A chuckle. "Forest walking?"

"Hah. You've got a loudmouth forest."

Soft laughter from all four.

"Mmmh, I should have the harp. Awas, would you let me borrow that?" She pointed at the large gourd.

"Why not?" Awas hefted the gourd. "Watch out, it's heavier than it looks." She tossed it to Shadith, who grunted with surprise when she caught it, then watched in interested silence as Shadith plucked at the strings, listening to the various sounds she could elicit, tapped and slapped at the belly to produce assorted tunks and booms, gradually putting what she learned together until she got a complex music going using about every possibility for sound the gourd possessed, a feat not as remarkable as it looked, since she'd done this sort of thing again and again on one world or another in that first part of her life when she was still in her original body. She let the music die, looked at the expectant Avosinger faces, then closed her eyes and sought through her memory of Shayalin patterns and finally chose one that seemed to fit the things she'd felt during her lucid periods as she walked through the fringes of the forest. She drew her hand over her face. "Right, walking through the forest." She looked down at Linfyar. "Come in when you feel it's right, Linfy."

She began with a muted strumming, clicking her nails against the varnished surface of the gourd, humming almost inaudibly, gathering up the stillness of the room, the night sounds drifting in, watching the flickers of the dying fire; she let the humming expand into the pattern song, the word sounds twisting and turning through the rhythms her hands were coaxing from the strings and body of the gourd; she stared at the flames and did not see them, saw instead her sisters in a circle swaying beneath the giant tress of Avosing. Giant trees stretching out before her, away and away and away and away, canceling wall and window, caught in an elusive balance between stillness and motion, there in all their thereness, their extension into time-was and time-will-be, grazing the sky and sounding the underworld. Her sisters dancing in their shadows, singing polyphonic patterns, singing tranquillity in power, singing forest heart and forest folk and how they twine together, strong in serenity, quiet in deed, gentle in their power, singing the miners of the amber, the fragrance of the amber, the shine and shimmer of the fires in amber heart. Her sisters dancing in light and shadow, life surging up through them like sap rising. The energy of the croon built and built, Linfyar weaving his liquid lilting whistle through her voice and hand-music, then it broke off.

Linfyar broke off at the same moment, leaving the room to a shattering silence.

Shadith sat blinking, holding the gourd with trembling hands, her mouth dry, her throat a little sore, her body drained of energy.

Perolat was lost in dream still, staring at nothing, tears drifting unchecked down her angular face, a slight smile curling her lips.

Ticha and Derek swayed together, faces slack and quiet, lost utterly to a dream it seemed they shared, her hand resting in his, her lips moving with his in brief smiles that lifted the slack muscles of each face at the same time in much the same way. Shadith was startled. Two clients linked in a common dream—that she couldn't remember ever happening even when her mother's sisters, master weavers, wove the dreams; similar, yes, variations on a single theme, never the exact same dream. Well, she wasn't truly a weaver, and her family had never visited a world like this. She blinked, startled by a sudden thought—or worn the body of a mindrider. Could she possibly do this without the pervasive pollens of Avosing? Was her dream back in the k'shun not just wishful thinking but a real possibility? Did she even want it to be?

As Shadith sat silently watching, Awas came swimming up out of dream. She looked around, dazed incomprehension on her face for the first few breaths, fixed her eyes on Shadith, wariness and a little fear in them, then she grinned, her dark eyes disappearing into nests of laugh wrinkles, her nose and cheekbones suddenly prominent. "I'll be humbler next time I play that," she said, half amused, half serious, nodding at the gourd.

Shadith flushed. "That's silly and you know it. What you heard was part suggestion and part funny-dust."

Perolat blinked slowly, looked around, raised her brows at Derek and Ticha, turned to Awas. "I didn't really believe it."

"The Po' Annutj."

"You too? You think them?" Perolat nodded at the still-dreaming pair.

"I expect so."

Perolat switched her gaze to Shadith. "And you don't know what you did, I'm fairly sure of that."

"Did?"

"Showed us the Po' Annutj."

"I know what the words mean. Forest Heart. But . . ."

"Loudmouth forest." Perolat chuckled.

"Hunh."

Ticha and Derek began to blink, eyelids clicking to a different rhythm, their eerie synchronization lost.

Perolat looked relieved. "Where did you learn that music?"

"Part of it from my mother, part of it's improvisation, things I've learned in my wanderings."

"Shayalin. That's what you called your homeworld, isn't it? I have not heard of it."

"It doesn't exist any longer. I'm a double orphan. Lost my family, lost my world." She yawned, almost not getting her hand up to cover the gape. "I said that before, didn't I?"

"You're tired," Perolat said.

Shadith grinned sleepily at her. "Understatement."

"Go home and get some rest. Your meals are on me tomorrow. Thanks for tonight."

Shadith swallowed a second yawn, her eyes watering. "If you could tell me where it'd be all right to perform, I'd appreciate that." The words were clear enough in her head, but slurred and slowed when they came out.

Perolat looked around at the others. They nodded. "Any k'shun that's not being used." She hesitated. "But you won't be in the k'saha long—the doawai will be calling you into the cathedral soon as he hears about you. Inside the walls."

"Walls?" Shadith shook her head. "No."

"You'll take in more coin."

"Depends. I know those places—lot of strings on your take. At least, that's what I've seen before, and I don't expect it's different here. I could have had lots of berths like that otherwise. Un-uuh."

"You might not have much choice."

"Warning?"

"Too strong. Just be careful. City"—she jerked her head toward the north where the walls were—"and doawai, he'll invite you first. Turn him down, he'll make your life a misery. Keep turning him down, he'll send his engiaja after you.''

Shadith yawned a third time, got heavily to her feet. "Then I'll move on." She stirred Linfyar with her toe. "Wake up, Linfy, time we got to bed. Too bad if that happens, Perolat. I like it here, like to stay awhile." She patted Linfyar as he got groggily to his feet and stumbled against her. "No use inviting trouble." She yawned a fourth time, surprising herself.

"And you're asleep on your feet, child—no don't tell me again you're older than you look. Derek, carry the boy. Ticha, give young Shadow your arm. Sleep as long as you need to, child, then come see me and I'll fry you up some breakfast.''

A nineday passed.

Shadith lounged about, getting to know the place, saying little, listening much, picking up threads here and there, finding nothing that would get her to the Ajin without him suspecting what she was after. Hints of rebellion, yes, whispered gossip, harangues by rebels sneaking into the bebamp'n trying to stir up excitement and anger and recruit Dusters into their cause. Nothing enough to give her a line on him.

Church spies snooping along the talishi, the wandering ways that were the local streets, and through the k'saha; church enforcers stumping arrogantly through the bebamp'n hunting down the negligent. These men wore respirators and protective clothing; even so, one of them would slide into a trance now and then and whoever he was harassing would take off before the rest of the troop could react. Enforcers never walked alone. Too many disappeared the time they tried that. Avosingers yielded before these troops, fading into the narrow talishi, vanishing into houses, shops, factories, taverns, whatever; vendors who couldn't wheel their carts away tuned out on the world. Behind the troop, life took up its ordinary ways, a touch of wariness in the most casual conversations.

A pervasive resentment of all church and Authority forces,

outright hatred in some quarters. The amberminers and their kin standing aloof—except when they helped the kin of those that disappeared or provided escape routes for those the enforcers were after.

As the days passed, she confirmed what she'd suspected that first night. Perolat and the twelve were the invisible government in Keama Dusta. They took care of order in the bebamp'n, sentenced thieves to tending the local gardens, repairing the water system, doing just about anything that needed work to keep the community life flowing smoothly, they warned wifebeaters, took rapists into the forest and left them (these weren't seen again, not hide hair or bone), warned merchants who were cheating customers, especially folk in from the grasslands with money to spend, and if they didn't listen, they disappeared; they settled boundary disputes and quarrels about goods and kinship problems with nothing but moral force to back their decisions, moral force and community consensus, an elaborate system of obligations, a web of services that bound man to man, woman to woman, built up wholly outside the oppressive Colonial Authority and the officials the Pajunggs appointed to uphold homeworld law.

Sing us a sad song, Shadow, they called to her, make us weep, Shadow, sing of thwarted lovers and heroes dying young, sing us a sad song, Shadow, oh Shadow.

Nineday. Market day. Farmers and ranchers in from the grasslands to the north, flying in with produce to supplement the kitchen gardens, red meat and fowl; fishermen with loads of fish, foresters in with herbs and tonics and flasks of fancy liqueurs, loads of fine woods, new flowers and plants. Shadith is mobbed, they won't let her stop singing, won't let her sing anything but the Shayalin patterns, mobs of listeners filling the k'shun and overflowing into the talishi.

Sing us a mad song, Shadow, Shadow, sing a nonsense to make us laugh, sing us silly, oh Shadow, oh Shadow.

           *   *   *

A miner came in from the forest with a pack full of amber. Tjepa confided to Shadith that he'd cached ten times what he brought in to spend with smugglers after he'd fixed up his family and sated Pajungg greed. Everyone knew about it, no one said anything.

Sing us of triumph, oh Shadow, oh Shadow, sing to us songs of silk and sweet ease, sing of our dreams, oh Shadow, wise Shadow, sing us of triumph, oh Shadow, our Shadow.

An emissary came from the doawai, a minor hiepler in the cathedral hierarchy accompanied by a decat of enforcers. He pushed through the listeners and stopped in front of her. "Singer," he said, "this is korbeday. On sukanday you will sing for doawai."

"Fine," she said. "On sukanday I sing in Sebela k'shun. Harin's tavern edges it. If your doawai wants to sit and see, he can rent one of Harin's balconies."

"No, no," the hiepler said hastily, "you will sing in the cathedral."

"No, no," she said, "I most certainly will not."

"What?"

"I don't like walls. The doawai wants to hear me, he comes outside."

"The doawai doesn't come to people, they come to him."

"Too bad. He must miss a lot that way. He's going to miss hearing me sing."

"It's an honor to be summoned."

"It's an honor I'll live without."

"You refuse?"

"Good, it's finally sunk in." She ran her hand across the harpstrings, the sweep of sound a period to the discussion. "Now go away and let me sing to these good folk."

He looked around him, saw the numbers, felt the hostility there. With a jerk of his head in a parody of a polite bow, he stalked off, pointedly ignoring the crowd that parted before him and the silent enforcers stumping along behind him.

*   *   *

Sing us a song, oh Shadow, sing us a dream of owning our
world, sing us, oh sing us of freedom, oh Shadow, of living
the lives that we want to have, sing us, oh sing us out of our
apathy, sing us, oh sing us out of our fear.

It was the excuse she needed, almost the excuse, anyway.
The next time the hiepler came, Perolat warned her, he'd
bring a summons to a hearing before a heresy judge and the
offer to avoid it by coming with him then. But he wouldn't
arrest her; that would come later when she didn't show up for
the hearing. If she fled Keama Dusta, well, wasn't that what
everyone did? If she ran into the outback and did her singing
in forest and grassland villages, who could say it was all a
plot? From the bits and pieces she'd picked up, she knew the
area where the Ajin was most active; if she voiced her
resentment and her fondness for the world, if she sang pro-
vocative songs and moved on before the Authority could land
on her, chances were she'd be recruited by the Ajin's men.
He might even order her brought to him directly. She grinned
into the darkness. *Why not? What a propaganda artist I'd
make.* She slipped out of bed, careful not to disturb Linfyar,
and padded into the other room, thumbed on the light, found
the book she'd been reading and settled down to wait the
coming of the dawn. For one accustomed to four or five
hours of sleep, these sixteen-hour nights were a penance to be
suffered far from gladly. She curled up in a chair, opened the
book and lost herself in the extravagant fantasy, amused by
the way the writer toyed with treason in the guise of litera-
ture; the book had the church's imprimatur—probably a lazy
or stupid censor passed it for publication, someone whose
mind was on other things. Or maybe he was a sympathizer;
odder things had happened. She relaxed and let the words
carry her along. Four hours till dawn. No more thinking, just
go with the flow.

Early morning in the smugglers' market.
A k'shun larger than most, within the miners' quarter
where enforcers never came and even spies were rare. Pember
k'shun, deep in a maze of crooked talishi. You had to know

where it was before you could find it. If a church spy dared
show up there—they were all known, even the youngest
miner child knew faces and names—groups of men and women
and children began nudging and shoving him toward the edge
of the k'shun, working him away from the tables, never
acting directly against him, all done with the blandest
innocence—but he was out of the market within minutes of
his arrival, and if he was too persistent at trying to get back
in, he was gently clipped on the head and removed, waking
up later in some other part of the city, usually drenched with
one of the more odorous liqueurs.

Leaving Linfyar to running about with Tjepa and his friends,
Shadith wandered among the tables, astonished by the amount
and variety of the offerings, most of them forbidden by the
church. She wasn't much worried about Linfy getting into
trouble; like most young animals, Tjepa was a trifle wild and
could be thoughtless, but he knew from much painful experience that anything too bad he did would be reported with
copious incriminating detail to his mother. Minor irritations
the Avosingers would let slide, but there was a line he knew
better than to cross. It was a fuzzy, ill-defined line, and
sometimes he misjudged it—to his sorrow and sore behind.
He came to their morning practice session a few days ago,
fidgeted a bit and wouldn't sit down, then rushed out an
explanation; seems he'd tied two jinkas' tails together and
dropped them in old Kaus's chicken coop—an unrepentant
grin, you should have seen the feathers fly and the noise was
loud enough to wake a wino after a wet night—but the jinkas
were Dihann's pets and she didn't think the joke was funny at
all and old Kaus was foaming at the mouth. "Mam, she *tore*
up my behind and I got to work a nineday doing whatever old
Kaus tells me. And go comb the jinkas' fur and take care of
them for Dihann." He sighed. "All day. Except Mam says I
can still come for my lessons. If you don't mind." His
friends were much like him, three miners' sons and a lone
wild girl who was all legs and hair and audacity, a version of
what Perolat must have been at that age. She almost envied
that girl's freedom; her own childhood had been strictly

disciplined, little play allowed, no one to play with; her sisters were almost adults by the time she hatched.

She wandered among the tables, bought some books and a sack to carry them in, thought about a silver filigree headband set with moonstones, but it was too fragile to last through the turbulent times ahead. Enjoying the bustle and color, she worked her way to the section where the bolts of silk and avrishum, brocades and broideries were, loving the sheen and shimmer of them. She rounded a high pile and stopped, her mouth dropping open. *I don't believe it. Arel and his pet killer Joran. Vannik must be guarding the ship*.

She strolled by the table, suppressing a smile. Here and there among the offerings she spotted a bit of the old Queen's jewelry. She looked at the delicate gauzes and rolls of brocade, sneaked another look at Arel. His bony sardonic face was much the same in spite of the years that had passed since he left Aleytys on Maeve. *I'll have to tell her I saw him. He's looking prosperous. Not really so strange he's here—this is smugglers' heaven. Wonder what he'd think of her now. She's changed from that naive mountain girl he bedded so sweetly those days*. Shadith felt a heat growing in her and quickly shifted her thoughts. Joran hadn't changed much either. Those cat ears still twitched all the time, some streaks of gray in the black hair, no lessening in the aura of deadliness that clung to him. Funny to think she knew so much about them and they wouldn't have a clue about her. She sighed. *They'll be gone in a day or two. Maybe after this job is done I can hunt him up and say hello. Be interesting if . . . Hah! Shadow, get your mind on your business. Grey comes first*.

She ambled on, picking up more about the Ajin in snatches of conversation about her . . . a jaktar robbed of revenues from the church casinos in Windsweep and Sapulake . . . a flier vanished over the forest somewhere north of the Ular River . . . a customs boat sunk in Moster Bay . . . enforcers dropping on Kotican just two hours after the Ajin cleared out . . . a truck convoy of enforcers and their gear vanishing between two checkpoints. . . . *Every day I linger here*, she thought, *that's another day of torment for Grey. But if I rush around like a fool, what good does that do anyone? I need my cover, my excuse to get the hell out.* She glared up at the administration towers. *Come on, you, I've defied you, do something! Come at me. Give me an excuse to cut out of here. I have to go slow, I have to be covered all the way, I have to keep out of Kell's trap, or all this is wasted, Grey's wasted, I'm wasted, do I have to kick you in the gut? Do something....*

Shadith's second nineday. She has just finished a performance, is getting ready to join the celebration of the Amun-Bar. The hiepler pushes through the stirring crowd around her, stops in front of her, reads from a paper that she is required to present herself in the court of the Impor Melangg to defend herself against charges of heresy and suspect activity; if she agrees to come with him and perform in the cathedral while she listens to the wise and benign teachings of the doawai, the hearing will not be necessary.

"I have said to you I will not come behind walls."

"If you refuse again, your chattels are subject to confiscation. That instrument"—pointing at the harp—"your pet, the singing beast"—pointing at Linfyar—"everything you own." The hiepler stared at her, face set, eyes hostile. "Perhaps we should take them now." He lifted his hand.

"No." She leaped to her feet, thrust Linfyar behind her. "You will not."

Before the hiepler could react, the crowd started pressing in on him and his escort, a low angry growl coming from a thousand throats, a thousand pairs of cold angry eyes fixed on him and his entourage.

He knew Dusters well enough to understand what was not said, so he contented himself with the pronouncement that the church considered all minor children without adult relatives, Pajungg or not, as wards of the state, under its authority and protection. Then he swung around and stalked off, his escort scrambling after him, losing a good portion of their dignity in the speed with which they departed.

Shadith grinned and dropped back down, began a comic song she'd translated into Avosinger Pajunggeesh, the tale of

an extraordinarily maladroit but lucky spaceman. With Linfyar
whistling and clapping in accompaniment, she sang the Saga
of Jigalong Jon until well into the Amun-Bar, the miners and
their friends clapping and shouting out the refrain while she
caught her breath and got ready for the next verse.

That night, after supper, she took Perolat aside. "Whatever
you all do about this," she said, "don't do it for me but for
yourselves. I don't want to seem ungrateful, but I just as
much don't want that kind of responsibility on my head." To
herself she thought, *All those years of living in Lee's head,
some of her fussing has rubbed off on me.* She tried to mock
herself into her usual easy glide through life, but she couldn't
manage the trick anymore. "Don't push too hard, you miners, you'll drive the church into crushing you. I've seen it
happen before. I won't be even a proximate cause of such a
disaster."

Smiling, Perolat drew the tips of long fingers across Shadith's
brow. "Such a serious child. We keep our freedom day by
day, act by act. If we don't exert ourselves now and then, we
certainly will be swallowed up. We don't allow our friends or
our own to be harassed within the bebamp'n. Outside, you're
fair game to the predators. Remember that."

"I will. If I leave, you'll know I've gone freely and will
take the consequences."

"May they be small and light. The blessing of Po' Annutj
on you and your reason for coming here."

"Pero . . ."

"No, no, what we don't know, we can't spoil. You mean
us no harm, that's good enough."

"You're sure of that?"

Perolat laughed. "Come back sometime when you're not
tied into fancy games."

Shadith watched her go back into the kitchen, shook her
head. "Loudmouth Forest," she muttered to herself, and
started walking back to her cabin. *Another day of singing to
satisfy pride and make the Pajunggs think I'm going to hang
around defying them. Tomorrow night, late, steal a flitter
from the Flying Man and hit for the back country. Have to*

leave the flitter's price with Perolat; don't mess your nest, she says. Umm, better leave most of the take with her, she'll keep it safe until I can pick it up, god knows what thieves they've got out there. Damn you, Kell, I hope Aleytys takes your skin off an inch at a time. This is a good place; why'd you have to ruin it? Tjepa, you crazy little jinka, I'm going to miss our sessions. You've got a gift, don't waste it, make your mam find you another teacher. This is going to get tricky. Wonder where I should head. Kotican? Don't think so, spies there, called the enforcers when the Ajin showed up. Still, he did show up. Cabin's dark. Linfy must be asleep already. Maybe Windsweep. Nice name. Hey you out there, you in the forest, give me a clue, huh? Chuckling, she palmed open the door.

Dull crunch . . . exploding pain . . . nothing. . . .

SHIBURR ON GYNNOR

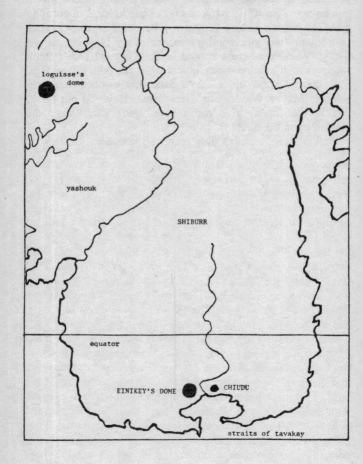

VRITHIAN
WITNESS [1]
A MISTRESS IN SHIBURR

My name is Xanca. I am not young. I am not pretty. I have
found being neither pretty nor ugly something of an advantage. Rich men marry beautiful women to show the world
their virility and their power, then they fill houses in back
streets with women like me. I work hard to learn my patron's
needs and satisfy them. Half the time he doesn't know himself what he wants. How stupid these powerful men can be.
Yes, I have great contempt for all my patrons. How . . . oh,
you can tell from the tone of my voice. Most days I am more
careful how I speak. It's the puatar, I usually don't indulge
when I have company, it makes me careless. Your company
too, and the funeral. Yes, my last longtime patron died. With
what he left me and with what I've saved the past years, I am
finally free. Like the undying. I have seen how their women
walk, arrogant as any man, not even their own men ruling
them. I want to walk like that. Me. Xanca. Well, I won't,
I'm not foolish. Free to be myself but not that free.

The undying. They rub the gloss off everything. One thing
I noticed, whatever my patron said, whatever he did not say,
the undying were always in his mind, the demon mistress in
that dome up there on the mountain. He boasted to me of his
wife. The most beautiful woman in Chiudu, a frail creature
with the prized fire in her hair. A most unpleasant woman if I
believed what he said about her, and I did. Some of it. Pour
me another drink from that bottle; being honest like this is
cold, like I was stripping myself bare in an ice-wind. Where
was I, oh yes. I believed some of it, though not like he
wanted me to. I believed his tales because in her place I

would have done much the same. There. You see? Isn't that honest? Cold, greedy and arrogant. I used to dream of being her after I had to spend a long time with him being soft and submissive, using every trick I knew to make his flabby member hard, cooing at him, lending a soft accepting ear to his whining. She was supposed to have demon blood in her. Now and then the undying have taken women from Chiudu, but I've never heard there was issue from any of those couplings. None of the women came back with child, the few that did come back. Still, the brightheads are rare enough among us to raise the possibility and they've played that card to lift themselves high, oh yes.

He had another mistress, the one he showed off when he was with the other big men in the city. A beautiful child, fourteen at most. He showed me her photo. They envied him, those hungry greedy friends of his, that was the point of his having her. She is truly quite lovely, being kept by one of his closest friends now. He told me she was like a beautiful beast, soft of skin, very alive, filled with an energy that exhausted him almost beyond bearing. Except that she was always at him to buy her things, he said he wouldn't know she could speak, hadn't an idea in her head. Animal. That's what he thought of her. I tell you he knew nothing. He understood nothing. Not me. Not himself. He would change nothing in his life even though the way things were made him ill. Killed him too, I suppose. He bragged to me once how he and his friends had sniffed out and secretly executed every member of a plot to sneak up the mountain and attack the demon mistress there, drive her and her kind from Shiburr. He feared the undying, but that was not the reason he was so adamant against the plotters. He feared more losing his place, his wealth, his position, in the shaking out if the demon fell. If he could, he would not drive the demon from the mountain. If he could. Hah!

You say if I know all these things, if I despise my patrons so much, why do I submit? I survive, my friend. I live as I must. If you seek to lay blame on me for the way I live, if you seek to shame me for growing comfortable with the humiliations I have endured, then I say to you that you are no different. If the demon on the hill says to you lick the dust off her feet, you will fall on your belly and lick.

I have little more to say and your bottle is almost empty. But there are those among us who try to cast off the foot of the demon, who have tried before and will try again. Me? Don't be stupid. You know what I am. Who would trust me with such things? I speak of rumor and tales you hear in the street, and out of my most secret dreams, no more. I dream and I wait, my friend, I dream and I wait.

VRITHIAN
on the oblique file [2]

Willow ran along the edge of the lake, her long thin dawn-shadow jerking and gesticulating like a stick parody of a person, her feet kicking up flirts of rain-wet sand, pounding a rhythm up through her body to the top of her head, her breath coming in easy pants. She ran through ragged patches of shorebirds scratching about for grubs and worms, startling them into raucous, whumping flight, hardly higher than her head before they settled back behind her. A freshening breeze tickled the water into pointed, tight-packed ripples that whispered to the sand beside her beating feet; armadas of kimkim cousins twisted in dark funnels out over the shallow lake, their high singing hum floating above the water noise; fish leaping for the kimkim cousins beat the water into a continual boil under these dark tourbillons.

She joyed in the dawning, in the sheen of sweat on her skin, the drive of her small body, in the smells around her, wet earth, rock and sand, the clumps of cattails in the shallows, old stems and leaves rotting into silt, the sweet-sweet-sweet yunyiun flowers growing where rocks sprayed into the water, stiff white, pink and crimson stars on rope-wide spongy stems, arrowpoint leaves as thick around them as spines on a nagri's back. Rotten fish, bird dung, wet feathers, rich strong smells she sucked in with the clean clear morning air.

She stopped running when she saw dimpled sand ahead of her, and began kicking it up, searching for kimkim grubs. Hyaroll provided ample meals for his zoo, but Willow sometimes preferred to find her own breakfast. In a way it was a reassurance that however much she'd lost to time and distance, she could still keep herself. And sometimes she simply had a craving for the kinds of food he would never think of providing. She found a heaping handful of the grubs, rinsed them in the lake and strolled along, cracking their shells, stripping out the plump white flesh and crunching it with relish between strong square teeth. When she finished the grubs and brushed away the fragments of shell, she kicked up a flake of stone and hacked out a long piece of tuber from among the yunyiun plants. She washed off the tuber in the lake, scrubbing away the silt, the fine white rootlets, the papery outer skin. When she was satisfied, she moved a few paces down where the water was clear, knelt again, drank deeply, washing away the aftertaste of the grubs and the last bits of flesh stuck in her teeth. Then she got to her feet, shook off as much of the water as she could, scowled at the sun, pale and remote as if it wasn't ripe enough to let the warmth loose.

Holding the tuber in her left hand, she began running back the way she'd come. The sand was a little drier now and the edge was off her enthusiasm, she didn't push herself but loped easily along, the weight of the tuber adding an odd tic she rather enjoyed into the rhythm of her going.

When she dried off and warmed up, she slowed to a walk, took out the folding knife Hyaroll had given her and began peeling away the fibrous inner bark of the tuber, working with meticulous care and the attention she gave every physical act. Hand-thinking, Hyaroll called it in the long-ago times when he still bothered to talk to his zoo. The pale tan skin came away in long strips, exposing the creamy inside little by little. When she peeled away the last strip, she started to toss it aside as she had the others, but checked her hand, caught by a sudden thought, stopped and stared at the length of skin. Then she tucked it over her waistrope, winding it several times about the rope to make sure it wouldn't work loose, started walking again, slicing off slivers of the sweet crisp tuber and eating them as she went back around the lake toward the sheltered oval lawn where Sunchild and Bodri would meet her later in the day.

*   *   *

She sat on the grass, passing the rootskin from hand to hand, rolling it between her palms, chewing at it, gently, so she wouldn't break the fibers. By the time Bodri came poking along, she had separated out most of the long tough hairs and was examining them with satisfaction, regretting that she'd taken a less than active interest in the hodgepodge of plants and trees Hyaroll had collected along with his mobile specimens and set out where the whim had taken him, leaving them to the care of the ironheads and the lizard people who lived here already. At her first waking she thought these folk were more specimens in the zoo, but when she'd followed her need to know the land and traveled to the edge of the dome, exploring along it until she circled the park, she saw them all around outside, working in fields, passing to and from a clutch of low houses just visible on the top of a hill some distance away. Not specimens, just slaves for ol' Stone Vryhh, who made them do whatever he wanted.

"What are you fussing at now, Willow?" Bodri came stumping around a bush, settled himself with a thump on the grass. She stared at him, startled. He never called her by just her name without adding a bit of fond embellishment. There were dead and yellowing leaves on the miniature bushes in his back-garden, and a flowerstalk held several withered blooms, a sure sign he had sunk into one of his rare melancholies.

She held out her hand so he could see the fibers. "I gonna make me a cord," she said.

His mouth worked, settled into an almost smile, and some of the dullness left his eyes. "A very short one."

"Seein if I could. Seein if these'll hang together." She began teasing the fibers with her thumbnail. "Old Stone Vryhh, he got poison plants around here too?"

"Why?"

She shrugged, began rolling some of the fibers against her thigh, twisting them into a thin tight thread. Fiber by fiber she added length to the thread, holding it up now and then to see how well it was bonding together, how tight the twist was, how firmly it was set. She continued working, clicking her tongue in a work song, deeply satisfied with how her experiment was turning out.

"A noose for old Vryhh?" Drawn out of his gloom, Bodri had edged closer to her and was watching with an intentness he usually gave only to his plants.

"Mmmp. Maybe. Maybe bowstring."

"Ah." He unfurled his antennae to their full length, waved them in slow graceful arcs, curled them back again. "Better not say any more." Absently, still watching her, his tentacle arms came from under his shell and the thin strong fingers at the end of each began to prod among the garden rooted into his back, nipping off the dead leaves and gently stripping away the withered flowers.

She watched that from the corner of her eyes as she rolled and twisted, rolled and twisted, happy that she'd roused him from his sorrows. Though she hadn't expected much from them, seeing the fibers in the rootskin had started her thinking and remembering. Hands going quiet, she looked full at him, frowning a little, then turned her head to look over her shoulder at the house rising behind the treetops. She finished adding the last of the fibers and wound the thread about her left hand, feeling a strength in it that was changing her mind about its possibilities. "Old Vryhh," she said, "he like watchin you me makin plots. Like my folk laugh and clap hands at a song-dance. He won't do nothin long as we workin. He tell hisself I stop the funny ol' things come time they ready to take me." She fiddled with the thread, feeling the hard twists. *Fishnet maybe if the water don't loosen it too much. Somethin to do, anyway.* "I thinkin, " she said, "all kind plants here. I thinkin you know how makin them grow, maybe you know what ones make poison. Otter, other men back-back when . . ." She fluttered her hand in a broken wing drift meant to say long-ago, far-away, lost to me, oh lost to me. "When rains come, they hunt papkush and dofuffay. Dry time they sit around makin bow, arrow, chippin stone for point. Little arrow. So big"—she held her hands about the length of her forearm apart—"and dofuffay he make two Bodri, some left over." She laughed. "So women we boil kakoya root till it sticky glop in the bottom of the pot, poosha

for the arrow. Poosha not for killin but for makin sleep.
Dofuffay hit, he run and run, then he fall over." She flicked
her fingers out and up like a beast rearing, then made her
fingers legs that ran and ran, then she slapped her hand flat
on the grass. "Then the men blood him, cut him up. I thinkin
we make poosha for Old Stone Vryhh."

"Be ready for you, now he's heard you say it."

Willow wrapped the ends of the cord about her thumbs and
tugged sharply at it, grunted as it cut into her flesh. "Let 'im
watch. Take a while to make poosha right, try it on Vryhh-
size beast. Then we figure somethin." She canted her head,
grinned at him. "Sunchild and me, we makin one piece here
one piece there, now you make your piece, eh-huh?"

VRITHIAN
action on the periphery [2]

Amaiki came to the garden early that morning, riding her skimsled from the small neat house in the workers' quarter tucked up next to the downcurve of the dome, a delicate lacertine figure standing on the small round platform, five long long fingers (narrow crooked thumb tucked neatly under) resting lightly on the squeeze controls at the ends of quarter-circle arcs coming from a narrow column rising before her, a smooth pebbly skin, mottled gray-green, long soft folds of loose skin draping gracefully about her neck and along her sides, those delicate seductive vertical folds seen and not seen through the openings between the front and back of the brown-black tabard she wore, a tabard with no decoration but subtle patterns woven into the cloth, patterns that shifted with each movement she made, each push of the wind against the cloth, a silent music in the play of light and shadow.

She came to the garden early intending to work on the circle of tazukli bushes, coaxing them to grow in the candalabrum form that gave maximum scope for the flitter-blooms that were even now budding on the side branches. It was sensitive, demanding work that the androids simply could not do, requiring the deftness of Conoch'hi fingers and Conoch'hi aesthetic intuition, it was work she liked, the kind of work she needed after the dreams that plagued her last night; three times she dreamed of fire and death and each time woke not knowing if what she'd heard the odd ones saying had seeded the dreams in her or if they were tomorrow dreams. If her family were here, she'd know, through the lots

123

and the echoes. She thought of calling them to the com-kiosk near the workers' quarter. *I will tonight; maybe the dreams won't come again*. She maneuvered the skimsled into a rough shed built next to the wall of Hyaroll's house, took the toolbag from the shelf at the back of the shed and went walking slowly through the clean clear morning to the tazukli ring.

After she'd been working for around half an hour, on her knees before a single tazukli, softening the strongest branches, straightening them, curling them up at the ends, painting on the porous hardener that would hold in place the curves she wanted, she heard the pat of the little woman's feet, the tongue-clicking rhythm of her walking song. She was always singing or dancing, even when she sat she danced, except when she was absorbed in some bit of handwork. One of the odd ones, but not so odd as some. Amaiki finished the shaping with the click song in her ears, lending her some of the happy calm of the woman on the far side of the shrubbery, began carefully pinching off buds the wrong shape or in the wrong place. Death and fire, a bad time coming for the Conoch'hi, if her triply repeated dream was true, but one conc's dream had little validity, it took a consensus of family, then line, then the whole to reach reliably into tomorrow, to send the whole acting as one. In the life weave of her line mother, the patterning of the whole was rare, once twice no more. A single dream was nothing, born perhaps of a belly-ache, a quarrel with a co-wife or the naish of the love group, of fears or shame or a thousand other things. She kept telling herself that, her mind knew it was truth, but the cold knot in her belly would not go away.

She moved on her knees to another tazukli, deliberately choosing a bush near where the odd one sat on the other side of the bushes. She'd heard the three talking here some days ago when she came to assess the tazukli and see how ready these were for shaping. Now she both wished and feared hearing more. Her pointed leaf-shaped ears shivered; there was a strain in her neck as she worked with the bush, cutting away the side shoots and sealing the cuts with the graft tool. The beetleman was right, the sunthing was right, Hyaroll was

sinking into a lethargy that threatened them all whether he
died or not. The year she left Shiosa the upland rain was late
and thin; this winter and last, there was no rain at all. Wells
were drying up, especially close to the dome, where Hyaroll's
pumps sucked away every spare drop. For the first time in
memory, for the first time noted in the life weaves of the
upland Conoch'hi, the Vryhh Hyaroll broke the Covenant and
did not bring the winter rains. Her folk were beginning to
leave the land; whole villages would be emptying soon when
all their wells ran dry. The line mother of the Yumoru in
Dum Ymori came to the caller kiosk, but Hyaroll would not
talk to her. Old Stone Vryhh, the little woman had called
him. She was right. Heard nothing, saw nothing, wanted
nothing. Last year and this, Naish Ha-erdai, speaker of the
fifteen, went to him at the double full of the moons, saying it
is in the covenant, O Vryhh, give us rain or let us go. No rain
came. They could not go. Amaiki tended the tazukli with
gentle care, listening to the exchange between the odd folk,
hearing the seriousness behind the words. With Hyaroll watching over their shoulders they were going on with their prepa-
rations to attack him, working slowly, meticulously, feeling
their way along toward their final plan, knowing it might be
futile because nothing they could do would be secret from
him, Old Stone Vryhh watching their twists and turns with
a rusty amusement, letting them go on because their energetic
activity filled the emptiness in him.

Amaiki let her hand fall onto her thighs as anger flushed
through her; the tazukli had not harmed her, though it was
taking water that her people needed. She closed her eyes and
sat very still until her trembling stopped. Though the beetleman
and the little woman continued to talk, chewing over what
they'd said already, she no longer listened, concentrating all
her attention on the tazukli, working calmly, steadily; she had
to finish what she'd begun or harm the plant, and she would
not do that; she curbed her impatience, shut a mind-door on
frustration and shaped the plant to the pattern in her mind,
sealing the cuts, stabilizing the curves, pinching away buds
growing in the wrong places. Again she dropped her hands on
her thighs, closed her eyes. Again she trembled all over as the

rigid controls came off her emotions; rage and fear flashed through her, strangling her, shaking her until she thought she was going to fly to bits. She dropped her head onto her knees, whimpering softly, until the spasm passed. She stayed folded up like that for several breaths, then straightened her back in time to see a patch of golden light slipping behind the trees, Sunchild joining his companions, whose voices still sounded beyond the leafy screen. For a moment she thought of listening to see if this creature would have anything to add, then she shook her head; no point in it. Besides, she wanted rather desperately to reach out to her family, to feel the gentle soothing mind-touch of the naish Se-passhi, who was their far-speaker and the tie that bound each to each and all to all.

Moving with silence and precision, she collected her tools, cleaned them, inspected them, then set them neatly back into their loops in the bag. She knelt listening a moment to the noisy argument between the three odd ones, smiling, thinking that they'd given over caring anything about what they said or who heard them, knowing that *he* heard everything. They were trying to find a way to trap Hyaroll, each punching holes in the plots of the others, everyone getting nowhere. She stood, looked around at the ring of tazukli, the two plants shaped stark and elegant next to the fussy prolixity of the others, a sigh her sole farewell to a project that would have given her much pleasure.

Amaiki sat on the hykaros jewel rug, a gift from one of her mothers, meant to help her feel back into family warmth while she was exiled inside the dome. It made it easier for her to reach out to the far-speaker of her own mate-meld. She crossed her legs at the ankle and looked slowly around at the room with its muted earth colors, the intricately knotted grass mats, the cushions, their covers weaving of her own and gifts from Kimpri, the panels carved in low relief that Kimpri and Keran had made, the bubble glass in the round windows, the scattered lamps, no two alike, giving off a soft golden glow, making as many shadows as patches of light, perfuming the room with their scented oils. It was becoming her place finally, after nearly two years of nesting there. She sighed, closed her eyes. One by one, she brought the faces of her mate-meld to her mind, dwelt lovingly on each: Keran, long and narrow, eyes like amber fire, tinkerer extraordinary, builder of anything; Betaki, round and chubby, sleepy-eyed and sensual, nurse and nurturer; Muri, tiny but strong, fast enough to catch lightning on the leap, handler of the family finances; Kimpri, dreamy and intense, a shaper of form and texture, weaver and carver; Se-passhi, tinier even than Muri, the naish of the meld, deeply loving, the bond in flesh.

Se-passhi touched her, folded round her, drawing in the others, she knew them, whispered their names, felt behind them the ghost touches of the hatchlings, one two three four—four?—a new hatchling, she poured out her joy to them, absorbed their joy . . . she sighed and opened her sorrow to them and her need. . . . "Come," she whispered, "come to me, I need to speak to you. . . ." Whispering the words knowing what they received was not exactly words. . . . "Come, I need you, I need you all. . . ." Se-passhi's whisper came to her, not words exactly, but when the murmuring was done, she knew with certainty that the mate-meld would be at the com-kiosk two days from this at noon, knew also that they needed to see her almost as urgently as she needed them . . . she sent them love and a sigh of loneliness, caught the return then felt the touches fade, felt the ache of loss that never lessened.

She opened her eyes, sighed again, her need for them as strong as it was on the first days in the dome. More than three years of duty left before she could hold them and be held. She drew her knees up, draped her arms over them, rested her head on her arms. *Two days. I will see them and hear them. Can't touch them, but at least I'll hear their voices, see their faces. Two days. How can I wait? Two days.* She closed her eyes and let the longing take her and pass away, sitting on the silky rug until she was empty and calm again. Then she got to her feet and went into the small kitchen to fix her evening meal.

THE ISLAND CHAIN SULING LALLER

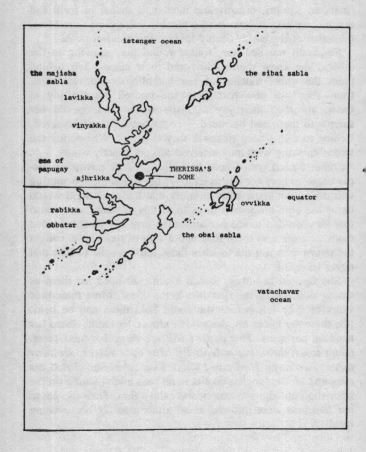

VRITHIAN
WITNESS [2]
THE BLINDNESS OF TRUTH IN SULING LALLER

My name is Binaram Kay. Please, it is the only thing my own. I am a reader of truth, rather what someone thinks is truth, this is the curse born in me, yes, curse. You are skeptical, that is easily read, you think this is a great power, to know when others are truly saying what they feel or lying to you, I tell you there are as many reasons for lies as there are lies, no I am wrong, at least twice as many reasons, and many of them are kind, many of them come from a need to defend oneself from someone more powerful, someone who can hurt mind or body. I am old, this is a thing I have come to understand after many trials, many mistakes that hurt more than me. Blind? Yes. Not born blind. I was just discovering the pleasures of babbling about anything and everything, just able to run without tripping over my own feet, able to climb on things without help, but not old enough to understand discretion, that lying by silence. My mother was beginning to suspect my curse and tried to teach me to keep quiet in the presence of my elders. Ah yes, I have to admit she had little success in this, Juntar was a small village in the mountain spine of Rabikka and every third person was an uncle, aunt or cousin. But you know the truth of this, some cousins are closer than others. I made the mistake of telling a cousin he lied when he denied sleeping with another cousin and getting her pregnant, then proving it with the truth that lay behind his face. Therissa's men came for me that night and took me to Obbatar. They tested me for days. After the first few days I began to enjoy all the attention. I knew they were truly interested in me, I was petted and cosseted and let show off in ways I found very pleasing, I was much too young to understand what lay behind that interest. Ah well, I cried myself to sleep often enough from missing my mother and my goat and my brothers and sisters, my uncles and aunts and cousins, and everything I'd known in my short life, but that too happened more and more rarely as I settled in to life at the Center. After three months of testing they put me to sleep and gently blinded me to be sure I wasn't merely a muscle reader. Therissa was not interested in those. Oh it was done quite painlessly and humanely, if that word can be used about such a procedure, I was anesthetized and the optic nerve surgically severed, I was kept half unconscious till the wounds healed. I can remember no pain, but you must see I am very far from that child. Therissa? No, I've never met her. Of course I have not, think about it, my friend. Are you truly comfortable this close to me? Yes, I mean you to ask yourself that question knowing I don't need the answer. You see the value of a lie? If I had kept silent, you wouldn't feel this uneasiness. So you understand why she doesn't come near her pets, only watches us. Yes, yes, I am blind, but there are things I don't need eyes to know. Pets? Yes. What else are we? Kept in luxury. Look about you. Is not this a pleasant world for an ancient blind man? How delicately they decorate for us, such marvelous textures, such intricate but undemanding sounds, the falling water, the wind chimes, the rock hollows that sing in storms and are silent when the wind is gone. Close your eyes and use your ears, your fingers, and find how pleasantly we are housed. Kept in luxury and bred at our keeper's command. As soon as I reached puberty they started bringing women to me. It's quite laughable how gullible I was then. I was far from the first truth-reader Therissa put in her zoo; she knew better than to send the women unprepared. They loved me passionately, all of them, I read the truth of that and responded, how could I not? Each time one of them became pregnant, she was taken away and replaced by another equally in love with me. How many children? I have no idea. After the first dozen or so were removed, the wrench of parting became too painful, so I stopped trying to see them with my fingers, stopped trying to keep the voices straight, stopped learning their names, they were shadows, vessels of my pleasure, they came and went like shadows. And after a while even that became too painful, my body rebelled and would no longer perform the act. Ah well, that too was a long time ago. My duties? Simple enough. A good watchdog sniffing out weaknesses in my owner's defenses, bringing her profit from renting me out. Do two merchants conclude their deals, I am there to assure both that both intend to live up to the bargain. Is there a question of theft or wrongful death, then I am there to read the truth behind the faces. Is there trouble on any of the sablas, I am led through the streets, my nose twitching, to point out the plotters. No more. These old legs have too little spring in them. But there are many to take my place, my own sons and daughters among them. How many? Look about you. This place grows every year. Why? I have thought about that often these past years. A whim. Nothing more than that. Something to pass the endless years. And when she is finally bored with us, no more velvet mosses and wind chimes, no more fine wines and fine food, no more shelter from the malice of those whose lies we've ripped apart. A whim. A playtoy to pass the time. That's what we are, my friend. And all I can hope is that I die before Therissa's interest does.

VRITHIAN
opening moves in the primary attack

Shareem clicked her fingernail against the glass of the screen. "That's Loppen, that crab-shaped island there. The Mesochthon is on the south coast, by the bay that's rather like an old-time keyhole. Middleground. Only spot on Vrithian where Vrya can meet without worrying that one will try to kill the other."

Aleytys glanced at the screen, but she was more interested in watching Shareem. Her mother was babbling, throwing out snippets of information as if they were chunks of meat churning to the surface of the stew in her head. During the fifteen days out from Wolff, she'd been calm and sure of herself, showing off her ship, reminiscing about the happier times in her past, but as soon as she saw the gas cloud around Vrithian, she started getting jittery about their reception. Aleytys listened to her with a sudden intense surge of affection. Shareem clearly preferred not to look ahead more than she absolutely had to, yet against her nature she had worked long and hard to set up the arrangements that were giving her fits right now, forcing her to confront anxieties she'd refused to think about before.

The lander circled down through the thin scumble of clouds toward a force dome like a dewdrop shimmering on the chalk cliffs above the water. Aleytys watched the ground come surging closer and was herself uneasy about what waited down there. She'd tried schooling herself to expect very little. Ibex had taught her about the grubbiness and trivia that could lie beneath the golden glow of myth; Shareem's jitters were wiping out any lingering hopes she might find a home here.

Home. She thought of her house on Wolff, then of Grey. *What am I doing here, not . . . no, I won't think about that.* She tightened her lips in a brief unhappy smile. *Shareem's daughter. Oh yes.*

The dome flickered. The lander passed smoothly through, settling on a white ceramic target that looked absurdly like a giant porcelain dinner plate laid carelessly on the grass.

A gleaming white tube snaked from the gleaming white cube whose polished faces (two hundred meters on a side) were opaline with pale images of everything around them, even the clouds flowing raggedly by overhead. From the exterior sensors, a soft sucking sound, the tube mouth fastening over the lock.

Shareem straightened her back. For a moment she looked bleak. Then she stood, shook herself, pasted a smile on her face, willed a gleam into her eyes and in a breath or two was the feckless ebullient creature she showed to Head and Shadith, though never to Aleytys. "Come on, Lee," she said, laughing. "Time to meet your loving kin."

A cavernous room. All white and black. All shape and springing form, arch on arch, falls of frozen white laces, twists of thready black lace, breaking the interior cube into irregular space. Spare white chairs scattered on an asymmetric spiral of black and white tiles. Elegant backdrop for what Aleytys saw at first as a horde of identical faces and forms, the same shade of red hair, the same translucent pallor, the same green stares. A fantasy fugue of peacock colors in their robes and tunics and trousers, this single difference emphasizing how alike they were, male and female, sibling and non.

All those pale faces turned toward her. Some scowling and hostile, others blank, waiting. No sign of welcome, no acceptance there.

As Aleytys followed Shareem into that intimidating silence, the sense of clotted numbers dissipated. Maybe fifty Vrya, no more than sixty. Her kind, all right, though her skin was shades darker, her eyes bluer. She lifted the corner of her mouth in a half-smile, mocking the dreams and hopes that had lingered after all in spite of her deliberate lowering of expectation, stared back at them with those bluer eyes, throwing a silent challenge into their silences.

The Vrya turned away as she moved passed them, took up the conversations interrupted by her arrival. She caught snatches as she walked behind Shareem.

". . . local shamans had a witch-smelling last week. Nallis and I got together and played a joke on them, dumped a load of phosphors on the head boneshaker, he was getting uppity anyway, you should have seen it, how they turned on him and . . ."

". . . Dromms crowned a new king. Went, of course, can't let them think they can do that sort of thing without one of us. Tedious, you don't know . . ."

". . . there was this idiot preaching against us all up and down The Sheng, and believe it or not he was starting to get a following; turned him into a torch, that stopped . . ."

". . . the Fospori they've developed this marvelous batik process, it takes an age to make a meter square of it, I've set a couple thousand working on . . ."

". . . Poyeska, Zeia and I, we came out of the clouds over a shevorate herd, startled them, should have seen those idiot beasts run, went for stadia without stopping, trampled a plavine camp, turned it into mush . . ."

". . . boring, Lally, you wouldn't believe how boring my Vrithli are, lumps that grunt at you, I tried to get them working on something simple as woodcarving but they . . ."

Shareem stopped at the elbow of a man who looked appreciably older than the rest of the Vrya. He was a head taller than most, with heavy shoulders, powerful arms and legs, a lined, ravaged face, expressionless now except for a hint of impatience as he listened to a woman with a fanatical intensity to face, eyes, voice.

". . . you must admit, Har, my breeding programs are more effective than your neglect. What have you produced in your orpetzh but a vague sort of foreseeing that takes statistical analysis of large samples to produce anything reliable? Now I've got six lines of truth-readers and ten of dowsers and three PK specials, though I have to admit I've got inbreeding problems with the PK bunch, but I've had the last cadre of infants collected, put my best surgeons to work on them. Thing is, gensurgery is such a chancy thing and the talent is so elusive and androids are so limited. Har, I wonder if you . . ."

"No." He turned so abruptly he brushed into Shareem, shoving her into a stagger backward. He caught her arm, held her up until she had her balance again, then looked beyond her at Aleytys, his eyes intent, momentarily bright with interest. The brightness dulled again in a breath or two. "Chasing dreams," he said, dismissal in his hoarse voice. "You're a fool to come here, girl. Give me your hand so I can play my fool's part in this."

He took her hand, bowed over it, straightened, spoke loudly. "Welcome to Vrithian, granddaughter. So that you have a seat here, Synkatta's dome and domain is yours, my gift. The transfer is logged, Synkatta's androids and Vrithli await your arrival." He dropped her hand, muttered, "Much good it'll do you, but I've kept watch there, purged the place for you. Kell and his herd can't get past my security. Call me when you're ready to move in. My advice, if you want it, is to get out and don't come back. It's a trap, girl, and the bait's not worth a handful of shit." He stalked away before she could get a word out, leaving her with her mouth hanging open, feeling foolish.

"Well, that went better than I expected." Shareem sounded almost complacent.

"Better!"

Shareem fluttered a hand. "Listen, Lee, he never bothered to acknowledge me as his daughter even after he took me in, but look what he's doing for an offworld brat."

"Reem . . ."

"Oh, I don't mind. He was fond of me before he got so strange, he helped me when I needed help . . . never mind, we shouldn't talk about such things here. Come, let's get the rest of this over with."

They wound through silent staring Vrya toward another corner of the room, moving in a cold and hostile atmosphere meant to be intimidating; it only made Aleytys angry enough to burn away any trepidation she'd been feeling. She no longer cared whether these people accepted her or not; she'd get her birthright confirmed, deal with Kell, then do what she wanted, Aschla take the lot of them. Well, not Shareem. She smiled at her mother's back.

Filiannis waited near the wall, seated in one of the free-form chairs, a pair of identical Vrya silent at her shoulders. The twins watched her quietly, their faces impassive, lowering their eyes as she came closer. *Don't they realize they reek hostility and jealousy?* Aleytys wondered suddenly whether any of the fifty or so swirling around her ever connected in any way less superficial than casual sex. The predators she'd come across in the roundabout course that brought her here— *deadly little Joran; wonder what made me think of him?*—the scavs on Nowhere, assorted company reps, whatever, all of them had about as much feeling for others as a pack of hungry silvercoats, yet even they knew more about reading nonverbal clues than this bunch. She examined the twins thoughtfully. Her mother's hand dropped onto her arm. "Don't say anything about them," Shareem whispered. "Don't talk to them, don't even seem to see them. They're clones. Not very successful ones, short-lives, limited minds, she just does them over when they fade." Aleytys nodded; *I've seen worse,* she told herself. Shareem smiled. "We'll talk later."

Filiannis the poet, or so Shareem said. Hadn't written anything new for centuries. *But I could have missed something,* she admitted, *seeing her as I did only every hundred years or so. And I've never been much interested in poetry anyway.*

Filiannis leaned forward with considerable eagerness as Shareem and Aleytys stopped in front of her. She didn't wait for Shareem to speak, but stood and held out her hand. When Aleytys clasped it, Filiannis said (speaking so fast she was almost jabbering): "Welcome to Vrithian, Vryhh daughter, Vryhh born to the Vrya." Her hand was dry and smooth; the skin felt like fine paper. She dropped back onto the chair, the twins retreating to stand once more at her shoulders. Aleytys found herself thinking of them as children in spite of their developed forms; they had an unfinished feel to them as if they weren't whole persons. Unsuccessful clones and aware of it, forced to stand before her, the whole-person Vryhh-daughter they could never be. She fought back a sharp stab of anger; it was unnecessarily cruel to create these half-persons, even crueler to bring them here.

Shareem glanced at her, stepped quickly forward. "Hello, Filiannis. Fia and Lia are looking especially well today. The blue suits them." Aleytys was startled and annoyed to find Shareem doing what she'd forbidden Aleytys to do. *I'm still an outsider until this business is over,* she thought.

Filiannis smiled, but the energy with which she'd greeted Aleytys was draining out of her. "They are well. We are well. Your absence this time was short, Reem."

"I had a good reason for returning." She put her hand on Aleytys's shoulder.

Filiannis looked vague, then alert again. "Ah yes." She turned to Aleytys. "Yes. Karos and Agriotis were here a year or two ago. They told us some exciting tales about your adventures, Vryhh-daughter."

"Rumor, anassa. Don't believe all you hear." Aleytys lifted a hand, let it fall. "Most of the time I was hungry, filthy, confused, bored and frightened half to death. It wasn't anything like exciting."

"No. No." Filiannis closed a hand about Aleytys's arm, closed it so tightly her nails cut into Aleytys's skin, a naked greed in her face and voice that astonished and repelled Aleytys. As if the Vryhh woman was a leech getting ready to suck her dry. She stood without moving, waiting for the woman to collect herself. "No." Filiannis straightened out her fingers, letting go of the arm, and with the falling hand seemed to lose most of her energy. She stared past Aleytys at something, perhaps only a fragment of some ancient memory, or a brush of suddenly recalled emotion. Her crumpled lips stretched slightly; she turned her head, seemed startled to see Aleytys and Shareem still near her. "You come and visit me, Vryhh-daughter, you be sure and do that."

"Yes of course, thank you, anassa."

Filiannis got to her feet. "My dome's in Beyinne. Shareem can tell you how to find it." She walked off with Fia and Lia trailing silently behind.

A cold knot in her stomach, Aleytys watched her walk off.

Filiannis looked almost as young as Shareem, time had left her shell intact, but the inside was rotted out. When Shareem had told her of the suicides that thinned Vrya numbers, Aleytys hadn't understood, in a sense hadn't quite believed her, but she began to understand them now. If chance or nature didn't kill her first, she promised herself as she watched Filiannis vanish among the other Vrya, if she ever came to such emptiness, she'd dive her ship into the nearest sun. She turned to Shareem, started to say something.

"Not here," Shareem said.

Aleytys looked around, sighed.

Hrigis was another ancient spirit within a preserved shell, the youthful elasticity of her body wrapped oddly about the ancient spirit sitting like a shriveled nutmeat inside it. Though Hrigis was brighter and sharper, more energetic than Filiannis, her green Vryhh eyes had all the warmth and welcome of polished jade; perhaps she'd used up her whole store of emotion so long ago she couldn't even remember how feeling felt. Her voice was a rather musical soprano, practiced and precise, counterfeiting the life she lacked. "Welcome to Vrithian, Aleytys Shareem's daughter, daughter of the line of Tennanth, kin and kind." She took Aleytys's hand briefly, dropped it. "Go warily, Aleytys, you have enemies here. Once Kell issues his challenge and you leave the Mesochthon, you'll be a target. I expect he'll show up as soon as this tedious little ceremony is completed. Do be careful. You're more interesting and I'm sure far pleasanter to have about than he is."

Shareem caught hold of Aleytys's arm and led her away. Her hand was shaking; she looked frightened. "I thought we'd have more time," she murmured, "I should have known someone would get word to him I was bringing you."

"It had to come sooner or later," Aleytys said quietly. "Better now while we're expecting him. Besides, it gets him away from Grey and Shadith."

"You don't know what you're talking about. At least he can't attack you until he announces his challenge, but I thought we'd have more time to get dug in before he got here." She pulled her hand down her face, wiping away the worry with it, the effort concealed behind the smile evident in the rigid set of her shoulders.

Aleytys looked around. "We're more than slightly outnumbered."

Shareem sniffed. "These? They're terrific when they're beating up on unarmed Vrithli, but show them a real fight and they'll dive for cover."

"Even mice are bad when they've got numbers on their side."

"They won't touch either of us here. Now shut up, one more to go." She raised up on her toes. "Right, follow me."

Loguisse was the last of the Tetrad, the same mix of age and youth, she was smaller than the other two women, with sharp but delicate features, and (according to Shareem) a tendency to retreat into the intricacies of her own mind. She was a mathematician working in realms so esoteric no one else on Vrithian could come close to understanding what she did. Unlike the other three Tetrarchs, she continued to work in her field, even left Vrithian to attend conferences with other mathematicians. She maintained a steady contact with a web of her peers across known space, using Ibex as a transfer node for com-calls, since she could not speak directly from Vrithian without revealing its location, something she was not about to do. Of the four Tetrarchs, Loguisse was the one most fully committed to accepting her. Among other reasons, she preferred Aleytys to Kell because he was too turbulent and too unpredictable, too apt to destroy Vrithian and all the Vrya in his attempt to fill the holes in his soul. Her hand was cool and dry, her fingerbones like birdbones; they felt so fragile Aleytys was afraid of crushing them and glad when Loguisse took her hand back. "Welcome, Aleytys Atennanthan, daughter of Vrithian." She smiled a little vaguely, then drifted away.

"Well, that's it, Lee. You're now a Vryhh of Vrithian."

"Any reason to stay here longer? If I'm the excuse for this party, I'm certainly not its shining light."

"Let's find Hyaroll and get him to let us in Synkatta's. Forget this bunch. I didn't expect much from them, though I did hope Aglao and Ruth and a couple others would be here.

They sort of promised . . ." She looked around. "And Rodyom, rats gnaw his toes, he probably forgot what century he's in." She wrinkled her nose. "That's one thing you're going to have to live with, Lee—the best of us isn't all that reliable when it comes to remembering engagements."

Aleytys chuckled. "Poor Mama—stood up by how many?"

"Hah, respect for your elders, child." She began scanning the crowd for the massive figure of the Tetrarch; with his size and width he should have been easy enough to locate, but there was no sign of him. Absently, Shareem said, "I didn't want to give you a total disgust of your kind; I thought I'd pull in some of the Strays, add some flavor to the mix." She chewed on a knuckle a moment, then started moving. "Help me find him, Lee. We've got to get you installed in your new property."

Aleytys followed her mother as she went quickly from divider to divider, circling the huge room in her search, growing more and more anxious as it became clear that Hyaroll had already left. "I didn't expect a house given to me," she said. "Thought I'd have to buy one. As on Wolff."

"Har's head of Tennanth-line, Lee. Never mind what Kell told you. Synkatta's dome came to him when Kata climbed onto his funeral pyre and lit the match. Hyaroll shut it down. Wasn't anyone around he liked well enough to bestow it on. Damn his thick head, he's left us floating."

"Well, well, it's mud-face. So you squirmed your way here."

Aleytys turned slowly, trying to control the surge of fear and anger that shook her when she heard that deep fluid voice, a voice she'd heard only the one time waking, a thousand times since in nightmare.

He was still thin, but it was a healthy leanness, not the papery skin over chalk bones she'd seen on Sunguralingu. When she cured him of the disease that was eating his life. His smile became a grimace as she took her time examining him, that assessing gaze reminding him too vividly what he'd been and what she'd done. She felt the fever in him, the need to wipe away the memory of his weakness, but she wasn't ready to deal with his rage. Or her own. Not yet.

"As you see," she said temperately. She heard Shareem's breath catch, felt her mother's fingers closing warm on her shoulder; she covered the hand with her own, grateful for the silent support.

"Mud," he said, snapped his mouth shut. A moment's tense silence. "Look at that, all of you." His voice was hoarse, slipping out of his control; again he clamped his mouth shut. Another silence. Soft scuffle of feet as the Vrya came closer. "Look at what you want to call Vryhh. Wash it till the sun's a cinder, you won't get it white." Another exploding silence. "I will not, I will not have that slime call itself Vryhh. I will *not*." Silence. "To the death, Mud." Silence. "I declare war between us. I declare that you and any who try to help you, Mud, will die at the hands of me and mine."

Aleytys sucked in a breath, let it out. "To the death, cousin," she said quietly, flatly.

His face went taut, his head back; she thought he was going to explode and attack her, but he swung around and strode away, vanishing into the nearest exit.

For several breaths after he left, there was total silence, then a murmur of comment growing louder and more excited as the room began to clear.

Aleytys felt chilled to the bone, anger gone ash inside her; she was suddenly tired to death of all this, the sheer stupidity of it like stones crushing her. "Looks like the party's over."

"I knew it would be bad, but he's . . ."

"He is that."

Shareem opened her mouth, closed it, looked helplessly around.

Aleytys moved her shoulders, shook her arms, straightened her back. "What comes next? What do I do?"

"The ship, I suppose." Shareem took a few steps toward an exit, hesitated, came back. "My dome's in Guldafel, but . . . there's almost nothing. no defenses . . . couldn't stop a hungry mouse . . . I'm almost never there. I thought . . . I don't know . . . I thought Hyaroll might take us in. But that's . . . he's not here. I'm sorry, Lee."

"He gave me Synkatta's dome. Why not go there?"

"We can't get in until he unpeels it for us. That maggot-head, what good does it do to give you the place if he doesn't . . ."

"I'll put you up until you can get old Stone Ear's attention." Loguisse. She'd come up behind them shadow-silent. "He'll talk to me most times even when he shuts out everyone else. I wouldn't mind guests for a few days, and Kell knows better than to worm about in my domain. Besides" —eyes alight with silent laugher—"my androids will love having someone to do for. They complain I need so little that half their circuits are rotting from disuse." She strolled away, leaving them to follow if they wanted.

Shareem brightened and started after her. "Thank whatever gods there are, Lee, we'll make it through the next two three days." She was almost dancing, her spirits soaring out of the mucky swamp they'd been plodding through for the past several minutes. Aleytys followed, smiling, unable to resist her mother's pleasure. They stepped into the tunnel a pace or two behind Loguisse.

"I've forgotten too much, Lee, tried to forget it, I suppose. I'll do better after this, I promise."

"Forget that too. We should talk soon. I need to know how this war works. What about the lander?"

"Best to leave it right here. He's probably got in and trapped it already."

"But you said . . ."

"Huh? Oh. The Mesochthon truce ground is just the hall floor."

"Aschla's hells." Aleytys caught hold of Shareem's arm and threw her back down the tube, ran ahead, flung a startled Loguisse after Shareem. "Harskari," she cried, "help me."

The amber eyes come open and alert.

A weight about her head. The diadem begins chiming.

The air thickens about her.

A few steps ahead the floor cracks open, pieces of the tube start to fly up and out, then they slow. freeze in place.

She struggles against the intractable weight of the air, kneels and pushes the pieces of the floor aside; they resist her briefly, but her strength is augmented in this state. She reaches into the hole, gets her hands around the bomb, a black egg with narrow jagged cracks in the heavy casing, the heat inside glowing a murky red. The bomb is small, about the size of her two fists, but its mass almost defeats her. With Harskari urging her to a cautious haste, she manages to pry the bomb loose and stagger to her feet, cradling it against her stomach.

She lurches along an endless white tunnel until, with a relief that almost undoes her, she sees daylight ahead and the green of grass. Kell or his minions had pried the tube loose from the airlock when they introduced the bomb. Wondering how she is going to dispose of it, she staggers into the sunlight, Harskari warning her she is running out of time and strength. She keeps moving. Past the landing saucer. Across the grass. She bumps into something that feels like the skin on old gelatin, pops through it, realizes that the skin must be the force dome. She slows, stops, remembering that the dome is very close to the cliff edge. She blinks the blurring sweat out of her eyes and finds that the third step on would have been a very long one indeed.

Throw it, Harskari says. *I can hold the stasis a few minutes longer.*

Arms shaking, she takes another step and heaves the bomb over the cliff edge, wheels and races for the dome, pops through it a breath before Harskari lets go. The explosion finishes itself partway down the cliff but is shunted away from her and the others by the force dome.

Feeling like a watery pudding, she crashed to her knees and gasped in mouthfuls of shivering air.

Shareem came running to her, Loguisse following more sedately.

Aleytys looked up, smiled wearily at her mother. "I wish you'd mentioned a bit earlier that the neutral ground stopped at the hall's edge."

"What a thing . . ." Shareem pulled Aleytys onto her feet. "You look whipped." She steadied Aleytys, pulled her daughter's arm around her shoulders and started walking with her toward Loguisse's flier. "What did you do?"

"Time for that later." Loguisse's cool, calm voice. She

moved past them, stepped onto the landing saucer. "You live up to your reputation, Hunter." She touched the lock. Over her shoulder, she said, "Wait there a minute."

Aleytys clasped her hands behind her head, swayed back and forth, stretching her muscles, feeling a treacherous euphoria flooding her. She'd just been a hairline away from death. Cloud shadows swam in lyrical silence across the shining white face of the cube, but nothing else moved, there wasn't a stray sound. "I'd have thought there'd be more fuss, Reem. A bomb just exploded, but no one seems to have noticed that."

"Oh, they did. They went the other way fast."

"That's how it's going to be?"

"Till this is over."

"Mmm. Why pick this tube?"

"Chance, maybe; or they mined all the tubes and only touched off the one you went into. Does it matter?"

"I suppose not."

Loguisse reappeared in the lock. "Come in now."

Water from horizon to horizon, bright glittering blue, small tight bumpy wrinkles packed close like pleats in a fan.

Three black midges come leaping at them from three directions. Loguisse does nothing. They sizzle and phutt out before they come near the flier. Other fliers dip in and out of clouds, so far away they are guesses on the viewscreen; they don't try to get closer. More missiles. Loguisse sits quietly before the console, a bored look on her still face; the flier handles whatever is thrown at it; nothing comes close enough to shake the air about them.

As soon at the flier moved over the land, Loguisse woke from her dream; a slight smile on her face, she bent over the console, reading the flood of data, responding with a swift dance of her fingers over the sensor panel. Apparently she guarded her domain as tightly as her dome. The flier lifted, dropped, turned in a complex saraband across the dry harsh land of Yashouk.

Loguisse's dome was in the high uplands of Yashouk, in

bleak but austerely beautiful canyonlands. Wind-sculpted stone and narrow tortuous canyons with water glinting silver at the bottom of a few. The dome spread over the whole of a broad mesa whose precipitous walls were being gradually eaten away by wind and water and time. Loguisse had lived there most of her ten thousand years; in another ten thousand she might have to move if she didn't do something to stop that infinitesimal erosion.

The flier hovered over the dome while she did a final glissade over the sensors, then it dropped slowly, merged with the dome, dropped further into a hole uncovered as a pool slid to one side, dropped down and down the stone shaft, falling into thick darkness, down and down until it feathered to a halt in a vast cavern deep inside the mesa. Light bloomed about them as it settled onto an oval platform some meters above the stone floor.

Loguisse spoke a single word. "Krasis." Without bothering with explanation or instruction, she swung her chair around, stood and walked toward the lock, which opened smoothly as she approached, stayed open behind her. She stepped onto nothing with a calm assurance that was immediately justified as a white ceramic disk materialized under her feet and began lowering her to the floor of the cavern. Rather impressed, Aleytys smiled and relaxed. Kell hadn't a hope of getting in here. A step ahead of Shareem she went to stand in the lock, watching what was happening below.

As Loguisse drifted downward, a tall golden metal man came with feline grace from a side tunnel and stood waiting. Another of the fantastic androids of Vrithian. It was delighted to have its mistress back, she could feel that—but how could a thing of circuits and crystals feel so intensely about anything, how could it feel at all?

Loguisse stepped off the disk and sent it back to the lock with a flutter of her fingers. "Kell," she said. "You know his tricks. Keep him out." The android walked away, vanishing into the darkness from which it had come.

Shareem brushed past Aleytys and stepped onto the disk, letting it take her down. Aleytys gazed after the android, puzzled by the relationship between Loguisse and her constructs. She certainly didn't fuss about ceremony. Robots, androids—not so complex and, well, beautiful as these—existed otherwhere than Vrithian, but most folk who built or owned them demanded servant manners from servants shaped like men. She rather liked the absence of that mindset in Loguisse, but it made her uneasy, made the Tetrarch more enigmatic. She stepped onto the disk Shareem had sent back for her and floated down. *It begins,* she thought. *I'm learning the possibilities wired into me.* She stepped off the disk, started to speak, then decided she had nothing she wanted to say. Loguisse looked around, nodded, then started walking up the tunnel the android had taken.

"Rest as long as you need." Loguisse tapped a sensor by the door. "If you want anything, this will call your attendant." She smiled vaguely and left.

Aleytys poked about the small bare room. Perfect order, pleasant enough, but it looked as if it had been wrapped in plastic for a long time and someone had only just broken the seal. She nodded. This only confirmed what she'd felt about Loguisse. The Tetrarch preferred her androids to people; they went quietly about their tasks and left her undisturbed. She didn't want visitors. Aleytys and Shareem were unwelcome as fleas infesting her extended body no matter what she said; they'd better find a way to leave soon if they wanted to keep her friendly. Aleytys yawned. The long day had left her exhausted. She stripped and showered, then climbed into the narrow bed and dropped into a heavy sleep.

Glass strips tinkling in the wind, chimes sliding into her sleep.

She began to wake.

Soft female voice replacing the chimes: *Aleytys, Aleytys, join us for dinner. Aleytys, Aleytys, you've slept long enough. Aleytys, Aleytys, let Korray bring you to us. Touch the caller when you want her.*

Aleytys turned over, murmuring drowsily, rubbed at her eyes. The voice shut off. Muttering a little, she got out of bed. While she slept, someone—presumably Korray—had brought a selection of long dresses to the room and hung them on the air at the foot of the bed. She ran her hands through her tangled hair and stared at them. One was blue-green, the color close to matching her eyes, a soft clinging silk, cut to skim the curves of her body. one side slit to the thigh for ease of movement, a scoop neck, long loose sleeves. She wrinkled her nose at it. The second was so dark a green it was almost black; it glowed with the sheen of fine wool. A looser fit; the skirt flared to flow like water about her as she walked. The third was white, a stola made of a supple silky material she didn't recognize, heavy enough to hang in graceful folds from the round gold brooches that held back to front at the shoulders. Nice to have a choice. She looked about for the comfortably familiar shipsuit, but whoever had brought the dresses had gone off with it, presumably to give it a good cleaning. *Lovely service, but I want the suit back. I damn well couldn't do much fighting or running in any of those.*

She got to her feet, stretched, did a few breathing exercises that woke her body up but did nothing much to clear the cotton wadding out of her head. Rubbing her eyes, massaging the back of her neck, she walked to the snug fresher and stood for a dreamy while with the shower beating down on her.

I won't stay here.

Amber eyes blinked open. *Certainly not here,* Harskari said, acerbic amusement in her voice.

Aleytys shut the water off, stepped from the cubicle, began scrubbing one of the blanket-sized towels over her body. "I meant Vrithian."

Going to run? He'll be after you.

"I know." She dropped the towel on the floor and went to make faces at herself in the steamy mirror. "Afterward." She began dragging a comb through her soggy hair.

Leave afterward until you're finished with now.

"Oh, profound."

Mock how you want, you're still running. It's time to face about and attack.

"How? Where? Give me time to get my head organized."

No time left.

"Loguisse bought me some. A day or two. I've bought time for Grey. And Ticutt. Kell's here."

Shadith should be on Avosing by now—the distances from Wolff are roughly the same.

"I know." She pulled the comb a last time through her hair, looked at the snarls of wet red caught in it, threw it at the tiled wall across the room, watched it bounce. "Attack, hah! Attack what? Pin him down? Where? A world's a big place. And it's his world. Only advantage I have is that I know sooner or later he's coming after me." She edged a hip onto the sink, closed her eyes. "Got to let him do that and hope to catch him hopping. Got to switch his ground to mine. How? I can't just go out and say here I am, hit me. Either he says no thanks or he squashes me; too likely he puts his thumb on me and turns me to a smear on the stone if I give him an opening like that. Leave me alone. I'm trying to work it out."

Touchy.

"Yes. I am."

If you don't want me around . . .

"Now who's touchy?" She smoothed her hair back. looked around for something to tie round the queue she circled with her fingers, shrugged and let it go, walked back into the bedroom. "What about our canceling out the bomb? Think that jarred him any?"

The missiles were a weak follow-up . . . could have been deliberate, make you underestimate him, maybe point you away from where the attack's really coming. In any case, he'll be regrouping and planning something worse.

"I know." She walked around the robes, felt the material, then pulled the dark green dress off its invisible hanger, gathered up the skirt into loose folds and tossed it over her head. A wriggle or two and it slid down over her body as if it had been made for her, which it probably had. "Send a prayer to your gods whoever they are that Loguisse can give me the data I need." She smoothed the closures shut. "Data we need."

Thanks for remembering.

"Sarcasm is not at all attractive."

Remind yourself of that, Lee. Remember, I'm here until you get around to finding me a body.

"How can I forget?" She slid her feet into the heelless slippers that matched the dress. "Keep your eyes open, oh wisest of mentors. Once this war gets moving there should be a wide choice. Pinch me fast when you see one you fancy. As Shadith did. I wonder what she's doing now."

Up to her ears in a mess of her own making, no doubt.

"I suppose so, but I'd a lot rather be there than here."

Really?

"Aschla's hells, I don't know. Leave me alone."

Korray took her to a room that was an elegant but chilly concoction of glass and stainless steel with a floor that repeated the design of the walls, white cloisonné filling brushed steel outlines. Vines with heart-shaped leaves the palest of greens wove through open spaces and took some of the visual coldness from all that white and silver, but not much. Through an unglassed arch came the sound of water playing lazily through the lobes of an angular steel sculpture, dropping musically into a cylindrical basin, its bricks glazed a bright blood red, their mirror surfaces a shout and a shock in all that glassy glitter and washed-out green.

Shareem and Loguisse sat in separate silences at a glass-and-steel table with three place settings laid out on it. Loguisse was gazing abstractedly at the fountain, putting some problem through its paces; Shareem was silent also, the lightness gone out of her face. She looked drawn and tired as she folded and refolded a bright red napkin. *If that is an example of Vryhh homelife, no wonder she prefers to stay away.* As she walked toward them, Aleytys found herself wondering what Shareem's childhood had been like, the time before Kell, long before the death of her mother. Sudden thought (sparked by the sight of the fragile-seeming silver-metal Korray moving ahead of her): Were all Vryhh children raised by androids? That would explain a lot. The elegant little android pulled the third chair out from the table and waited to help her sit. She settled herself, then looked up through the dome at the sky. Cloudless, pale blue, no sign of the sun. Was that east? It was hard to say; she wasn't adjusted to this world yet. She tried a tentative smile.

Shareem winked at her, startling her. For an instant, just an instant, her mother was the lighthearted laughing woman she'd been on Wolff. Loguisse continued to look abstracted.

"I'm still half asleep." An apologetic turn of her hand. "What time is it?"

Loguisse blinked, slid round to face her. "Six hours after noon. A twenty-eight-hour day."

"Then it's supper you're offering."

"More or less, though my staff can provide anything you feel like eating."

"I was a time coming. You've eaten?"

"We waited for you. Tell Korray what you'd like."

"Oh. Umm, meat of some sort, green vegetable, bread. Local produce. I'm not fussy about how it's fixed. Cha if you have it."

Korray shifted slightly; the new angle, altering the patterns of light on the angular planes of its face, made it seem as if it was smiling. It walked away with a delicate grace, a fluid almost fleshly flow. And it was quietly happy; like Krasis it centered its happiness on Loguisse's return. Aleytys gazed at her hands. Programmed into them? Or something that had slowly, slowly developed over the millennia androids and maker had lived together. She hoped it happened that way; the other made her rather sick.

"Korray and Krasis were both designed by Synkatta; he had an elegant touch with androids." Loguisse was smiling at her, amused.

"Synkatta. If he could do that, why . . ."

Loguisse shrugged. "He ran into the limits of his gift."

"Oh. Where can I find Kell?"

"You don't waste time."

"I've wasted too much. I need information, anassa, I can't fight in the dark or sit around on the defensive too long. Fight him on his terms, well, that's not a good idea, I've got to shift the war onto my own ground."

Loguisse nodded. "I'll set Krasis to making extracts for you, what I know of Kell and his resources. Will that do?"

"How can I say until I've seen what comes up? Is it too late to try reaching Hyaroll?"

"You're in a hurry to leave. Should I be insulted?" Cool voice, spark in the greenstone eyes, irritation a fog rolling out of her. A jolting reminder that Aleytys was taking too much for granted the great favor Loguisse was doing her.

Aleytys opened her mouth to explain that she knew Loguisse was uncomfortable with them there, but swallowed the words after another look at the Vryhh woman. After a moment's thought, she said, "I'm a danger to you, Loguisse anassa. As long as I'm here. You've been very kind taking us in despite that danger, nearly got blown to dust for it. How can I repay you by putting your life more at risk?"

Loguisse said nothing for a long moment, her face unreadable, her mind and emotions so controlled that Aleytys caught almost nothing from her but a general skepticism. And a touch of relief. "I've been trying to reach Hyaroll," she said finally. "He won't answer my calls." She leaned back as a trio of androids came in with a serving cart. "I'll try him again after we eat."

Loguisse had no luck that night; it was midmorning the next day before she got a response. Hyaroll looked as if he'd bitten into something sour and couldn't get the taste out of his mouth. "What do you want, Loguisse?"

"You present Aleytys with dome and domain and forget to key her in," Loguisse said calmly. "Kell could ignore those defenses you boast of and take her while she is scratching about trying to get in."

An impatient grunt. A crabbed gesure with one hand. "So keep her there."

"I'm willing. She's not."

"Take a pattern, flip it over to me."

"Don't be absurd."

He scowled at her, chewed on his lip. "You know where it is. Meet me there. Two hours. Local time. Got it?"

"Got it."

The screen blanked. Loguisse swung around. "We'll get you keyed in, then we'll come back here, Aleytys. You need to learn more than Shareem can tell you about how to manage a kephalos.''

Shareem laughed, spread her hands. "I've spent too much time offworld. Listen to the woman, Lee.''

Loguisse slid from the chair. "Come," she said. "You don't need anything beyond what you're wearing. Kell will keep his head down while Hyaroll and I are around.'' She walked briskly to the door and the bubble within a bubble that protected this room, the heart of her dome, the point where kephalos and Vryhh had closest contact, then turned and stood fidgeting impatiently until they reached her.

They passed through the double membrane into the smothering darkness of the maze. Aleytys took Shareem's hand, reached for Loguisse's and let her lead them through the twists and turns ahead.

They emerged into the cavern close to the shrouded machinery, the silent sealed workshop, nearly halfway around from the place where they entered the maze. Apparently the maze changed shape and entrance at established intervals following some principle known only to Loguisse; she'd suspected it was changing again even as they passed through it, she had had a feeling of movement, of oppression in that thick stifling blackness as if walls were pushing at her, even though she saw and heard nothing.

She followed Loguisse toward the bulkiest flier, Shareem trailing silent and unhappy behind her. Shareem wanted to be away, out of this delicate steel paradise made for one. More than anything else, she wanted to take Aleytys away and go back to the universe outside the cloud where things were confused and perilous, but less hurting and certainly less confining; out there she had space to move, she had her ship and her talents, and if things got sticky or boring she could pick up and go somewhere else. Vrithian oppressed her and Kell terrified her. Aleytys knew all that, was thinking about it as she rode the disk up to the lock, and when she looked down she saw Shareem looking down also, her shoulders slumped, her body radiating unhappiness. When Shareem came up, she put her arm about her mother's shoulders, hugged her hard, then moved quickly to the passenger chairs. Shareem looked startled, then smiled and followed without comment.

Symkatta's dome was on the southern coast of Kebelzuild, high on granite cliffs above a narrow beach where surf pounded endlessly, white foam about black rocks, the bright blue sea stretching out to the horizon. This ocean had a wider, wilder feel to it than the one they'd crossed to reach Loguisse's dome; perhaps because she was closer to it, perhaps because the dome was farther north, the ocean here seemed to have more energy, more anger to it. *And I'm using this nonsense to avoid thinking about what could happen to us if he doesn't come.* She glanced at Loguisse. The Tetrarch was silently fuming as she kept the flier circling above the dome. Fifteen minutes passed. Twenty. Thirty.

Aleytys squirmed in her seat. *Ay-Madar, here I am, helpless again. Hanging on one protector's arm while I wait for another. Like with Stavver and Maissa on Lamarchos. Hauled here, dragged there. Kicked about by the whim of others. Even Arel took me where he wanted to go, dumped me when I wanted something else.* The last few years she'd been making her own decisions and running her own life; right now she was seeing more clearly than she had when she was immersed in it how much control she'd had in spite of the Hunts more or less forced on her, Hunts she had to admit, if she was really honest with herself, that she'd enjoyed, dangerous and dubious as they were. She fidgeted as quietly and inconspicuously as she could. Where in Aschla's stinking hells was Hyaroll?

Loguisse leaned forward. Hyaroll's scowling face filled the screen. "Gnats," he grumbled. "Had to swat 'em. You ready to follow me down?"

"Ready. Go."

The face vanished; the image was a lumpy armored flier that darted down at the dome, a dark streak moving so fast it dropped off the screen before Loguisse could move. She dropped her flier after him, followed him through the dome. Then both fliers were sitting on landing saucers not far from an odd whimsical structure it was difficult to call a house and a series of gardens as disconcerting and prankish and lovely as the house.

Hyaroll walked stiffly the few steps to join Loguisse, Aleytys and Shareem. He pointed at Aleytys. "Come." Without waiting for a response from her, he started for the house. Over his shoulder he said, "You two wait here. She can do what she wants when the thing's finished."

Loguisse tapped Aleytys on the shoulder. "Go. No use trying to argue with him. We'll be over there by the fountain." Shareem nodded agreement and strolled away toward the fountain, a fantasy in twisting looping bronze tubes spitting up spurts of water in a comical lilting strongly rhythmical dance. Loguisse dropped beside Shareem on a bronze bench and sank into the intricacies of some problem. Aleytys ran after Hyaroll, caught up with him and walked along beside him. What she got from him was a feeling of terrible weariness. It smothered almost everything else about him. Somewhere inside that weariness was a hint of irritation, but even that was hollow and without force. She walked beside her grandfather, saying nothing because there was nothing he wanted to hear from her. She had the feeling that the slightest obstacle, even a wrinkle in a rug, might stop him and he'd just stand there and turn slowly slowly into stone. Yet he'd bothered to acknowledge her as his granddaughter and fit up this dome for her. She found it hard to understand why he'd stirred himself, what given when she felt in him. She thought of asking, but that might be the metaphorical wrinkle in the rug.

He led her through flow-spaces, past doors and open rooms maintained by the house androids, who were nowhere in sight right now; she couldn't even feel them ticking away around her, they must tuck themselves away in closets somewhere after finishing the eternally repeated cleaning chores about this house of ghosts. They wound deeper into the house through those empty, echoing . . . well, halls, slipping down and down into the stone of the cliffs. A brief darkness, a sense of *waiting* around her, a maze of her own once it was activated and deployed. A brief double tingle as he took her

through the inner pair of membranes and into a brightly lit
all-white room similar to the heart of Loguisse's dome, though
the instrumentation was less complex here. Which was natural enough, given the differences between Loguisse and
Synkatta.

Hyaroll put his big hand on her shoulder and guided her to
the command seat, a heavy black swivel chair fixed before
the console. Without letting go of her, he used his free hand
to drag the dust cover off that chair. "Sit there and don't
fight what happens." He urged her toward the seat with small
pushes that made her feel like a bit of rag caught in the jaws
of a large angry dog. Annoyed, she resisted, tilted her head
up and around. "Fight what?"

He dropped his hand. "Probes. Need to read you, get your
patterns into kephalos. Sit."

"I don't like things messing with my head."

"Sit or forget it. Up to you."

"Hunh." She settled herself in the chair, felt it come to
life around her as Hyaroll began moving his fingers stiffly
over the sensors. The back moved, flexing and bulging,
rising like a cobra hood over her head, coming over and
down, shaping itself to her skull. She tried to relax. Not the
time to wake the diadem. *No danger,* she thought at the
thing, *stay quiet, I need this.* The diadem did not manifest.
She relaxed some more. The hood closed over her face,
shutting off light and air so suddenly she almost panicked,
caught herself just in time. She sat still, breathing as deeply,
slowly, steadily as she could. Probes came slipping into her
head, tickling and stinging, wriggling around. An obscene
feeling. As if some repulsive stranger had tied her so she
couldn't move and was feeling her up and she couldn't do
anything to stop him. After those first ugly moments, though,
she learned as much from kephalos as it learned from her and
she knew with a comfortable certainty that she could destroy
chair, console probes, everything, the whole of kephalos—if
she wanted to. This certainty gave her sufficient sense of
control that she didn't need to destroy anything. All this was
happening because she let it happen. It was enough. She sat
still and let kephalos read her.

Time passed. Finally the hood retreated, collapsing into the chair. She moved her shoulders, straightened her back, swung around so she could see Hyaroll.

"Not yet. Stay there." Hyaroll was frowning at a screen. "Odd readings. Very odd." He continued to work over the sensors, stopping occasionally to stare blankly at nothing as if his memory had halted on him and he had to dig deep to find what he needed. As he worked, she felt the room and the house coming alive about her. More and more of the console lit up; numbers and symbols began to flow across the screens. She didn't attempt to read them, though she did wonder if her translator trick would work with numbers and number codes as well as it did with words and language. She didn't especially want to find out right now; her head ached enough already.

Hyaroll took the metal strip that slid out of a slot under the sensor panel, stepped back. "It's yours now. Or will be once I'm outside the dome." He gave her the finger-length strip of bluish metal. "Hang onto this. It's your key if you have to leave the dome. Come." He started for the membrane, waited for her without trying to pass through it. "Up to you now," he said. "Order kephalos to let me through."

"How?"

"Say the words."

"Aloud?"

"If you want. Or subvocalize."

"I hear you."

He put his hand out, tested the membrane, started off at a much faster pace than he'd used coming here. Swearing under her breath, she ran after him.

In the baronial great hall with its massive door, its playful windows that were abstract patterns in crimson-and-sapphire stained glass, its rugged ceiling beams and huge fireplaces, its rows of chandeliers, Aleytys, feeling like the heroine in some ancient melodrama, caught his arm. "Wait."

He walked three steps more, dragging her along, then turned to scowl down at her. "What?"

"Why are you doing all this?"

"Finishing something."

"What?"

"My business."

"Mine as well since it involves me. This isn't idle curiosity, anaks. I've a hard fight ahead. The more I know the better I fight. I don't understand you. I need to."

He stared at her a moment, then shifted his gaze to look past her at one of the bright windows. To her surprise, he smiled—a twist of his large mouth, a glint in narrowed green eyes. The glint faded, his face sagged, there was nothing left. "Blood," he said. "Promised her mother I'd take care of Shareem. Ianna, her name was, Shareem's mother. Promised her that after she pried Reem loose from Kell. Knew he'd go after her, wanted her to stay with me. She wouldn't. You're a lot like her, Lee; saw that soon's I saw you. Did the best I could for Shareem after Ianna was killed. Reem'll never amount to much. No, no, don't argue, girl. She's not the worst, cares a lot about you, that's something." He put his hand under her chin, tilted her face into the red-and-blue light. "You're a good child, Aleytys; you hurt when you see hurt. Shareem showed us. Proud you're my kin." The words were fine, made her glow, but there was so little feeling behind them that she ached for him. He must have seen something of this, because he backed away a step, hand dropping to his side. "Say it one more time. You shouldn't have come, this world is too small to fit you. I wind down to nothing, entropy embodied, soon unbodied." Another step away from her. He caught hold of the door's latch. "You're too full of life, girl. Like sandpaper on an ulcer. Don't call me again." He tripped the latch, pulled the door open and stalked outside.

By the time she followed he was halfway to his flier. She stood in the doorway watching until the lock closed behind him, then walked across to join Shareem and Loguisse by the fountain, the rising whine from the flier drowning the water's laughter. The flier rose and hovered just below the apex of the dome, waiting.

Aleytys looked at the strip of metal in her hand. "What do I do now?"

Loguisse blinked, squinted up at the flier, shading her eyes with both hands. "Tell kephalos to open the dome."

"Then whoever is out there waiting lobs an egg through and boom."

"Warn kephalos that you expect trouble, that the defenses are to be at maximum alert. They should be adequate—Har set them up."

"Thanks." She thought a moment, getting the phrasing right, then reached for kephalos as she had when she let Hyaroll out of house-heart, gave the order.

Hyaroll's flier shot up and darted away, taking out a missile that pounced on it the moment it left the protection of the dome, and kephalos ashed a pair that streaked for the hole. Then the flier was gone, the dome was intact, and the fountain was playing its comic song loudly enough to be heard over the wandering breeze and the very faint popping noises as the remnants of the missiles hit the dome and sizzled down its sides.

Aleytys ran her thumb across the featureless strip of blue metal. "Will this work for anyone who holds it?"

"No. Your brain and body patterns are coded into it. Holder has to match those. As long as you're alive. Once you're dead, anyone can use it."

"Right. If I lose it when I'm outside, I can't get back in?"

Loguisse looked thoughtfully at her. "You?" Her eyes crinkled with her silent laugh. "The rest of us would have to find someone we trusted to make a duplicate, not something especially easy on this world." She sobered. "If you lose it, come see me. I'll make the duplicate."

"That's a relief." She looked up at the last faint sparks of the debris. "That was rather obvious of him."

"Don't disdain the obvious."

"But don't employ it." She reached out a hand to Shareem. "Let's go back now, if you don't mind. The sooner I learn all there is to know about this dome, the sooner we'll stop making a target of you."

She stood alone in one of Loguisse's gardens, a fantasy of crystal and steel, three tall spindly trees with whippy limbs and diamond-shaped leaves, a small crystalline fountain in the center, the water making spare, simple music as it fell onto crystal leaves and ultimately into a shallow crystal basin. The late-afternoon sun was low in the west, the tree shadows were long scrawls across the short grass, dark wavery bars across the fountain.

Stuffed into her head, outlined on a handful of flakes in her belt pouch, she had all that Loguisse saw fit to tell her of the general functions of the kephalos in each dome and instructions about how she could probe her own kephalos to find out its idiosyncrasies, since the kephaloi were programmed according to the whim of their masters and creators, so that they all had surprises set up to trap the wariest of intruders. Loguisse was terse about this, and Aleytys didn't push her. Her head ached already with the heavy dose of Vrithian's history, sketchy though it was, covering the ten millennia Loguisse and the other Vrya had lived here, even sketchier when it came to the hapless Vrithli used by the undying as toys to enliven the endless march of days. She'd been given a skip-stone look at the two species native to this world, their various cultures, and how those cultures had been distorted by the presence and interference of the Vrya. It wasn't a pretty story. It infuriated her, though she said nothing of her feelings to Loguisse. Because the Tetrarch's interests were so detached from experimentation and ordinary life, she allowed the Yashoukim within the boundaries of her domain to develop as they chose, only emerging from her retreat when the intrusions of neighboring domains grew too blatant, too annoying. Other Vrya, with less to occupy hands and minds, kneaded their Vrithli like clay, punching and pulling them into the shape they chose by whim or curiosity or obscure internal needs, ruthlessly squashing or lopping off any attempt of those Vrithli to grow in forbidden directions.

After watching the water for a while as it shot up and fell back on the crystal leaves, a pleasant soothing sound, she dropped to the grass and sat dreaming for a while more, listening to the water and the breezes teasing the pale green leaves at the end of threadlike black stems. Kell first, no choice there, then. . . . She yawned and smiled. Just as well Loguisse didn't know about her plans or she might change her mind about who'd disrupt Vrithian most, she or Kell. She watched the water falling, changing color with the sky about the setting sun, and felt a relaxing, pervasive relief, a sense that an immense weight had rolled off her shoulders; she had discovered a task important enough to keep her working for those uncounted years that lay ahead of her, something to keep back the tides of entropy that had eaten Filiannis and Hrigis empty, that was turning Hyaroll to dead stone. Prying Vryhh fingers loose from Vrithli lives. She had no illusions about the transcendent joys of such freedom; most Vrithli were probably quite satisfied with their lot and would be extremely unhappy if they were forced to think for themselves. Too bad. They'd just have to learn. *Let them make a few tyrants of their own and learn how to pull those down. I'll be taking away their certainties and their security. Not kind. Not even doing it out of moral outrage. Using them like the rest of my folk have used them, entertainment.* She smiled drowsily. Not so bad as it might be. *Maybe just as well I'm not going at this filled with moral outrage and sure my way is right. Results of that kind of mind-set aren't so good. Some outrage, yes. Can't get calloused or complacent. Long hard job, and isn't that nice.* She stretched and yawned, looked around, oppressed by the lack of color. Even the varied greens after a while lost vitality and might have been only shades of gray. Everything in the dome was exquisite, and after the first glance boring. *Aphorism,* she thought, *unrelieved elegance is ultimately boring.* Loguisse wouldn't notice; when she was here she evidently spent most of her time talking with kephalos, going endlessly though esoteric concepts Aleytys found incomprehensible and as boring as the landscaping. More boring. When Loguisse tried to describe one of her current obsessions, Aleytys waved her to silence. You lost me with the second word, don't bother going on, she said. Loguisse sighed, her momentary vivacity fading. Pity, she said. Aleytys nodded, understanding well enough. There must be very few people she could talk with about the things that interested her most. She bent over, pulled loose a blade of grass and began tearing it into thin strips. *Loguisse misses conversation, I miss Wolff.* Her friends there, her house, her horses, she missed most of all unplanned accidental color, bright and dark, pale and saturated, and the ebb and flow of people with all their ragged edges. Maybe if she lived as long as Loguisse, she'd change her tastes, but she doubted that. Maybe Loguisse had started out like her, relishing the variety of life. She doubted that too. Ten thousand years. Impossible to say what a world would be like after such a time, even more impossible to tell how a person would change after that much time, though that person was yourself.

She sat awhile longer, listening to the water and the leaves, curbing her impatience to be on her own again. That meant she'd be hauling Shareem about—no big problem; she liked her mother and was occasionally amazed at her flashes of courage, staying here when she could so easily by somewhere else. Aleytys sighed, feeling guilty because she was irritated by that courage, that effort. Everything would be so much simpler if Shareem would just take off and let her get on with the fight. Unfortunately that sensible course would destroy Shareem. *Destroy. Melodramatic word, but I can't think of another that would fit. Well, once this is over, she'll go her way, maybe visit me now and again. The world will weigh lighter on both of us.*

She got to her feet, brushed herself off and went inside for the last uncomfortable meal in Loguisse's dome.

While Aleytys spent hours down in the heart room, plugged into kephalos, Shareem moved about the whimsical house of Synkatta. Bedrooms sitting like oranges impaled on thick stalks, reached by clear glass tubes extruded from the greater mass of the house; an infirmary like a soap bubble painted with mirrors, filled with light inside, the outside reflecting everything that fluttered past; and when you were tired of whimsy, sedate and comfortable rooms of stone and wood and leather: a reading room filled with books from a thousand worlds, a fieldstone fireplace, a sturdy desk of some light tan wood with a tight grain; a music room; a kitchen filled with stainless steel, more practical than aesthetic; that baronial great hall with its rough-hewn beams and colored windows; a house that was an absurdity of allusion and metaphor and with all that, comfortable. Shareem explored it, happy to

have something to do, opening the sealed rooms, bringing life
back into the emptiness, activating the androids, designing
the meals (when she could pry Aleytys loose from Kephalos
long enough to eat anything besides sandwiches and cha),
feeling cozily domestic, content to do this minor bit of mothering. She knew she was playing games with herself, but she
was also happier than she'd been in a long time.

Each day the flying bombs struck at them, others came
digging at them from beneath, but kephalos ashed the fliers
and melted the diggers, filtered out clouds of corrosive gas.
At Aleytys's instructions, kephalos had warned the local
Vrithli that absence was the safest defense in this war between two undying. The fishing village was deserted, the
farms were left with their crops going to weed, the livestock
was gone with the farmers. All the Vrithli left without argument; they'd heard too many grisly tales about those caught
up in a death duel.

On the fourth day after their second arrival Shareem lay
stretched out on the grass staring up at the cloudless sky,
hands clasped behind her head. She winced as the daily
missile whipped down at the dome, dissolving as always
before it came close enough to bother anything. Same time as
yesterday, same two prongs air and earth, same everything.
Every day she expected Kell to try something more complex,
more inventive, expected him to use the pattern he was
establishing to catch them off guard, but each afternoon, the
same time, the same spot, the diggers came digging, the
missiles came arching in; each afternoon both prongs were as
routinely destroyed. She frowned. Loguisse could say don't
condemn the obvious, but it wasn't like Kell to be that
obvious. He could be patient, that was certainly true; he'd
waited ten years to go after her mother. He might be counting
on using up their supplies, then overwhelming them with an
all-out attack. But that would take years, and Aleytys wouldn't
give him those years, he had to know that; besides, the Tetrad
would resupply her if she asked. There had to be something
else he was after.

She grimaced and forced herself to think carefully and
seriously about her mother's death. All these years she'd fled

from taking a close look at it, reacting to grief, to guilt for being the survivor, to a fear that thinking about it too much would force her to challenge him or forfeit her last shreds of self-respect. Ianna and she had been closer than most Vrya and their children. Ianna had carried her to term, though most Vryhh females decanted their fetuses into android wombs and left the children's care and education in the cold capable hands of their androids. Ianna had given birth to her in the old old way, had suckled her and kept her close until she was old enough to go into intensive training in the labs and automated factories that turned out the starships and other equipment the Strays needed and the Stayers coveted. Close. They fought a lot and laughed a lot. And that day she stood with Hyaroll looking down on the desolation that had been her home, feeling . . . well, it was certainly a good thing Hyaroll was there with her.

She didn't remember much after that. There was a time, part of it in the autodoc, part being coddled by androids, when she was only loosely connected with her body, a time after that when Hyaroll put her to work in his manufactury. She was better at model-making than he was, neater-fingered. The work helped her regain her confidence. Later he took her out on his collecting runs, got her fascinated with the cultures he inspected, the people he snatched. Took a long time . . . she was startled by how long. Nearly two hundred years until she could stand on her own. She gradually drifted away from him, understanding finally how relieved he was to see her go, though he'd never said anything about her leaving. That still hurt. Her father. He'd never said it. Never. Even now he said nothing to her, though he'd named Aleytys his granddaughter. For a shaming moment she was jealous of her daughter, hated her a little, then she pushed the feeling aside and scratched irritably at her arm. She didn't like feeling uncomfortable. No help for it. Ianna's death. It made her queasy to think about it. Abruptly she knew as surely as if he'd flashed the diagrammed plan in front of her eyes, that he'd set a trap for Ianna, a trap in her homeheart where she'd be most off her guard, set that trap in those quiet years before she knew he was coming after her. He hid the bomb or whatever it was

years before he called challenge to a death duel. It wasn't
supposed to happen that way, it wasn't supposed to be so
unfair a fight, but Kell was . . . was contemptuous of any
rules he hadn't made. *I ought to know*, she thought, *I ought
to have seen this centuries ago. I didn't think. . . .*

She sat up, sick with sudden fear. All those stupid missiles
banging away that couldn't hope to get through, all those
diggers slagged, those gas clouds rendered harmless . . .
misdirection. The magician's stock. Look over here so you
don't see what I'm doing over there. Distractions from a
danger already planted within the dome. To be activated
when they were lulled by the futility of his attacks. Thirty
years, more, time when he knew Aleytys would be accepted,
time to watch Hyaroll. She knew how Hyaroll worked; who
could know him better? A putterer. Off and on, as his interest
waxed and waned. How many years to put Synkatta's dome
in order for Aleytys? How many years was it vulnerable
before Hyaroll did his final checks? Twelve years, and more,
when Kell knew what Aleytys was and was becoming, time
enough to learn to fear her. To learn her weaknesses as well
as her strengths. A dozen years to make his final plans.
Probably discounting Shareem. *He knows me too, he knows
how futile I'd be in this fight*. She sat up, her skin crawling,
shrinking from the lightest touch. If she could have floated in
midair, she'd have felt marginally safer. What was waiting
for them? Bomb? Most likely. Disease? Fire? Poison? He had
a universe to draw on. She got to her feet, moving as slowly
and delicately as she could. She couldn't float, that was
dreamwork, she had to walk, her feet had to come down on
the ground, had to bear her weight. She had to breathe,
though each warm ragged exhalation might be the key to set
the thing off. Whatever it was. *Whatever gods there be,
please please please don't force me to be the one who kills
my child*. She walked slowly stiffly impossibly into the house,
hesitating for an agonizing time before she worked the latch;
she had to get to Aleytys, had to warn her, warn her of what?
Kell, Kell, always Kell. She left the door open, but that
might be the cue, closing it might be the cue, who could tell,
walked across the shining parquet floor—*which one of those*

*inlaid bits of wood might be the trigger? where did I walk
before? should I pass that way again, is it safe, or should I
take another way?* She crept along the flow-way to the reading room, remembering pain, remembering the hard, hard
birth, remembering the baby dark against her breast, her tiny
golden baby with a mass of bright red curls, stubborn even
then, even when she was a few days old, demanding, small
fists kneading her breast as the baby sucked with such uncon-
querable determination—all the memories she'd shut away so
many years ago. She reached for the sensor plate to open the
door of the reading room, a comlink in there tied to the
heartroom. She hesitated—*Is this the one?*—palmed the plate
and walked inside with that same slow stiff eggshell walk.

The desk. The link at one end, a tilted screen set into the
wood, a sensor panel. She reached out. Stopped her hand
above the sensors without touching any. A dozen times before, more than a dozen, she'd talked to Aleytys on this link,
scolding her into coming up for a hot meal. What if this was
the call that triggered the thing? She started shaking. If she
called . . . and if she didn't . . . and the thing activated and
killed Aleytys . . .

Whatever she did or failed to do could trigger the thing.
Anything at all. Action or omission. She nearly screamed
with frustration. And even that, noise, that could be the
trigger. The sound of her voice. She sighed, cut the sigh
short, froze a moment not breathing, then gazed down at the
comscreen. If action and inaction were equal risks, then it
was easier to act than to refrain, better to do something than
just sit waiting. She tapped the code into the link, sweat
rolling down her face, sweat oozing from her palms, making
her fingers clumsy, slippery. Very slowly, very carefully she
tapped the code into the link, waited without breathing, didn't
relax appreciably when her daughter's face appeared.

"What is it?" Aleytys looked tired and irritable.

Shareem licked her lips. For a moment she couldn't talk
around the lump in her throat. She worked her tongue, tried
to swallow, gave a short dry cough. "Lee." It was a squeak
that broke in half. "Lee, come up here, it's important."

Aleytys looked at something out of range of the viewer,

then she leaned forward and shut down what she was doing. "Be there in a little, Reem." The screen emptied.

Hand shaking again. coated with sweat, Shareem tapped the link off, then stood where she was a moment, hugging her arms across her breasts, hands closed tight on her upper arms. Nothing happened. She walked to the door, stepping as lightly as she could, afraid to put a foot down once she'd raised it, but she had to and did, afraid to lift it again, afraid to stir the air with her breath. Anything could be the trigger, anything at all. Yet she could no more stay in that pleasant room than she could stop the neurons discharging in her brain. She stood waiting in the great hall until she heard Aleytys calling her.

"Here," she said. It came out a whisper; she had to clear her throat and repeat herself. "Here, Lee. In the hall." She waited tensely until she saw Aleytys coming toward her, then she moved in that stiff-legged reluctant walk to the front door, reached for the latch, forced herself to grasp it, then shove the door open with a single smooth push. Then she was outside, wiping sweat from her face. They should be marginally safer outside.

"What is it, Reem? You look terrible."

Shareem looked nervously at the door, then took another step away from it. "Lee, I . . . I . . ." Startling herself and Aleytys, she began sobbing, caught Aleytys in her arms and held her daughter tight against her, her face in her daughter's hair, the daughter who was taller and stronger than she was, stronger and more alive, so wonderfully against all odds alive and back with her.

But it wasn't a baby she held. only a woman she didn't know all that well, and when the first helpless reaction had passed, she stepped back from Aleytys, flushed with embarrassment. "I . . . I'm . . ." She looked frantically about, saw the patch of grass where she'd been lying. ". . . sorry, Lee. It was just . . ." She started toward the grass, and Aleytys followed without saying anything.

Shareem dropped to her knees, swung her legs around until she was sitting cross-legged, knee to knee with her daughter. "I was afraid . . ."

"I saw that. What is it?" Aleytys leaned forward, took her

hand and held it between her own. "You're still shaking. And sweating rivers."

"I'm a fool."

"No."

She pulled her hand free, laced her fingers together. "Don't talk about what you don't understand." She looked at her hands, then past Aleytys at the house. "I told you Kell challenged my mother to a death duel and killed her."

"Yes. So?"

"I run away from things. I ran away from that, never thought about how my mother died. Until now, just now. I was stretched out here. The missile came. Third hour after noon. Like yesterday, day before, day before that. Kephalos took it out. Like yesterday, day before, day before that. Four days, Lee. How long does it take me to get the point? But I finally started thinking." A small tight movement of her mouth, more a grimace than a smile. "I do think. Now and then. Kell is never obvious. So what is all this for? Every day I've been expecting some devious attack that takes everything we've got to stop it. If we can. But nothing happens. Just those idiot missiles, and a few frills to keep kephalos honest. But he got into my mother's dome. Ten hours after the challenge she was dead, the place was molten rock and miscellaneous debris." Her stomach was churning, and there was bile burning her throat. "I always assumed he got through her defenses somehow." She drew her hand across her mouth, then scrubbed it along her forehead, scraping away the sweat, pushing her hair off her face. "Ten years, I thought, so Ianna would forget how he hated her, so she'd get interested in other things. A distraction. And I thought, these stupid attacks, it's the same thing, really. A distraction. And I thought, why? And I thought, it's obvious, if you look at it the right way. He's got something planted here waiting for us or him to trigger it. Could be a bomb. Doesn't have to be. Disease. Poison. Anything. And we've been here four days. Anything could trigger it. Anything. Maybe time triggers it. So many days, boom. Or whatever. Maybe the missiles trigger it— kephalos wakes his defense nodes, and boom. Tomorrow? Any day after that? No way of knowing, except it's probably

not today's, though it could be on a delay circuit. You can't
know how I felt, Lee. Lying there thinking all this, thinking
I've got to warn you, but anything I did might be the trigger,
or anything I didn't do. I was about falling apart.'' She
looked down at shaking hands. ''I still am. The thought of
going back in there . . .''

''Ukh.'' Aleytys closed her eyes. ''Worms eat his festered
soul, I think you're right, Reem. It feels right. It feels like
something the man I met would do. Hah! sitting out there
somewhere gloating. Ay-Aschla, what a time for Shadith to
be on her own. I could use her instincts and training.'' She
smiled at Shareem's frown. ''She's not the child she looks,
you know.'' She closed her eyes, and her lips moved. *Talking to the other one,* Shareem thought, abruptly and absurdly
jealous of that sketchy bundle of nothing. Aleytys opened her
eyes. ''Reem, your flier. It's armored, isn't it?''

''But we left it sitting for a couple of days at the Mesochthon.
I know Loguisse went over it, and she's the best there is after
Hyaroll, but Kell's . . . well . . . Kell.''

''And I am Aleytys.'' She blinked, smiled. ''That sounds
. . .'' She got to her feet, took Shareem's hand and pulled
her up. ''I don't care how it sounds, I've got more resources
than he knows.'' She frowned. ''On second thought, he
knows I have the diadem, but he doesn't know its uses, even
I'm still surprised by . . . Never mind. Come on.''

Shareem sighed for what she'd lost. Aleytys liked her well
enough, that was comforting, but she could remember too
vividly the child who had filled her arms. She knew none of
the vague dreams that flitted through her head had many ties
with reality. Babies grew up and as often as not left wreckage
in their wake; she could remember all too well the times
when she'd choked even under Ianna's loose restraints, choked
and kicked and said things she nearly always wished unsaid.
And there was this diadem thing, a reminder of all the ties
Aleytys had with other people, people she knew nothing
about. But . . . *Forget that, Reem,* she told herself. *Futility
lies down that street. You did what you did for Aleytys's
health of mind and body. And,* she told herself, whipping
herself with it, *because this so dearly loved baby was a drag*

on you. You could have kept her. You could have gone back for her anytime. You could have raised her on the ship, kept her away from Vrithian. You didn't do any of that. It's over. You can't go back. Live with it. She looked at the house, shuddered. Out here in the garden, the summer sun beating down on them, she could put her fears aside and almost forget them. She glanced at her daughter. Whatever Aleytys feared, it wasn't physical danger, physical damage. Her daughter walked with that alert serenity Shareem had seen now and then in the faces of the short-lives she moved among out beyond the cloud, men, most of them, though there was a woman or two that came to mind when she thought hard, a look that said without boasting they could handle just about anything that came up. Not courage, not exactly physical competence, more a state of mind. She didn't know precisely what it was, but Aleytys had it. Nothing Kell could do to her now would frighten her. Shareem felt a touch of envy, even resentment. She pushed them away hastily—*no no don't think about that, no no too upsetting*.

The flier sat in the landing dish, squat and angular and ugly without fuss or pretension.

"Wait here," Aleytys said. Her eyes were fixed on the flier, her hand warm, her touch hasty, rather rough as she stopped Shareem. She approached the flier with taut, wary interest, vanished around the flier's far side, came back around the tail. Shereem knew she was forgotten, that Aleytys was wholly concentrated on the flier. Aleytys dropped to a squat, went very still, hands on thighs, eyes closed. Shareem sighed and dropped to the grass to wait.

Time passed slowly, the afternoon filled with the mewls of sea birds, the brush-crash of the surf, the sound of the crazy fountain, wind chimes somewhere behind the house, and a low breathy booming sound from the house itself. Aleytys didn't move. Shareem was content not to move. Her eyelids drooped, she dropped into a half-doze. And started, nearly falling over, when Aleytys got suddenly to her feet and climbed into the flier. She stayed inside a few breaths, then came back out with a small black ovoid carefully cradled in her hands.

Her face intent, she carried the ovoid to the cliff edge close to the shimmer of the dome field. She stopped a moment. Opening a hole, Shareem thought. She gazed at her daughter's back, chewed on a knuckle as she waited.

Aleytys flung the black egg through the hole, stood watching. Nothing happened for what felt to Shareem like an age, then there was an explosion that shook the cliffs. Nothing came through the screen, and the earth settled rapidly back to stability. Silence. Then the patter of water hitting the screen and rolling down it, flowing back to the sea.

Aleytys came slowly back, her face thoughtful. "That wasn't it," she said, "if there is an it. That's another distraction." She stood with her hands on her hips, frowning at the house. "Hard to know where to start." She flashed a grin at Shareem. "I can understand your dithers. 'S going to take some doing walking back in there."

Shareem returned the smile. She stayed where she was, sitting on the grass, watching her daughter, contented and at ease now, trusting Aleytys to take care of this threat—as empty a threat now as the bomb that had blown a hole in the ocean. Aleytys was her shield, like the dome that kept out missiles and gas, but more flexible and even more effective.

Aleytys moved her shoulders, slumped a little. "Can't find it from out here."

"What are you going to do?"

"Think. Got a feeling looking for the thing is the best way to set it off."

"Depends on how you look."

"Mmm, tell me something. Vrya aren't empathic, that's obvious. Any PK, manipulation at a distance?"

"No. For sure, no." Shareem chuckled. "That you get from your father's side. What a thought, that I should ever be pleased by anything that man had."

Aleytys ignored the last part of that. "Good. Limits the places Kell can put things."

"He knows what you can do?"

"He's had painful personal experience with what I can do. Mmm, it won't be shielded, just hidden. I wouldn't have to go looking for shielding, it'd be shouting at me *here I am*.

Hiding's better—then if his misdirection fails and I go looking, he could use that to trigger the thing. Plenty of psi detectors about, easy enough to tie them into the detonator. Kell, worms eat your liver, why wait so long? Why four days?" She started pacing back and forth. "Reem, what am I missing? If it'd been me, I'd have blown the thing no later than the second day. Why give us this much time to think about what's happening?"

"Something you haven't done, something I haven't." She pulled a blade of grass, used the stiff, pointed end to scratch along her nose. "Hyaroll's really the best, Lee. He'd spot anything too complicated, even a timer, anything that took energy. Has to be something activated from outside, probably mechanical. Like your psi detectors. No psi about, the detectors play dead. Hah! That damn silly missile shower. Activates the same portion of kephalos every day, say it advances a ratchet one notch each day until boom. If we leave, he stops the missiles—logical, isn't it?—and the trap's set for next time we're here. Could be the fifth day, the sixth, the tenth, who knows but that spider? Him sitting out there gloating. Pfahh!"

Aleytys said nothing, gazed past Shareem at nothing. "Nice problem," she said finally.

"Why don't we just leave? Even if he doesn't stop the count, we're safe."

"Where do we go?"

"Hyaroll? Loguisse? Filiannis said to visit her."

"Filiannis?" Aleytys chuckled at the expression on Shareem's face. "Right. And Hyaroll won't let us in." She tilted her head back, gazed at the faint shimmer of the dome. "You know, I've got a feeling we'd better not try leaving again. Maybe you're right. Maybe he'd shut down the count until we got back. Have to activate kephalos to get out. Want to take the chance? No, me either." She dropped to the grass beside Shareem. "If I can't come up with something between tomorrow and noon, I'll get us both out without opening the dome. Funny, in a way it was Kell who showed me how to do that—well, made it necessary to learn. Thing is, though,

that would leave us on foot and more or less unarmed on
ground he knows better than the both of us. I like the odds a
bit more even. Mmm, let me think. . . .''

Harskari, Aleytys subvocalized, *we've got a problem.*
Amber eyes opened. Voice dryly amused, Harskari said,
*Interesting. If you could find the bomb, you could disarm it,
but to find it, you'll have to probe for it, and if you probe for
it, you'll set it off. If it's a bomb, it will come close to being
a planet buster. To make sure he gets you.*
Could you hold something that powerful? Just in case?
*Don't know. If I'm close enough, if you can feed me
enough power.*
*Can't stay. Can't leave. Can't do nothing. Can't do some-
thing. So what do we do?*
*Getting to be suppertime. A pleasant warm evening. Have
your androids serve a hot meal out here.*
What? I couldn't eat.
*You have to, Lee. High-energy food. Much as you can.
Force it down if you must. Nothing is going to happen for a
while. I have a glimmering of an idea. I need time, Lee. I
need to consider the resources of my craft and the possibilities of the diadem. No reason for you to sit around moaning.*
I'm glad one of us sees some light. She stretched,
opened her eyes, spoke aloud to Shareem, who was sitting
and watching her. ''Reem, my head's going around in circles
for now. Anyway, I'm hungry. Get the Ikanom out here and
have it arrange an alfresco supper for us. Steaks, I think, a
big salad, anything else you'd like. You do that kind of thing
better than I do. I'm going to start thinking on my feet for a
while—maybe that will be more profitable.''

Aleytys emptied her cup. ''I was hungry.'' She set her cup
beside her and lay back on the grass.
''Walking help?''
''Not much. Reem?''
''No.''
''What no?''
''You can't sent me off without you.''

"Reem, if I have to waste energy protecting you . . . ."

"No. If I'm here, you'll be a lot more careful."

"I'm not about to get myself killed."

"But you'll be that little bit warier if you've got me to worry about."

"Reem . . ."

"No."

Aleytys got to her feet and began pacing about the lawn, saying nothing more, turned inward, brooding as she walked. Shareem dipped a leaf of crisp green thrix into a pool of coldsauce and crunched it down, drowsily content. She'd made her statement, put her foot down, and that was over. She chewed and swallowed, feeling like one of the more placid ruminants.

Aleytys came back to the remnants of the meal, dropped into a squat and scowled at Shareem. "At least you'll spend the night in the flier."

Shareem fished another bit of thrix from the salad bowl, grimaced at it. "My aching back."

"Please."

"You're trying something tonight."

"I have to, don't I?"

"Oh, all right. I can throw some blankets in the back, and I suppose Ikanom can find some sort of padding so I don't wake up with bruises on my rear."

"Thanks." Aleytys got to her feet and went back to drifting about this section of the garden, automatically avoiding obstacles, back in her somber brood.

Shareem looked at the thrix again, popped it into her mouth. She wasn't worried. Aleytys would come up with something. She looked around her at the debris of the meal. then tapped the caller, summoning the Ikanom to clear up the mess. She wiped her mouth on a napkin, dropped it, drew her legs up and sat with her back against one of the boulders scattered about the wild garden, watching Aleytys wander about. *What's she going to do after this is over? Stay here? Not likely. She'd be bored to stone here. Wolff? Probably. If young Shadith—how good was she?—found Grey and got him loose from Kell's trap.* Grey. She winced. But he was a

short-life, a mayfly, nothing to worry about. She watched her
daughter fondly, dreaming of times to come when they could
be together, passing the decades, the centuries together, as
she and Ianna might have done if Kell had given them the
chance. A long gentle dance of friendship, visiting each
other, going their ways, coming together again. Aleytys was
a shadow drifting through shadows. *I should be terrified,*
Shareem thought, *but I'm not. Not anymore. Funny. Me and
that dirt-grubber—what did he call himself?—that Azdar. We
produced her. It doesn't seem possible.* She settled back
against the boulder while Ikanom directed kitchen androids
that were clearing the grass of the supper leavings, a tall
silent graceful male figure, burnished bronze, the light of
Minhas sliding along the wonderfully crafted face whose
shifting planes and hollows could be remarkably expressive. *I
never knew Synkatta. Wish I had. The man who built those
androids and that house* . . . She made a mental note to ask
Ikanom about him when there was time.

Minhas swam full overhead through cottony clouds while
Araxos was a fat crescent low in the east. The house was a
complex burr-edged blotch in the darkness, silent and drowsy
in the cooling night. Aleytys sat slumped on a wooden bench
by a small rambling stream, rubbing bare feet over the grass,
waiting with a mixture of impatience and reluctance for Harskari
to come out of her retreat. Nothing Aleytys could think of
stood up to critical evaluation, developing large uncomfortable holes as she tried playing out the line of action. She
stirred restlessly on the bench. "What am I doing here?" she
said aloud. "I should be getting Grey loose."

Harskari's eyes came open. *Shadith is quite competent,
Aleytys. You can't do everything.*

I could try. She laughed, but quit that when it started
getting out of hand. *Sure Shadith is competent, but she's not
me. I know what I can do, I need to get my hands on
things. . . .* She opened and closed her hands, wanting Kell
in those hands right now; she wanted to pound Grey's location out of him. She gripped the edge of the bench. *Did you
come up with something?*

Yes.

Well?

The amber eyes slitted, Harskari projected an intense reluctance.

Well? Aleytys knew Harskari wouldn't be hurried, but she couldn't help prodding a little.

You've thought about passive detection.

You know I have, but . . .

You couldn't see a way to make it work without first knowing what you'd be using it to find out.

Yes.

The diadem phases in and out of this reality depending on the pressures you put on it. There's no way anyone these days can detect it when it's phased out—

Aleytys interrupted her. *The RMoahl. They've never had the least difficulty keeping track of me.*

Innate sense, I think. Harskari made an impatient sound. *Kell's no RMoahl. Where was I? Oh, yes, no one but the Rmoahl can detect the diadem when it's phased out, yet Swardheld, Shadith and I are able to touch you, use you in spite of being an inseparable part of that concatenation of forces. I've had a long time to study it and intimate knowledge of it; it was constructed by one of my people, a product of our common skills and the uncommon skills of Traivenn. I think I know a way to tie your body temporarily to the diadem so you can phase out with it. In a sense you join me in this parody of existence. You should be able to pass through ordinary matter without disturbing it. I've considered all the possibilities I can think of. Seems to me the one place he could put the bomb—I think it's probably a bomb—where kephalos couldn't detect it is inside kephalos. Out of phase, you should be able to pass into kephalos without registering on any of its sensors or alerting the psi detectors. Once we find the thing, I can half-phase you and hold it in stasis until you can disarm it. That's why I wanted you to eat and rest. Isn't going to be easy on either of us.*

Aleytys wrinkled her nose. *Pass through matter. Hunh. What happens if I start sinking slowly and inexorably into the center of the world and stay there as ash for eternity when our strength gives out?* She thought a moment. *Or go floating off and end up an icicle in the gas cloud up there?* She waved a hand at the silver mist making shimmery background for the moons.

Aleytys, don't be silly.

I feel silly. She sighed and reached for the symbolic power river, tapped into it and drew as much of the energy into herself as she could hold without burning to the ash she'd mentioned a moment before. *I'm ready. Let's try it.*

The diadem chimed. She felt the familiar weight on her head, then a strange chill passing through her body, starting at her feet, going up through a suddenly tight throat; it made the back of her eyes itch and shivered the roots of the hair at the crown of her head. An odd fluttery feeling like wings beating inside her. The garden and the house fluttered like the wings within. The air got darker as if the gas cloud were quenched and the two moons had gone dark. Then it seemed she pushed through a membrane like that of the field that guarded the househeart and found Harskari standing beside her, a tall and slender woman with white hair and dark skin, wearing a slim dark robe embroidered in jewel colors with designs that seemed oddly, disturbingly familiar, though Aleytys knew she'd never seen them before. She knew she was seeing Harskari's memory of her former self, yet the figure seemed real. Solid. There was a sourceless thick light around her. There was color, rich color darker and more saturated than the colors she remembered in the garden; the foliage was green ultramarine, stone and earth and wood were dove-gray, russet and tawny, the textures about her mostly visual but no less rich for that, like those in a brocade print made from forty blocks. No smells. And after a short while longer in that eerie state, she was startled to find she wasn't breathing. Or perhaps it would be more accurate to say the shadow she cast in this other reality wasn't breathing. The relation between the sensing shadow and the body she could no longer feel was something she didn't understand and only made her head ache—her shadow head—when she tried to work it out. Weird, she thought. Weird.

Harskari controlled her impatience and waited for Aleytys to grow accustomed to this state.

Aleytys turned her head. Her shadow head turned and she supposed her body's head turned too. She saw, somehow, the garden around that body, the house, and grew confused about just who or what was doing the seeing. *I'm here . . . whole . . . inside my own head.* She willed herself to stand and sensed that she was moving. Felt as if she was operating something made of marshmallows and gristle. Enough body-sense left to let her move. Frightening not to know exactly where her real hands and feet were. Frightening to have so little sense of her own reality. *Do ghosts feel like this? If so, I'd rather never be one. So I'd better get busy.* She willed herself to walk. Felt herself bouncing on ground that was rather like good-quality foam rubber.

Harskari beckoned to her, turned and glided away.

For a moment Aleytys felt like a centipede deciding what foot to start off on, then she was gliding after Harskari, not precisely walking; it felt rather like the times in the fall before the worst of the snows when the children in the vadi Raqsidan made ice slides and wore the bottoms off their boots.

The house looked solid. Dauntingly so. The texture of the stones was powerful before her.

Harskari—or her dream form—walked into that wall. As if it were no more solid than a heavy fog.

Aleytys followed, found herself struggling to breath; she scolded herself, telling herself she hadn't been breathing for . . . how long? Impossible to say. The wall had the rubbery feel of the earth, it made little resistance to her passing, but she was very glad when she emerged into the book room. The things in the room had a strong presence, unreal, yet at the same time their surfaces were energized, solid. As if they were finely made holographic images that were perfect and at the same time obviously what they were. She was gliding through a hologram, gliding through the dreams that the floor and the walls and the furniture were dreaming.

She followed Harskari along the flow-ways as she'd followed Hyaroll, down and down through the cellars with their racks of wine bottles, jars of preserves, past the shrouded machines in the workshop that seemed to exist beneath every Vryhh house. None of these dusty, nothing ever seemed to get dusty in these domes, pity the poor android with its endless dustmop rounds. Down yet further through the open maze—she found the fuss of threading through the thing so annoying she left it undeployed, though Shareem scolded her about that. Through the membranes without the membranes noticing her.

Through the face of kephalos.

Into another sort of maze. Snapping neurons of woven wire and silica flakes and painted panels and a shimmer of continuous happenings, almost visible thoughts. Kephalos dreamed too, hummed and sang conundrums to itself, needing to use the parts of its enormous capacity that defense and the care of the house and grounds left unused.

During the past four days she'd gotten used to the aspect of kephalos that communicated with her, but what she perceived now was so much greater that she faltered, disoriented, almost lost herself. Harskari came back to her, touched her arm. Calmness and assurance flowed hand to arm. She looked at Harskari and thought: *I love her. This is my true mother, the mother of my soul.*

On and on. Growing astonishment at the sheer size of kephalos. Growing sense of personhood about her. Kephalos as something far beyond machine. Not it, yet not him not her. Kephalos thinking, dreaming. Then . . .

Darkness thick, massive, ugly.

Tumor on the brain.

Death embodied in darkness, waiting.

She felt it before she saw it.

She knew it before she saw it.

When she saw it, it flooded her with fear.

Harskari moved to it, stood beside it, her hand on it.

Aleytys shuddered. Felt herself shudder. Like touching suddenly and without warning a slug, feeling it pulse alive under your fingers.

Harskari's voice came like another shock. "Hurry, Lee. Look at it. Know it. Time runs away."

She had to force herself to move closer to the thing. She put her hand on it. Holograph hand, hollow and insubstantial. Hand sliding over it. It was heavy, dark and solid even in this reality. Warm and vibrating, purring along, not a real sound, but something slipping through the whole of the body she was beginning to feel again as if the bomb was so powerfully present in both realms that it gave a sort of reality to her dreamform, though she also knew that was Harskari bringing her up to half-phase so she could handle materials in the outside world. Harskari's hand warm on her shoulder, she touched and traced, found the psi alarms and pulled their sensor flakes, found the electromagnetic sensors and pinched them free to hang dangling down the sides of the bomb, found the tremblers, the scaly patches of the other alarms, and peeled them loose, felt out the internal mechanisms of the bomb and found what she thought was the ultimate detonator. Once again she began the slow tracing of connections. Heat gathered in her. At first she didn't notice it, then she ignored it, then it was an agony that she couldn't ignore, but she kept on with her slow, thorough trace. Harskari drained off some of the heat accumulating in her, but couldn't do that much.

The bomb began to change. The heat seemed to be forcing her into phase with it, or maybe the weight and malevolence of it was changing her angle to reality. She muttered a quick warning to Harskari, not knowing if the old one heard her, then began untangling and undoing all the traps, concentrating fiercely, little strength in her hands and a clumsiness that gave her fits. The bomb was reacting to her while she worked, arming itself, her work was a race against that, a race where she had a slipping edge. Her fingers fumbled on, she sobbed, felt rather than heard herself, drew on the remnants of her strength, removed a section of the bomb's skin, set the plug on the floor by her feet, then began pulling flakes in the sequence she'd determined. Hands trembling, no feeling in her fingers, every movement guided only by the sense that was not sight. Until she finally bared the detonator and pulled it with an ease that seemed to make a mockery of her pain and terror.

The bomb died.

She felt it die under her shaking hands.

She felt a great numbing release; her body quit on her as her will quit.

Harskari slapped her, shouting: "Quitting, are you? Lying
down on me. Letting Shareem down. Finish or it's all for
nothing. Finish. On your feet or kephalos dies too. Take the
detonator farther away from the bomb. I can't do it. I'm a
phantom even here. Your hands are the only ones can do it.
Move, Lee. *Move!*" The last word was a shriek, Harskari's
eternal irritating calm shattered at last. It broke Aleytys out of
her lethargy, prodding her to one last effort.

She pushed onto hands and knees, felt about for the detonator, twisted some broken wires tight about her wrist. She
stayed there awhile, her mind drifting off whenever she tried
to focus on anything. Harskari's hand came warm on her
shoulder, guiding her, comforting her. Dragging the detonator, she crawled under the maze of kephalos, nothing in her
mind but slide her knees, move her arms, slide-slide the
knees, pat-pat the hands, hear the detonator scraping, tum-
bling along beside her. On and on. No sense of time passing.
Slide-slide the knees. Pat-pat the hands. One-two. One-two.

A warmth on her forehead, a pressure halting her. "Lee.
Lee. Lee." For a moment she couldn't make sense of the
sounds. *Lee? Oh. My name. Yes. My name.* She lifted her
head. "Lee, you can rest now. I'm phasing you back. It's
over. You've done the job. Rest now."

A wrenching and a twisting of her body. a flash of fire
over her skin, a pain more intense than any she'd known
before. She was briefly aware of a small dusty room. Dust? A
cold stone floor. Real darkness. Thick. Almost tangible.
Weariness swept in waves over her. She plunged into a deep
dreamless sleep.

LOPPEN VAR ON SAKKOR

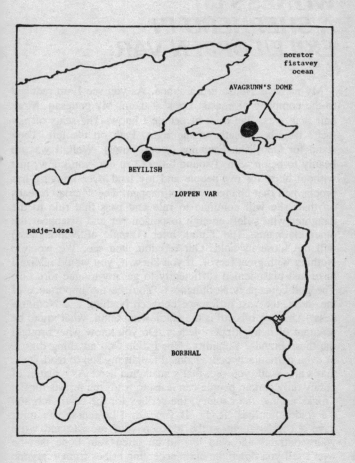

VRITHIAN
WITNESS [3]
A SHEPHERD IN
EXILE/LOPPEN VAR

My name is Hattra lu Laraynne. As you see I am reduced to the company of beasts. Look at them. My gettesau. More hair than wits, like a lot of people I know. The scars on my face? Brands. Oncath on the right, Fath on the left. They stand for Oporlisha Faerenos (rebel traitor). Well, I was no beauty to begin with. I sound bitter? I'm not, you know, just without hope for my people and my land. Our undying has proclaimed that change will not happen. The Matriarch leans on that; she will continue to rule and pass that rule to the daughter who's deft enough to poison her and disappear the other claimants. The T'nink Intet (Temple of Nothingness) will not loose its hold. Our religion, you see. We worship Nothing with great fervor. If you knew it, you would realize I have just blasphemed sufficiently to get my tongue torn out. The god-concept is Nothingness. You see the importance of the -ness, the vast difference between Nothing and Nothingness? Ah, how blissful is the unknowing mind, what joy to be ignorant of itchy slippery letters. Do you know what brought me these brands? Stupidity. No, I didn't do anything drastic or even particularly courageous; I taught my son to read. Yes, that's all. Well, you see, that's anathema here. As a matter of policy only certain people can learn to read, the priests for the t'ninks around the country, the scribes for the Matriarch and the trader families. Right. If you run a business, you must have a t'nink-taught scribe to keep your records and write your contracts and you live in an often vain hope that he won't sell you down the drain accepting bribes from everyone about. But the lu Laraynnes have always been rebels. Oh, not overt rebels—that trait vanished quickly from Loppen Var.

Anyone who stuck her head up was killed. Among other things we did, mother taught daughter to read, this from way back in the mists of forgotten times. Because of this lu Laraynne prospered, though we let ourselves be cheated now and then for the look of it; word got around we were lucky. I don't mind telling you all this; the line is wiped out. Cousins, aunts, grandmothers, mothers, all gone. Our undying, our living god Avagrunn, she saw to that. She wants no changes in the rules she set down for us. For longer than anyone can remember, she comes down from her dome when there is unrest and adjusts the folk to suit her pleasure, slaying the intransigent, punishing the others. Why am I alive? I don't know. A sign perhaps of the consequences of rebellion. Not much of a sign. I seldom go near other folk, only go into the village when I need something I can't make for myself. Don't talk to anyone, no one talks to me. Why did I do it? Ah, if you'd seen him, you'd know. My firstborn, a beautiful loving boy, gentle and kind, but with a hunger in him to know things. His father? You really don't understand how things work here, do you? Nothingness. He came out of nothingness, a gift of the Great Nothing. What that means is pubescent girls go to the t'nink in their town when they are ready for children and their mother allows it. They spend thirty days there doing t'nink service in the day and lying with whoever comes to their rooms at night. The priests? Didn't I make it clear the priests and scribes are always women? No. Every thirty days a levy is made of village men in the middle range of ages, they do heavy work for the t'nink in the day and go to the rooms appointed them at night, a different room each night so no one, not even the priests, knows who sired what child. Afterward? Well, associations do form between men and women, though they are not supposed to. As long as there are no children of that association, no one says anything. My son, my Juranot. I tried to keep him on one of the family farms, gave up my place on the ruling board to stay with him. He didn't mind, he had a deep and abiding love for wild plants and animals, he made sketches of them in a little book I had bound for him. And kept notes in that book about their habits. It was dangerous, but I could not deny him that gift. Then priests came and took him away, took him to do his service in the village t'nink. I warned him to say nothing about the reading when I taught him. I had just time to warn him again when they took him away. I wasn't terribly afraid for him; he was quick and wary when he had to be. But ah, he was beautiful.

That was the thing I feared. That was the trap that snared him.

The undying came through the village when he was in the t'nink.

Avagrunn saw him and desired him. Took him.

I had friends then. One of them saw what happened and came to tell me, comfort me as much as she could.

He betrayed his teaching. How could he not—he was only a boy and she is ages old in treachery and terror. He didn't tell her anything, I'm sure of that, but somehow he let her see he knew his letters. That was all she'd need. They brought his head to me, priests and a squad of harriers. They branded me and drove me from my home. They burned everything, killed my kin, everyone except me. Me they left alive to remember and grieve over what I had done. Oh yes, they sterilized me first to make sure none of my tainted blood would be passed on. What can I do? Avagrunn won't change. As long as she is there, as long as her power supports the Matriarch, nothing will change. You must understand, hope's the only pain I couldn't endure. I have no hope. I will walk my quiet rounds the rest of my days. I will shear my gettesau each spring and trade the fleeces for what I need to keep me for the year. When the time comes I will die up here and rot and finally I will be some use again, fertilizing the trees and feeding the scavengers. Regrets? I regret nothing. What I did before I would do again. My beautiful boy, how could I cripple him with unnecessary ignorance? Would I break his leg to make him limp, would I pluck out an eye to destroy the lovely symmetry of his face? How much less could I stop the reach of his mind? I accept no guilt for what I did; the guilt lies with the undying, with Avagrunn. If I could get my hands around her throat, I would test how undying she really is. But there is no hope of that, so I have no hope. Ah, I'm tired of talking about this, it's all foolishness and futility. Go away. I've nothing more to say to you. Go!

VRITHIAN
action on the periphery [3]

Amaiki touched the screen to life, clasped her hands to stop them trembling as she saw the loved faces: little Muri up front; Kimpri leaning over his shoulder; Keran towering over all of them, a half-smile on her narrow face; Betaki leaning against her, amusement warm in his slitted eyes; Se-Passhi, their naish, in the curve of Muri's arm. Dear, most dear, all of them. Seeing them like this, unable to touch or smell them, was almost more than she could bear. Then Betaki held up the newest hatchling, a tiny gold naish, the blessing of blessings to a mate-meld. She gasped and bent closer to the screen, her hand up to touch the little blind face, her heart so full that she couldn't speak. She made the blessing signs, the joy signs that should have been made touching the soft soft skin, aching because she could not feel their naishlet, could not smell the sweet-sour scent of the infant.

Muri cleared his throat, tapped his skinny forefinger against the screen, finally catching her notice. "Haven't named our naish yet, Ammi-sim. Waiting for you."

"Ah why? Muri-sim, I'm stuck here three more years."

"We want you to tell the undying to let you go. He's broken his side of the covenant, two winters with no rain. Why should we keep our side?" His high tenor roughened to a low growl; there was a general murmur of agreement from the others.

Amaiki closed her eyes and breathed slowly until she had control of herself; she hated fusses, hated getting into a flutter. Keeping her voice low and quiet, she said, "It will be difficult. He does not listen to our speaker here—why should he listen to me? I'll try to make him hear me. Muri meld-

brother, have there been dreams in the Dums around here, dreams of fire and death that could be reaches into tomorrow?''

Muri smoothed his hand over his lacy crest. ''No one but us left in Shiosa, Ammi. We had dreams, but who can say what they mean?''

''No one left?''

''The deepest well in Shiosa is sucking mud. We could drill deeper yet, but what's the point?''

''Ah. The meld dreams?''

Kimpri leaned over Muri, ignoring his disgruntled snort. ''Blood and death, Ammi. You remember Tamakis in Dum Hayash? Who was my nest-sister?''

''Kimp-sim, I've only been gone a year and a half, not half a life.''

''Feels like a life—the flavor of the meld needs your spice, love-sister. Anyway, she called me before her mate-meld left, a pretty good far-speaker she is too, says she felt blood dreams all over the uplands.'' She straightened, brushed affectionately at Muri's crest, flicked a finger against the tip of an ear. ''All right, all right, little cricket.''

Amaiki swallowed. ''How long can you wait?'' she said, her voice hardly louder than a whisper.

Muri looked uncomfortable. ''We thought we could stay out your time, Ammi, but we can't do it alone. Wolves prowling. Four-legged and otherwise. The other night we talked things over and called line-mother in Shim Shupat. She's got space we can have on a ship for Bygga Modig. It leaves with the tide Minha-new-moon. That's seven days from today.'' He fell silent, drooped sadly, his quicksilver spirits gone suddenly dull.

Keran made an impatient sound, leaned forward, taller and more angular than any of the others; she wasn't a talker, was far more expressive with her hands. ''Am, uplands're empty. Pinbo m' cousin Likut's line, taken the year after I hatched, she a far-speaker, touched our Se-passhi, says come and be welcome. Guldafel. Lot of taken there.'' She raised a long hand, signed love and retreated.

Amaiki signed back, then stroked the folds of skin about her neck. ''Nothing else you can do. I agree. Give me three days. If I'm not out by then, Hyaroll won't let me go. That gives you four to make the coast.'' She smiled at Keran, reached out touched the glass where her meld-sister was. ''My love, no one can convince me you've let our flier go out of shape, so you all can spare me three days.''

Keran smiled gratification, nodded.

Muri erected his crest, opened his eyes wide. ''We'll be early and wait the whole day.'' He spread his hands, long fingers flickering with signs for amplitude and good living. ''A grand last picnic to say farewell to the uplands. The hatchlings will love it.'' He sobered. ''And if the undying won't let go?''

Amiki moved restlessly, shifting her feet on the beaten-earth floor of the com-kiosk. Nothing here was secret from the undying. Nothing at all. But what did it matter? She had to do what her fate decreed, so let him hear. *Let me be as bold as the odd folk.* ''If he will not let me go, I will get free somehow and come after you, my loves. Leave signs behind to tell me where you are and I'll find you no matter what. No matter how long or hard the journey, I will find you.'' That last was a promise she meant to keep, a promise implicit in the formality of the words. She backed half a step from the screen, fighting to control the emotion erupting in her; she was turning into a stranger she didn't quite like.

The meld made the love signs, the waiting and faithful signs, then the farewell signs; Betaki held up the hatchling and moved the little naish's hand in a fluid farewell sign, the baby cooing and making small sucking sounds. Amaiki gave the signs back, her eyes blurring, her control deserting her again. She brushed at her eyes, blinked to clear them, unwilling to miss a second of seeing them. Understanding this, Muri broke the connection and all that was left was darkness.

Amaiki moved quickly out of the kiosk and went to stand by the wall. She watched her family move out of the other side and climb into the flier, stood leaning on the top stones while the flier lifted vertically and turned toward Shiosa. It hovered a moment. She waved. It dipped a stubby wing at her, a quick precarious move that could have been a disaster with anyone but Keran at the console.

She stood watching until she could see the black speck no longer, then trudged wearily to her dwelling to eat a light meal and gather her courage before she tried to reach Hyaroll.

VRITHIAN
on the oblique file [3]

Willow sang: "This and this and this and this and this and this," scraping carefuly at a shaft a little greater around than her biggest finger, smoothing it, gradually tapering a portion at one end to the girth of the tapestry needle set in that end.

Days ago, after she left Bodri brooding over the properties of roots and how they could possibly get at a man who knew exactly what they were doing, she rambled about the whole of the domed enclave hunting out and collecting branches of the proper tight grain, girth, strength and straightness. She brought these back to the hillside where she had her camp, cut them into roughly equal lengths, then dried them on a frame over a smoky fire. When they were ready for working, she sent Sunchild foraging for her. In the lizard folk's village he found a dozen tapestry needles, in Hyaroll's long-unused workshop he found glue, hones and an assortment of cutting tools. He was limited in the weights he could manage, but he absorbed patience from Willow and found what he considered a perverse satisfaction in the task.

She took the hone and began sharpening the blunt needles; Sunchild squatted beside her, the squeaks and squeals of the hone affecting him as catnip did a cat.

When the needles were sharp enough to prick a thought, Willow chose twelve shafts from among the cured branches, reamed holes in one end of each, then glued the needles into them.

Willow sang: "This and this and this and this and this," and handed the finished shaft to Sunchild.

He heated up one hand and rubbed gently along the shaft until it was polished smooth and hard as stone. He set it on a cloth beside him and waited contentedly for the next.

Bodri was burming along to himself, a low rumbling tuneless hum, working as intently as Willow, borrowing her worksongs to pass the time in his tedious experiments. He was cutting up several different kinds of roots and pods, tossing the chunks into the pot hanging over a small hot fire. While Willow was hunting her arrow shafts, he'd been prospecting among the plants, sniffing and tasting, bringing back samples to the camp, making decoctions of them and testing these on birds and fish. He wasn't satisfied yet with the toxicity of his mixes or the speed with which they acted. The decoctions that acted quickly enough killed just as fast in very small doses; the ones that only stunned took too long to do it. They certainly didn't want to kill the man—that would ruin everything.

Willow's camp was a dirt flat on the hill behind Hyaroll's house, trees thick on three sides, large boulders sprayed in an arc about the downhill side. A small stream sang through the trees, ran between two of the boulders down the long gentle slope to the lake. Beside that stream was a small hut built of bark and wattle where Willow slept at night, where she kept her tools and anything else she didn't want rained on.

She handed a finished shaft to Sunchild, reached for another, glancing downhill as she did so. Hyaroll was walking toward the landing saucers. She held the shaft across her thighs, frowning. The back of a flier was just visible over the kadraesh trees. "Old Vryhh, he going somewhere."

Sunchild set the shaft with the other finished ones. "Kepha said he would. To meet that woman. You know, the one the Vryhh bitch was yelling about."

"Hmmp. Yelling." She clicked her tongue, danced her fingers on her thighs, over and around the shaft. "Singing her into the clan, huh?"

"In their way."

She lifted the shaft, then set it aside and climbed onto one of the larger boulders, waiting to see the flier jump up and dart away.

One of the lizard folk stepped from behind a bush and put a hand on his arm, stopping him. Willow could hear their voices, but couldn't make out the words. The slim lacertine figure was filled with passion, talking fast, demanding something. He listened briefly to it, then brushed it out of the way, more roughly—maybe—than he intended, went on to his flier. The slight figure lay crumpled on the grass.

A moment later the flier passed through the dome, then darted away to the northwest.

Willow stood on the boulder, looking from the vanishing flier to the creature below. It stirred and sat up. She hummed the paka cat song, moved her feet on the rock, curiosity growing in her. An impatient snort. A quick jump from boulder onto grass. She ran downhill to the shuddering shape.

The creature was trembling all over, incapable of speech, unable to stand. Willow moved cautiously closer, touched its shoulder. It jumped as if her touch stung, then collapsed again and struggled for control of the emotions wracking it. It wasn't hurt as far as she could tell, just filled with a seething mess of anger and frustration and fear. She remembered seeing this one working here and there in the garden all summer, handling the plants with a delicate touch that reminded her of Bodri. She squatted beside the creature, frowning, humming snatches of song, trying to find a way to comprehend the hurt and help it. Finally she began one of the go-'way-hurt songs she used to sing to her children, faltering at first because these were songs she hadn't sung since Old Stone Vryhh ripped her from her family—but something about the pain in this creature struck deep into her and drew from her responses she'd denied till now to save her sanity. Singing that string of magic meaningless sounds, she ignored the creature's feeble attempts to push her away and gathered it into her arms, across her legs, and patted its back and rocked it as she would have rocked her babies. After that first resistance it went limp against her and began sobbing, something that startled a tiny part of Willow because she didn't know lizards could weep. She continued to sing her go-hurt song, continued to comfort the creature. No no, folk not lizards, no no, folk can cry, no no, folk have ears not lizards. The sunlight shone a light leaf green through the creature's large pointed ears, the skin as fine and thin as the newest spring leaf. *Man or woman?* she thought suddenly. *Which is this? Cries like me when I hurt. Can't just look with folk, not like run-about beasts. Have to ask. Yes, I ask.* She let her song die and loosened her arms as the creature's shuddering diminished, then stopped.

The man? woman? pulled back, stiff with embarrassment. At least that was what it looked like to Willow. Its face was a light olive green with a smooth pebbly texture; ordinary eyes except they were shiny like melted gold; a nose like a knifeblade with wide flared nostrils, a long mouth, thin flexible lips delicately curved; high cheekbones, rather hollow cheeks. Almost no chin, but that didn't make the face look weak. Mobile pointed ears much larger than Willow's. She watched the sun shine through them and reminded herself again, this was another place and these were real folk, not spirit creatures with animal forms. She shifted around so she was sitting on her heels, her knees spread, her hands resting on her thighs, palaver stance among her people. "You man or woman?"

The creature looked startled, then offended, then faintly amused. "I am female," she said. Her voice was clear, its sound very pure. Willow sighed with pleasure hearing it. "My name is Amaiki," the other went on. "I am a conc of the Conoch'hi."

Willow bowed her head, snapped her name sound on her fingers, then said it in the common tongue Hyaroll's teaching box had given her. "Willow," she said. "Old Stone Vryhh, what he doing to you?"

A film slid over Amaiki's gold-foil eyes. Her impossibly long thin hands closed into knotted fists. She bowed her head, the trembling back again, but only for a moment this time. She smoothed her tabard about her narrow body, pulling out the wrinkles, tucked her legs under her, set opened hands neatly on her thighs. For several heartbeats longer she was silent, staring past Willow at the wind-teased grass on the hillside. When she spoke again, she was outwardly composed, but in her voice was an angry helplessness that found a powerful echo within Willow's breast. "For many and many generations have Conoch'hi served Hyaroll, for many and many generations has he shaped our lives and made us depend on him, has he taken our children from us and changed them or sent them away. He gave us peace, he gave us rain, he took our naidisa from us. Look around you, Willow from far far away. How green and lovely it is in here. But go to the dome's edge and look out, then you will see dust and death and a sun without pity. He does not call the rain for us, he sucks the ground dry to feed his trees. Our children grow hungry, our children thirst, our plants and beasts they die. Six days ago, oh Willow, my mate-meld came to the caller kiosk. They are leaving the uplands, Willow, leaving me behind. They are taking our newest child and our other four and they are going to the far side of the world. They cannot stay and starve. I went to Hyaroll and asked him to let me go with my mates-in-meld. He would not. I begged him to let me go. He would not. I asked again and again until he would not see me, until he would not come out of the house for fear of seeing me. I asked again today and you saw his answer." She stopped speaking, calmed herself, went on in a low quiet voice. "If I could leave the dome, I could follow them still. They must be deep into Istenger Ocean by now, but I could follow them. They promised to leave word for me as many places as they could, so I could find them if only I could leave the dome. I must . . . I must . . . I . . ." Her throat fluttered as she fought for control; her fingers moved in small gestures Willow read as distaste for her own excesses—or what she saw as excesses.

Willow scowled at the dome, its faint flicker close to invisible against the cloudless sky. "He gone, but he leave ears behind." She lowered her eyes to Amaiki's face, her hands touching her own ears, dropping, clutching hard at each other; she hissed and pulled her hands apart. "Time was once, I have a man, my Otter; time was once, I birth my Sparrow my daughter who sing before she talk; time was once, I birth my Mouse, my son-baby, my hurry-about baby. Before he walking good, hah!" She hugged herself, rocking

on her toes. "Before he walking, he still on tit, Hyaroll
snatch me away. Ay be-be, ay-yii, my Mouse. No more. No
more." She straightened her back, dropped her arms. "Can't
go back, me. But you, hah!" She lifted a hand, made a blade
of it, chopped the blade down. "Him! He don't do it again. I
get you out." She spread her hands. "Don't know how. Not
now." She got to her feet. "You come, huh?"

Willow told the tale with hands, feet and body while
Amaiki sat primly on one of the boulders. Bodri was dour,
resisting her passion and insistence with his own; again and
again he said, if we help her, Whisper in the wind, we could
wake Old Vryhh to work against us, let her wait, time is coming
when we're ready to go against Old Vryhh, when we win,
we'll get her out, wait, wait, he said, don't kick up dust for
Hyaroll to see, it's safer when the thing is over, it's safer and
more sure.

Willow only grew hotter and more determined. In a sense
all that they were doing now, the shafts she was fashioning,
the bow she'd make later, Bodri's boiled messes, Sunchild's
erratic poking and prodding and his small but useful thefts,
all these things were games they were playing with themselves, busying their hands and minds with what they could
do so they could hide from themselves their helplessness and
futility. This was different, this was something they could do
here and now to frustrate the plans of the man who'd stolen
their lives from them for his amusement. She danced all this
with body and hands and the oblique allusions of her songs.
"Now," she sang. "It must be now."

Sunchild watched the battle unperturbed; he'd seen others,
though none so deeply felt. He had several things to say when
the time came, but there was no point in saying anything until
Bodri stopped arguing, either agreeing to help or refusing to
listen to Willow any longer. While the argument raged on, he
amused himself trying out the shapes swimming so powerfully in Amaiki's mind. He felt her distress as he shifted from
Keran to Muri to Kimpri to Betaki to Se-Passhi and finally to
the infant naish, running them off like beads on a worrystring,
but that distress didn't bother him. His folk made very power-

ful emotional bonds but also very few. His family was three now and forever. Willow. Bodri. Kephalos. And the deepest, most intimate of those bonds was with the awakening kephalos; in its way it about matched his mind age and shared many of his interests, though its way of thinking was very unlike his. Beyond those three who he loved without reservation and forever, no one existed for him, not in any meaningful way. He could be confused and irritated with them; he would play with them one way or another, but as soon as his interest waned, he'd be gone; he felt no responsibility for them; they were images in dreamland.

The debate was calming down. Bodri nodded reluctantly, Willow smiled, turned to Amaiki. And saw her distress and saw Sunchild shifting. She gasped. Jumped the short distance to him and slapped her hand through his substance, not hurting him but startling him into cringing away from her, the flare of her anger washing over him, whipping him with its nettle stings. He cried out, a high keening whine like the sound the kimkim flies made late in the evening.

Her anger died. Willow knelt beside the quivering shapeless lump of light and for the second time that day sang her go-'way-hurt song. She stroked his outline, careful to keep her hand from breaking through the fragile membrane of his surface tension, controlling her own shock and momentary revulsion as he was first Sparrow, then Mouse, then Otter curled up on the ground beside her. She softened the song to a crooning whisper, "Ah-weh, be-be, ah weh." She gave him a last gentle pat, then got to her feet. "He only teasing," she told Amaiki. "He don't understand much about the way mamas feel." She nudged Sunchild with her toe. "I see you peeking, little sneak. Up. Tell this mama you sorry for fussing her."

Sunchild got warily to his feet, his form melting at the edges, caught in the contrary urges pulling from the two women. He sneaked a look at Willow, saw her hands moving in a scold-song, saw her smiling at him in spite of that. He straightened himself out and firmed up, then he did a graceful Conoch'hi bow with Conoch'hi signs expressing shame and repentance, then looked at Amaiki slantwise from those blank beautiful eyes.

Amaiki had seen Sunchild before as he drifted about the gardens, a butter smear of light half the time shapeless as any cloud; now, for the first time, she saw his beauty and was startled by it. And deeply moved by it, though it came in so strange a form. She saw him grin at her and take on hints of Conoch'hi, just enough to drive home the effect of his grace. Understanding then how little real feeling lay behind his charm, she grinned back. "Well done, kushi-su, I have never seen a more graceful apology."

Bodri snorted, then laughed, a papery rustle that sounded like dried leaves rubbing against each other, but he said nothing, only moved back to his fire and began stirring the mixture in the pot, his back turned to them, disassociating himself from what was happening.

Willow traced the blue lines of a design pricked into the dark brown skin of her side, then spread her hands, fluttering the fingers. "Me, I don't know nothing about getting out of here. Sunchild, he the one can talk to kepha." She turned to him. "So what do kepha say?"

Sunchild sidled up to her, pressed himself against her as hard as his lack of mass would permit. She stroked the golden semblance of her Otter and gave him the affection and acceptance he craved. Satisfied, he retreated a little, keeping close enough to her so his form could stabilize into the single shape. "Kepha knows he'll die with Hyaroll. He doesn't want to die, Willow. He'll do about anything he can to stop that. There's not a whole lot of things open to him. He can't do anything that will hurt Hyaroll, not anything. He can fiddle that some, make limits to what *hurt* means to him. We been working on that. I figure maybe letting this Amaiki get away is something he could decide won't hurt Old Vryhh; so unless Hyaroll has given him direct orders to keep her and the other Conochi'hi sitting in that village, maybe kepha can open the way for her. And maybe not." He scowled at Amaiki, showing his resentment at her being the cause of his scolding, but he smoothed out his face when he turned back to Willow. "Now Old Vryhh's gone, I'd better go have a talk with kepha, find out what he can do and what he's willing to do. Might not be the same thing."

Willow nodded, looked at the sun, then at him. "Good thing if this be done before Old Vryhh get back. How long he going be gone?"

"Till he gets back."

"Hah, you. Not funny."

"I don't know, Willow, and kepha doesn't either. Nothing like this has happened before."

"So go now." She flapped her hands at him. "Go!"

He drifted into the air, flowed out of shape into a streak of light, and as a streak of butterlight raced downhill and merged with a wall of the house.

Willow folded her arms, rocked them. "No big badness in him, he just a baby."

Amaiki dipped her head in graceful acknowledgment, but said nothing; she'd felt the bite of Sunchild's malice and knew what he did, he did for Willow, not her. There was a strong bond of fondness between these disparate beings, almost a mother-child link, and she would put no stain on that. And she would not stain her own being by speaking a lie she knew was a lie.

Willow sighed. Trying to help this one was like fighting against a haru-wind bringing in a spring storm. *Not for you, stranger, 's not for you I doing this, not just for you.* She snapped thumbs against fingers, looked at her hands. *I sticking pins in Old Stone Vryhh, hunh, he won't feel them, him, but I know they there. I know. Good 'nough.* She said, "Ev'ry time I see Old Vryhh go out, it up there." She pointed at the top of the dome. "You fly one of those things?"

Amaiki shivered, then came out of her withdrawal.

Willow watched her shuck her shell. If she hadn't seen and felt that outpouring of rage and fear and hate down the hill, she'd have thought Amaiki was as cold and unfeeling as the reptile she vaguely resembled. Not so. Despite the surface, not so. She and Bodri had a lot the same feel to them: neatness of hand and body—Bodri might look clumsy and sound like rocks banging down a hillside, but he got about the garden with a surprising deftness and never bruised a plant or even an insect he wanted to keep alive; precision of thought and motion—Bodri was looser about this than Amaiki, but the effect was the same, the control similar; dislike of fuss in all forms—which was why Willow almost always won arguments with him; *she* didn't mind noise and messy emotions and turmoil and tears, she rather liked them. And she had more staying power. She could keep on long after he was exhausted. Like today. He wasn't really convinced, he just didn't want to go on arguing.

"A flier," Amaiki said thoughtfully, then shook her head. "I can fly one, of course, but two things about taking a flier. One, kephalos might be willing to let me go, but I don't believe he'd let me take off with Hyaroll's property. Two, I suspect the controls of those fliers only respond to Hyaroll's touch. Hmm. Maybe one of the larger skimsleds. That's property too, but nothing like the cost of an armored flier. I could bypass the level control and hype the drivers to give me enough power for a jump through the dome. Hmm. Tricky. Might turn the sled into junk. If I set in a cut-off switch maybe I could save it . . . use heavy-duty batteries, switch them for solar . . . I could travel at night, lay up during the day, let them charge . . . less power, but a longer range . . . lot better than going on foot." She nodded. "That's what I'll do. I've been packed and ready to go for days. I'll shift my things to the sled garage." She stood, pointed downhill at a low blocky structure separated from the house by a thick planting of kadraesh trees. "I'd better be moving, Willow. No matter what answer your friend brings back, it's as well to be prepared." She hesitated, then gave an angular, formal bow with graceful hand gestures that Willow watched with interest, liking the fluidity of the movements. "You have fought hard for me, sister-friend, my line is deep in your debt. I shall knot you with pride into my life weave and your story and your kindness will be remembered through all generations that will be."

Willow inclined her torso, touched head and heart, straightened. "I have borne and lost, sister-friend. It pleases me to give a mother back to her children." She flung out her arms, laughed fiercely, smacked fist against palm. "And do Old Stone Vryhh a mischief where it'd hurt if he had any feeling left."

With a laugh and a last farewell sign, Amaiki moved through the line of boulders and started down the slope with that deceptively unhurried, gliding stride that took her quickly toward the sled garage.

"You weren't just arguing to be arguing."

Willow looked over her shoulder. Bodri had taken his mixture from the fire and was prodding at it with a limber twig from a murkka tree, putting a tiny fraction of its paralyzing poison into the mess. He poked at the decoction twice more and threw the twig into the fire. "I thought you were getting restless," he said. "But it means a lot to you."

"Yes, old beetle, it really do."

"You don't talk much about your children."

"No."

He gazed at her a moment longer, then heaved a huge sigh that set his back-garden swaying. "All right, Willow. Whatever I can do, that's yours."

She smiled and went to squat beside him and scratch up where his stumpy legs joined his body, her fingers working among fold on fold of soft silky skin. He sighed with pleasure, his tentacle arm looped around her shoulders and playing in the springy curls at the nape of her neck.

Willow was scraping with finicking care on the last of the shafts, Bodri was ladling the cooled decoction into test tubes and sealing them, when Sunchild came back. "This kephalos is almost as old as Old Vryhh," he said.

Hands going still, Willow looked up. "So?"

"So Hyaroll has been working on it, adding to it, changing it, multiplying its purposes, all that, for a long long time." He glanced at Willow, saw her scowl. "Like taking, um . . ." He looked up. Several of the many raptors inside the dome were riding thermals, coiling about each other as if for the game of it and nothing more. "Like taking a vekvem up there and putting more brains in his head, making him smarter and smarter and smarter until maybe he's smart as a person. Till he is a kind of person. You see?''

Willow shaded her eyes and looked up at the gliding circling vekvem. ''Can't,'' she said.

''But if you could?''

''Magic?''

''Something like that.''

''So. Kepha smart now and like a person, not a . . . a . . . an ironhead know-nothing.''

''You got it. Different too. You, me, Bodri, we can move around; kepha has to sit where he is—and well, Hyaroll keeps chains on him so he can't do much except what Old Vryhh wants.''

''Cut the chains.''

''Magic chains.''

''Thump Old Vryhh, make him take 'em off.''

''Kepha can't do that.''

''Us.''

''Kepha won't let us. He can't.''

''Magic, hah.'' She spat.

''Way it is.''

''We can't do nothing?''

''Didn't say that.''

''Well, say what!''

''Well, kepha's getting smarter all the time, doing it to himself now; he was just a baby, but he's growing up fast and he doesn't like being a slave.''

''Ummp. Big surprise.''

''You the one in the hurry. Listen. I've been talking with kepha since we started this.'' He waved a hand at the pile of shafts, swung it around to include Bodri and his labors. ''I figure what's the harm, Hyaroll knows what we're doing anyway. Kepha can't come right out and tell me what Old Vryhh is planning, but he lets me know when I guess right. So, for sure, it's a funeral pyre with us all following Old Vryhh down to hell. Kepha is not not not happy with that, but he can't stop it, not just him. Thing is, he is programmed, umm, he has to do whatever Hyaroll tells him to do. Old Vryhh's got careless. Doesn't think much of us either. He just told kepha to make a summary of anything we do he might find interesting. Might find. Hear that? Leaves the choice up to kepha. Lot of things he can do with that. Like what we're saying now. Or the time I talk with him. He just tells himself it's all too boring, that Hyaroll wouldn't be interested in it, so he doesn't have to report it. He'd stop us hard if we tried to hurt Old Vryhh, but as long as we don't touch him, we'll be all right.''

Willow made a hissing impatient sound.

"Thought you'd like to know."

She leaned closer to him, said very slowly, "He help Amaiki go?"

"Hurry-hurry. This is what he says. He can't open the dome when Hyaroll is gone. He can't open the dome anytime unless Hyaroll orders it." Sunchild paused a moment, touched her nose with a forefinger, danced back from her, teasing her, his silent laughter pulsing waves of light through his body. "But he can keep the hole open a short while after Hyaroll's through. Long enough to let the lizard lady hop out. If she can get up there. Kepha says if she waits until he's almost down on the landing saucer and jumps out fast, he won't notice anything's happened. So you go tell her to be ready fast. Old Vryhh's on his way home, be here in about a half hour." He bounced away, perched on top a boulder. "I'd better get back to kepha. He's nervous and lonesome. It's hard to be nervous and lonesome."

Amaiki looked cool as morning. standing erect but relaxed on the skimsled, a heavy dark cloak bound closely around her so it wouldn't get in her way, her long hands resting lightly on the steering bars. Willow squatted in the shade of a hairy lod-bush watching her, watching the dome.

A dark dot came darting over the mountains, grew into the flier, which hovered briefly over the dome, then sank through it, dropped for the saucer. The skimsled hummed. The hum rose to an urgent whine. The moment the flier slowed for the last meter before it touched down, Amaiki moved her thumb. The sled shot straight up for a kilometer, then slanted south and passed through the dome. For a breath or two she flew on

a level, then arched down and was on the ground again before
the flier finished its settling. Willow crouched where she was
and watched Hyaroll step down from the lock. Grim-faced,
but without hurry, he walked away from the saucer, heading
for the house. She tried to read his face, but he looked more
or less how he always looked. When he vanished inside, she
got to her feet and trudged uphill to her camp.

Sunchild came drifting down, squatted beside her, watching her cut vanes from stiff feathers. "She got away," he
said.

"Hmp."

"He didn't notice anything."

"Good." She set the feather down. "I need more glue."

"I'll look about."

She reached out, touched his face with her fingertips.
"You did good."

"Me and Kephalos."

"Hmp. All of us." She grinned at Sunchild. "We whip his
tail, Old Stone Vryhh."

BORBHAL ON SAKKOR

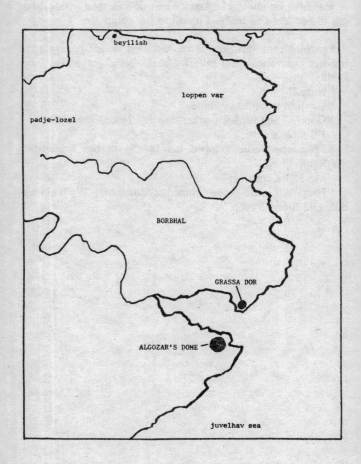

VRITHIAN
WITNESS [4]
A SHOPKEEPER IN
GRASA DOR

My name is Tensio alte Nariozh. My mother came from one
of the best families in Borbhal, but her father was a gambler
and lost most of the estate, so she had to marry beneath her.
My father was a good man in his way but he had no polish
and used to grate on her nerves with his loudness and his
crudeness; he never could learn to appreciate the gracious
style of living she found more natural. Though I shouldn't
say it, I know how it sounds, but really just coming into a
room he could make me wince. She wanted to send me to
Cabozh, to the University at Inchacobesh outside the capital,
but my father wouldn't hear of it, I had to go into the
business and learn it from floor to attic, and I do mean floor.
He had me pushing a broom with the slaves brought up from
Cobarzh. Tempestao, you wouldn't believe how they stank,
those turezh. And lazy, good for nothing. . . . I won't have
one of them in my shop, not to work and not to buy. It makes
me sick to my stomach to think of them putting their filthy
hands on my silks and laces and velvets. You see how fine
my goods are—look at the light coming through that window
and playing on the colors and the delicate textures; you won't
find such goods anywhere else in all of Borbhal. Perhaps
across the Fistavey in Cabozh, but nowhere closer. Demons?
Ah, you must mean the undying. Please, I must ask you not
to use that awful term in my presence. They come in here
several times during the year to look at my goods, no I am
not boasting, it is true, that's the noble Algozar's sign right
there, he had it etched in my window. You must have seen
his dome on the cliffs across the bay. He knows beautiful

things when he sees them, oh yes. He talks to me as if I'm one of the great ones, oh yes. The undying know, you understand, they feel the good blood in my veins. I've done all I can to rid myself of my father's crudeness and pattern myself on my mother's side of the family, and I flatter myself that I know the courtly ways the undying expect. In my circle they say I could go on very well at court back home. Why don't I go? There are jealous men, officials at court, who just won't let any colonials near the King. And my mother's family, who could intercede for me if they wanted, well, they live off the money I send them, but they won't acknowledge me. Bitter? No, no, of course not, just a little disappointed. I take comfort in remembering I am the one with the noble mind and heart, the true scion of our ancient line. Listen, the Governor himself comes to my shop when he wants something especially fine. And his wife sends her dressmaker to me. His mistress? I don't talk about the private affairs of my patrons. I'm sorry you asked, I thought you were another kind. I have said all I want to say. Please leave.

AVOSING
action on the second line [1]

Shadith woke to a throbbing in her head that blanked out everything else. She drifted in and out of consciousness, aware of little beyond a thick darkness around her and noises she heard and forgot immediately. Disoriented and nauseated, she was too absorbed by pain to wonder who she was and what had happened to her.

Gradually she grew aware of something outside the pain. Her wrists were tied together, a smooth pole passed between them. Her legs were tied at the knees and ankles to that same pole. He head hung loosely, bumping back and forth with the swaying of her body. She was being carried like a pig to a roast. Eyes slitted, fighting to ignore a headache that beat the worst hangover she could remember, she used the motion of her body to shift her head about and gain the widest field of vision she could manage without informing her captors she was awake and aware.

The darkness was gone. She was being carried through a thin greenish twilight. Forest. On the edge, as before. A man ahead of her, pole on his shoulder, looked like an amber miner. That couldn't be right . . . they wouldn't . . . no . . . forester of some kind. More likely. Man behind her, much the same. Big men, keeping up a smooth steady lope, used to being in the forest. More of them behind her carriers. She took a chance when they went around a slight bend, swayed out farther, fell back. Another pole. Probably Linfyar. *Poor Linfy*. Her stomach was turning flip-flops. She kept from vomiting by force of will alone. The nausea came and went in waves; once the worst was over, it retreated for a while.

When the last crisis was over, she tried thinking again. *Looks like I won't have to bother laying a trail to show I'm no provocateur. This has to be the Ajin's men, and isn't that a giggle. All my fussing for nothing. Wonder if old loudmouth is watching. Keeping his head down if he is. If I had anything to bet with, I'd give good odds these bastards found my stash and my hard-earned coin is sitting in their pockets. Shadow, my girl, this is a promise, if that's so I'll take it out of their stinking hides. Hunh, I'll take this damn pole and make 'em eat it, first chance I get. Lousy way to travel.*

She relaxed as much as she could, putting herself into a shallow trance so the bobbing of her head and the chafing of her arms and legs wouldn't drive her into trying something foolish. After a while the pollen took her and everything melted about her; she drifted in a dull throbbing state where nausea mixed with distant pain and a low-grade fever. By the time her bearers dumped her in the dust before a weathered building, she didn't much care who had her or what happened to her. Her arms and legs were rubbed raw from the ropes and the pole; her shoulders felt as if her weight had wrenched her arms from their sockets. Her mouth was dry and sour. Her head pounded with each beat of her heart. She wanted water desperately but knew she'd never keep it down. *Just give me something to wash my mouth out, that's all.* Cool water, rolling in her mouth, cool water to splash over her face and head. Somewhere, not too far away, men were talking; she could hear the different voices but they were too broken and blurred for her to make out the sounds. *Whoever you are, whoever did this to me, whatever you want, you aren't getting it. I don't care what happens.* Anger built in her, the heat of it energizing her, chasing away the depression of her spirits, driving off a good part of the fog in her head. She pursed cracking lips and whistled, just a thread of sound.

A whistle came back to her a moment later, cautious, brief, but familiar enough. She relaxed. He sounded all right, not too happy, but intact.

Footsteps behind her. She closed her eyes, lay without moving. A hand lifted her head. Pain took her so suddenly and completely she couldn't suppress a short sharp gasp.

"Jambi, you git, you hit her too hard. He'll skin you if she dies on him." There was disgust in the voice and a rough gentleness in the hands that soaked the crusted blood from her hair and scalp and applied a salve that spread cool comfort over her head, even seemed to soothe the pain inside her skull, though she knew that was nonsense. He dragged a pack of some kind around, put her head down on it, shifted his position. As he cut away the ropes around her wrists, she cracked her eyes so she could see him. A big man, with shaggy gray hair, a lined impatient face. Could be one of the Sendir. Tjepa had told her about them when he pointed out a Senda wandering through the market. They didn't like people much, came to Dusta maybe once a year to pick up things they couldn't make for themselves, to say hello to relatives, a friend or two, then go back to their jealously hidden nests deep in the forest. He scowled as he examined her bloody wrists, set them neatly on her body so the dust wouldn't get in the wounds, began working on her leg ropes. He went away when he had them off her, but came back a moment later, lifted her head and shoulders and braced them against a knee. He bathed her face, let her drink from a gourd dipper. She swished the first mouthful about, spat it out, took another few swallows, sighed with pleasure as the coolness bathed away the bitter dryness of her mouth and washed dust and phlegm from her burning throat. He only let her have a little, then peeled a hard candy and slipped it between her lips. "Give you energy," he said, "you need the sugar."

She didn't trust him all that much, but there was no point in spitting it out. She sucked at the candy. Sugar and a bit of mint for flavor. Maybe to cover what else was in the candy. *That's stupid. My head's not working. Why would he do that? And if he did, what does it matter?* She closed her eyes. *I wouldn't mind a short blackout right now, say about three days long.* He bathed her wrists, smoothed on more of the salve and wrapped bandages around the raw spots. *I should get the formula of that gunk. No more Lee to heal the hurts—that's one talent I wish I'd yanked along with me when I jumped into this body.* The Senda washed her legs, put salve on them, bandaged them, then got to his feet with a smooth

effortless lift of his big body. A moment later she heard
Linfyar squeal and go silent. Thanks, man; poor little Linfy,
maybe he'll change his mind about adventures after this. He
dealt with Linfyar's abrasions in that calm silence she found
almost as soothing as the salve, came back a moment later,
dropped a canteen beside her and went off, leaving her to
care for herself now that she could. His nurturance apparently
had severe limits to it.

She lay still a few moments longer, reluctant to break into
her comfortable lassitude, but curiosity was almost as great a
prod as thirst. She rolled onto her stomach, got carefully onto
her hands and knees, pushed up until she was sitting on her
heels, her hands resting on her thighs. *No double vision—at
least I'm not concussed.*

Some sort of abandoned settlement. The building beside
her looked like a trading post or storehouse and was well on
its way to rotting back into the earth. A stubby, shaky pier
jutted into the water, a number of planks gone, several of the
piles listing at precarious angles. Water stretched away from
the shore in a vast gray sheet, rippling a little as the breeze
freshened, then dropped again. Ocean? Can't see the other
shore. If there is one. No, not the ocean. Probably one of the
lobes of Tah Badu bay. She glanced at the pack her head had
been resting on, grimaced. *Mine. Harp case about a step
away from the pack. They scooped the lot.* She scowled at the
scars in the leather, the thick coat of fine red dust. The shore
here was mostly a heavy reddish soil whose top layers had
been baked and blown into dust as fine and slippery as a
graphite lubricant. What her harp would look like when they
finally got wherever it was they were going was something
she didn't want to think about. Linfyar was curled up in the
middle of the rest of their gear, looking miserably unhappy;
there was a rope about his neck, the other end tied to a stake
pounded into the dirt. Tethered like an animal. She closed her
hands into fists, bit down hard on her lip to keep her fury in.
Like an animal. Someone was going to pay for that.

Small groups of men stood about talking in mutters, looking repeatedly out across the water. One man stood guard at
the corner of the building, a projectile weapon hugged under

his arm. She saw the bore and shivered at the thought of that lump of lead making hash of her insides. The rest of the men had similar weapons, several wore laser pistols on their belts, most had belt knives, one—hunkered alone out at the end of the rickety pier—had something that looked like a meat cleaver with elephantiasis. His arms were thicker around than her thighs, his shoulders bulged under the sleeveless tunic that was all he wore on his upper half, he looked as if he could crash that cleaver through one of the forest giants with a single swing. No regimentation about this bunch of men, but a military patina on them that was enough to confirm her suspicion about who had her. She'd seen soldiers wait like this before with the endless irritable patience that had been drilled into them. *Well, he's done himself a mischief with this even if he's done me a favor solving my problems about locating him.* She looked at Linfyar tethered to the stake, breathed hard for some minutes, tears of anger and frustration prickling behind her eyes.

When she had control back, she drank from the canteen, then smiled to herself at the contrast between her angry ambitions and her present helplessness. With a wary eye on the sentry, she crossed to Linfyar, squatted beside him. Using his home tongue, she muttered, "How you doing, Linfy?"

He lifted his elbow, flashed a grin at her.

"Want me to get that rope off you?"

"Not now," he whispered. "I can get loose anytime I want, Shadow. Creeps didn't find the blade in my belt. I figure the more helpless they think I am, the looser I'll be." He rolled over, put his hand on her knee. "Don't fuss, Shadow. Let them act stupid as they want—makes it easier to clobber them later."

She caught hold of his big toe, shook his foot. "I might have known," she said.

A hastily muffled giggle. "Yeah, you shoulda."

She'd forgotten what his life had been like, threatened with death from the moment of birth when he made the mistake of being born visibly mutant. He'd learned to scramble and connive almost before he could talk. And when she and Aleytys had found him on Ibex, he'd been running from a gelding meant to keep his voice from changing, leaping into the unknown with an unquenchable zest and a shrewd trust in his ability to survive anything that life threw at him, nine years of faun charm and deviousness. He didn't waste time on pride or worrying whether other people respected him, he concentrated on surviving. "How'd they get you?" she said.

"Dropped a sack over me. Used my hand to open the cabin's door. Brought you in a bit later. Cleared the place out. Took off with us. Boat first, couple hours in that, then they walked, us on those . . . those poles." He snorted his disgust. "I thought about yelling when they took us through the city, but they were a bit too efficient and you were limp as a dead cony, so I thought better wait till they got where they were going and relaxed some. And till you woke up." He hesitated. "Maybe I shoulda yelled."

"Glad you didn't. Look, Linfy, I think these're the Ajin's men." She chuckled. "We spent all that time nosing about for a way to get to him and here he's fetching us right where we want to go."

Linfyar touched her hand. " 'S all right with me as long as they don't put me back on that dumb pole." His lips fluttered as he limned her with the echoes from his silent whistles. "Shadow?" He sounded anxious, was suddenly more of a small worried boy. "You sound a little funny. You all right? You were out a long time."

"A roaring headache, but I'll survive, imp. It's already starting to go away."

He sighed and straightened his legs. "I'm hungry, Shadow."

"When aren't you? Well, I'll see what I can dig up."

She got to her feet, feeling as creaky as the ragged building before her. The Senda was nowhere in sight. She started for the sentry, stopped as his face went slack. He stared at nothing, mouthed soundless words at that nothing. A second sentry was immediately there, taking the rifle from the slackened grasp. He strolled to the storehouse, leaned with elaborate casualness against the cornerpost, watching her without seeming to. She walked over to him. "We're hungry," she said. "You planning to starve us too?"

He ran dull eyes over her, produced a grunt. When she didn't go away, he said, "You eat when we do."

"And when, O Jewel of Eloquence, will that be?"

"When we get where we're going."

"Oh joy. Any objection to me getting out some trailbars? I see you brought my gear." She waved at the heap beside Linfyar. "And you may recall I haven't had anything to eat for quite a while."

"Don't try nothing."

"How could I, O Jewel of Wit? I don't even know where the hell I am."

He grunted again and shifted the rifle to a more secure hold, the barrel swinging around to point at her.

She decided to take his silence as assent, walked cautiously away from him, keeping her movements open and slow, knelt beside the pile of gear and went through it until she came up with the fruit-honey-nut confection Linfy liked so much. She peeled it, then squatted beside him. "We seem to be headed somewhere else before we settle for the night."

Linfyar nodded. "Heard," he said, the word muffled by the mouthful of bar.

Shadith looked over her shoulder at the empty water of the bay. "Hurry up and wait," she muttered. "Military mind never changes, I don't care what the species."

"Huh?"

"Never mind. Hot air, that's all."

She sat on her heels and brooded. *Taggert, where are you now? How are you coming in? I suppose it's just as well I don't know, considering where I am right now. Wonder if he's already snuggling up to the Ajin; probably he'll even get Grey and Ticutt loose before I get anywhere close. Just my luck, the Ajin won't want me for propaganda, probably wants me to sing lullabies to his harem or something just as vital.*

The long day trickled endlessly on.

Shortly after sundown the soft splutter of a motor broke the silence; not long afterward a broad-beamed boat nosed up to the dock and a big man jumped onto the planks with a careless physical competence meant to impress anyone watching. Shadith swallowed a giggle. Enter the Ajin. Lovely.

He strode up to her, stood looking down at her. How much he could see was questionable; the sky was overcast, there were no lights, not even a campfire. She looked up, nodded at him, looked away.

He bent closer, caught hold of her hair, turned her face up, looked startled, let her loose and stepped away. "Manjestau."

A smallish wiry man came out of the shadows. She made out a lined harsh face, one she hadn't seen before.

"You sure this is the one?"

"I watched her do it."

"This child?"

"Her and the freak."

The Ajin moved over to Linfyar. "Why the rope?"

"So it wouldn't run off. We figured the girl wouldn't run without her pet."

"How good is she?"

"Good enough. Did it to me, and I was ready."

"Interesting." He walked around Linfyar and Shadith. "How long does it take to put a crowd under?"

"Three-four minutes."

"That fast?"

"I'd say."

"And they all more or less see the same thing?"

"From what I hear. Didn't want to ask too many questions. Miners hanging about. Perolat. She doesn't like us a whole helluva lot, and she knows me. Didn't want her thinking we were interested in the girl. Hiepler came while I was there, wanted her for the church, threatened her. I figured this was a good time to take her. Perolat would figure the kid ran to get away from the engiaja."

The Ajin came back and stood looking down at Shadith. "We'll burn honeyfat to the Lady tonight, Manjestau. Luck smiles on us today." They walked off together exuding satisfaction.

Hunh, pair of self-inflated prickheads. She dug at the dust with her heel, stirring up a cloud of dust that made her cough. For the moment there wasn't much she could do except go

along meekly with what they had in mind for her. Thank
whatever gods there be, there didn't seem to be any pedo-
philes among them. She didn't feel up to coping with that sort
of complication. *If they want me enough, maybe they'll cod-
dle me a little. Have to wait and see what develops.*

The men on the shore broke up into a number of different
squads; some vanished into the shadow under the trees, others
moved swiftly to haul boxes out of the storehouse and load
them onto the boat, taking Shadith's gear aboard in the
process, walking around her, brushing against her, ignoring
her and Linfyar, not quite stepping on them.

The Ajin himself cut the rope from Linfyar's neck, lifted
the boy to his feet. For the first time he saw the shallow
hollows where Linfyar's eyes would have been if he'd been
born with eyes. Distaste strong enough to smell rolled out of
him, though he controlled it immediately and patted Linfyar
on his sleekly furred shoulder. "Sorry about that, boy," he
said, a smile in his voice. A deep warm flexible voice he
could manipulate with an actor's skill. "Some of my people
are too scary for good manners."

Thinking, *Get your bigoted hands off him, you bastard,*
biting her tongue so she wouldn't say it, Shadith jumped to
her feet and pushed between them, trembling with the resur-
gent fury that threatened to burst out of her control. There
was a sick twisted loathing in the man that ran along her
nerves like vomit; he hid it well enough from everyone but
her, but it was foul. Linfyar put his hand on her arm. "Oh
Shadow," he wailed, doing his pitiful act so well that for a
heartbeat she was almost fooled, then had to restrain herself
from slapping him so violent was her relief. "Oh Shadow,"
he repeated in a trembly, die-away voice, "What's happening? What is he doing?"

She sucked in a breath, let it trickle out, patted his hand in
silent gratitude. "Nothing bad, Linfy," she said, injecting
into her voice the cooing condescension she felt the Ajin
would expect from her, a semi-adult calming the fears of a
deformed child. "He's going to take us someplace where we
can be more comfortable and have a hot meal and a bath."

The Ajin smiled, a broad, charming almost-grin, his eyes

twinkling at her with an intent warmth that would have been
more convincing if there had been anything behind it but
calculation. Her mind-riding gift was developing rapidly into
a full-blown empathic sense; Shadith wasn't too sure she
liked that. There were things she absolutely didn't want to
know, and she resented other people's emotions—or lack of
them—making demands on her. She didn't want to know
about the Ajin's xenophobia. Know about it! Feel it was more
like the truth; it was spreading its slime all over her. *Have to
remember to ask Lee how she blocks out this kind of thing.
God! What's she doing now?* The Ajin put his hand on her
shoulder. She stiffened a little, couldn't help it, but he seemed
to find that reaction quite natural. Conceited slime. "Come,
child," he said, wooing her with that voice like dark suede
burnishing her senses; he turned her toward the boat, walked
beside her while Linfyar was left to follow behind. "I'm
sorry about this." He touched her bandaged wrist. "Once
you understand why, I'm sure you'll forgive us."

She gave him an awkward little nod, her equivalent of
Linfyar's pathetic act. *Oh yes, O mighty conqueror, I'm just
a pore little singsong girl flustered by your attentions.*

He was very good, kind and solicitous, settling her and
Linfyar on cushions in front of the wheelhouse, tucking
blankets about them, bringing them cups of hot spiced cha.
She suspected there were drugs in it meant to put her out so
she'd not see where the boat was going. His prime base, if
her luck hadn't run completely out. She drank. The cha was
hot and clean and refreshing. With a slight undertaste that
told her she was right. *Hah! Play your games; I wouldn't
spend a rotten eyelash to find out where we're going, I just
want to get there.* Linfyar sniffed at his tea; she saw his ears
twitch, then he emptied the cup with innocent gusto, set the
cup down beside him and began singing softly, a plaintive
lovesong from his home city; he sang just loud enough to
blend his clear pure voice with the sounds of wind, water and
the boat's motor. When he began interrupting himself with
yawns, he curled up with his head in Shadith's lap and went
peacefully to sleep.

Shadith finished her cha and set her cup down; she leaned

back against the wheelhouse and felt the motor's vibrations the length of her spine and across her sore shoulders. It seemed to crawl into her bones and was as soothing as whatever that drug was in the cha. Aleytys was suddenly on the bow rail smiling at her, then the figure melted into a fragment of mist. Half asleep, she saw the Ajin take up the cup Linfyar had used and toss it over the side, but didn't bother getting angry again. He was a nothing. He didn't matter anymore. Hollow man. Hollow. Hollow. Hollow man. *Aleytys on the bow made out of mist, she's realer than you. Real, oh real, what's real, am I real? A voice in Lee's head, a knot of forces in an ancient trap. Got a body now. That's real. Gonna have fun with this body, won't lay it down till it's old old old, you hear that, body? Old old old.*

Hello, oddity.

Hello yourself. She giggled. *Who you talking about odd?*

You're plotting something.

Plot, plot, got no plot.

Sounds more like got no brain.

You're messing in it, you ought to know.

Ah. Sobering up a bit.

Sleepering up a bit. She yawned. *Noble knight up there drugged me.*

You didn't have to drink the cha.

Ah well, keep your illusions. I thought I'd be polite.

What do you intend?

My business.

My world.

So?

Be more respectful of your elders, infant.

Why?

(chuckle)

That's no answer.

You first.

Why?

I was here first.

Can't argue that.

Well?

My business.

We've been around that way once. Once is enough.

He your boy? I don't think so.

You're right.

Two great minds beating as one. How can I bear it?

You, ancient child, are a saucy snip.

Yeah. She giggled. *A needle in the ass of authority.*

The Pomp of pomposity.

Soulmate.

Not likely. I sigh with delight that you don't know the location of my hindquarters.

Oh, you have 'em then?

In a manner of speaking. I don't offer them for your prodding.

Keep it clean, I'm underage.

Under what age?

Fourteen. Fourteen thousand. Take your pick.

Why are you here?

Ah. Now that's a question I've never heard answered satifactorily. Why am I? Why is anything? Or is all this a dream? Are you a dream, O loudmouth forest, O Po' Annutj?

(an indescribable sound like solidified irritation)

Tell me why you want to know.

(sigh, long and long, with prickles of annoyance in it)
Enough of this nonsense. Because, ancient child, I want the Ajin off this world, I want him either dead or stopped. My friends suffer now, will suffer more, and in the end, this world will burn if he has his way. Parts of me will die beyond my power to repair and replace them. What grows between me and the soft folk here will die. I think that would be a shame, a loss of richness in the All.

Yes. (a long pause while Shadith struggled with the sluggishness of her brain, the drug tightening its hold on her) *I came to pry two friends out of his claws.* (pause) *Hunters. They came to get him.* (pause) *He . . . no, not him . . . Kell . . . the Vryhh . . . set a trap, caught them.* (pause) *Going after . . . no . . . that's it. I get them, they get him.*

The Senda who tended you is mine.

I wondered . . . I didn't . . . why?

Liaison. Spy.

(sleepy laughter) *That's good gunk he has. One I owe you.*

There are others like him. They'll know about you, help when they can.

Know? No.

Only that you're mine.

Not yours. Not anyone's.

Quibble. Friend, then.

All right.

(feel of almost-maternal amusement and affection) *Go to sleep. That's a good child.*

Up yours.

Keep it clean, ancient child. Remember my age.

What age is that?

Not half yours. Sleep. Sleep.

How can I with you yelling in my head?

Sleep. Sleep.

Good night, Po'. Go away, Po'.

(laughter fading into silence)

Interesting, she thought, and drifted deeper into the drugged sleep.

She woke to darkness and thought at first she'd slept through the day and into night again, then realized the boat was burbling along inside a cavern, plowing heavily against a powerful but sluggish current. She sat up, looked around, then shook Linfyar awake. Bending down to him, she whispered, "How big is this wormhole?"

Linfyar rubbed at his nose, yawned. His ears quivered. He rolled out of his blankets and squatted beside her, listening intently. After a minute he said, "They're using radar to find their way; I'm trying to read their beeps." Another short silence. "Roof comes down close to the water ahead," he murmured. "About twenty meters. Boat'll just scrape by." He wriggled uneasily. "Shadow, there's things in the water."

"What things?"

"Don't know. Big things. Talking and making my ears hurt."

"Come here, imp. Don't listen to them."

He curled his ears shut and climbed into her lap, sat with his face pressed into the shallow valley between her small breasts. She pulled a blanket up around them, then reached out and touched the things. Raw hunger. Fury. A force too primitive and diffuse for her to control. Far too deadly to challenge. "We sure don't swim out of here, Linfy," she murmured.

Some shapeless sounds from him, a sleepy shift of arms and legs, then he was heavy against her, wholly relaxed, asleep again. The blackness closed down tighter. The boat slowed until it was making little headway against the current; she heard creaks and rasps where it was scraping against the rock.

Then there was light ahead, blooming green and gold in water smooth as glass. She rubbed watering eyes and sighed with relief as the weight of stone lifted away.

They drifted into a round lake inside high craggy walls. There were patches of lush greenery, but the cone of the ancient volcano was mostly heaps of mottled stone, slides of scree slanting from the precipitous walls. One of those slides jutted into the deep black water; after a moment she saw it was a camouflaged wharf with a slot where the boat could slip in and rest unseen from above. Beyond the wharf were more structures, massive stone buildings built up against the wall, camouflaged like the wharf by the sweeps of scree.

The Ajin helped her to her feet and with smiling courtesy lifted her onto the dock, then stepped after her, leaving Linfyar to scramble up how he could. *Poor old bigot, no use getting mad at you anymore, silly old fool, escorting your enemy into the heart of your power*. He put his hand on her shoulder and guided her along the wharf and into the largest of the structures. The walls were not as thick as she'd expected, but these buildings weren't meant to live through a bombing; that was the meaning of the camouflage. If the Pajunggs found this base, they'd flatten it, but a world was a huge place, even so small a part of it as a continent, and they didn't have the tracers to locate him. Not yet. And they were terrified of the forest. No native intelligence here. Hah. What they told themselves so they wouldn't have to go into the forest hunting it. She wondered about the other worlds the Pajunggs had colonized, what they'd found there and quietly destroyed. Respect for life and the rights of natives, all that was the luxury of settled peaceful lands long after those natives had either been assimilated or destroyed. Unless they had the power to resist cooptation. In the end that was what it came down to, the possession of power in one form or another. Where law didn't exist, the survivors were those strong and smart enough to prevail. Kell and Aleytys, it was the same thing. Po' Anuutj, the miners against the Pajunggs and, yes, the Ajin.

The hand on her shoulder turned her away from the main corridor down the building and urged her down a side way that went out of the house into the living stone of the mountain. She thought about his loathing of Linfyar, who was recognizably of kindred stock, a handsome little faun with more charm than was good for him. What would the Ajin be like once he had complete authority over this world and came against the Po' Annutj? They went back and back into the mountain until she had the feeling she walked on a surface precariously spread over a seething sink of molten stone; with a shrug of its shoulders the mountain could drop them into its heart. She shivered.

The Ajin patted her shoulder. "Not much farther," he said. "I want to keep you close to me, make sure you're safe."

She did her awkward childish nod, but said nothing. *Treating me like a kid*, she thought, *being the tough but gentle father. Hunh. I want a father like I want another head*. She'd lived with Harskari far too long to relish acquiring another mentor, especially this condescending bag of air planning to use her and her gifts for his own purposes. *I said it right, out there on the bay. Hollow man, only his needs to drive him, no real contact with anyone else. The rest of us are shadows cast on his desires*. She thought about Perolat and Tjepa. She thought about the Ajin selling himself to Kell in return for support in his ambitions. *I'd bet anything Kell built this place for him and stocked it too. Wonder where the trap is? Won-*

der what it is? Taggert, she told herself, *I hope you know what you're doing. Another Hunter in the trap. Would that bring Kell running? God, I hope not. I know when I'm out of my weight.*

The Ajin palmed open a door, urged her inside. A huge false window took up most of one wall, a viewscreen showing the mountainside with its immense trees, the solemn silent beauty of the forest, the sunlight streaming through occasional breaks in the canopy, bat-winged birds soaring and singing; forest sounds came through subdued and faintly magical. Bright hangings broke the chill of the black stone walls. The floor was dull metacrete, but a silk rug hid its ugliness, echoing the abstract patterns in the hangings. A black glass table with food steaming on black glass plates, cha in a pot covered by a quilted cozy. Steel-framed chairs with black leather seats and backs. A black velvet divan piled with brilliantly colored silk cushions. A cheerfully inelegant room decorated by someone with a liking for color and no pretensions to taste. The Ajin stepped aside to let Linfyar in, moved to the center of the room. "These will be your quarters, singer. Bedroom and fresher through there." He gestured at a black velvet curtain between two of the hangings. "Rest and take care of your body's needs. I will return to talk with you tomorrow. No need to worry about anything. No one will hurt you here. Just relax. I'll explain everything soon." He smiled at her, a warm beaming smile, his brown eyes twinkling with goodwill and appreciation, then made a rueful face, lifted a hand in an apologetic gesture. "The door will be locked—I'm afraid it's necessary. For your protection, child, I promise you, that's all. Some of the men here aren't as gentle with women and children as I'd like." A last smile and he left, the door closing behind him with a slight pneumatic hiss.

Shadith looked around, raised her brows. Their gear was piled against the wall at the end of the divan. "Looks like we took the scenic route."

"Huh?"

"Never mind. Private joke."

Linfyar twitched his ears, turned in a slow circle. In his home-tongue he said, "Busy-busy, crawling with bugs."

"Man wouldn't trust his own mother. Better not count too much on talking this way, my young furry friend. Your language is a variant out of a large family; might not know it, but you come from the cousin races and if their computer has translating capability, it won't take them all that long to get a good idea what we're saying. Besides, if they get curious enough and decide to stop being polite, all they really have to do is hook one of us to a psychprobe."

Linfyar shrugged, began moving about the room, his lips fluttering to read what was around him, his nose twitching, all his senses operating as he explored this new place. He followed his nose to the table, slid into one of the chairs. Switching languages, he said, "Not going to starve us, anyway. Mmm. I'm hungry."

Shadith chuckled. "Me too, imp. Be with you in a minute." She left him sniffing at the dishes and pushed past the curtain.

A bedroom with another screen tuned to the same image. She was grateful for those screens; they made the stone more bearable, though she suspected they were two-way viewers. She dragged her hand hard across the screen, made the glass squeal, grinned at the trees and birds she couldn't touch. *Voyeur*, she thought, but didn't say it. She circled the wide bed and went into the fresher. It was small and neat, with a flush toilet and a shower cabinet, a large mirror over a basin. She took care of the ache in her bladder, stripped to use the shower, annoyed that there was some fool somewhere watching her. She started to step into the shower, then frowned at the bandages on her arms and legs; she stripped them off and inspected the abraded flesh. Most of the red was gone. Cautiously she touched her head. No swelling, no soreness. Great gunk. *Yeah, I owe you one, old Po'. Hate to wash it off, but I'm too grungy to stand myself any longer.* She found a cake of soap with a pleasant herbal scent in a niche in the shower, laughed as she turned the water on and adjusted the temperature. *VIP treatment. Looovely. But you walk eggshell-light, Shadow, you're frosting on his cake; he can get along quite well without you if he has to.*

The water came hot and hard. She found herself singing,

enjoying the feel of the spray, then of the soap as she spread lather over her body. She lingered awhile after the soap was rinsed off, letting the hot water beat against her back, but she was hungry, so she finally shut it off and stepped out.

She scrubbed one of the thick nubbly towels over her body until she glowed, then wrapped herself in the toweling robe that hung on a hook beside the cabinet. She tied the belt and went strolling back into the sitting room, rubbing at her hair, humming the song she'd been singing.

Linfyar was eating neatly but steadily from a plate heaped high with bits of meat and vegetables, washing down every other bite with a gulp of heavily sweetened cha. "You sound happy," he said. He sniffed. "And you smell good."

"A change for the better, huh?" She filled her plate, settled into a chair across the table from him.

Linfyar stopped chewing, put his fork down and rubbed at his nose. "You think maybe . . . um . . ." He shifted languages but was still careful in his choice of words. "What we're looking for, you know . . . maybe it's right here. Funny if that's right, don't you think?"

"I think that's something we don't talk about, you hear?"

"I expect you're right."

"Funny or not, I expect you're right too, Linfy."

He picked up his fork, tapped a bouncy rhythm on the edge of the plate, then started reducing the mound of food on it.

Shadith sat in the middle of the wide bed and began going over her things, checking to see what the Ajin's men had brought along, harvesting a small collection of metal burrs from various parts of the clothing wadded into the bags. She set them aside, continued with her inventory and came across her hoard of coins. "Hunh, honest kidnappers." All her possessions were here, even an old polish rag she'd meant to throw away. She looked at the clothing with distaste. *All of them, underthings and everything, handled by those creeps and invaded by a horde of bugs, worms eat his liver. Wonder who does the laundry around here. I can wash a few things in the fresher basin, but I want this whole mess cleaned before I wear any of it.* She wrinkled her nose at the small pile of

burrs. *Sneaky, yeah, and don't he think he's clever. I'm
supposed to find you and feel oh so confident. Happy to
oblige.* She scooped the bugs up and flushed them down the
toilet, then went back to the bed and unsnapped the harp
case. Someone had wiped the dust off the outside, but more
than enough had managed to ooze inside. With a grunt of
disgust, she lifted the harp out and set it down carefully, then
slid to the edge of the bed, flipped the case over and shook it
out on the rug. She set the case down. *Have to go over it
later with a damp cloth.* She dug into the pile of clothing,
found that decrepit polish rag and began to wipe the harp,
working very carefully so she wouldn't scratch it. When she
was finished with the frame, she wiped the strings, then
plucked each of them to get the last grains of dust off. And
found another bug tucked up high on the inside of the frame
where she wasn't likely to see it. She went to the sitting room
to fetch a fork, detoured to check on Linfyar. He had squir-
reled deep into the pile of silk pillows on the divan and was
asleep, snoring a little, almost like a loud purring. She smiled
at him, shook her head and went back into the bedroom.

Harp on her lap, she probed for the flat little patch and
finally managed to scrape it loose. It looked a bit battered,
but she suspected it was still in fair working order; they built
those things to take a lot of knocks. She held it close to one
of the strings and made that string shriek at it. *Hunh, you
bastard, hope that wrings your ears for you.* She took the bug
into the fresher and flushed it after the others.

The Ajin came back the middle of the next morning.
Shadith sat on the floor gazing at the image on the screen,
hands moving idly across the strings, making a portrait in
sound of her restlessness. She looked around as she heard the
door open, scowled and turned back to the screen, putting an
acid jangle into what she was playing.

He laughed, strode over to her, plucked the harp from her
hands, tossed it onto the divan, pulled her to her feet.

For a moment Shadith could not speak. She was so furious
her throat closed up on her, so furious she could only stand
there shaking. She stared at him blankly; when she could

move, she marched to the divan, picked up the harp, ran her hand over the frame, then the strings. She squatted, set it on the floor and came slowly back up, turning to face him as she rose. "Don't ever ever do that again," she said flatly. "Touch it again and I'll kill you."

"Watch your mouth, girl."

She stared at him, said nothing.

"Sweet little girls don't go around killing people. Didn't your parents teach you that?"

She kept staring, still furious, though she'd calmed enough to start thinking again. The little girl act—she could go on with it, but was it worth it? She looked into that handsome smiling face and decided it wasn't. *Might as well test just how much he thinks he needs me; let him start walking over me and he'll keep on tromping.* "They taught me a lot of things," she said, her voice still flat and as cold as she could make it. "They taught me it's both stupid and discourteous to handle other people's belongings without permission." She rushed on, drowning his attempt to speak. "They taught me that kidnappers are thugs and men who steal girls are perverts or pimps and a pimp is lower than a pervert. They taught me that real men treat other men and women, and children, with the respect they expect for themselves and those who act otherwise are only cheap imitations."

He took a step toward her, hand raised, then checked himself. As clearly as if she read the words on a tape issuing from his head, she knew what he was thinking: *Look, never mind what she says, she's only a silly little girl who doesn't know what she's talking about; anyway, there's no one to hear it.* His eyes narrowed. She read the codicil in his face: *But be damn sure she's not going to say such things in public.* "Come, child," he said, "not so much heat. I'm sorry about the harp. Let me be honest and confess it, I didn't understand how important it was to you." He patted her shoulder, quite unaware of the effort she made not to knock his hand away. "Sit down, please. I promised you an explanation today, and I've come to give it. Ah. Good." He smiled at her as she slipped from under his hand and seated herself on the divan. "We aren't kidnappers, child. Or pimps.

We fight for Avosing's future, child, we fight to drive the tyrant from our world. We need you, child, we need your gifts. I want to show you some of the things the Pajunggs are doing to us. They aren't pretty, and if this were the world I dream of, you wouldn't have to see these things, but I want you to understand us. You saw for yourself what the Pajunggs wanted to do to you in Keama Dusta, you know how the hiepler threatened you. We saved you from some of the horrors I'm going to show you.'' His voice was low and gently persuasive, a seductive murmur caressing her ears, but she took no pleasure from it, was too aware of the deep dislike he felt for her. *Shit on this talent,* she thought. *I can't even enjoy my illusions anymore. No fun to be courted by someone you know despises you.* He sat beside her, careful not to touch her, providing a low-voiced narration for the succession of images he cued into the screen.

The forest scene vanished.

Shaky, grainy pictures took its place, images captured by hidden cameras under difficult conditions.

"This is where you would have performed." The church casino, great and noble room, low-relief sculptures ten times life size, the pantheon of Pajungg gods, overlooking the games of chance; intent worshipers bending over boards or watching lights flicker, playing their games in reverent anxiety; hooded and robed croupiers; white-robed serving maids; hum of recited prayers rising above the assorted clicks and clacks and slaps and rustles of the games. "And this." Whoever carried the camera followed an attendant through the players and past the private rooms and out the back of the church. After winding through a dizzying series of turns and twists he stepped into a cozier milieu where child whores of both sexes dressed in filmy short robes displayed themselves to men with a shared patina of wealth and power. A few of the children were her apparent age, but most were younger, even a number barely walking. "Slaves, all of them, sold by their parents."

Another scene. A house burning, dark-clad enforcers standing about, two of them holding the arms of a weeping man, others keeping the man's wife and children herded together.

"He never went to church, had several warnings; a bad season, wilt in his gancha grain, disease in his stock, got into debt; next year, prices were low, couldn't pay his creditors; church seized the land and goods; he's the one set the fire, wouldn't let them have his house. See what happened to his sons and daughters.'' Scene change. A slave auction, the children going one by one to the highest bidder.

New scene. Twisted, savaged bodies barely recognizable as something that might once have been human. "Some are men who joined our fight; they were captured by enforcers. Some are men denounced to the church for heresy.''

A miner who'd been caught hoarding amber, his body jerking as massive jolts of electricity hit him.

More images documenting the cruelty of man to man.

Meant to evoke horror and disgust in her. Meant to convince her to serve the Ajin and his cause. If she'd told him he was not so different from the men he wanted to replace, he would have been angry, perhaps a little hurt, but he wouldn't have understood what she was saying. Because of his background, Head and Taggert and even the Pajunggs had seen him as a cynical manipulator only after power, but he was more than that. She remembered Head saying the thieves are heretics, not unbelievers. He believed in what he was doing, and like most true believers he was willing to use any means no matter how repulsive to achieve his goal.

He grasped her shoulders, turned her to face him. "You see how the Pajunggs corrupt and oppress us. We have to change that, child, and to do that we have to convince all the Avosingers that change is possible." Bending closer, he went into a short harangue about morality, the sacredness of home and tradition, sketching out a world where men and women knew their place and stayed in it, where there was no disruptive change, where life went on in calm comfortable channels. *All very lovely,* she thought, *if you happen to be a man. Perolat wouldn't like it much, and Dihann, well* . . . She lowered her eyes and swallowed a giggle at the thought of Dihann's reaction to being told she ought to subordinate herself to any man no matter how forceful and dynamic he was. She listened and kept her eyes down, resigned to playing the role he kept insisting on. *It's not for that long,* she told herself, *just until I find Grey and get him loose.* It made her feel like vomiting, but she told herself she'd done worse things before this and survived them, she'd survive this.

The Ajin led them back to the outer building, into a glare-free white-tiled space, filled with banks of computers and viewscreens relaying images from satellites even her lander's sensitive detectors hadn't noticed. *Kell, worms eat your liver, by god, you really want Aleytys, you're paying high for the chance of catching her.* Men working with stone-faced dedication at consoles, looking up to nod a quick greeting at the Ajin as he moved past them, Shadith at his heels, Linfyar trailing behind.

They passed through into a darker quieter hall and finally turned into a side room equipped as an infirmary, more gleaming white tile, white-enameled machines and other instruments, many of them new-made antiques in her eyes; like a lot of Avosing, a confusing mixture of late industrial and contemporary technologies. It was a large room with uncertain echoes, the bounding sounds making her itchy. It was a lot worse for Linfyar; he nudged closer to her, trembling. She dropped her arm around his shoulder, hugged him. "Roll 'em up, Linfy, and hang on to me." She looked from the Ajin to the small dumpy man he was talking to, made a small hissing sound, cut it off as it started to echo. "Hey," she yelled. "I don't like it here. I'm leaving."

The little man turned spectacled eyes to her, the harsh light glinting off the lenses making him look more machine than flesh. He stepped to the bank of black rubbery switches, clicked one over, and the echoes hushed so suddenly she almost stumbled as if she'd been pushing against some force removed without warning. He came around the examination table and stood in front of her, peering at her through those thick glasses, the pale yellow of his eyes intermittently visible, the thin almost white lashes. "This child?"

"Apparently."

"Mmm." He stumped around her, his hands folded over

his tight little paunch, high for a man, so high he looked pregnant. "Collar her?"

"No. Nothing showing."

"Hm." He took hold of her shoulder, started prodding at her back.

She tried jerking away, but he held her too tightly, his fingers digging into her muscle. With a grunt of effort, she caught hold of his little finger, twisted it, then twisted away as he yelped with pain. "Keep your hands to yourself, fool."

"You . . . you . . . you . . ." He raised a fist.

"Try it," she flung at him.

The Ajin got a grip on her hair and jerked her back, snapped to the other two men standing quietly in the background, "Take care of him."

After the melee was sorted out, the man's finger restored to its joint, the Ajin swung her around, pushed her against the bank of switches. "I'm getting very tired of your insolence, girl."

She glared at him, all resolutions forgotten. "Biiig man, oh I'm so scared. Ask me," she yelled at him, turned it into a chant. "Ask me ask me ask me. If you want something, ask me, don't maul me about, ask me. I'm not stupid, or deaf— don't treat me like I am. Easy little words, ask me." She grew a bit calmer. "You didn't like it when those creeps were fooling with the kid whores—how come you're treating me like a whore? Like you can do anything you want with me and I shouldn't complain? Huh?"

He stared at her, pulled his hand away from her hair and rubbed it absently down his side. She'd hit something in him, she could feel that, but she wasn't quite sure what it was, and she was more than a little startled and ashamed of her reactions. Lee'd told her a number of times she was letting this body make her forget what the years had taught her; for the first time Shadith was ready to concede she might be right. She'd gone through this sort of scene more than once with her mother in those difficult days around her first puberty, and here it was again. *Oh god, do I really have to go through all that misery again?* She pulled her mind back to her present predicament and waited for what he'd say.

"You are a child and female," he said. His voice was cold and flat, devoid of emotion. "You will do as you are told and create no more disturbances or you will be punished. You will behave as a proper young girl should behave; you will speak when you are spoken to and remain silent at other times. You will be modest and quiet in your manner. And you will understand that you are less than dust when compared to the great dream you are privileged to play a part in. Do you understand me?"

Come on, Shadow, take a lesson from Linfy. She sneaked a glance at the boy crouched out of the way under the examining table, silent and inconspicuous as a small furry ghost. It took a minute, but she swallowed her loathing and said, meekly, "I hear."

They poked at her and prodded at her and sampled every fluid they could think of (the yellow-eyed doctor watching her with angry spite, his left hand bandaged, the little finger in a brace), recorded brain emissions while she was silent and while she was running off scales and a song or two, they fed her drugs and watched the results, put her under various sorts of stress. For her own pride's sake she made the results as meaningless as she could, her mind and body control sufficient to let her duplicate results when necessary, but it was a strain trying to keep the readings logical and remember what she'd done before. A strain, yes, but also healing to her self-respect. For the most part they ignored Linfyar; these were technicians, not real researchers, and she was glad of it for his sake, since they had little of the explorer's driving curiosity and were willing enough to leave him alone as long as they had her to play with.

Those tests lasted all that long day and most of the next morning, then they announced that they were finished for the moment; it was time to evaluate their accumulated data. She went back to her rooms and let herself be locked in. Linfyar was asleep again on the divan. She scowled down at him, wondering if she should be worried about the amount of time he was spending in sleep, not certain her itchiness was anxiety about him or just jealousy that he found such a satisfac-

tory way to pass the endless days. She was about ready to
shriek from boredom. She'd already read through her handful
of books twice, she didn't feel like sleeping, and she certainly
wasn't up to fooling around with music, not in the mood. She
went into the fresher and made faces at herself in the mirror
until she got tired of looking at herself, then stripped and
stood in the shower letting water as hot as she could stand it
beat down on her body, first her front, then her back. After a
while she shut the water off, wrapped the robe around her and
ambled into the bedroom. She threw herself onto the bed and
lay with her head on her arms, breathing in the dry dusty
smell of the velvet bedspread. Body. Body. Body. *Oh god,
it's so easy to forget when you don't have one what happens
in the body. Easier to dream when you're a knot of nothing in
a bit of sorcerous headgear gathering dust somewhere.* She
went back to her earliest memories and began reliving them,
struggling to recall the smallest and most insignificant details,
drifting gradually into a heavy, nightmare-ridden sleep.

The doctor laced his hands over his paunch and blinked his
weak yellow eyes at her while his acolytes attached sensors
about her head and body, careful not to interfere with her
ease of movement, making her rock and sway, reach and
fold. Other silent white-clad men were setting up micro-
phones about the chair. She watched all this without protest;
even if she sang a real croon, nothing much was going to
happen in this sterile room with its scrubbed air and literal-
minded technicians. No pollen. No Linfyar to broaden the
range of the sound. But she wasn't going to take any chances,
she was going to give them something that sounded similar to
her ancient songs, but it would be enough off, enough of the
harmonics and overtones missing, that even with the pollen it
wouldn't work the way they wanted. *You're not going to
replace me with a flake player.* When one of the men sig-
naled they were finished, she looked around, straightened her
back and resettled the harp. "Nothing's going to happen, you
know. I've been about more than you think, and this is the
only world where I sing dreams. Must be the pollen." She
drew her hand across the strings, making a soft drift of

sound. "This air." She shrugged. "And the acoustics here are foul."

"Play." The light glinted off the doctor's glasses and showed the silver stopples in his ears as he adjusted them to shut off yet more of the sound in the room.

Frowning, she plucked a series of single notes from the harp, then what she could do patterned itself in her mind and she slid into the almost-croon and sang it through. There was no trance effect even among the acolytes; with the echo killer on, the song dropped dead into the sterile air. She stilled the last sounds and sat with her arms curled about the harp, saying nothing, waiting for the Ajin to show up, wondering just what he'd say to her. If he said anything to her. He'd been conspicuously absent the last several days.

The doctor opened out his ear stopples and darted busily from dial to drum, muttering with his assistants, chattering into a flake recorder, ignoring Shadith, who was quite happy to be left alone, though she'd have been happier with something to occupy her mind and keep her from wondering how much she'd given away that she'd rather keep to herself. She knew well enough how much information a skilled researcher could tease out of a pile of apparently unpromising data; her first owner had been an itinerant trouble-shooter with a genius for spotting weak links. He had little use for women in any sense of that word, but a passionate love of all forms of music. He bought her for her small deft fingers and because he'd heard her playing a tin whistle she'd sneaked into her cell. She traveled with him, getting from him everything he could teach her, winning from him a reluctant affection and a generous admiration for her tenacity and the speed with which she learned. She grieved when he died, killed in a quarrel with a lover, not just because now she'd be sold again, but because she was deeply fond of him and for the second time in her life she was losing all she had of family.

The Ajin came in and stood frowning at her. "Why?"

She dropped her eyes to her hands. "I played what I've played before."

He took a step to one side. Behind him was his skinny aide, Manjestau. "Well?" he said.

"Sounds like it." Manjestau came closer, looked at the harp, looked around at the room. "Probably right. Probably needs the pollen." He looked at her again. "And the freak."

The Ajin walked over to her, smiled down at her, his eyes twinkling, his good humor apparently returned. "It looks like we should have listened to you, child."

She moved a little, stiffened as he started to frown. "My name is Shadith," she said quietly.

"Well, Shadith, I still need to be convinced you can do what the reports say. Hmm. Tomorrow, I think. Outside somewhere."

She plucked at a string, waited until the note died. "We need to talk deal, Sikin Ajin. I don't play this thing out of the goodness of my heart. It's my profession. My skills are for sale, I don't give them away."

"Right now I wouldn't take them as a gift. Persuade me."

"All right. Tomorrow. A free sample. After that, pay me."

"If you're worth it, we'll work something out. Right now there's something I want you to see."

"Shall I bring the harp?"

"No need."

"Allow me time to put it in the case, please."

He inclined his head.

She began stripping away the sensors. With muttered imprecations one of the assistants hurried to her, collected the ones she'd removed and slapped her hands away as she reached for another. She sat quietly letting him peel them off with slow care, watching the Ajin move about the room, stopping a moment to speak to the doctor, looking at the readouts, killing time, she was sure of it, until she was ready, looking grave all the while as if he knew what he was seeing. Apparently he'd forgotten the laws he'd laid on her the last time they'd met—at least he seemed willing to allow her a certain degree of independence as long as she didn't push too hard. All right. She knew now she wasn't Linfyar; body aside, she wasn't that young or that flexible; she knew too much about what she'd turn into if she let her self-respect corrode too badly. The assistant went away, cuddling his sensors to his bosom as if they were favored children. She slipped out of the chair, snapped the harp into its case and left it leaning against a chair leg.

He took her to the end of the corridor and into the mountain again, only a short way this time, and stopped before a heavy steel door. He palmed it open, then stood aside until she walked in, following her, closing the door behind them.

It was a high domed room with tool marks still on the walls. Naked stone, exposed wiring, complex flake boards that looked as if they'd been painted by an ancient ink master, a rough but powerful scrawl, compulsion worked so intimately into the pattern that it drew her eyes and would not turn them loose. She made an effort and turned to face him. "What's that?" Even with her back to the thing it was burned so deeply into her memory she saw the webbing of darks and lights shadow-cast across his face and form. It made her dizzy and uncertain.

He wasn't looking at her, he was gazing at the thing with a proprietorial satisfaction that told her he hadn't the slightest idea what he was seeing.

She glanced at it again, forced herself to look away. It was disturbingly like the diadem—not its innocuous outside, but the way she'd seen it from inside. Anyway, the closest any construct of this age had come to that ancient trap. Kell. *Worms eat his liver, why does he have to be such a . . . god knows . . . when he can make things like this?* "Well?" she said.

"Have you heard of the Hunters of Wolff?"

"Who hasn't?"

"My enemies sent them after me," he said, a blend of triumph and relish in his voice. "They didn't know I have a patron greater than any Hunter, a man who supports our cause without counting the cost in time or goods. A Vryhh master designer made this, young Shadith, set it here as a trap for my enemies. If I had to pay him for his time and work, it would have cost me the total income of this world for a year. He gave it freely."

"That's his choice. You left me none. Me, I want to be paid."

He ignored that. "A trap for my enemies, young Shadith. Look at it."

"No. Makes me dizzy."

He laughed, pleased by what he thought of as her weakness, just one more proof, if he needed it, of the power of his mind. "Never mind, then, look at this instead." He put his hand on a bluish oval sensor, and a viewscreen lit up at the back of the chamber. "There they are, the great and indomitable Hunters of Wolff." Two men hung in grayness, turning, writhing, horror and pain graven into their faces. "There they hang, young Shadith, my enemies. Hunters. In a nothing where they are neither dead nor alive, but fully aware of what has happened to them. Where they listen to whispers from their most secret fears. And it goes on and on, child, it never stops. That's where anyone who betrays me will find himself. Or herself. Do you understand?"

Shadith nodded, still staring at Grey. Alive. She shuddered, but horror wasn't a luxury she could afford right now. "Umm . . . is that permanent or could you bring them back? Say someone wanted to ransom them. Or you maybe wanted to put them on trial to embarrass the Pajunggs, once you take over here."

"An interesting thought, child. You have a devious mind. I'll have to remember that." He contemplated the two forms, smiling with quiet satisfaction. "I could. Yes, I could. And I'm the only one who could. You might think on that during the long nights, young Shadith. Right now, I feel better with them in there where I know they won't try spoiling my plans." His hand on her shoulder, he turned her to the door. "And there's plenty of room for more in there, that's another thing to think about." He touched the door open, followed her out, took her back to her rooms.

Inside, he swung around one of the chairs from the table, sat with his arms crossed along the back, facing the divan. He waved a muscular arm. "Sit, child. Do you still want to bargain with me?"

She settled herself among the pillows. "I won't do you

much good in that place, Ajin. And let me be candid. I will be even less use if you try forcing me. I'm stubborn. You're not a fool; don't act one. Consider me a mercenary and ply me with gold. Or the local equivalent. I don't give a mouthful of spit about your noble cause, but I do appreciate hard coin. Nice cool rounds that rest heavy in the hand. That's a cause I can put my heart into. Slide a few my way and you'll see fervor like you wouldn't believe.''

"You're young to be so cynical."

"Not so young as I look; all species don't mature at the same rate."

"Is there anything you believe in?"

"A full belly and a warm secure bed. That today will end and tomorrow come whether I live to see it or not. I prefer being alive to being dead, being rich to being poor. That's about it.''

"You know what I want you to do?"

"I got a pretty good idea."

"Can you?"

"All right. Honest again. I think so."

"I won't haggle. Conditional on the success of your performance tomorrow, five kilos sweetamber, passage offworld, your word not to return with the understanding that if you break it you join my pets in that pocket of nowhere."

"The price is right. Name the terms of service."

"Five Avosinger years. You sing where, when and what I tell you."

"Three."

"I told you, no haggling. Take it or leave it."

"If I leave it?"

"Do I need to say it?"

"No. One small change, if I may. It's for your benefit as well as mine. *Where* and *when* is your business. *What* is mine. Tell me the effect you want and let me decide how I'm going to get it."

"That makes sense. You understand, I'll have observers in the audience."

"I never expected anything different."

"Deal?"

"Deal." She smiled at him, knowing full well that even if she did serve him faithfully and fervently for the next several years, all she'd get out of it was a berth beside Grey. Honor was between men; breaking a promise to a woman was as heinous a sin as farting in public. He got to his feet. "Tomorrow, second hour after the noon meal," he said. "That suit you?"

"Suits me fine."

He nodded and left. After the door slid closed behind him, she sat for some time without moving, eyes shut, hands pressed hard on her thighs, using breathing exercises to calm her mind and sort out the whirl of joy and fear and hate and rage roaring through her. Finally she sighed and let herself fall back among the cushions. *Taggert, where the hell are you? Grey's alive, he's really alive, but oh god, I've got to get him out of there. Ticutt, poor old Ticutt, what a hell that must be for you. What am I going to do? Never thought I'd miss witchface's scolds, ah, Harskari, I wish you were here, I'll never tell you, I suppose, oh god, I wish you were here.*

They were waiting for her, restless and close to hostile, routed from card games and sleep, taken away from their screens and scanners, their leave time, mercenaries that were the Ajin's personal guard, the core of his army, and the better part of the technicians that lived and worked in the camouflaged buildings. Taken from whatever pleasure they were immersed in and forced into the treacherous outer air to listen to some flat-chested halfling sing at them.

The Ajin looked at them and smiled. "If you can get them, you're better than good, young Shadith. Look at them—won't even sit together." He frowned. "Mercenaries. Tough men. Good fighters. But they'll always retreat just that fraction sooner than men fighting for something they believe in. They're here for coin, and coin is no good to a dead man."

"My kind of people," she murmured.

He was not amused. "Make them love Avosing," he said. "Make them cheer me. Make them ready to follow me into fire."

"It won't last."

"You can do it?"

"I can but try."

"Remember what you're working for. Remember the five kilos sweetamber."

"I hear you." She shifted the harp, got ready to play, then lifted her head. "Don't forget I told you. The effect wears off fast."

"Play."

"Linfy, you ready?"

"Yah, Shadow."

She nudged him with her toe. "This one has to be good."

"Gotcha."

She sneaked a last glance at the Ajin and saw that he believed in her enough to have filters in his nostrils and distorting plugs in his ears. *Cheer him*, she thought, *damned if I do, damned if I don't*. She discarded what she'd planned and riffled through her stock of song patterns. *All right, sing a song of fierceness and glory, weave it around the Ajin, that should do what he wants*.

She began to play on the harp, the sound thin and swallowed by the wind, then ripening into richness as Linfyar caught the mood and added his whistle. She could feel the men resisting her, still resenting her, determined to punish her with their indifference. She smiled to herself and began the croon, the ancient words ringing out with all the power she could put into them. And her sisters were finally there for her, spinning the dream out of their ghostly substance as they made her voice theirs. She sang first yearning for home, not the real home but the dream home men made for themselves when they were far from that home in every way that counted, in years, miles, a multiplicity of sins and sorrows. She watched the hard faces soften, shallow eyes mist over with tears, not surprised by this; the mercenaries she'd known had been easily sentimental when it cost them nothing. She teased them from that sentimentality into dreams of glory and honor, all the things they wanted to be or thought they were, fierce bold men of matchless skill, loyal to their brothers and to a stern code no outsider could understand. A dream even the most cynical and treacherous among them cherished deep in some

corner of his shriveled soul, though he knew in mind and gut
that it had very little to do with the real order of things. At
first she'd been bothered by her complicity in this manipulation of men for purposes other than pleasure, but by the time
she finished the croon and stilled the sound of the harp, she
felt better about what she was doing. At least, with this
bunch. They lived quite comfortably with the chasm between
the ideals they professed and the things they did to outsiders
and each other.

The Ajin leaped onto the rock beside her and began a
rousing speech; after a few words he had them on their feet
cheering. She stopped listening and frowned at her hands.
One thing to play on these men, but what about the Avosingers?
One time wouldn't make that much difference—what if he
made her do it over and over again? *I want out of this now. I
can't . . .* But she had to. Until she could figure a way to
break Grey and Ticutt loose, she was stuck here, she had to
compromise, had to do things that were hard to live with. The
Ajin squatted beside her, whispered, ''Sing them quiet and
reinforce what we've done.''

We, she thought and felt her stomach curl into a knot. She
settled the harp and began a rousing song Swartheld had
taught her, one he'd picked up in his wandering since he'd
acquired Quayle's body; she had them clapping with the beat
and shouting out the chorus, then she cut it off and sang a
gentle, sentimental song of home, ending where she began,
ignoring the calls for more when she finished, sitting slumped
and weary over her harp as the Ajin sent them back to what
they were doing before he'd ordered them out here.

When they were gone, he came back to Shadith. ''No more
'conditional'—you've shown me something I wouldn't have
believed. Would that work with any crowd, one with women
and children in it? More of a mix?''

She straightened, forced herself out of her gloom. ''Once I
get the feel of the crowd, I think so.''

''Then you can't just push button A and get result A.''

''No. People change. If you brought that bunch out again,
I'd have to sing something different. Slightly different. It's
nuances that make the effect work. Or fail.''

He gazed at her skeptically. He didn't want to believe her, but he was out of his depth with music and didn't know how to question what she was telling him. She kept her face calm, smiling a little, tried to project passivity and lack of interest in what he was thinking, though she read all too clearly that he was a little afraid of her now and his dislike and distrust of all women was working on that fear. *I'd never last the whole five years even if I meant to stay. When his fear gets too strong, I go into the trap with Grey. Something to think about—how long have I got? How long before my value is outweighed by the danger I represent?*

He nodded, held out his hand. "Right. Come. There's one more thing we have to do, then you can get some rest. You look tired."

"I am." She let him pull her onto her feet, then followed him back into the building, Linfyar trailing silent and forgotten behind them.

In the infirmary again. He stopped her beside the examining table, stood looking thoughtfully down at her.

"Mess with my head and I can't do that anymore."

He nodded. "I believe you. Nuances."

"Well?"

"You worry me. I haven't got a handle on you."

"The sweetamber. I stay bought."

"Easy enough to say that here. Out there you might change your mind." He shook his head. "I don't leave loose ends, Shadith. That's why I'm alive now and not bones in a crypt." He made no apparent signal, but a tangler wrapped around her. She heard Linfyar squeal with outrage and fear, forgot her own fear as she screamed curses at the Ajin and fought to tear free from the strangling bonds. A sting on her shoulder. Darkness knotted about her; she heard a last whimper from Linfyar, then nothing. . . .

She woke lying on her stomach on the table, the Ajin looming over her. He stepped back as she spat at him, so filled by rage she wasn't thinking, only reacting. Looking past her at someone on the other side of the table. "Turn her loose."

"She's knotted up, ready to attack."

He laughed. "That child? Am I so weak? Turn her loose."

She felt the straps loosen over her back and legs, then fall away. The interval had given her time to remember where she was and why she was there. She sat up, winced as she felt a sharp twinge between her shoulder blades. A tall thin man came round the table and held out her tunic. She pulled it on with angry jerks, smoothed it down, then slipped off the table. "What did you do to me?"

"Come over here."

She followed him across the room to a tilted screen a meter above her head. He touched a sensor and she saw herself stretched on her stomach on the table. She saw the thin man make an incision in her back and insert a small oval object among the bared muscles, sew it in place with a few knots. He pulled the flap of skin over it and sewed that down, slathered on some greasy liquid, covered it with a gauze pad held in place with adhesive tape, an antique procedure that appalled her. The Ajin tapped the screen dark.

"Miniature thermit grenade," he said, "tied to this." He held up a blob of back plastic threaded on a chain, let it dangle in front of her a minute, then dropped the chain over his head. "You're safe as long as you stay less than a kilometer from me. And as long as I'm alive. If I'm killed while that's still in you, too bad. I won't be worrying about anything or anyone after I'm dead."

She pressed her lips together, hugged her arms across her chest.

He smiled lazily at her, calmly content with what he'd accomplished. "It'll come out as easy as it went in when your time's up."

"Oh, thanks," she murmured. "How kind."

His smile escalated into a chuckle. He was very pleased with himself. "Come along, singer. You've had a hard day. Time to rest."

She started after him, then remembered Linfyar. She stopped, looked around. "Where's Linfy?"

"What?" He stopped in the door, turned his head, impatience limned in face and body.

"The boy. My companion. He was here. Where is he?"

"Oh. The freak. He started acting up, so I had him hauled out. He's back in your rooms." He didn't wait for an answer but strolled out, knowing she'd follow.

She closed her hands into fists, looked around at the carefully blank faces of the surgeon and his assistants. Then she followed him. There was nothing else she could do.

Linfyar charged her and wrapped his arms about her in a desperate hug, nearly squeezing her in half. She freed herself, laughing, surprised and touched by the fervor of his greeting, glad the Ajin had delivered her to the door and left without coming inside, though not without locking her in.

After he satisfied himself she was intact, Linfyar backed off, still vibrating with a harrowing mix of emotions. "What'd he do, Shadow? What'd he do?"

"Creep was making sure I have to stick close to him." She hesitated, uncertain about what to say; he'd better know, for it colored everything she'd do from now on. She sighed and told him what the Ajin had done to her.

He went very quiet. Then he screamed, a harsh tearing yell whose only sense was in its sound, and started racing about the room in a frenzy, banging himself against the walls, the floor, anything that got in his way, shrieking obscenities and threats. She finally managed to catch and hold him, shocked by the strength of his slight body and the fury churning in it; it was as if all the things he'd let be done to him, all the tricks and little betrayals he'd used to stay alive, all the humiliations he'd suffered had come to a head at that moment, all that poison came spurting out of him. After a short struggle, he collapsed against her, muffling soft wails against her breasts, shaking all over, so hot he almost burned her arms as she held him tight to her, rocked him gently, until the shaking and the whimpering stopped. She held him awhile longer. held him until he pushed against her, wanting free.

When she saw his face she was startled in a way she hadn't expected. No tears. No signs left of his distress. Easy enough equation—no eyes meant no tearducts. Obvious. But she'd never thought of it, accepting him with as little understanding, almost, as the Ajin. She wrinkled her nose, watching him as he dug among the pillows on the divan and settled himself, hysteria passing like a summer storm, leaving little behind but a touch of weariness. He yawned, stretched, wriggled about, then demanded more details about the insert. "Let me feel it," he said. "I want to feel it."

Shadith stripped off her tunic and let him feel the bandage, but stopped him quickly when he wanted to peel off the gauze and dig out the bomb. "You'll blow us both up, imp. Besides, it hurts. I don't want you messing with it."

He darted around behind her and began feeling the bandage again. "I can do it, I know I can."

She scrambled away from him, caught up her tunic and pulled it over her head. "Hai-ya, imp, calm down, will you? I mean it—you try anything like that, and ka-boom, kid."

"But I want to help, Shadow."

"You are helping, Linfy."

"But I mean . . ." He broke off as she laid her hand gently on his mouth.

She took the hand away. "I know, Linfy. It's hard sitting around waiting like this with nothing to do but fret."

"What do you want me to do, Shadow?"

"Pay them no mind and sing when it's time." She switched languages, sang the next words as if they were a snatch of song: "I've got a plan, I think it can work, you know what I told you, he's alive and he's here. But it's gonna take time, my friend, and it's gonna take thinking and it's gonna take remembering we can't talk at all." She added a few more sounds, meaningless noises, and stopped singing.

Grinning, ears twitching, hands beating time on the pillows, Linfyar sang back to her: "Oh yes, we'll do it, we'll fool them like silly fish, oh yes, we'll do it, I understand now."

She held out her hand, smiled when he took it, said in common Avosinger, "Besides, we're getting good pay. Think about it, Linfy—five kilos of sweetamber and our passage to wherever we choose. Not bad, eh? Better than we usually get. So what's a little glitch in the working conditions? Like the man said, it'll come out as easy as it went in.''

''Oh yeah,'' Linfyar said; he slid off the divan, yawned and groaned as he worked his small body. He stuck his tongue out at her, danced away. ''Not like that other time when we got stranded and if we didn't stow away on that half-wit's half-dead ship we'd be there still.'' He giggled and dived past the velvet curtain into the bedroom.

Brows raised, she stared at the swaying curtain. *Wonder where he picked that up? Nine going on ninety, so help me.* She yawned. *Ai-iy, I'm beat. Linfy's right. Might as well sleep—there's nothing else to do.*

He was already asleep when she reached the bed, curled up in a small furry tangle of legs and arms. She nudged him over, stretched out beside him, lying on her stomach, her head on her arms. The anesthetic was wearing off and the middle of her back felt like a sore tooth; as the thought drifted through her mind, she giggled softly, drowsily. Odd place for a tooth. The giggle made her back muscles move and stirred the wound, so she stopped that and lay very still. A few breaths more and she was drifting into a dozing dream state.

Well, ancient child, you've landed yourself in a mess.

Old Po', what you know?

That you've got a bomb in your back. What are you going to do about that?

Get rid of it when I'm ready to.

How?

Why don't I leave that up to you? One of those spies you were talking about.

When?

Not for a while yet. Don't want to make our conquering hero feel insecure.

You saw your friends.

You knew about that obscenity?

How could I not?

You know about Kell?

''How could I not?* (feel of amusement) *Besides, you told me about the Hunters and the Vryhh the last time we spoke.*

My memory's a bit hazy, but I don't recall your saying anything about any of this then.

You went to sleep on me.

Plenty of time before. Well, it's done, no use wearing a rut in my head. Why don't you talk to me other times? When I'm awake.

Good question, oddling.

Which means you aren't going to answer it.

You got it.

What I'm getting is rotten jokes.

Hard to do good ones in someone else's language.

What are you?

What?

Should I say who?

It would be courteous of you to assume a who rather than a what.

You're the one invading a stranger's head. Not me.

Not because you didn't try.

One eensy time.

Mmm. Do you trust the Ajin to keep his word and take the bomb out?

Course not. What I expect he'll do, if he doesn't put me in that glop with Grey, he'll take me someplace, Angachi maybe, and shove me out when the flier's over two three kilometers off the sand so he can see me splatter when the bomb goes boom. Like he said, he's a careful man.

Ah, you softsiders, you busy little murderers. You'll be the death of me, ah weh, you will. Unless, unless you're part of me. Help me, ancient child, help me live, help Perolat and Tjepa, Awas and all the rest, stop this Sikin Ajin before he brings the bombs on us, the fire from the skies. Did you know, only a dozen others can talk with me like this—the rest hear me as siren song, a dream they long to find. Are there more like you out there, on those worlds beyond my reach?

(sleepy chuckle) *Not hardly, Old Po', but yes, a lot of folks with gifts like mine.*

You give me hope, ancient child, hope someday I can talk with all of my soft sides. If I have the time. Give me the time, little oddling.

Time for what? Are you any better than the Ajin, driving these folk for your needs not theirs, playing with them, breeding them like pets, sucking them into you?

The Ajin wants stasis, my oddling; what good would that do me? The Ajin wants slaves worshiping him; what good would slaves do me? Worship, what foolishness. I want friends to talk to, ancient child, my oddity. Is Perolat a slave? Dihann? Awas? Any of them? Not likely. What I want is time to bloom the latent powers budded in them. Make them more themselves, not less.

(sigh) *Don't sell so hard, Old Po'. Me, I've got no choice. But I sure wouldn't turn down a bit of help now and then.*

(vast relief) *I like you, ancient child. Before you leave perhaps you can find time to come visit me and we can talk without the pressure of time and need.*

*I'd like that. And, hey, call me Shadow. *Oddity* and *ancient child,* huh, I'm getting very tired of those.*

(warm amusement) *Go to sleep, little Shadow; I'll find you a surgeon, just call Old Po' when you're ready.*

Tikumul.

Grasslands stretching away on three sides, a low bank of clouds beyond the low coast range, white fleece against the blue of a vast sky soaring above a flat featureless land, a sky that filled the eyes and left little space for the endless shimmer of the grass.

The k'shun in the center of the village.

Dust everywhere, no clovermoss to keep it down.

Families, single men, shifting restlessly about, talking in small groups, killing time until the Ajin arrived. Children running about, shouting, chasing each other. Trucks ringing the k'shun, women setting out earthenware bowls on braced tailgates, chewy yellow gancha grain, meaty stews, fowl bits fried in batter, crisp stir-fried vegetables, steaming pitchers of spicy belas. Under the trucks, tubs of ice with kegs of beer, ale, and hard cider.

The women working at the trucks took time off now and then to gossip with friends they hadn't seen face to face for months, only on the com circuits, friends they wouldn't see again for more months.

A hay wagon in the middle of the k'shun. Someone had hung a painted tarp about the sides and set a truss of straw at one end. It waited.

The grasslanders waited with the same stolid patience.

The grasswinds blew golden whorls of pollen into the sky and let it fall again, covering everything and everyone with a misting of yellow that the sun turned to glittering gilt.

The Ajin arrived an hour late, greeted with shouts and laughter and much excitement. As he passed through the crowd to the wagon, mothers and fathers lifted their younger children to their shoulders so they could see the man who dared to rebel against the government. Shadith walked behind him with Linfyar trotting half a step ahead of her; she felt battered by the exuberance around her and wondered how much they were committed to him and how much he was simply entertainment, an excuse for this get-together. They took the minor risk of coming to hear him—would they take the major risk of fighting under his leadership? She began to understand more clearly the reason he'd spent so much time and effort on her. She was there to find the fervor in them and heat it up, to wake the anger in them and turn it to the Ajin's benefit. That thought was a sour taste in her mouth. She watched Linfyar scramble up onto the wagon bed, followed him, stepping from hub to tire to flat. *I can't do it . . . ah, no, why bother trying to fool myself? I'm here. I'm going to do what he tells me and hope I can finesse a little self-respect out of this mess.* A little forlornly she listened as the Ajin began speaking.

He was different out here, his weakness gilded over like the farmers' faces. He was a powerful speaker with an instinctive grasp of things that reached deep and moved his listeners. He spoke to them of home and children, of hard work, of savoring the fruits from that work. He spoke quietly at first, but built to passion, and for that moment at least he believed fervently in everything he said. Truth was raw in every word, and the grasslanders felt it; she felt them responding. It was almost funny—the slickest thief on Pajungg praising the virtues of hard work and meaning what he said with every fiber in his body. Like the mercenaries, he knew what he knew, but exempted himself from his strictures. She hunched her shoulders, hugged herself and felt miserable.

He roused that crowd until they were cheering, whistling, stamping, then quieted them, introduced Shadith and brought her forward. She settled herself on the straw and began playing the harp, starting quietly, as the Ajin had. There was a spark of recognition somewhere in the crowd; one or more had been in Dusta and heard her sing. Linfyar settled at her feet and eased his whistle into the flow of the music. She began singing, using a pattern poem she'd written during the week the Ajin gave her to let the incision heal, a song like the other croons in the ancient Shallal tongue. She was nervous; this was the first time she'd departed from memorized patterns, and she didn't know if it would work. For her soul's sake, she was trying in a subtle way to undercut what he was doing to these people.

Laughing with her, sharing her daring, her sisters danced among the golden whorls of pollen. The new song brought them even more intensely alive. She let herself relax and threw herself into the pattern, singing love of land and home, love for everything that ran on that land and flew in the air above it, love for their families and their neighbors, singing love of freedom and need for self-respect, reinforcing everything in them that made them sturdy, stubbornly independent, walking a tightrope as she struggled to satisfy herself and confuse the Ajin about what she was doing. Yet when she finished the pattern poem and saw the rapt faces, she was afraid of what she had done; she had tried to insulate them against him, but there was nothing precise about the patterns, not before and not now when she hadn't sufficient data to judge the responses. She settled back and watched the Ajin take them in his hands and work them back into a frenzy with hatred of the Colonial Authority and the fumbling ignorant homeworlders who tried to run Avosinger lives, then he switched keys and painted a warm golden picture of life after independence, finishing with a low-key call to follow him when the time was right.

His flier swooped down, hovered a handbreadth above the wagon bed until the Ajin and the rest of his party were inside, then it darted away.

Half an hour later church enforcers descended on the village, scuttled futilely about, irritating the folk there and winning more converts to the Ajin's cause than his speech and Shadith's croon.

In the days that followed, they zigzagged across the grasslands and the coastal savannas, touching down at town after small town. Seteramb. Simbelas. Debaua-ben. Perkunta. Windsweep. Sulata. Tobermin. Hatti-hti. Dubelas. Dabatang. Even Rhul and Rel just across the bay's mouth from Dusta. Stirring up the locals, skipping out ahead of angry and frustrated enforcers, sometimes with hours to spare, sometimes in a desperate scramble into the treetops where the enforcers feared to follow. Several times they returned to base, where the Ajin saw reports of the rising anger in the villages, the hardening opposition to the Colonial Authority. For the first time he was keeping hold of more than a tiny core of supporters. He began working harder, going farther and faster, pushing Shadith and Linfyar close to exhaustion, riding a stronger and stronger high. And by some peculiar twist of his psyche, he began seeing Shadith as a talisman, his good-luck charm. "You're my luck," he told her and stroked her head, missing the flare of anger in her eyes. "Soon, yes soon, the time comes soon."

She was afraid he was right and wondered how she could reconcile herself to her part in it. Toward the end of the third nineday, she'd had enough of exhaustion and self-loathing. She waved her hands in his face, showing him her battered fingertips. "No more," she said. "Listen to me, I'm croaking worse than an arthritic frog."

He smiled at her, patted her hands. "Magic little hands. Would a nineday do you, Fortune's Child?"

"It would help."

"It's yours." He chuckled. "I've work waiting for me that will more than fill the time. And it would be as well to let the church calm down. Don't want them yelling for help from home."

* * *

Shadith wandered unchecked through the base, speaking to no one, only waving and passing on when a technician or a mercenary called her name. She was Ajin's luck; none of them would dare touch her or stop her from going where she wanted. She stayed away from the Ajin as much as she could, though he liked to have her near so he could touch her. Nothing sexual in it, there was that small blessing, but she hated those careless pats and strokes. *I'll have a dozen ulcers before I'm through,* she thought, but kept a firm hold on her temper and said nothing. *A thumbstone, that's what I am, a bunch of worry-beads, a wela's foot to rub for luck. Bad enough, but, ah, if only he'd keep his fuckin mouth shut. He talks to me much more like I'm a halfwitted infant, I'm going to . . . oh god, I don't know. Damn. Damn. Damn. Grey's so close and there's no way I can think of to get to him.*

She thought up plan after plan, but nothing had a hope of working. Time pressed in on her. She had only these nine days to do something; after that he'd have her on campaign with him, then fighting his idiot war, and no way she'd have enough free time to think of some way to break this stalemate. Three out of the nine gone already, and her head felt like solid bone. Ear to ear. Linfyar kept out of her way. Slept most of the time. That irritated her, though she tried not to take her irritation out on him; it wasn't his fault she had a billiard ball for a head. Then there was the ultimate frustration. She could see half a hundred lines of attack—if she had still been inside the diadem and had the use of Aleytys's body and her talents. For a dozen years she'd helped Lee develop and hone those talents, and had had the use of them when her knowledge and training were needed. No more. Never again. *I boasted about my wits and my long training in survival. Hunh. Maybe the Ajin's right to treat me like a feeble-minded twit. Fourteen thousand years' experience. Still, most of that was spent gathering dust in that stinking RMoahl vault.*

The Ajin could get Grey and Ticutt out.

No one else.

I don't know what the trap is. He won't talk about that. (She'd tried getting him to show it to her, playing the pretty

250   *Jo Clayton*

child for him, but he'd only laughed at her and told her not to bother her little head about such things; that day he was very close to dying, but she bit her tongue and let him walk away.) *It's instinct. It has to be. He's not that smart. And I'm not that stupid. I'm not. And I'd feel it if he was suspicious. He's not. But he just slides away.*

How can I make him bring them back? I can't. No lever. Torture? Doubt if I could do it enough to make him talk. And he wouldn't give in to a child no matter how much he hurt. To a girl child. Taggert. Worms eat your pea brain, where are you? Drugs? Maybe Old Po' could help with that. What do I want? Something that would make him babble, get past his defenses. Damn, I'm no biotech, even if I got enough blood and cells to run tests on. High up in the shadow government on Pajungg, hunh, he's probably protected every way possible from folks trying to make him talk. Still, it's a thought. And the only one that has any chance of working.

By the time the fourth day neared its end she was ready to explode from frustration. He wouldn't let her out of his sight, even made her sleep in his quarters. "Tomorrow's an important day," he said and passed a caressing hand over her wild tangle of brown-gold curls, then touched her nose and pulled an ear. "I want my luck close to me."

She paced the room he put her in ("I'm locking you in," he said, "it's for your protection, child of fortune, there are traps and alarms all about this place, I don't want you hurting yourself"); for one hour then another she charged about that room trying to work off the jags of anger and fear and frustration that wouldn't let her relax enough to sleep. The more she tried the angrier she got; the Po' Annutj couldn't talk to her when her mind was tense, she had to be tired, and it was best when she was half asleep. But she couldn't sleep. When her body was exhausted, she lay down on the bed and spent more hours staring at the ceiling she couldn't see in the thick darkness that came when she turned the lights out. Finally she crawled under the covers and tried blanking out her mind. She concentrated fiercely on it, so fiercely that before she knew it, she was fathoms deep in sleep.

          *   *   *

A hand touched her shoulder, shook her gently. She came swimming back to awareness, lay blinking up at the beautiful empty face of the woman bending over her. One of the Ajin's concubines; her brain was too stuffed at the moment to remember the woman's name. Didn't matter. What mattered was getting in touch with Old Po'. When she saw Shadith was awake, the woman bowed slightly, then left.

Shadith pushed up, feeling as tired as she had when she lay down last night. She scrubbed a hand across her face, rubbed at her eyes. A breakfast tray on the bedtable. The smell of eggs and toast nauseated her. She got up and stumbled to the fresher, splashed cold water on her face, then spent some minutes staring numbly at her reflection in the mirror. Dark blotches under her eyes, teeth like moldy tombstones. She inspected her tongue. Finest thing in fur coats. At least with a hangover she'd have had some fun to remember, but this . . . With a groan filled with weariness and more than a little self-pity, she pushed away from the basin and stumbled into the shower. With hot water beating on her back and steam cleaning out her head she began to feel like just maybe she wanted to live.

She rubbed herself dry and wandered back into the bedroom. Her tunic and trousers were gone, in their place one of the soft white robes the Ajin kept trying to make her wear. Which she kept tossing out, wearing her own clothes instead. *Wanted to make sure of me today*, she thought. *Prickheaded idiot, I bet that's why he kept me here. Making sure I'd have nothing else to wear this once*. She pulled on the robe, went and looked at herself in the door mirror. *Isn't that too too sweet*. She hesitated, thought about making a fuss and insisting once again on her own clothes, but she simply didn't have the energy. She went back to the bedtable, took the covers off the food and stood staring at it, then she sighed again, pulled up a low stool and began eating her breakfast.

"Three men are coming to try selling me their goods. I want you to tell me which of them I should trust. And which might be spies hired by the Pajunggs or junk dealers who sell rotten wares."

"What makes you think I'd know?" She asked that with a cold knot tightening in her stomach.

"You've got a good ear for sham and fakery—you saw through mine soon enough."

"Well, why do you think I'd tell you if I spotted something wrong? I'm not exactly fond of you, you know that."

"Ah, but you're my luck, you can't help yourself. Besides"—he smiled that lazy complacent smile that always made her want to bite him—"you have a strong interest in keeping me alive."

"So I do."

"Well then, keep your eyes and ears busy, Fortune's Child." he wrapped one of her curls about a finger, then slid it off again, a gesture that could have been intimate and affectionate but wasn't; she was the thumbstone again, the talisman whose touch brought luck. She pulled away and settled herself on the hassock by his desk.

He laughed and tapped a sensor. "Send Harmon in."

Harmon was a little wizened man, a few strands of no-colored hair combed across a freckled dome. He fingered his sleeve cuffs after he settled himself in the client chair. Plastic slivers in his cuffs with compressed-air bulbs to spit them out. Some fairly potent poison on them, no doubt. That went with the cold malice pouring out of him. He wouldn't go anywhere completely unarmed; he had to have his poison sting. He slipped a flake from a slit in his cuff, tossed it onto the desk. "A summary of what I can offer that is immediately available. Numbers and quality of all items are indicated, along with the possibilities of resupply in case of need. More exotic weapons are available on special order. They will, of course, take longer to procure."

Gunrunners, Shadith thought. *My god, he's ready to go.* She watched as the Ajin slipped the flake into a player and projected it against the wall. A catalogue of hand weapons, energy and projectile. Tactical nuclear weapons and delivery systems. Conventional explosives. More delivery systems. An assortment of poisons, disease vectors, gases, mechanical traps, mines, implants for personnel control, illustration of the use of a human bomb, tangler fields, plasticuffs, a wearying list of similar items with an exhaustive description of uses and capabilities. A final section with costs and delivery times.

The Ajin withdrew the flake and set it on the desk in front of him. "Most impressive. I'll let you have my decision by tomorrow noon. If that's agreeable?"

Harmon got to his feet. "No later, if you please. You'll understand I do not like to linger away from my ship." With a short jerky bow he left.

The Ajin picked up the flake, ran his forefinger around the outside, a dreamy look on his face. He set it down again, turned to Shadith. "Well?"

"What can I tell you that you didn't see for yourself?" She moved her shoulders impatiently. "A weasel. Running just a bit scared. Probably won't last much longer in this game. I'd say his goods would be as advertised, though not prime quality of their kind, and you might have trouble with resupply. Against that, you can probably get more from him for a lower price than you could from a more secure dealer. Depends on what you want."

He laughed and ruffled her hair. "Ajin's luck," he said, touched the sensor again. "Send in Sapato."

Sapato was a genial golden man, a deep smooth tan, laugh lines radiating from the corners of soft chocolate-brown eyes. Easy laughter, the motions of gregarious fellowship, but everything he said or did was just a little off. After he'd chatted with the Ajin for a short while, she decided she didn't need to be an empath to be careful of this one. With a smile just a trifle too confident he tossed his flake onto the desk and sat back as the Ajin inserted it in the player.

Shadith watched it for a few beats, then went back to studying the man; there was something about him, she couldn't quite put her finger on it . . . until she glanced from him to the Ajin and back. She nodded to herself. Didn't matter what she said, this one had lost his sale. The two men were too much alike to tolerate each other. A lot of repressed hostility behind those easy smiles. Sapato was a less successful version of the Ajin, something he picked up as a subliminal message that left him angry and nervous, though he worked hard to keep it from showing. And the Ajin saw the man he might

have been if circumstances had been only slightly different;
like the runner he wasn't conscious of that. She watched them
both, nodded to herself. In a way Sapato was also a forecast
of what the future held for the Ajin if his revolution failed and
he survived it. She glanced at the screen, listened as a traped
voice described the use of the weapon pictured, a multishot
rifle with exploding pellets, then presented demonstrations of
the rifle's speed and accuracy and stopping power on everything from a charging man to an angry changrain hornbeast.
Sapato's was a far more thorough and effective presentation
than Harmon's, showing the weapons in action as well as
describing their specs. Gunrunners had the most dangerous
profession in known space; instant death if any government
caught them. No trial, not even a farcical one. Worse if they
were caught inside Company territory. Profits were enormous, of course, but the field was a small one, its members
constantly changing as luck ran out for old ones and newcom-
ers took their places. It was a tribute to the rarity and worth
of sweetamber that the Ajin had attracted three of them and
managed to get them bidding against each other. She glanced
at the screen, shuddered. A reenactment of an actual battle,
the fighters and eventual corpses provided by contract-labor
bosses, according to the narration. *I'd like to turn Lee loose
on those*, she thought, then suppressed a sigh. Just like the
runners, take one boss out and a dozen more would pop up
fighting to replace him.

The Ajin slipped the flake out and set it on the desk.
"Most impressive," he said. "I'll let you have my decision
by tomorrow noon. If that's agreeable?"

Spato got to his feet, waved a hand in an airy dismissing
gesture. "Take what time you need. You won't find better
than that." He sauntered out.

The Ajin scowled at the flake, pushed it away from him
with the tip of his finger. "Well?"

"Full of himself, isn't he?"

"Very."

"I'd say he runs a tight business, you'd get prime goods
for your coin, resupply's probably fast and accurate. It'll cost
you top price and maybe more. And he'll have enemies. That

could complicate everything, might even have repercussions back here. A dangerous man, a little unstable, a very bad enemy. Definitely what he says he is—that's no Pajungg spy or tricky swindler.''

''Right.'' He touched the sensor. ''Send in Colgar.''

Taggert! She caught back a gasp, concentrated on breathing steadily, her eyes on the floor. *So that's where he's been. Setting up background. It'll be deep and solid.* She chanced another look that made her wonder how she'd recognized him so swiftly. The thick head of white hair was gone, his skull polished to a high gleam. He looked hard and gray and mean, a statue cast from metacrete. Nothing left of the smiling man who liked children and could sit for hours with his own, making up fantastic tales to amuse them. This man was dangerous as an ancient blade quenched in the blood of thousands. Dangerous to her too, though he didn't know it. He'd have to act fast, taking the Ajin out at the first opportunity. His time here was strictly limited. *Damn! If only I knew where and what that trap was, I could warn him about it. Maybe he'll be lucky. Hunh. His good luck is my bad.* If he killed the Ajin or hauled him off to Dusta, that meant a very messy and altogether premature end to her tenure in this body, an appalling waste of healthy flesh. While she was resigned to dying eventually as this body wore out, she wanted to put that eventuality off as long as possible, meaning to celebrate a lively old age. What a bind. She glanced at the projection. First cousin to Sapato's, same slick presentation, same blood and gore. *Gah, Taggert, how could you. Don't be silly, Shadow, he's doing his job. Time you did yours.*

The flake finished its run; the Ajin slipped it from the player and set it beside the other two. ''Most impressive. I'll let you have my decision by noon tomorrow. If that's agreeable?''

Colgar/Taggert got to his feet, gave the Ajin a grudging nod and walked out with the lithe, noiseless stalk of a hunting cat.

The Ajin leaned back in his chair, smiling. ''Well, Fortune's Child, what do you think of that one?''

''If you cut at him, he'd dull the knife. Got the charisma of a rock, probably as efficient as they come, good merchandise, top price, no bargaining, take his offer or leave it and goodbye to you. Not a man to like or dislike, use him like a machine, won't trick you, won't give you a speck of dust you don't pay for. What else he is, god knows, I don't.'' She waited to see how he'd react, feeling reasonably secure; he'd shown no signs before that he was particularly adept at reading behind her smiles.

He played with the flakes, pushing them about. "Which one, Child of Fortune, which one shall I buy from?''

She was suddenly confronted by temptation almost too powerful to resist. *Tell him to stay away from Taggert, send him away immediately, save my life. No, I can't. Might be a death sentence for him. God!* She gazed up at Ajin. *Worms eat your miserable soul.* Aloud, she said, "I can't tell you that.'' She sucked in a long breath, let it explode out. "I won't.''

He bent over and stroked her head. "Little luck . . .''

She jerked away, got to her feet with some difficulty, cursing under her breath at the narrow robe that hobbled her movements. "Look,'' she said when she was steady again, beyond the reach of his hand, "I'm a singer, that's what I know. I don't know shit about that stuff.'' She waved her hand at the desk and the flakes.

He stiffened. "You will not use that kind of language, child.'' It was an order, his heavy teasing banished as he moved around the desk and came to loom over him. "Do you hear me?''

She shivered, forced herself to lower her eyes. "I hear you.''

He cupped his hand under her chin, lifted her head. He was smiling again, the stern father banished. "Little luck, you have to be perfect, don't you see?'' He drew the back of his hand along the side of her face, then stroked the tip of his forefinger along her mouth. "You have a great destiny, dreamsinger.'' He took hold of her shoulders, turned her around, guided her to the door. "Go back to your quarters, Fortune's Child, and think about what I said.''

*   *   *

She palmed her door open and went inside. Linfyar was curled up on the divan, sleeping again. She sighed, ripped off the white robe and threw it on the floor, strode through the bedroom into the fresher. With barely controlled violence, she twisted on the water, yelped as she scalded her arm and hastily adjusted the temperature. She stepped in, folded her arms on the tiles, rested her forehead on them and let the water beat on her back. *My god.* She banged her head against her arms. *My god. What a mess. That creep. That curreep. You have to be perfect. My god. Little luck. I'm going to throw up if he doesn't stop that. You have a destiny. Yeeuch.* She shivered all over, shut the water off and started soaping her body, scrubbing at herself vigorously until she began to feel clean again. She rinsed the soap off, stood letting the water beat down on her some more until the heat melted the tension in her muscles and left her feeling limp. She rubbed herself dry, wrapped the toweling robe about her, went into the bedroom and threw herself on the bed; the hard night finally catching up with her, she drifted into a doze.

Well, Shadow, interesting developments.

Hello, Old Po'. Tried to get through to you last night.

Beat yourself, didn't you?

I know. Too well, I know. Listen, what I need from you, it's even more urgent now, I need something that'll knock out the Ajin's defenses, make him babble, or maybe make him suggestible enough that he'll do what I tell him even though he knows it's dangerous for him. Can you do that? I mean, do you have some sort of juice that will do that?

No, Shadow. I'm sorry, but . . . no.

Shit. All that funny dust and there's nothing like what I want?

Shadow, remember, the Avosingers have been here only a few hundred years. There's been no systematic study of the plants here; the foresters have stumbled on a few things, the grasslanders, but it's been trial and error and mostly error.

But you . . .

Me? I have capacity but almost no experience. Shadow, I didn't even know what writing was before you soft sides came. Have you any idea how strange and marvelous and exciting I find that controlled and directed curiosity of your kind? I'm sorry (sad and rueful self-mockery), come back in a few hundred years and I'll supply you with whatever you need. Now . . . (sense of massive shoulders shrugging)

Hunh. That about sinks my only plan. Taggert's here.

Your friend.

One of them.

He'll act against the Ajin.

Right.

Then you'd better get that thing out of your back.

I had thought of that. Yes.

Best not wait any longer than you have to. You've been fidgety as a nervous flea the past few days. No one would take much notice if you went wandering around the lake.

"Haven't before. Ummm. Might be a new problem. Ajin's got plans for me; they might include notions of keeping me pure. So to speak.*

And he knows you're virgin.

Huh?

He had the surgeon examine you after he tucked that grenade in your back.

Creepy bastard. Eckh. If I bit him, I'd probably poison myself.

No doubt. He's quite pleased at how you keep yourself apart from the other men here. One of the reasons you've had so much freedom this time. You don't have to worry about him for a while yet.

That's comforting. All right. I can probably get loose and stay loose for a while. What then?

There's a sourberry vine by a stand of jemara trees on the south side of the lake, near where it comes to a point. You brought in a spray of its flowers two days ago.

Yes. I know the one you mean. Flowers didn't last.

Isn't a house plant. Inside the grove you'll find a small glade, clovermoss growing thick there. By the time you get there it should be mostly sunny, very pleasant. Quite private. Parrak will be waiting for you.

Parrak?

He tended you before.

Oh. Him. Good enough. He'll do the cutting?

Yes. You can trust him—he trained as a doctor before he came to me.

Nice to know. Ah, what a load off, getting that thing out of me. But it means I go after the Ajin tonight. (shudder passing along her body) You never said—have you any idea how that trap works?

None, I'm afraid. Shadow, be careful. I've gotten quite fond of you and I'd hate to see you hurt.

That's two of us. Umm. If everything falls apart and Taggert and me, we have to run, swat anything that comes after us, will you?

With all I've got. You'd better start waking now, Shadow.

Yes. See you later, Old Po'.

Later. . . .

She came out the door, sauntered casually past the squatting guard and made her way to the water's edge; she climbed over a flow of rocks, circled another tumble of detritus, stopped as she heard voices. Manjestau and the Ajin. She dropped onto a boulder and sat listening.

". . . had to cut off the input; those vibrators scrambled everything so badly the receptors were heating up, going to burn out if I left them in circuit much longer. Luck knows what they're getting up to in here."

"I need them, Manjau, can't rub them wrong until the bargain's made. Look, it's only till tomorrow, then they'll be gone. Once they're settled in for the night, put guards on the fliers and on the door to the guesthouse. Only one way in or out, and no windows; that should keep them honest."

"Talto's in from Rhul, he says the Authority has put a squad of enforcers in the Rumjat, says the pollen scares them into staying half drunk and they're starting to mess with the women, but you'd better talk with him yourself, it might be worth taking a chance. . . ." Manjestau's voice began to fade as the two men walked off, heading back to the main building.

Shadith kicked at the boulder and grinned at the bright blue water smooth and glassy as a mirror on this warm quiet afternoon. Clouds were beginning to gather overhead, but as yet they blocked very little of the hot glare of the sun. *What a giggle. The only place in this whole damn base where I can talk without the Ajin's voyeurs watching me is the room of the man who's come to kill or kidnap him. Well, Old Po', hope you're enjoying that little irony as much as I am.* She slid off the rock and began rambling toward southpoint.

Perrak spread a white cloth on the clovermoss and began setting out his instruments. "Get that tunic off and stretch out on the moss." He bathed his hands in a liquid from a rubbery gourd, spread some on her back and felt about with quick light touches of his fingertips. "Going to give you a local," he said. "The thing's not in deep—I can feel the lump under the skin. You must sleep on your stomach these days."

"Umm."

"This won't hurt." She felt a small sting, then for the first time in days lost her awareness of the lump in her back. She almost went to sleep as he worked, tension she hadn't been aware of draining from her. Death coming out of her body, control of her life coming into her own hands once again. *Never again,* she thought, *never again will I let someone do something like this to me. Never. Never. Nev . . .* Perrak interrupted the flow of thought. "It's out. I'm going to put some stitches in your back. Don't worry about having them out later. There's a plant in the forest that provides a tough fiber I've used before in things like this. It'll gradually be absorbed into the body without marking it." A low chuckle. "I'm sure you remember the salve I used on you before. I've got a tin of it for you. Have your furry friend put more on each morning." He picked up a rectangle of flesh-colored plastic and pressed it down on her back. "Don't take a shower for a day or two. This is going to hurt some when the local wears off; the salve will help a little, but it won't kill all the pain, you'll just have to live with it until you heal. If you can avoid it, don't go jumping about much the next few days—don't want to tear the stitches loose. The wound's in a nice place, though. Not too many pulls there unless you try weight-lifting. Where's your tunic? Ah. Here. Put it on. Appreciate it if you amble about more before you go in, give me time to get this stuff packed and hid and take myself somewhere else. Mind?''

She smoothed the tunic down, laughed as he helped her to her feet. ''Say hello to Old Po'. It's a grand day for a walk, isn't it? Did I thank you, no, well I do. Believe me, I do.''

He looked at the bloody grenade resting in a shallow dish. ''Like to make him eat it.''

''A lovely thought. See you.'' She waved and went into the shadow under the trees, feeling light-headed and rubber-kneed and altogether delighted with the day.

Around midnight.

Shadith woke from a heavy sleep, sat up, winced as the movement pulled at the stitches Perrak had put in her back. She moved her shoulders. No big problem. She knew the cut was there, but it wouldn't slow her down if she had to run or fight. She frowned at Linfyar, limply asleep beside her. *Better not get separated. If we have to run, I want no hostages left behind.* She shook him awake, whispered in his hometongue, ''Get up and get dressed, Linfy, we're going visiting.''

She glanced at the night-forest image on the screen, sniffed with contempt and slid off the bed; she was taking a chance that whoever was supposed to be watching them had gotten so bored he didn't bother anymore. Wasn't much of a chance; except under the Ajin's eye, discipline in the base was a joke. Besides, all the time she'd been here, she'd done nothing in these rooms but eat and sleep, read and fool about with her harp. She dressed quickly in the black sweater, vest and trousers Aleytys had found for her, checked the pockets in the vest. Lockpicks, a couple of hollowed-out coins that fit together and made a rapid-play probe for electronic locks, a long plastic blade with an edge that could cut a thought in half, a harpstring with wooden grips at each end. She found the tin of salve that Perrak had given her, slipped it in the pocket with the garrote, dropped to her knees and pulled her backpack from under the bed. Its stiffening ribs were thin but

strong metal tubes about as big around as her little finger.
One was nothing but a tube with one end finely threaded; two
others came apart into compressed-air cylinders that screwed
onto the tube to make a simple but efficient airgun; the fourth
held a dozen small darts, crystallized sova that dissolved into
the target's flesh and put him to sleep. It worked slowly, took
ten to fifteen minutes to put the target under, but it left no
trace in the blood and the slow action meant that the victims
of the darts usually didn't connect the tiny sting they made
with what happened later. She slid the tubes into the vest
pockets constructed to hold them, got to her feet and looked
around. Unless her luck turned really sour, this was the last
time she'd see this room. She regretted having to leave the
harp behind, but a harp was a lot easier to replace than a
friend or her life.

The guard at the entrance to the main building was taking a
leak against the wall and staring dreamily at nothing. They
slipped into the dark, overcast night without disturbing him
and worked their way silently among the rockfalls to the
isolated guesthouse.

The guard at the guesthouse was more alert; if the runners
got out and made mischief, it was his skin and he knew it. He
walked back and forth in front of the door with a dedication
that made her grimace. She moved her head close to Linfyar's
ear, breathed, "Wait here; should be about time for a guard
change." She pushed on his shoulder, went down with him.
"Keep flat till I get back. Might be a while." She assembled
the airgun, slipped in one of the darts, then crawled carefully
forward until she had a clear view of the guard. With the
patience of a cat, she watched him pace back and forth, back
and forth, dull steady trudging. *Got the brains of a slug, tell
him to do it, he does it till you tell him go away.* Ah for a
nice imaginative man, someone with intelliegnce enough to
get bored, someone convinced of the stupidity of all this.
Time dragged by on feet as leaden as the guard's. Back and
forth, back and forth.

Footsteps, quick and crisp, coming along the path. The
sentry lifted his rifle, waited.

" 'S me, Bigo, Jambi the goat, got to crawl out of a warm bed and warmer arms to watch a rock grow."

Bigo grunted and went stumping off.

Jambi shifted restlessly about. After a minute he shrugged, yawned, started swinging his arms.

The airgun made the faintest chuff. A second later Jambi winced, slapped at his neck; she was close enough to hear him curse the lake midges. She smiled and settled herself to wait some more.

A soft brushing sound. Shadith lifted her head.

The guard lay crumpled in a heap in front of the door. She scowled at him. *First you bang me on the the head, fool, now you haven't the sense to get out of my way.* She eased another dart into the gun, went back for Linfyar.

The corridor inside the guesthouse was dimly lit and deathly quiet. She stopped at the first door, *reached* in and felt at the sleeper inside. Harmon. Next door. Taggert. Awake and alert. She tapped the announcer.

A growly voice thick with sleep answered her. "Who is it and what you want?"

She grinned into the shadows. "An old acquaintance come to talk."

The door slid open. Taggert bowed her in. "You show up in the strangest places, young Shadow." He looked past her, shut the door behind Linfyar. "You and your friend."

"Don't we all. Got some things to tell you."

"Thought you might." He settled in one of the chairs, waved at the divan.

"Grey and Ticutt are alive. I've seen them."

"Ah."

"It's tricky. They're hanging in some kind of bubble universe, no way to get to them unless we get sucked in too." She smiled at the look on his face. "Don't need to go that far. Ajin can get them back. He told me. Just needs persuading." She grimaced. "By a man. I could take the skin off him a strip at a time and he wouldn't say boo."

"Any idea what the trap is?"

"He wouldn't tell me, the slippery fool. Here's a giggle,

Tag—I'm his talisman, his lucky charm. He rubs my head and expects the world to drop in his lap.''

"From what I hear, it is."

"He's riding high, all right. Tag, can you move tonight? Look, I'm pretty sure he's going to buy from you; he was after me to pick his supplier, but I wouldn't then. I can let him push me into doing it in the morning if you want, give you a way back in. So you don't have to jump tonight, but, Tag, I have to tell you, you'll not get a better chance."

He got to his feet, went into the bedroom, came out with a slim metal case. "Take a look." He touched his thumb to the lock, turned back the top. "Figured I might have to ask some hard questions."

She touched the woven metal cap, wiped her hand down her side. "A psychprob. They're really getting the size down. I suppose it operates from local power. Hunh. I thought Wei-Chu and Co kept those close to home."

"One of the advantages of being a runner, Shadow. You get access to all sorts of interesting things." He smiled. "And no need to explain them to anyone. Salesman's samples."

"Devious. Hmmm. One of the Chus used something like that on Aleytys once. A lot bigger, though. She blew it to blue smoke and cinders."

"Ajin's not Aleytys."

"Not even close. Tonight then?"

"No use sitting around watching the walls erode." He set a tablet and a stylus on the table. "Give me some idea how this place is set up."

She pulled a chair to the table, bent over the tablet. "Landing pad here. They stick the fliers in under the trees. Camouflaged sheds there and there. Manjestau, number two boy, he's put guards on the sheds, but I know about where they'll be—we shouldn't have any trouble with them. Here. Here. And here. Won't be changing again until dawn. Here's where we are. Guard here. Got him with the airgun and a sova dart. He's out for at least four hours. I snugged him against the wall with his rifle on his knees. He'll be more concerned with covering his ass when he wakes than he will be with what he's supposed to be guarding. Main building here, you were

there this morning, no, I suppose it was yesterday morning.
Guard here. Have to take him out. If he's not already curled
up sleeping. Here's the command center. Got some kreopine
and detonators in those samples of yours? The more confusion we can leave behind us . . . right, I'm teaching a silvercoat
to smell blood. That's the barracks, but we don't have to
worry about that, it's shut off from the offices, has a separate
entrance. There are the technicians' quarters. The brothel.
Down the other end, here, that's where the mountain starts;
so many wormholes in it, it'd look like goat cheese if you cut it
open. I don't know where half of them lead; I expect the Ajin
doesn't either. This is where he put me. Around this twist and
up a little higher, that's where he has his cozy little hole. No
guards anywhere around there. He likes his privacy. During
the day he brings in one of his women to clean the place and
cook for him . . . umm.'' She tore the page off, pushed it
along the table to him, began on the second. ''Kitchen here,
study here. I'm the only one he's ever taken in there, not even
Manjestau. He tells me his plans, strokes my head like I'm
some fuckin dog—hah! Forget that; I get a little hostile when
I think about how . . . Anyway, he likes to boast of trapping
two Wolff Hunters, I don't know how many times he's told
me he'd do the same to anyone who crossed him, and how
he's like brothers with a Vryhh master designer who built all
this for him and comes when he waggles a finger. Where was
I? Right. This is the room where his woman sleeps if he
keeps her overnight. Locks her in when he leaves her, I
expect. Did it to me when I stayed there. Sitting room. And
that's his bedroom. Nobody but him goes in there. Ever.
That's where this gets sticky. The portal to the pocket universe has got to be in there. Nowhere else it could be. One
way or another, I've got in just about everywhere. No sign of
any funny business. Umm. I forgot. Here's where he goes
when he wants to see Grey and Ticutt or show them off as
sorry warnings to anyone who might want to jump him.
Ordinary sort of lock on the door. I got in without any fuss.''

"Risky."

She put the stylus down, rubbed at the back of her neck.
"Not really, Tag. Technicians were used to me snooping

about, Ajin thought I was just being female, so that was covered. A chance I might get sucked in, but I figured it wasn't likely. Seems to me either he keeps the portal's trigger on him, say it's small enough, or like I said, it's set up in his bedroom.'' She leaned over and tapped the sketch in front of him. ''The machinery that works the thing, that's here.'' She straightened. ''I thought about lifting kreopine or something like it from the arsenal . . . um . . . forgot about that, that's around on the other side of the lake. Anyway, I thought about blowing up that bit of engineering, but there was too much chance that would strand Grey and Ticutt where they were. Which doesn't look like a very good place to spend eternity. Or whatever.'' She tapped her fingers on the table. ''Our problem tonight is getting at the Ajin. I don't feel happy about going into that bedroom.'' She shivered, scratched at the back of her hand, the side of her neck. ''Makes my skin itch.''

She sat frowning at the spidery sketches with the scrawled words dotted over them; after a minute he smoothed a big hand over his polished head, pushed his chair back and went into the bedroom. She heard him moving about in there, heard some scrapes and squeals, a thump or two, then he pushed past the drape carrying two heavy cases. He set them on the table, thumbed the locks open and lifted the lids. ''Come take a look.''

What a relief it was just to be herself without the complications of sex and rigid gender roles. With a rush of pleasure and gratitude, she went to stand beside him, looking down at the neatly racked weapons in the cases, rifles of several sorts, handguns, a dozen dark small grenades. Understanding finally just how cramping the Ajin's mindset had been. Except for a few times when he was particularly obtuse and offensive she'd gotten so used to being annoyed it was like having a low-grade fever. As with a fever, she made allowances and lived at a lower rate, forgetting what being healthy felt like. Until Taggert blew in and blew away her blinders, reminding her what it was to be treated as a reasoning and responsible adult.

Taggert unclipped a fat-butted laser pistol. ''Waste of time,

all this. Didn't even make me open the cases." He twisted
the gun apart. A shell. With fiber packing. He stripped the
packing away, set the items on the table beside the case.
"Tanglers. Shock grenades. Sleep gas." He popped one of
the rifles, cleaned off two thick rods about the length of his
forearm. "Extensible claws. Hunch to bring them paid off. I
like that bedroom about as much as you." He lifted one of the
rods, tapped the end. It expanded in half a breath until it was
stretching across the room. Another tap and curved claws
spread from the end. He clicked them against the door,
twisted the end. The pole collapsed as rapidly as it'd expanded. "What do you think? Stand in the doorway, don't set
foot in that room, toss in one of the sleep-gas canisters, pull
the covers off him with a claw, make sure of him with a
tangler, use a couple of the claws to haul him out of there.
Doesn't matter if we damage him a bit—Pajunggs won't
mind. Me either, as long as he can still talk." His pale blue
eyes narrowed to slits, his long, off-center nose twitched, he
grinned at her.

"I think you're absolutely wonderful, oh man." Giggling,
she dropped into a deep curtsy. "I worship at your shrine."

"Snip."

"Hush, you." She looked at the case. "What else you got
in there?"

With a rumbling chuckle, big hands moving swiftly and
surely, he assembled a multiphasic probe and lockpick, assorted alarm sensors and overrides. The Compleat Burglar Kit
guaranteed to get the possessor into most places he had no
business being.

Taggert glanced at the readout cupped in his palm, thrust
out his other hand. Shadith stopped Linfyar, shifted her grip
on the psychprobe's case, watched Taggert dig out one of the
overrides. He set the squat cylinder in the center of the
tunnel, eased back and stood waiting, his eyes on the readout.

Linfyar curled up his ears and pressed himself against
Shadith.

Taggert began pacing back and forth, watching the light
bead hop about on the face of the readout. After a tense few

mintues, he walked back to Shadith. "Too much," he muttered. "Ajin's got that hole covered like an arkoutch expecting a cold winter.

"What's the problem?"

"Field isn't wide enough."

"Two?"

"Can't. They'd cancel. Maybe we'd better."

"Cancel? No." She went silent, frowning at the cylinder, trying to remember all she knew about that sort of override. Pulsed subsonics. Supposed to overwhelm the alarm, confuse it, keep it too occupied with what was happening to its own circuits to notice the sound patterns it was supposed to listen for. Obsolete alarm system, too easily countered. Couldn't be Kell's work. Must be something the Ajin had bought for himself. Got cheated too. Or maybe not. "All this stone?"

"Could be."

"Mmm. Linfy."

He stirred against her.

"I know it hurts your ears, but do you think you can listen to that thing, then make the same kind of pulses, only louder? Well, louder to you—we don't hear them."

His mouth shifted through many shapes, his ears unfurled a little. He moved few steps away from her and stood poised like a deer on the verge of flight. He stood like that, ears full out, body quivering, one moment, two. Then he flashed a grin at her. He nodded, opened his mouth. His throat began to quiver like a bird in full song.

Taggert glanced at the bead, lifted his brows, then nodded to Shadith and started walking down the tunnel.

Shadith followed slowly, supporting Linfyar with one arm, clutching the probe case with the other, slowly slowly along the dark tunnel diving into the mountain's rock, moist with seepage, thick with cold musty smells, slowly slowly, every scrape a thunder in her ears, slowly slowly, Linfyar straining, shaking, draining himself into the pulsing subsonics, slowly slowly, Taggert stalking ahead of them, his eyes on the light bead, laying another override, Linfyar struggling to hold the match, fitting himself into the pulses as subtly as he fit his whistles into her croons.

The door to the Ajin's room. Ponderous. Laminated plasmeta. Complex internal lock. Shadith stretched out her mind-rider senses, felt for the Ajin, found him, a ghostly touch, just enough to recognize him. As far as she could tell (he was at the limit of her perceptions), he was sleeping, sunk in the slough between dream states. Taggert knelt by the lock, examined its external parts without touching them, then eased the electronic lockpick over it. He sat on his heels and waited.

The pick flashed through families of settings.

Linfyar's fingers dug into Shadith's arm, and he sagged heavily against her, but he kept the pulses surging out of his reedy throat.

The door started sliding open.

Taggert snatched off his pick and stepped inside, alert, ready to counter anything set to jump him, though Shadith had told him the Ajin didn't trust any of his men enough to leave them loose in those rooms, preferring to guard himself with more incorruptible mechanicals.

Shadith half-lifted Linfyar into the room as the door begain sliding shut. When she let go, he coughed and dropped in a heap; she set the probe case down, knelt beside him, rested his head and shoulders against her thigh. "You all right?"

He massaged his throat, managed a weak grin, amplified it with a nod that made a soft brushing sound on the black cloth of her trousers. He didn't try to speak. She could feel his fierce pride. They wouldn't be here without him, and he knew it.

Shadith tapped his nose. "Yeah, you're doing fine, eh, imp?"

He nodded again, pushed away from her, using her shoulder as a prop to help him get back on his feet. With a little shake of his body he brushed away fatigue and stood with ears twitching, waiting for what happened next with the exuberant anticipation he maintained in spite of all hardship.

She laughed softly, got to her feet. "Wait here if you want, Linfy. This shouldn't take long now."

He produced a faint scornful hiss and moved to join Taggert, who'd been prowling about the room watching the bead dance in his readout. When Shadith came over to him he murmured, "Dampers in the wall. No hand weapons will work in here." He smiled at her, his pale blue eyes shining with a gentle amusement. "Just as well we didn't bring any. He always leave the lights on?"

"Not in the bedrooms, but out here?" She shrugged. "I suppose. The one night I spent here, I didn't go exploring."

"Right. Which way to the bedroom?"

Shadith started past him, but he caught her shoulder, stopped her. "Together. In case of surprises."

With Taggert keeping a close eye on the readout and Linfyar coming close behind, Shadith led them to the door into the Ajin's bedroom. No alarms, more dampers in the walls, some weapons, but they lay quiet; whatever the three of them were doing, it wasn't enough to trip their triggers. Behind his locked door the Ajin slept the sleep of the just man he knew himself to be, serenely trusting in the gadgets he'd installed to ensure his security, undisturbed by what was happening around him. Shadith found she was looking forward to seeing his consternation when he discovered he'd been trapped by the girl child he thought he had cowed; she savored every moment of his quiet sleep. When Taggert knelt before the lock, she stepped aside laughing to herself; if he was the Ajin, he wouldn't trust her with such delicate work, but because he was Tag, she knew he was only indulging himself in one of his favorite activities, teasing a lock open, not thinking of her at all. *At least the Ajin's paranoia isn't rubbing off on me.*

He stood, touched the latch and waited until the door was completely open, then moved the readout along the posts and lintel, being careful not to move into the doorspace. No reaction. He slipped the readout into his pocket, turned to Shadith, raised his brows. She shook her head vigorously, moved to stand beside him looking into the bedroom.

It was dark but the darkness was not complete. Glow strips stuck low on the walls provided a bluish light that was sufficient to show shapes without detail. The Ajin lay on his back, his arms flung out, his chest bare, blankets pushed into a crumpled roll across his waist. He was profoundly asleep.

Taggert handed her one of the extensible claws, took out a sleep-gas canister and the tangler, transferred the tangler to his left hand, lobbed the canister onto the bed, tensing as it passed through the doorway. Nothing happened. The canister plopped down beside the Ajin's shoulder and popped open. Taggert slapped Shadith's shoulder lightly, grinned at her. She squeezed his hand, then listened to the Ajin's mind, felt the rhythms change from sleep into unconsciousness. Taggert held up the tangler. She nodded. Holding her breath but not as tense as she'd been before he'd thrown the canister, she pointed the rod at the Ajin, touched the trigger. The rod shivered against her hand; the end shot out and out until the knob was bouncing lightly up and down above the sleeper's stomach. She twisted the base. The claws sprang out, opening like the segments of an orange. Working with extreme care, she lowered them until they were nearly touching the blanket; she eased the needle points into the blanket, twisted the claws shut and drew the blanket off the bed, moving slowly because she didn't want to touch his flesh, she didn't know why, but she listened to the impulses and kept the pole clear of him. She opened the claw, dropped the blanket on the floor, retracted the pole.

"What's that around his neck?" Taggert's voice was low, but he'd given up whispering.

"Nothing to do with the trap. At least I think it isn't. It's supposed to be a control; he planted a thermit grenade in my back that he said would explode if I went farther than a kilometer from him. Or he died. No problem. Friend of mine cut the grenade out yesterday."

"Nice timing."

"Meant to be."

"I don't see anything else on him. Not even a ring. He was wearing one yesterday."

"On the table by the bed, I think—at least, there's something small there."

"Careless, if that's it."

"Maybe."

"Better get on with the fishing." He transferred the tangler to his right hand, narrowed his eyes, swung his arm a few times to get the feel, then tossed the tangler onto the Ajin's chest. The sticky translucent threads whipped out and bound themselves around his arms, his neck, winding down around his pelvis and legs. Taggert sighed and took out another extensible claw. "You get a wrist, I'll go for an ankle, then we reel him in."

Shadith nodded. The feeling came again stronger than before. *Don't touch*. She ignored it, extended the pole and positioned the claw over the Ajin's wrist. A click of Taggert's tongue told her he was ready. She lowered her claw as he lowered his, edged the prongs under and over the wrist, then twisted them tight, the needle points sinking into the Ajin's flesh.

"Right." The word was an explosion in her ear. "Pull!"

Together she and Taggert began hauling the unconscious man along the bed.

There was an odd humming in her ears. The faint blue light seemed to waver. One moment she could feel the butt of the pole pressed against her hand, then there was nothing. Nothing there. No light either. She shouted and could not hear her voice. A horrible sucking feeling. Then she was drifting in grayness, nothing but grayness, no smells, nothing to touch, no sounds not even the sounds of her own body, nothing. . . .

COBARZH ON ASKALOR

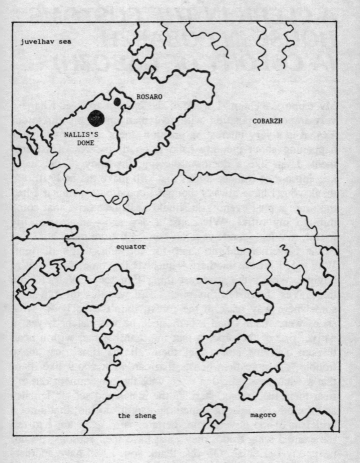

VRITHIAN
WITNESS [5]
A CLERK IN THE CUSTOMS HOUSE IN COBARZH (A COLONY OF CABOZH)

My name is Peixen. I work in the customs office. I have a very important position with five men under my direction. Yes, it is a very interesting position, there are always things happening about me, my hand is on the nerves of government, I am like a doctor protecting the body of the state, keeping out of it those things that will make the body ill. Oh thank you, I have always thought I could be a writer if I had the time, a poet even. You should hear the stories that come through my office. Why, just a day ago—ah-ah, no, my friend, that is a secret, you can't entice it from me; I am loyal to the Governor and too sharp for you. Oh, that's all right. Why yes, I'll have another. A quechax this time, since you're buying. What's the strangest thing I've seen? Well, let me think. Yes, I can tell this one. There was this turezxh from somewhere way back in the forest, didn't even know what shoes were, hadn't had a bath since he was hatched, yes, a native, one of the orpetzh that infest this place, with a head thicker than his stink. Get them all the time, just make trouble, no more than beasts that can walk about like men, that's what they are, don't see why the government doesn't treat them like beasts, sterilize the males and set the females and the others to doing something useful, no, no, that's not a criticism of the government, certainly not, who am I to tell the exalted what to do, they must have their reasons, no no, never say I criticize. Oh yes, thank you, I will have another. A warm apology for sure. Another quechax, crizhao, and

don't take so long about it this time or I'll complain to your
employer. Where was I? Oh, yes, thank you. This turezxh.
He wanted to go to Fospor, at least that was what we got out
of him. He had this big wicker basket and he didn't want to
open it. In the end we had to call the guard to hold him.
Turned out in the basket was the biggest snake you ever saw.
Big around as a man's thigh, and heavy! You wouldn't
believe how heavy that obresh was, all wrapped up in coils
until it filled the whole basket. Well, I ask him why is he
taking that thing to Fospor and he says a cousin of his has a
circus there and wants the snake to make the Fospri gape.
That sounds reasonable enough, doesn't it? But I didn't like
all the fuss he made about opening the basket. I said to
myself he's hiding something. So I made him take the creature out of the basket and stretch it on the floor. You would
have laughed to see how nervous my underclerks were, backing away, looking over the counter with just their eyes showing. Even the guards backed off. I'm sure they felt foolish a
bit later, because the snake was sleepy as a raw recruit back
from his first leave. Thank you. I think the comparison is
very apt. There was nothing in the basket but some leaves
and grasses, I had them emptied onto the floor and went
through them with a stick, you never can tell what vermin
these dirty turezxh will bring with them. Nothing there. Even
the captain of the guards wanted to let the mushhead go with
his torpid beast, but I smelled something wrong. Yes, I've got
a good nose for that sort of thing. There was a lump about
halfway along the obresh's body. I ask the turezxh about the
lump, he says it was a porzao he fed the snake so it would stay
quiet. And that seems reasonable, doesn't it? Wouldn't you
believe that? No, you're right. I didn't. My nose was telling
me there was something there, something more. The guard
captain wouldn't touch the obrezh, but I take his sword and
slice open the snake and there's this porzao inside all right,
and inside the porzao there's a sack with fifteen emeralds in
it, big enough to choke a man. Well, the turezxh he tried to
run off when he saw that, but the guards jumped him. I did it
to serve my country, it was simply my duty, you know, but
to show you what splendid types they are who rule us, they

awarded me a bonus and an extra day off when they didn't
have to do any such thing. The turezxh? The governor was
more merciful than I would have been, just cut his thieving
hands off and let him go find a living how he could. Just goes
to show I was right a while back, should clean them all out of
the jungle, get rid of them, worthless beasts. Some softheads
say those beasts, nothings like that, they got rights, some of
those traitors in the 'versity, sitting there with their books and
salaries paid by the government, paid out of taxes folk like
you and me pay, traitors got no gratitude, no feel for real life,
looking down their stupid noses at an honest working man
who could be a poet or writer if he wanted to, anytime he
wanted to, if he could take the time from his work, and it's
important work too, keeping out the filth that would corrupt
sosh . . . sozheety . . . you know. Better poet even so than
them, a man, you bet, not a gutlesh ol' woman. . . . Got to
go? Sh . . . sorry 'bout that . . . good company's h . . . hard
to fin' . . . Tempestao ble . . . blesh you 'n y'r f'mly.

VIRITHIAN
action on the periphery [4]

Dum Ymori. One hour from the dome. Silent, deserted, a mourning wind blowing dead leaves into broken dead houses. Looted houses. Muri said it, wolves on two legs prowling. Amaiki tried to grieve for the lost life of the Dum as she guided the skimsled past the empty houses, but all she could feel now was her own fear. The last time she reached to touch her mate-meld, she'd sensed anger and frustration and alarm overlaying their welcome-warmth; then she thought that blend was aimed at Hyaroll, now she realized how blind she'd been; this was what they'd been living with, this desolation and danger. That they'd waited as long as they had was a measure of their love for her. She felt shamed by how lightly she'd held that love, by the anger she'd felt when they went off without her. Sitting comfortable and well fed—and safe—in Hyaroll's dome, she hadn't the least notion what was happening outside, what the little less than two years she'd been away had done to the uplands and the people living there.

She left Ymori behind and moved off the produce road into the fields, but there were too many fences; they slowed her badly and she was afraid of getting lost. She dug into the toolkit and found the graft tool, adjusted the cutting beam until it reached out a body length from her, then she took the sled back to the road, the tool ready for use if anything came after her.

The rest of the day she rode stiffly alert along the gradual sweep of the road, circling wide about two more deserted villages, seeing no living thing except a few raptors gliding high overhead. Death and desolation. How could he let it

277

happen? It must have been coming for years; all this couldn't happen overnight. Could it? She could remember water getting short, the planted acreage shrinking gradually, year by year, but the families were still comfortable, everyone had enough to eat and hope that next year would be better. The rains came, though they were shorter and lighter each year. Life had diminished a little when the lot chose her to be one of the fifteen servers, but with a bit of care there was enough to go around for everyone, sometimes more than enough.

The day darkened swiftly once the sun went down; because of her late start she'd planned to travel all night, but after she'd gone off the road twice and nearly wrecked the sled, she crept along until she came to an abandoned farm. Afraid to sleep in the house, since that seemed the most obvious point of attack, she found an empty shed (it smelled like a tedo cote, though her flashlight showed her walls and floor swept carefully clean; not a wisp of straw or a tangle of fleece left behind) whose walls were tight enough to keep any light from getting out and betraying her presence. She ate a cold meal, heated water for tea on the porta stove, sat in the doorway sipping at the tea, watching a waxing Araxos swim across the faint glow of the skymist. *The difficulty,* she thought, *doesn't lie in the amount of light, but in how it is focused. I hadn't noticed before how much I depend on shadows to judge distances.* She wrapped her hands about the cup, the warmth sliding down her arms to join the warmth in her belly. In the distance one edinga howled at the moon, then others joined the chorus. She shivered and gulped at the tea, emptying the cup, desperately glad she needn't force herself farther into that half-dark with its deceptive shadows. She felt her aloneness in her bones and wanted to howl like the edinga; she'd never been so alone in her life, not ever; even in the dome there was a naish to curl against when the ache of apartness bit too deep. *No naish here. If I stay like this any longer, I certainly will start howling.* She pushed onto her feet, feeling every ache in every weary muscle of her body. *I wonder if Hyaroll will bother looking for me . . . who's to remind him . . . not the odd folk.* She patted the earth with her foot, a reverent caress. *Earth mother bless them and what they are trying.* She pulled the door shut; there was no catch on the inside, but she pushed the sled across the opening and scattered metal tools along it so she'd have their rattle to warn her if something or someone tried to get inside. In the light of the flash she snapped her sleep-pad out of its roll, wound a quilt around her and lay down clutching the graft tool. With weary patience she disciplined her whirling thoughts, and once the quilt warmed the chill out of her aching body, she dropped into a heavy sleep.

She woke shortly after dawn. The morning air was cold and dry, though the sun was beginning to warm the chill away. Something brushed against the boards near her head, there were other furtive rustles and slithers; she lay stiff and frightened until she identified the noises: tikin, tí-besh, mikimiki and others, small furry nibblers pattering about the business of finding food. As she rolled out of the quilt she saw a flash of pale green, a jiji darting under the skimsled, tail thrashing, skinny hairless legs working frantically. A moment later it backed out with a thimble-sized t'ki pup in its mouth. Holding the pup down with its slim, six-fingered forepaws, ignoring Amaiki with the casual indifference she remembered with affection from the jejin in her childhood home, it proceeded to swallow the pup, then grunted itself in a comfortable sprawl on the end of the sleep-pad, a film descending over its golden eyes as it began digesting its breakfast. Chuckling, her loneliness temporarily assuaged, she tugged an end of the quilt from under the jiji, laughed aloud at its squealing protest; she rolled and strapped the quilt, packed the scattered tools away, turned the cock on one of the water cans to draw water for her morning tea. Jejin had lived on Conoch'hi farms from the time Hyaroll stopped the clans' wandering, moving unhindered through the houses and barns, the cotes and sheds, shaping nests in haystacks and cornbins, eating insect eggs and larvae, chasing snakes away, keeping down the population of various sorts of nibblers. Amaiki hummed contentedly as she checked the monitors on the batteries. Left the dome midafternoon, quit traveling two hours after sundown. She was surprised to see how little of the power she'd used,

pleased too. Still humming, she moved the sled aside and
pulled the door open. Bright cloudless sky. *I might as well
stay here awhile,* she told herself and felt an immediate relief.
The thought of plunging into that unknown ahead turned her
stomach sour; she liked things to stay the way she knew
them; strangeness intimidated her. It was pleasant to have a
viable excuse for clinging to familiar things and places. She
eased the sled outside and unfolded the collector films.

After breakfast, she checked the monitors, sighed when she
saw the charging almost complete. There was still a hint of
chill in the air, so she tied on her cloak, then went wandering
about the stead. A barn built of wood and fieldstone, several
corrals, a stripped kitchen garden where even the weedgrass
was dry and dead. She lifted the well cap, dropped a pebble
down; it rattled against the sides of the hole and stopped with
a dull thud. Not even mud left. The house was locked up, but
the shutters had been pulled off and the windows were smashed;
what she could see of the inside was a mess. The wolves had
been here, cleaned out anything worth taking, spoiled the
rest. In the whole long span of the Conoch'hi life weave, the
only thing that came close to this sort of destruction was the
hints and fragments of stories before the coming of the undying, stories about raids by shevorate galaphorze, hairy tribes
living around Lake Serzhair. Maybe, after these thousands of
years of peace and safety, they were raiding again. No stink
of galaphorze about, but this place had been empty for a long
time, and scent didn't linger in air as dry as this. Might have
been Conoch'hi gone wild. It happened. She didn't like to
think about that. Everything she knew was breaking apart.

She went back to the shed, her enjoyment of the morning
gone. Instead of the comforting familiarity she'd felt before,
there was nightmare, an edge of ugliness to everything about
her. She eased an annoyed jiji off the sleep-pad, rolled it into
a tight cylinder and tied it to the sled; she folded up the
collector and guided it back into its slot, checked the packs
and cubbies, the water cans, made sure the taps were covered. From the look of things the water would have to last her
until she reached the river. She took a last look around, saw the
marks of her sandals in the dust. The wind was beginning to

rise, coming out of the southwest with that low keening howl she knew too well, the zimral that leached the soul and maddened the brain; that hot persistent wind would blow away those tracks before night fell, she knew that, but leaving them behind, there for anyone to see who came in time, was like leaving bits of herself lying about. She found a long-stemmed weed and went about the stead brushing away old footmarks and new; when she reached the sled she stepped up on it, brushed out the last mark, broke the weed into small bits and cast them away. She pulled her cloak around her, laced the front together, drew the hood up and snapped the dust veil in place, then started the sled and left the farm without looking back.

All that long day she saw no one, though she passed more abandoned steads, more empty villages. Overhead a few raptors rode the zimral, but any tedo or other large animals left in the uplands were hiding from the wind and the sun. After all the millennia the Conoch'hi had lived here and turned the soil and left their bones to make it richer, the uplands were going back to wilderness, dusty, dry and secret. She paised orchards where dead leaves rattled before the zimral and dead limbs creaked a dirge for the dying of the land. She passed vineyards where dead vines were a calligraphy of despair. The uplands had come to life on the rains Hyaroll brought to them, stayed alive because he continued to bring them, year on year, steady as the ticking of a clock, year on year without fail, the centuries piling up, one, two, three, ten, fifty, one hundred centuries of winter rains coming without fail; what wonder no one thought to study the natural seasons of the land or build reservoirs against the time when the rains might fail to come. Who could remember what the natural seasons were? Not even the life weave went back that far. *We planted what we wanted and forced the land to shape itself to our needs. What had been would always be. As long as the undying lived in the dome there would be peace and plenty. Sometimes we railed against the hardness of his hand when he took our sons, our daughters and most of all our naidisa, but no one dreamed of doing without him. We were pampered pets, Hyaroll's jejin, charming in our way and*

*useful, and like the jejin on that farm, we are left to make our
own lives when he nears the end of his. At least the jejin have
instinct to guide them. What do we have? The land takes back
its original face. So fast it takes it back. And we fly away
from it as fast, hunting for another master to make all right
again.* It was a bitter lesson she read that day in the writing of
dead vines and the rattle of dead leaves.

Two hours before sundown she came across another abandoned steading. She stopped the sled and checked the monitors. Down by two-thirds. She looked around. Clouds low on
the horizon ahead, just a few ravelings but more than she'd
seen since she left the dome. The grass was sun-dried and
parched but not dead yet, and the orchard stretching away
behind the house had a faint flush of green to it; the tree limbs
bent with a lively spring before the push of the zimral; more
than guess or elapsed time, these things told her she was
nearing the edge of the high plateau. Graft tool ready in her
hand, senses as alert as she could force them, she sent the
sled humming down the driveway toward the house.

She felt the emptiness of the place before she came to a
stop. Heavy shutters were closed over the windows in front,
three rows of them; the house was asleep, it wouldn't wake
till the line families came back. She started the sled around to
the back, easing it along at a creep. No sign of a break-in; the
wolves never left such neatness behind them. That made her
nervous; they hadn't come here yet—was tonight the night
they hit? There were several barns and a silo. Well built and
well maintained. The Conoch'hi who held this land worked
hard and were proud of their home and loved their land. She
looked about and mourned with them the need to leave what
generations of their line had built. It hurt because she was
conc and sister to all Conoch'hi and because it reminded her
all too sharply of the home her meld and line had left to wind
and sun and filthy wolves who'd break and mess what they
could not use. She looked about, wondering what shelter
would be best. Not the house. Silo? No; if they rode kedoa—
which seemed likely, not many sleds or trucks left up here—
they'd be looking for any bits of grain left. Sheds? No.
They'd try every door looking for what they could find. A

shed was too confining, and even if she could latch it somehow from the inside, the fact that it was closed against them
would make them all the more eager to get inside. She took
the sled over to the largest of the barns; it had double doors
on the upper story, a heavy beam jutting out from the roofpeak
and a hayfork swinging from a pulley screwed into that beam.
She stepped off the sled, hesitated, then unfolded the film. Be
safest to go to ground immediately, but the batteries needed
charging, and for that the sled had to be out in the sunlight.
She looked around. Trees and a pair of small neat sheds
between the barn and the house; it wasn't exactly hidden, but
someone would have to get within a few meters of it before
he saw it. She pushed up the hook on the smallest of the
barn's doors and went inside, leaving the door open so she'd
have light enough to see what the inside was like.

More light came in through airholes high up the sides of
the loft. The side where she walked was paved with heavy
stone flags, worn down by centuries of tedo hooves. Milking
barn? Probably not; more likely shelter during winter storms.
The air had a dry musty smell, old hay and worms in the
wood; dust motes danced in the light beams streaming down
from high above. She pushed apart one of the stanchions,
stepped into the old stone manger, stepped over the lip onto
ancient flooring that creaked and groaned under her sandal
soles. The center of the barn was a huge empty space with a
thin scatter of rotting straw spread out over the floorboards.
As she'd hoped, the loft floor came about two thirds of the
way to the front of the barn, then stopped. She could jump
the sled into the loft and leave no sign anyone was about. If
the loft floor was strong enough to hold the weight. She
walked under it and scowled up into the dim twilight; the
floorbeams looked strong enough to hold a flier. She came
back from under the floor, went quickly up the ladder and
swung out onto the planks. Stamping and hopping about,
suddenly more cheerful because of the sheer silliness of what
she was doing, she started dancing with the sunbeams, kicking up swirls of strawdust, until she slipped and landed on her
coccyx with a thud that jarred her brain. "Motherlost planks
are hard enough," she said. Groaning and rubbing at her

tailbone, she got to her feet and managed to reach the barn
floor without falling, though the tumble she'd taken had
shaken her more than she liked to admit. "What now? Take a
look around, I suppose, then fix some supper. It's a cold
meal for you tonight, Ammi-sim, no hot tea to chase away
the sorrows of the soul."

She stopped by the sled and checked the monitors. The line
had crept up a little, how much was hard to tell, but there was
still a long way to go before the batteries were topped off.
She did a few loosening-up exercises, but they didn't help
much; she was bone-sore and getting sorer by the minute.
*Stupid. Stupid. Stupid. Motherlife, I'd love to soak in a hot
tub for hours and hours and hours. Maybe I can fiddle some
sort of hot compress with the porta stove. Maybe all this is
useless pother, no looter coming, no danger closing in on me.
Can't take the chance, Ammi-sim, you know that. The least
they'd do would be take away the sled. With it you're reasonably sure to make Shim Shupat, without it who knows. . . .*

There was an elaborate garden behind the house; generations of love had gone into its shaping. A small stream had
run through it, falling down a miniature mountain vista to
murmur in meandering calm through a series of pools where
waterflowers had grown. Fed from the well, water had been
pumped into a mossy wooden tank; a small weir could be
opened to let a constant stream run down the tiny exquisite
vista to the stream and the pools and finally around to the
troughs where the tedo herds had drunk. No water now, of
course; the waterflowers were gone, other flowerbeds had
been dug up and replaced by mossy rocks in a desperate
attempt to hold on to some semblance of garden; most of the
shrubbery had been cut back or removed, a few ancient trees
remained, their leaves a withered green, small and dying.
They held out as long as they could. How much they must
have loved this place. She was suddenly happy she hadn't
seen her home again. *I have good memories*, she thought,
better memories than any of my line can have; I am blessed.
Her own life-strip was packed away in the sled, but she
knotted the thought into her mind for working later into the
weave.

*   *   *

In that gray light that comes when most of dawn's colors have faded, she woke from a chaotic, terrifying nightmare, filled with jagged flashes of fire and dark, with blood and mangled flesh, with screams and crashes, with shouts and curses, opened her eyes into that cold grayness, unsure whether she was awake or still dreaming, listened to sounds that seemed to belong to that nightmare: high, hooting squeals from kedoa, shouted curses and whinnying laughter, thudding scuffles of split hooves, shriek and squeal of tortured wood, dull thumps, crash of breaking glass. As the sounds clarified and she oriented herself, she began to understand what she was hearing. The looters had come.

She drew her legs up, pulled the quilt more tightly about her. Sour fluid flooded her mouth; she swallowed several times, drew her tongue across dry lips as she sat listening to the sounds the wolf pack made as they swarmed over the stead. Even worse than the fear that paralyzed her was the sick understanding that these ravaging beasts were Conoch'hi, unmelded manai. *Motherlost females like me. Oh-ah, how? How? What happened to them that they could do such things?* The big doors rolled open suddenly; she shuddered and clutched at the graft tool, sat without moving, almost without breathing.

"Mothercursed leeches, they licked the place clean." A hoarse wild voice that brought her rudimentary crest erect and flooded her with an equally wild hate that appalled her when she realized what was happening. *As fast as the land,* she thought, *we go back to what we were. Ah-weh, ah mother of us all, help me.*

"What about the loft, Napann? Want me to take a look?" A lighter, easier voice, not so troubling, but the words brought Amaiki onto her knees, the graft tool lifted and ready.

"No, anything worthwhile was in the house. This place is too open—look at it, not even fresh straw left." Footsteps going away. "Some good stuff in the cellar, we'll feast today . . ." The voice faded with the steps, though the mana kept on talking.

Amaiki sank back on her heels. After a minute she pulled the quilt up around her, clutched it tight to her, but the

shivering that shook her, jammed her teeth together, blurred
her sight, it wouldn't go away. The air warmed about her,
grew brighter as the sun rose higher, but the chill still lingered in her bones. A simple thing. Just follow her meld to
the coast. Getting out of the dome would be the hard part, the
rest . . . with a little caution and the proper preparation, how
hard could it be? Wild manai . . . how soon before they
begin raiding for naidisa and tokon? Everything she knew and
cherished was falling apart around her, even what she knew
of herself. *Rotting,* she thought, *dead and rotting. Mother-of-
all, what will happen to us?* She sat without moving for a
timeless time—until her stomach groweld and reminded her
to eat. Throughout that interminable day she heard the wolf
pack moving about. They tore a shed down and set it on fire
to roast something. The sickly stench of half-burned meat
drifted into the barn; she would not think about what it might
be. As the sun sank lower and lower, she began to wonder if
they meant to settle in for several days. She couldn't survive
that; already her bladder had proved a problem. She'd pushed
a pile of straw ends into one of the back corners of the loft
and voided on it, but her urine was thick from two days of
keeping her water intake to a minimum. The smell of it was
strong and lingering; anyone with half a nose coming into the
barn would know someone was there. If they ever settled
down and went to sleep . . . no no no, they'd have sentries
out, they'd chase her down, the sled wasn't fast enough to
outrun even a runty kedoa. *Go away,* she thought, *go away,
this is too close to the lowland, it's not safe to sleep here, go
go go*. She loathed being afraid, being filthy and stinking; her
sense of her own worth shredded away as the hours passed
until she despised herself as much as she did those beasts
outside, but most of all she was terrified by that fierce animal
part of herself that was drawn to them. It was not only fear
she felt that time the mana Napann spoke. *Go away, leave me
alone, let me get on unhindered, go.*

The interminable day finally ended. She voided her bladder
once more and was sick with the stench of herself and
terrified someone would come into the barn and smell it. The
wolf pack rioted about some more, making noises that sounded

as if they were celebrating the moonrise, then grew quiet as the night deepened. In the long silence that followed, Amaiki wrestled with herself, finding in that silence and the night's shadowed darkness the strength to face her needs and fears, her new and unwelcome knowledge of herself. *This is what I am*, she thought into the darkness, *these possibilities are truly within me; in the years of my life so far I have not had to find out so much about myself as I have discovered this single day. Tonight (and probably only tonight) I have a choice of paths. I can forget what I have seen within me and confine myself to that Amaiki who was gentle and loving, with—all right, admit it—a sometimes acid tongue, and a true gift for shaping and growing the green world. I can be that woman but not limited to her; I can put out other possibilities as a plant puts out sports, living with the good in me and using the bad to energize me. I can join this pack, run free and wild beneath the moons, answering to no one but my pack sisters, sloughing all those responsibilities that tug and twist at me and will not let me alone.*

Part of the choice was easy. The Amaiki of two days ago was dead; it would be like living in a rotting corpse if she tried going back to that one and denying what had happened. But the choice between the other two was far more difficult. Now—especially now—the call of the pack was terrible and powerful; even in the stillness she could hear their shouts and careless laughter, and feel the communion they shared.

In the end—she laughed at herself when she realized just what had made her choice for her, had to stuff the corner of the quilt in her mouth to muffle that delivering laughter—she put the pack aside also. No noble gesture, no reaching toward the rational, civilized self, no urge to duty convinced her. It was the stink of her body and her yearning for a hot soapy bath. She detested being dirty; her mothers used to tease her about her compulsion to neatness, saying even her diapers had been models of decorum. No long hot baths if she went running under the moons, no crisp fresh tabards every day, no cool clean sheets to slide between each night. As things were right now, it might be days, even as long as a year, before she had all those things again, but she would one day, that she promised herself. She'd never ever have them if she joined the pack. Toward dawn, at peace with herself again, she smiled into the thick darkness and thought of Keran's sardonic laughter when she told them all of this night, of Muri's vocal bewilderment, Betaki's understanding smiles, Kimpri's snorts and Se-Passhi pressed warm and pliant against her. Her breath came more quickly and raggedly; how could she ever entertain the thought of never seeing them again? It was all this mess around her, she was light-headed from not eating or drinking enough, that had to explain it, but she was honest enough now to admit to herself that there was a part of her that wanted everything the pack offered, that resented the others of the meld even though she loved them all and was bound to them with ties she would not and could not break.

In the gray light of early morning the wolf pack rode away from the farm without discovering Amaiki or even suspecting she was there. She stayed hidden a full hour after the last sounds faded, then jumped the sled down and set it in the sun so the batteries could finish charging. She got out a clean tabard, then used some of her too rapidly diminishing water supply to scrub her body clean. She climbed to the top pole of the nearest corral fence and sat there letting the sun scour away the last feeling of contamination as it dried her body.

By the time she'd fixed a hearty breakfast and downed it with several cups of herb tea, she was feeling better than she had in days, not only prepared, but relishing the challenge of dealing with the greedy, thievish and altogether detestable lowlanders between her and Shim Shupat.

Two days later, with no more shocks to her system, but her opinion of lowlanders thoroughly confirmed, she hummed into the port city, sold the skimsled to a dealer as furtive as he was miserly, and went looking for the hall of the line-mothers and news of her kin.

COBARZH ON ASKALOR

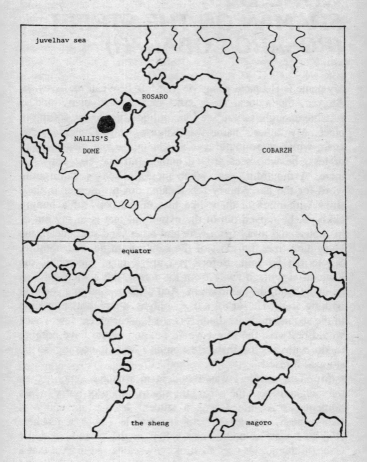

VRITHIAN
WITNESS [6]
SHAMAN ON THE STREET (ROSARO/COBARZH)

My name is Heomchi Kangavie, but folk here call me Aveyish. Ah yes, that's local street talk, means "old man" and is suitable enough; as you see I am antique, not to say rotting in place. My father's name was Kugapolush-je Omudda-popa-kush, which is a mouthful in any language and means, more or less, he who sees around corners no one else knows is there. A mouthful, yes. When the Ujihadda—a salimsaram word for the hurry-hurry folk—came down the river in their ships with roars in them like that in the belly of a hungry akko-yo, he moved out of the mawlihip, that is to say out of his house and away from wife and other, and sat beneath the Uyaggung tree. To most of the salimsaram he said nothing, but to me he said: Before you are a man, Heomchi, the Kwichi-jai will go away from the forest, the Kwichi-jai will go away from the salimsaram. And after he said that, he said nothing at all. He sat for a day, a night, a day, and sometime in the second night he died. It is so. I swear it. He saw what I would be, what the forest would be, and would have nothing to do with any of that. He couldn't stop it coming so he stopped himself.

Me? Oh, awhile I was a student in a church school, then the daughters sent me across the sea to the hurry-hurry men's homeplace. Awhile I was a student in the university at Inchacobesh outside the capital. Awhile I was a teacher. Awhile I was an author and a lion in the parlors, and the Cabozhi damazelas used to stroke my scales and marvel that a beast could talk like a man and so entertainingly too. But I had no kwi. I was like a tree flood-ripped from the soil that fed me. I went one way wrong, another way wrong, and turn and turn and it was all gone and I was a fat old fool dangling from the fringes of the hurry-hurry world.

So with one thing and another, here I am.

It is to laugh, my friend, it is the world's joke. The hurry men stomped the kwi out of the forest, and turned their back on the devastation they made, and kwi came to dance in the streets with the poor folk, hurry-hurry poor and salimsaram poor and other sorts of poor. The Ujihadda chased it from the forest and it ran here to live beneath their noses.

That's one thing.

The Ujihadda came with their storm-god boasting his dominion, I bow my empty head to him and go out of the forest. Now I sit here and see the undying flying about their mountain, the undying who make small the storm-god who makes nothing of hurry-hurry wailings and all their hurry this way, hurry that. I see the Ujihadda crawl to lick the toes of the undying and remember a forest boy not-quite-crawling to lick hurry-hurry toes and I see the Kwichi-jai dance in the street come rain-blow or bluest sky.

The undying? They walk like gods among the peoples of all lands. They even look like people, but they never change, never age; when they come strolling among us they put on light like a body suit and who touches them dies. They never bother to warn, what do they care? They care for nothing, we entertain them by our needs and our striving, then they go away again. They prick the bubble of hurry-hurry pride. You see? You see? And kwi lives in the street and laughs.

VRITHIAN
action on the primary line

Shareem slept restlessly on her pallet in the flier, woke with an aching head, soreness in her hips and shoulders where her weight had pushed them against the thinly padded floor, a stuffy nose from the dust. Muzzy and irritable, annoyed with Aleytys and Kell, she groaned up onto her knees, massaged her temples, patted a yawn, then crawled out of the flier feeling grubby and melancholy and wholly disgruntled with the fate that had brought her to this pass. She straightened and looked around. "Whatever you did, we're still in one piece." She stretched, ran her hands through her hair, rubbed bare feet on the cool wiry grass. "Lee," she called out. "Hoop hoop hoop, hey Lee, breakfast time. Up, my girl, your mama's hungry."

The mewls of the sea birds, the distant mutter of the sea, the drip of water in the fountains, that was all she heard. The house was silent, the gardens quiet, nothing moving, shadows stark in the early sun. Patches of frost lingered in the longshadows, and there was the smell of frost to come in the air, a hint that the short summer was nearing its end. Shareem pulled her toe across the powdery white, feeling the chill of it bite into her flesh, watching the black line her toe drew lengthen and fade as the frost patch faded. Abruptly she felt thrust back into time, into the primitive time where nothing changed with any permanence, where everything recurred again and again. In the seasons of her life it was Kell's time again, a time of flight and terror, but—or so she told herself and tried to believe it—the old theme was turned on its back, this time Kell would be the driven one. She stared at the silent house, suddenly frightened. "Lee," she called, urgency in her voice. *"Lee!"*

No answer. Shareem fought panic. Dead? Fled? What . . . She forced herself to walk slowly toward the house. *Slow and calm,* she thought, *slow and calm, slow and calm,* but she was breathing hard and almost running by the time she reached the door. She tore it open, slammed it back against the stone, but she didn't care, she didn't care if the noise triggered the menace, she didn't care about anything but Aleytys. In the middle of the great hall she scrambled to a stop and screamed her daughter's name.

No answer but the echoes.

She tried to control her terror, tried to think. Told herself: *Remember, you can precipitate the thing you want to avoid, you can kill Aleytys, kill yourself, reduce house and hold to slag, let Kell win.* She hugged her arms across her breasts and tried to calm herself, dragging up the ways she'd learned to shunt aside uncomfortable thoughts and shaming memories. "Ikanom," she called, her voice still ragged but settling into control. "Ikanom."

The android came from the back of the house, moving into the hall with that liquid grace that all of Synkatta's designs possessed. "You desire, anassa?"

She cleared her throat. "Where is Aleytys?"

Ikanom went quiet, consulting the kephalos, at first listening calmly, then turning its head so the planes of its face made a pattern of puzzlement, then it faced Shareem once more. "It is difficult to say, anassa. Within the dome, yes, somewhere, but precisely where is not at all clear."

Shareem swallowed, fought to control her fear. "Is she alive?"

Ikanom went still. Shareem's throat closed up. Its face made a pattern of puzzlement again. "Kephalos is confused, anassa."

Shareem waited, unable to speak.

"Aleytys archira is living but dormant."

Shareem swallowed again, stiffened back and knees. "It is certain?"

"It is certain, anassa."

"Then find her, Ikanom, bring her to me. It's important. It's more important than anything kephalos has ever done. Find her. Bring her to me." She looked around. "Here. I think here. When I see her I'll know better what to do."

"Kephalos searches, anassa. Would you care to eat while you wait?"

She stared at the shifting planes of the android's face. *How can I eat?* She pressed her hand against her middle. *I should. I don't know, yes I'd better.* "Yes," she said. "Bring me . . . bring me an omelet, toast . . . um . . . some shalla juice . . . um . . . a pot of cha. Over there." A small table and two chairs, in a deep alcove whose windows opened onto one of the gardens.

"In twenty minutes, anassa. If that suits you?"

"It suits."

Ikanom left. She walked with slow careful steps across the elaborate parquetry of the hall floor and sat in one of the chairs, her back to the hall so she needn't see how empty it was, her shakes changing into numbness, fear and anger blunting into passivity. If Aleytys failed last night, this afternoon's missile could trigger the tumor at the house's heart. Or tomorrow's. Or a thousand other things. She didn't care. Couldn't care. All she wanted was for this torment to be over, one way or another. If Kell walked in the next moment with a knife to cut her throat, she'd lift her chin to make his task easier.

Time dragged, each second an eternity. A few eternities later one of the house serviteurs rolled up and began setting out her meal.

She stared at the food. At first her stomach rebelled, but she forced herself to nibble at a piece of toast and sip at the fruit juice. In a few minutes her revulsion vanished, and her hunger returned so fiercely she had to discipline herself into eating more slowly.

Cradled by the quiet of the great hall, the hot meal scaring away the worst of her anxieties, she began to recover her composure and back away from that lethargy that was a kind of suicide. She sat a little longer at the table, watching the day brighten outside, expecting to hear at any moment that the kephalos had located Aleytys. After half an hour had slipped away, she got to her feet and began wandering through the house, room to room, kicking along the flow spaces, into closets and storage niches, prying into chests, not admitting to herself she was searching for her daughter's comatose body, just looking. She poked her nose into every crazy corner of that crazy house and found nothing. *If I get close enough to her, I'll feel her, I know I will*, she told herself; whether that was true or not, she felt nothing.

Midafternoon. She was in the bookroom passing a window when she saw the flare of light that meant another missile had been destroyed. She glanced at her ringchron. Right on time. Eyes closed, she listened. Nothing happened. Either it wasn't supposed to or Aleytys had pulled the thing's teeth. She dropped into the chair by the desk and sat with her head propped on her hands, thinking. *One place left. And I can't get in there. Householdeart. Tumor on the heart. Yes.*

Charged with sudden irrational certainty, she pushed way from the desk and ran from the room. Along the flow-way, down and down, through the cellars, across the vast manufactury with its shrouded machines and stores of raw materials, past the undeployed maze, down down until she bounced off the resilient membrane that protected the householdeart. She pressed herself against it; she could see the edge of the control chair—empty—a portion of the floor and console, nothing there. For the first time she felt that Aleytys was truly somewhere nearby; maybe it was imagination, maybe it was her need convincing her to feel what she so desperately wanted to feel, but she *knew* Aleytys was there. She had to be there. Nowhere else she could be.

Shareem pushed harder against the membrane. "Kephalos," she cried, "have you looked within yourself? She is here. I know she is."

No response. In a way that was comforting; as long as Aleytys was alive, kephalos's programming held and it would permit no one else into the house heart, would speak directly to no one but Aleytys. Calmed by the continuing silence, Shareem backed away from the membrane and began the long climb up to the living spaces.

*   *   *

Shareem was pacing restlessly about the great hall when
Ikanom brought Aleytys up from the cellars. She heard the
sound of the door sliding, swung around, caught her breath
when she saw what the android held cradled in his arms. She
hurried to meet him, touched her daughter's clammy skin,
made a soft distressed sound when she saw her daughter's
drawn face. "Infirmary," she said, then rushed ahead of him
along the flow spaces to the bubble room.

Ikanom laid Aleytys on the broad couch of the autodoc and
stepped back, stood by the door watching as Shareem stripped
the stained, filthy clothing off Aleytys, stared in shock at the
skeletal body, clicked her tongue at the raw groove in her
daughter's left wrist. "You look like the tail end of a seven-
year famine," she said aloud. Whatever had happened during
the night, it had cost Aleytys more than a third of her body
weight. Her hair was coming out in handfuls, her skin was
roughened and reddened, large patches of dead skin peeled up
and fell away at the lightest touch. Her pulse was strong but
frighteningly slow; the readouts said she was sunk in a sleep
so profound it approached coma. Over her shoulder, Shareem
said, "Ikanom, a sponge and warm water."

While the android was gone, Shareem looked more closely
at the readouts. Extreme fatigue and starvation. No serious
cell damage. What there was, Aleytys was repairing as she
slept. The autodoc was monitoring this and didn't seem inclined to interfere. It recommended frequent small meals of
thick broth and hot sweetened fruit juices. Hold Aleytys up
and let the swallowing reflex take the food down, don't try to
wake her. Keep her clean and comfortable. Nothing else was
necessary. She'd wake when she was ready. The autodoc was
almost purring as it contemplated its mistress. In spite of her
distress, Shareem was amused by the proprietorial pride the
machine took in Aleytys. Autodocs were like that. Even
Kell's. She shivered, jumped as Ikanom spoke softly behind
her. "The water, anassa." She took the basin and sponge and
began washing the dead skin and dirt from her daughter's
skin.

*   *   *

The days that followed were the happiest in all her long life. In this strange way she had her baby back, a very large baby to be sure, but that didn't matter. She washed and fed the sleeping woman, cuddled her, sang to her, told her stories she didn't hear, gave rein to the deep and possessive joy she took in her daughter. When Aleytys woke, their relationship would return to what it was before, a slowly developing friendship and undemanding affeciton, but for now she had her baby back, and she reveled in it.

The missiles kept coming, day after day, six seven eight nine. Same time, right on scheudle. And right on schedule kephalos destroyed them. Aleytys stirred and almost woke each time, but Shareem took her daughter's hand and held it tight, singing softly to her, calming her back into that revivifying sleep.

On the eleventh day there was no missile, so Aleytys must have done whatever was needed. After feeding Aleytys her fifth cup of broth for the day, she called Ikanom to the infirmary. "There was no missile today," she said.

"No, anassa."

"There is a bomb or something similar inside kephalos. Aleytys has defused it. I know this because there was no missile today; I know also that Kell understands Aleytys thwarted his plan. Kephalos should be wary these next days before Aleytys wakes."

"A bomb?" Ikanom sounded startled. "Kephalos knows of no bomb within."

"So I assumed. So Aleytys assumed. There must be something there, something dangerous, or Aleytys wouldn't be in such bad shape. Kephalos might police its innards, using the space where Aleytys was found as a starting point. Most of all kephalos should use all the tricks bequeathed by Hyaroll and Synkatta to guard against another penetration of its defenses. Kell would destroy us all to reach her. Are there questions?"

Ikanom shifted its head slightly; the sculpted facets of its abstract face seemed to smile at her. "Kephalos will be watchful," it said, "and kephalos will search within. This is a very disturbing thing. It must not happen again."

Amused, but careful to keep that from showing, taking pleasure in its grace, Shareem watched Ikanom walk out. *I say it again, Synkatta must have been a fascinating man. Hyaroll could tell me about him; they were friends.* She frowned. From what Aleytys had said after he left them, he wouldn't be around much anymore. Aloof as he'd been the past several centuries, she'd still miss him if he went. It was vaguely comforting to know Hyaroll was there if she needed him. He wouldn't like her bothering him, would most likely make her life a misery while she was with him, but he would take her in and protect her. At least, until now. She felt a touch of panic at the thought, then she shook off her malaise. His growls must be a temporary aberration; he had them now and then when he got fed up with people and shut himself in his dome refusing to talk to anyone for a decade or so. He got over those, he'd get over this. Aleytys mumbled something in her sleep. Shareem bent over her, then climbed onto the couch and sat holding her daughter's head on her thigh while she wiped away the sweat beading the sleeping face, then passed her palm over the stubble of regrowing hair; drawing the back of her hand in a gentle caress down the side of her daughter's face, she began a soft crooning lullaby.

Through the long quiet days Aleytys regained the flesh she'd lost; her skin regained its dark cream color; her new hair was as silky and red as before, an inch long already, long enough to fall in loose curls after Shareem shampooed and dried it and ran a comb through it. She worried off and on about the length of the sleep, but the autodoc continued to tick contentedly along and tell her not to fuss when she expressed her misgivings, so she relaxed into the dreamy pleasures of tending her daughter.

Kell called several times, but she refused to talk to him, instructed Ikanom to say nothing except that neither Aleytys nor Shareem wished to speak to him. There were other calls, but Shareem took none of them either—except the one from Loguisse. Even to Loguisse she said only that Aleytys was busy working with kephalos, getting her defenses in order. Loguisse nodded, then warned Shareem that they had better deal with Kell soon, since he was making considerable progress among the Stayers, turning them against Aleytys, and his converts were trying to pressure the Tetrad to revoke her acceptance. It was all extremely annoying.

On the twelfth day of her sleep, about midmorning, Aleytys stirred, opened her reyes.

Shareem felt a pang of loss, a rush of joy, sighed and patted her daughter's hand. "Welcome back."

Aleytys sat up, put her hand to her head, felt the short feathery curls. "What . . ."

"When Ikanom found you, you were a wraith, hair coming out, skin sloughing off. What happened?"

Aleytys looked down at herself, frowned at her wrists when she saw how thin they were. "How long?"

"Twelve days."

Aleytys swung her legs around, slid them off the autodoc's couch.

Hastily Shareem put her hand on her daughter's arm. "Careful."

Aleytys looked startled, then smiled. "I hear. Twelve days. Huh. Missiles still coming?"

"Stopped with the tenth. Kell's been calling, some of the other Stayers. I haven't talked to them. Except Loguisse. She says things are getting difficult out there, pressure on her and the others to revoke. So far the Tetrad seems to be holding. Harder Kell pushes, the stubborner they get."

"Good." She jabbed a thumb into a thigh muscle. "Mush. Twelve days on my back. Time I was getting into shape. Give me a hand, will you?" She wriggled toward the edge of the couch.

"You sure you should do this?" Shareem sighed as her daughter's hand closed about hers. "Shouldn't you rest some more?"

"Rested a dozen days already." Aleytys stood swaying. "Madar! I'm weaker than a just-born foal."

"Lee, you were almost dead."

Aleytys laughed, a grim sound with little humor in it. "With me, Reem, *almost* doesn't count." She closed her eyes and stood without moving for a moment, then seemed to shake herself as if she were shaking off the weakness that troubled Shareem; opening her eyes and letting go of Shareem's hand, she started for the door. Over her shoulder she said, "Tell me everything that's been happening while I slept. Loguisse is right—it's time I thought up some way to hit back at him."

Shareem followed quietly, wanting to cry a little. Her time was up, and it would never come again. She moved more quickly to catch up with Aleytys, then walked beside her, telling her what had passed since Ikanom brought her up from the heartroom.

The next day Kell called again.

After Ikanom told her, Aleytys turned to Shareem. "How do I locate him?"

"Set kephalos after him. And . . . um . . . unless he's changed things more than I thought, if he's in his dome, I should be able to tell from what's around him. Won't take much."

"Worth talking to him, I suppose." She swung around to face Ikanom. "Try to find out where he is, but keep it from him if you can. Transfer the call here, but give us a few minutes first." She settled in the chair, watched the android leave, then smiled at Shareem. "Maybe you'd better stand where he can't see you—he might be a bit looser."

"He'll know I'm here."

"Could be yes, could be no. Let's give it a try."

Shareem nodded, stepped to one side where she could see the screen but be out of the pickup's range.

Kell's face appeared on the screen, calm, smiling a little, the easy, confident, secretly assessing look of a salesman about to go into his spiel. "A new way of doing your hair."

"It's cool. What do you want?"

"To congratulate you."

Aleytys chuckled. "And make sure I survived your little joke."

"I knew that when the last missile blew."

"You were too slow, cousin."

"Not cousin, Mud, I won't have you call me cousin." he lost a fraction of his calm, then forced the smile back to his face.

Ignoring the interruption, she went on with what she was saying. "You were enjoying yourself too much, cousin, gloating over my end. You gave Reem time to remember how her mother died." She shook her head. "But I won't count on more stupid self-indulgence like that; I expect better of you, cousin. Or is that another mistake?"

"You made the worst mistake of your life, Mud, when you came here."

"Oh no, cousin, my worst mistake was threatening you like a human being. I really should have killed you then like the viper you are."

"Get out of here. Leave Vrithian. There's no place for you here, mongrel. You don't belong here."

"You get more boring each time I see you. Are you finally finished?"

The screen went abruptly dark, but not before both of them saw the fury in his face. Aleytys swung the chair around. "Well?"

"He's in his dome."

"For the moment, anyway." Aleytys frowned. "Something's bothering me. Why did he make that call?"

"I don't know. Not just to rant at you. To make sure you're alive?"

"Hmmm. The little I know of him, everything you've told me about him says he never aims where he's going to strike. He's so Aschla-cursed devious I don't see why he doesn't bite himself and die of the poison." She tapped her fingers on the chair arm. "I wonder if this whole damn world isn't riddled with traps he's set for me. Hunh. You said he called up two days after the last missile?"

"That's what Ikanom said."

"And you warned kephalos before that to be very careful not to trust him?"

"Uh-huh."

"Then it's a trigger. Problem is, for what?" She got to her feet, began pacing restlessly about the room. "What? What?

What?'' She ran her hand through her short curls until they were standing in twisted spikes about her head. "I was being so damn sassy, Reem, crowing at him like a fool. It was a mistake to talk to him. I hope . . ." She stopped by the door. "I don't feel comfortable in here, Reem. Come outside with me?"

Aleytys walked restlessly through the gardens scowling at nothing, forgetting Shareem, who moved quietly beside her, saying nothing, content to wait until her daughter was ready to speak. Aleytys scowled at the meticulously tended shrubbery. *Harskari,* she subvocalized, *what in Aschla's nine fancy hells is that man up to?*

Nothing Hyaroll could detect.

May his teeth rot and his tongue swell and strangle him, I will not believe he's got a whole string of bombs planted in here.

No. Not an attack this time. Information. Something that will let him plan a confrontation on his own terms.

Ah. A tap into kephalos.

Latent, like the bomb. Triggered from outside. A configuration of forces that wouldn't exist until it was triggered.

Harskari, Hyaroll checked the place.

He missed the bomb.

Yes, but . . .

He's ossifying, Lee; I'm surprised he can still make coherent sentences.

I don't know. . . .

You don't want to. Listen to me, dau . . . Lee, it doesn't have to be that way. For some reason—and don't ask me what it is—Hyaroll's running down; he wants to die and he's going to do it, but it doesn't have to be that way. Look at Loguisse—I don't say you'll be like that either, but at least she's sharp and very much alive. Kept her contacts with the outside, has an interest that keeps her brain exercised and excited. You could do worse.

Aleytys said nothing for several steps, startled by the small break in that impassioned speech. Harskari was jealous of Shareem. That sudden realization was so painful she shied away from thinking about it. *How much does Kell hear? Maybe I've said too much already.*

Depends on how much of kephalos he's gained access to. If you continue to make a fuss about your worries and make some really wild speculations, he'd probably discount your suspicions for a while. You told him it was Shareem who suspected the bomb and warned you about it. If I had to guess, I'd say you have a day or two to play the fool. And I wouldn't count anywhere inside the dome safe from observation.

Stinking voyeur.

Bothers you that much, look for the tap and pull it.

I could do that. Aleytys scowled at a flowerbed, seeing nothing of it. *I'd rather set some kind of trap for him . . . ummm . . . or go after him. Look. If he didn't know I'd left the dome . . . remember, you took me through the dome at the Mesochthon without having it opened for us.* She grinned, suddenly, fiercely. *As long as he doesn't know I'm out and roving, and he doesn't know we can pop right through his strongest defenses . . . ay-Madar, Harskari, do you know what he's done with this tap? He's located himself for us, tied himself to his dome. Not a chance he's going to be far away from the other end of the tap. I said it, ay-yiii, I said it, silly viper's gotten so devious he bit himself.* She laughed aloud, danced around in a circle clapping her hands, caught the startled look on her mother's face and settled down to a more sedate walk. "I've had me an idea," she said aloud. "Let me think about it for a bit, then I'll tell you." *Harskari,* she subvocalized, *we've got to do something with Shareem. I can't leave her here, she's too vulnerable. And I certainly can't take her with us.*

Loguisse. Would she help?

Splendid idea. Marvelous idea. Loguisse. of course. Even Hyaroll treats her with respect. Shareem will be safe with her. Got to have a good reason to send her, though. Mmm, if I could be sure Kell wasn't listening, I'd tell her about the tap and ask her if Loguisse might know how to root it out. That's a convincing reason for Shareem to go there, isn't it?

Quite convincing. It could even be true. Does it matter if Kell knows you know?

Good question. As a matter of fact . . . um . . . might even be a good idea to let him know. Convince him I'm focusing still on defense rather than attack. We could sit by the silly fountain and talk in low voices. I'm sure he's perfectly capable of filtering out that bit of interference, but it would look as if I'm trying to keep the plan a secret.

Sounds good to me. A brief silence. *If you're going to do it, do it now.* The amber eyes closed and the feel of the ancient sorceress vanished.

It's going to be lonely, Aleytys thought. *When the last soul's gone. When the diadem's gone. Ah, now, what's that going to mean to me, when the diadem's gone?* She realized suddenly that she could lose more than her last indweller when she shook the diadem off. Trap though it was, it was also an instrument of power, a focus for her own talents. Would they grow more diffuse, less accessible, when the focus was gone? How much of what she could do did she owe to the diadem, how much was her birthright? *I'll find out soon. I owe Harskari her body.* She missed Swardheld and Shadith very much, but she didn't grudge them their bodies, their separate lives. Harskari deserved as much or more from her. She thought of Shadith and smiled, but her smile faded as she remembered where Shadith was now and what she was trying to do. Suddenly irritated by all this devious convoluted maneuvering, she made a small angry hissing sound.

"What is it, Lee?" Shareem's hand on her arm drew her back to the unsatisfactory here and now.

"Just throwing a small snit, Reem, because of all the foolishness Kell is putting us through." She looked around. In her blind wanderings she'd brought them back to the smooth broad lawn spreading out in front of the house. She pointed at the fountain of absurdities. "Let's sit down over there; I've got some things I want to tell you."

"Yes, the water makes a pleasant noise. What is it, Lee?"

"I think I've figured out what that phone call meant. I think Kell's tapping into my kephalos."

"He couldn't, Lee. Hyaroll . . ."

"Guaranteed the place clean. I know. But he missed a bomb bigger than he is, and I think he missed this because the way Kell set it up, it didn't exist until he triggered it. A key word or maybe just completing the call."

"Sounds like something he'd do."

"I've had an idea. Does Kell know more about kephalos than Loguisse?"

"No one does." Shareem sighed. "Not me, that's sure."

"I can't leave here—he'd be on my back the minute I passed the dome. Comlink, well, he'll be listening to every word, and I don't think Loguisse would play, you heard what she told Hyaroll. You've got to go for me, Reem. It's dangerous, but he's not so obsessive about you. He'll know you're leaving, but not why, and I'll have kephalos keep an eye on you as far as it can. Will you do it?"

"You won't do anything rash while I'm gone?"

"How can I? I've got to keep close to kephalos and hope that snake doesn't figure out a way to take control and lower the dome."

"He couldn't . . . I don't know . . . it doesn't stop, damn him, why . . . all right, Lee, I'll go talk to Loguisse. And right now, if you don't mind." She got to her feet with a quick nervous push, started away, came back, touched her daughter's face. "Be careful, will you?" Without waiting for an answer, she swung around and ran for the flier.

Aleytys watched the flier leave, cold with a loneliness that surprised her. The dome seemed empty with Shareem gone. She hadn't expected it, but she'd found a friend. Not a mother. A friend. She'd expected to feel hate and rage when she saw her mother, but from the moment they met she simply liked Shareem. She enjoyed her mother's company. Shareem brought out the frivolous side of her, helped her slough the gloom-and-doom feelings that only made bad times worse.

She wandered restlessly through the gardens after kephalos reported that Shareem had reached the limit of its sensors unmolested. She was unable to settle to the planning she needed to do, even when prodded by a jealous Harskari. The old one didn't like seeing herself replaced in Aleytys's affections by her blood mother. That wasn't exactly true, but Aleytys knew Harskari had some cause for her bitterness. She realized after a while that she'd stopped calling Harskari "Mother" while Shareem was about. Though she seldom called Shareem "Mother," though Shareem couldn't hear or be hurt by the conversations inside Aleytys's head, though the old one had been her nurturer for longer and in ways Shareem would never be, in spite of all these things she could not call Harskari "Mother" any longer. And Harskari had noted the change; the old one noticed everything about her. She was hurt by the change and all that it meant. Aleytys was sorry for that; she owed Harskari too much, she was deeply fond of that stern old spirit and distressed now as she saw the growing disintegration of the strength that had sustained Harskari through the countless ages since her first so inconclusive death. Harskari needed a body, needed it soon.

Aleytys cursed Kell for thwarting any attempt to take care of that need now that she was aware how imperative it was, cursed herself for her complacency and blindness. Energized by that flare of anger, she stopped her aimless wandering and moved swiftly around the house to the landing disk. "Kephalos, bring up Synkatta's flier."

The disk sank into the ground. While she was waiting she tilted her head and frowned at the dome. *Harskari, when you're working that stasis trick, I can keep moving though everything else slows down or stops. What about a flier? Will its propulsors work inside that field?"

Slitted amber eyes, Harskari's frowning face sketched around them. *We had better try it on the ground first; I have no experience with that.*

The flier came smoothly up, its shrouds stripped away by Ikanom's surrogate hands; there was a blue-black sheen to its sleek sides, a grace and fluidity of line that was close cousin to the grace and fluidity of the androids. *Lovely, isn't it? Should be a dream to fly.*

Harskari wasn't willing to be distracted by aesthetics. 'If you can fly it. You can't ask kephalos to instruct you in its capabilities.*

No, obviously not. I suppose we'd better get busy finding out what I can do with it and what happens when you turn the diadem loose on it.

The flier was as responsive as a well-schooled horse, stopping, turning, dropping, darting, maneuvering through the treetops. There were no attack missiles; Aleytys could almost feel Synkatta shuddering at the thought. There was a strong defensive screen and a laser that seemed more suited to slicing stone samples to study in the laboratory than to defending the flier. Harskari held the stasis about it and they found it could make a creeping progress, enough to take it through the dome without alerting kephalos. They tried tuning it to the diadem; the propulsors didn't work at all, but Aleytys found she could move the flier a short distance by willing it forward. When they phased back into the original reality, she sat with eyes closed, shaking with exhaustion, almost unable to move body or brain. Roused by acerbic prodding from Harskari, she reached for her power river and drew in energy to replace what she had expended. After a careful look at herself, she was content to find she hadn't lost significant flesh this time. As she stepped off the landing disk onto the grass, she said, "A very pretty ship, yes. I wonder what Hyaroll did with the starship."

Kephalos might know. If you care to ask.

I think I might be expected to ask. Aschla curse all this fiddling around; as soon as I leave the dome kephalos is going to know something funny is happening.

Leave the key strip here.

Ah. She chuckled as she started for the house. *Tucked in my bed with a blanket dummy. Makes me wonder what you were like when you were a kid.*

None of your business. I was a very proper child.

Hmm. That's open to some interesting interpretations.

Hahh! go play your game with kephalos.

Seriously, when do you think we should leave?

*It would be a good idea to reach him about an hour or so

before the local dawn; his dawn is about thirteen hours ahead of ours. What's the local time? Fourth hour after noon, plus a handful of minutes. Traveling time, giving ourselves some play for emergencies, five hours . . . I'd say we should leave here no later than the first hour after noon.*

Tomorrow? Aschla's stinking hells, Harskari, you mean I have to wait a whole damn day?

Up to you. We could leave earlier, get there earlier. Or leave now get there around first or second hour after dawn. For more precise timing you'd have to check with kephalos.

And wouldn't that be a great idea. Hunh. She leaned against the door, frowning up at the faint shimmer of the dome. *I'm hungry. Let's make it tomorrow noon—that'd give us an hour to play with. I think we'll need to get past the outer rim of his defenses without tripping alarms.*

Good. The amber eyes closed.

Aleytys laughed and pushed open the door. "Ikanom," she called, "I'm hungry."

The rest of the day crept along as she sought for ways to make the time pass. She had a long rambling chat with kephalos about Synkatta's starship and found that Hyaroll had indeed taken it somewhere, but kephalos had no idea where that was; moved on to ways of strengthening the dome where everything she came up with either had already been done or was unworkable; went from that to talking about ways of pinning Kell down so she could do some attacking of her own rather than spending all her time and energy defending herself. "Think you can do that? It doesn't have to be precise, just give me the general area." *That ought to stir his juices,* she thought.

She left kephalos humming contentedly to itself; she could feel a strong glow of pleasure from it as it sank metaphorical teeth into the first hard problem it had had in years. Remembering her impressions as she drifted through it when she was searching for the bomb, she decided that the kephaloi could end up being the true immortals of Vrithian. Long after the last Vryhh succumbed to the crushing weight of the ages, kephaloi in empty domes would be talking to each other and forming a society that could last as long as the world itself. She thought about that awhile, speculating on the nature of that society, until her meanderings became so absurd she laughed at herself and went looking for a book to read among the many shelved in Synkatta's library.

About an hour after midnight she closed the book, a novel by a writer exiled from Shiburr. The Vrya were a darkly threatening thread through the narration, though they were seldom mentioned directly. The native Shiburri went about their lives in the shadow of the domes, always conscious of the undying, a consciousness that seemed to intensify all emotions, all struggles, all relationships. The characters in the novel could not escape from that awareness, though some tried to deny it; others shriveled into futility; a few retreated so far they denied the world as well as the Vrya; some laced themselves to the Vrya, letting the undying use them in return for power over their own kind; the strongest concentrated resolutely on getting the most out of their day-to-day lives, treating the Vyra like a storm or earthquake or any other force of nature they couldn't control but had to cope with. The main character was one of these last. It was a depressing novel, a catalogue of the disasters a good man could suffer, and it ended without hope, Shiburr unchanged and without possibility of changing. She pushed the book off the bed and turned on her back, lay staring into the darkness. After some minutes of chaotic thinking that led only to knots in her stomach, she began the calming exercises Vajd had taught her an eternity ago, cleared her mind and bludgeoned herself into a heavy sleep.

Aleytys . . . leytys . . . eytys . . . tys . . . tys . . . Aleytys . . . tys . . . tys . . . tys. She woke with Ikanom's slender hand shaking her, its voice echoing hollowly in her head. The nightmare-ridden sleep still clogging her thoughts, she pushed its hand away and sat up, scrubbed at her eyes, then emptied the cup of cha it handed her. "What time is it?"

Ikanom took the cup and refilled it. "Almost the ninth hour of the day, Archira. Five hours till noon."

Aleytys sipped at the cha, feeling some of the haziness warming out of her head. "Ninth hour? Why'd you wake me before the time I set?"

"Shareem anassa waits outside the dome, Archira."

"What? Let her . . . no . . . ahh." She rubbed at her temple. "No, let me talk to her first. Take this." She handed him the cup and tossed the covers aside, threw on one of the houserobes and padded across the room to the comscreen. "Reem?"

Shareem's face filled the screen. She looked weary and strained; her eyes had gone dull. "Loguisse came through," she said. Her voice was as lifeless as her eyes. "Lee, don't leave me out here. . . ."

"You look tired."

"I haven't slept. . . ."

"Just a minute." She blanked the screen. "Ikanom, is there anyone in the flier with her?"

"No other brain patterns register, Archira."

"Good enough. Let her through and fix us some breakfast, you decide what. We'll eat in the bookroom, um, yes, a fire, please, and get a bath ready for her."

She touched the image back on. "Come on in, breakfast's waiting, a bath and bed."

Shareem said nothing, just nodded and cut the contact.

Aleytys shook her head, pulled the robe tighter about her and tied the belt. *What miserable luck. Why couldn't she stay with Loguisse one more day?* She ran down the flow-way and into the hall. *Good thing she's so tired, she'll be sleeping when we go, I suppose it won't matter leaving her alone, Kell will be too busy . . . ay, Madar, I wanted her with Loguisse just in case . . . hah, better not think of that, I just have to win, that's all.* She pulled the door open and stepped out. The flier was quiet on the landing disk. Shareem hadn't come out yet. Aleytys ran a few steps, then walked more slowly, frowning. The lock iris began folding open. *Harskari,* she said, *I think I've done something really stupid this time.*

Harskari's eyes open, the diadem begins singing.

Shareem appears in the lock, a massive dark shape behind her; she moves like an automaton. Aleytys remembers what her mother said an eternity ago: "If he gets close to me, I'll do just about anything he tells me no matter how I hate it." *And I sent you out to him,* she thinks, *I was being so clever.* . . . The thoughts pass across her mind in a blinding instant, then she is screaming and running at the flier in a nightmare of slow motion, Shareem has come awake, suddenly, terribly, as the dark form's arm lifts she folds herself around it, fire explodes through her. *No. No. No.* The words scream in Aleytys's head, her mouth is open but no sound comes out, she runs and runs through the eerie outphase world as the fire burning through her mother's body passes through her without touching her. She runs up the flame as if it were a rope and drives her arms into that massive black form. It is like trying to feel about in cold bottom-of-the-barrel molasses, he has protected himself against her gift, the batteries are welded into their slots, if her tractor fields would work in this outphase world, she still would not have the strength to break the welds, the connecting wires are etched into the substance of the armor, paint on high-density metal like that used for the outer walls of starships, her hands scrabble about in him, there is nothing she can get hold of, she starts to panic, remembers the shattered body of her mother, cannot let him win, cannot, never, no, she finds the tiny drivers that power the joints, Harskari half-phases her hands, she snatches anything she can, breaks it, pulls it out, destroys those drivers, shoulders, elbows, wrists, down, hips, knees, ankles, *oh Kell oh Kell oh cousin, I can do this to you because you forced me to learn it,* up again, destroy the weapons, pull their packs, *you weren't so careful here.* Harskari there beside her, white hair whipping about her dark worried face, Lee, she calls, Lee, enough, tend Shareem, Lee, get away from him, I'm taking you back, Lee do you hear me. Harskari's voice finally is more than a mosquito whine in her ears, she finally comprehends what those words mean, she backs away, out the lock onto the landing disk and

falls on her knees when the world moves at normal time about her.

Shareem's body completes its fall, splatting down beside her.

The weight of her flesh is back on her bones, so heavy she almost cannot bear it. The stink of her mother's flesh is in her mouth and nose, she *reaches* for the power, fumbles and cannot find it, this has happened before, calm, calm, be calm, *reach* slowly and carefully, you're just tired, let the water come in, let it pool deeper and deeper in you, this is taking seconds, that's all, it's not wasting time, you can do nothing without the black water. . . . She moves on her knees to her mother's body, reaches out. Shareem seems to see her, or feel her, the residue of life in her flinches away from the hands that want to heal her, flinches, then flows away and there is nothing Aleytys can do to stop it. *She wants to die, she refused to let me make her live. She is dead. My mother is dead.*

Harskari was shouting at her. Something. For what seemed an eternity she couldn't take in what the old one was saying, then she did and was appalled. "No! You can't expect me to . . . No! it's grotesque, I won't . . . I can't . . . you can't be serious. No. Never. I won't do it."

Why?

"This is my mother, it isn't stray meat."

Is it?

"What?" Aleytys looked down at the cooling body; already it had the empty flattened look the dead acquire. "No," she said, "no, not any longer, never again." She began crying. For the second time her mother had abandoned her, and this time was far worse than before, this time she knew her.

I want that body, Aleytys. You swore you'd give me the body I chose. Keep your word, it isn't that much I'm asking. . . . On and on Harskari kept yammering at her; for some ghoulish reason she had to have Shareem's discarded flesh. On and on until Aleytys felt like screaming, until she knew if she didn't do this, she'd never again have a moment's peace. And there wasn't time for her to grow accustomed to the idea, already the brain was decaying and there was massive damage to the chest cavity that would have to be repaired. Either she acted in the next few breaths or it would be too late. *Let it be done,* she thought, *let me be.*

She bent over her mother and laid her hands on the chilling

body. Ignoring everything about her, she poured into it that power she'd been born to use, brought the obdy to a pseudo-life that halted the decay. Harskari gathered herself into a compact ball, wadding up the web of forces that was all the life she had. Aleytys caught hold of it and flung it into the empty envelope as she had done on Ibex with Shadith; no one to steady her this time, she had to do it alone, weary and unhappy. When what was empty was filled, what was on hold an instant before began to change. Stirred by the touch of Aleytys and the lapping flow of Harskari's minute fields, bones began to knit, seared flesh sloughed away to be replaced by new healthy flesh, organs began to rebuild themselves, the gaping wound closed swiftly, healed from the inside out, new skin spread across the muscle, alabaster-white like the rest of her, other cuts and bruises and burns healed, hidden by the remnant of the robe Shareem had worn. Harskari was dimly aware of these, though Aleytys wasn't, she was focused on rebuilding the damaged brain, a long and tedious task with no allowances for error. Minutes drifted by, an hour passed. The brain was more complex than the one Shadith had inherited, the damage was more comprehensive. There were places where there was so little left intact Aleytys had to use her own brain as a template, patching the new in with the old, working with hope and a prayer the new sections would meld with the old. When there was no more damage that she could find, she flooded the body with her power water, kicking it over from death into life, then she sat back on her heels and waited, ready to help if Harskari ran into difficulties.

The blaze of the old one's spirit grew stronger as she slid more deeply into the body. She blinked the eyes, moved the mouth, sucked in a long breath and let it trickle out. She lifted a hand, wriggled the fingers, let it fall back onto the grass, bent the knees, straightened them out, twisted both feet from side to side. The mouth curled into a small smile. She braced the hands against the grass and pushed herself up, straightened her back, squared her shoulders, lifted her head. The small smile broadened into a grin. "You've done it again, daughter." The voice was a little mushy and held to a deeper register than Shareem was accustomed to using, but there were enough similarities to make Aleytys wince.

"Don't," she said.

"What? Oh. Sorry. Habit, I suppose." With every word Harskari's control improved. She began a series of pulling, twisting, stretching exercises.

Aleytys watched for a breath or two, then was aware of a weight circling her head. She reached up, touched it, traced her finger about the delicate cool wires of a flower petal. The diadem, gone inert when the last of its captive souls escaped. She lifted it off, held it in front of her, draped over her hands, flexible, fragile, lovely; a circlet of jewel-hearted lilies spun from gold wire. She touched one of the jewels and felt somewhere deep within her a single shimmering note. Jewel flowerhearts catching the sunlight and splintering it into a thousand tiny gleams, it began to sing to her, weaving a spell of longing about her; it was waking again, calling out for new victims. With a cry half of pain, half of desire, she flung the diadem away from her. It landed in a heap on the grass, gone inert again when it no longer fed off the heat of her hands.

A pall settled over her mind. Hard to think. Her eyes blurred. *What* . . . Her symbolic black water seethed within her; she flushed the fatigue poisons out of herself, but that didn't help, the pall grew heavier, pressing in on her; her head felt like a pumpkin someone was stepping on. Someone . . . she slid around, frowned at the inert lump of armor blocking most of the lock . . . squeezing her brain . . . Kell . . . trapped in the metal that was meant to protect him . . . memory: Kell, wasted from disease, sprawling in the heavy embrace of his exoskeleton . . . she could feel him now, feel the malevolence pouring out of him, he'd tripped a switch, one she'd missed, and cut out his mind shields, the shields that convinced kephalos there was no one in the flier with Shareem, he'd cut them out and was attacking her. His body was prisoner but his mind wasn't. A massive blow shook her. She was pinned, she couldn't answer it. She wrestled with the hold he had on her. Stupid, stupid to forget him, to concentrate so completely on Shareem's body and Harskari's transference. She fought him, managed to move her arms, hugged

them across her breasts, bowed her head. She knelt in a
silvery bubble, fragile as smoke, inside swirling battering
forces . . . no escape . . . no escape . . . no . . . no . . .
creeping in like oil smoke . . . hate . . . anger . . . tendrils of
noisome smoke brushing against the bubble . . . it sagged
. . . she pushed against the weak spot . . . she was slow . . .
heavy . . . without the diadem, weaker, sluggish . . . the
bubble began to crumple as fear distracted her . . . no . . .
no! Fighting the pressure meant to snuff her like a candle
flame, she raised onto her knees, brought one leg up, put the
weight on the foot, leaned forward, laid one hand on top of
the other on the knee, pressed down, brought the other foot
forward, pushed slowly up until she was standing, leaning a
little forward. Step by step, driving herself against the hurri-
cane wind of his will, she moved toward him. He took the
pressure suddenly away. She stumbled, nearly fell, ran on
two steps, whimpering; instead of steady pressure, he was
pummeling at her, punishing blows that kept her off balance,
staggering. She tripped over the rim of the landing saucer,
jarred onto her knees; she could feel his triumph as he drove
in, smashing her defenses down, squeezing her smaller and
smaller. She curled up, knees to chest, strength draining from
her as he bore in and in.

Abruptly the pressure was gone. Only for a second. Something had distracted him. She didn't care about that; she built
her bubble back, struggled onto her feet and started for him
again, seeing nothing but him, that black beetle carapace
crouching inert and broken in the lock. A flash of red. His
head and shoulders were free. Another streak of red. Harskari
in Shareem's body kicking at his head from behind. Aleytys
ran three steps closer, plowed into the hate wind, leaned into
it, fighting toward him, one foot sliding forward, then the
other, closing faster whenever Harskari could break through
the wind and jar him with a kick or a slap before she was
flung back again, disappearing into the interior of the flier.
Anger turning to desperation, Kell writhed about, fighting to
trip the half-destroyed latches manually so he could free
himself from the armor, slamming brute mind-blows at her as
he worked. She staggered, crashed to her knees, fought back

onto her feet; she was on the disk, only two long strides from
the flier, but she couldn't cross that tiny space. Couldn't.
Driven by hate, using a skill he had honed through centuries
of killing, he was stronger, harder, faster; without Harskari's
intervention, she'd already be dead. He drove her back,
knocked her feet from under her; she crawled toward him, he
flung her back, she floundered, blood trickling from the
corner of her mouth. Harskari dragged herself to him and
slapped hard at his head; he struck at her, knocking her into a
sprawl. While he was distracted, Aleytys surged onto her feet
and dived at him, landing splayed out across the massive legs
of the battlesuit. Mind-fire seared her nerve ends, she screamed,
wept, clawed herself along. Behind him, Harskari pulled
herself onto her feet, stood leaning against the side of the
lock, a hand pressed to her stomach, breathing rapidly and
shallowly; she lifted her foot, pressed it against the wall. Her
face went blank with the intensity of her concentration, then
she uncoiled from the wall, one stride into a leap, a kick to
the head; in almost the same breath Aleytys was up and
surging forward; the kick drove his head forward and to the
right; Harskari twisted away, slamming into the side of the
lock before she could stop herself; the heel of Aleytys's hand
hit his jaw, drove his head back the other way; he was tough,
it only dazed him, he shook his head slightly trying to clear
it, but for the first time she was free enough to use her talent,
the talent muted by the discarding of the diadem; she *reached*,
put pressure on nerves until he stopped struggling, until he
almost stopped breathing.

She slid off the carapace, stood looking down at him a
moment. He'd changed so much after she'd healed him that
other time; if she hadn't seen him at the Mesochthon, if he
hadn't identified himself there with his words and manner, she
would not have recognized him. *I don't know you*, she
thought, *not at all. We've come within a breath of killing
each other and we're still strangers.* A groan distracted her,
and she went to kneel beside Harskari. The old one was
having trouble holding herself in Shareem's body; the breathing was harsh and uncertain, the eyes dull, the hands groping
without purpose, the mouth was making shapeless animal

sounds. The body was injured again, not quite so badly as before, only some cracked ribs and organ damage. Sighing, Aleytys *reached*, poured more energy into the envelope, supported Harskari as she tightened her hold, then closed her eyes and set the body to healing its hurts. That was just as easy as before and just as hard. *At least healing is my own gift, not something I got from the diadem.* Behind her she felt Kell begin to waken; with automatic speed and skill she tweaked the nerves again and put him back under, then was surprised at what she'd done. *Wonder if it'll all come back once I've practiced enough.*

Harskari pulled away from her, moved her shoulders experimentally, took a deep breath, expanding her ribs as far as she could, let the air explode out. She got to her feet and bent over Kell. "He's alive."

"Yes."

"You should have finished him."

"Well, I didn't." She pulled her hand across his face. "Things were happening too fast." His hands were plunged beneath the chest piece of the armor. "I need to know what he's done to Grey. I need . . ." She dropped to her knees beside him, tugged out one of his hands and began fumbling about inside that massive carapace for the latches that had resisted his fingers. "Help me get this off him."

"He's not going to tell you anything. What do you want me to do?"

"Maybe he will if he feels helpless enough. See if you can reach the latch for this front section—I think your side and mine have to be tripped at the same time."

"Right." Harskari began groping about under the carapace. "He knows you can't . . . ungh, I think I've got it. You ready?"

They unlocked the intricate pieces of the armor and laid them beside Kell. Aleytys wrinkled her nose. "Must have taken him an hour to get this on. Poor pathetic stupid wretch."

"Lee, he's dangerous."

"He's a better killer—you think that's strength?"

"It's the only kind he understands."

"How do you know?"

"I know his kind."

"What kind is that? Never mind, I was just thinking how little he and I really know about each other."

"You know all you need to know—what he did to you before, what he'll do to you afterward if you're silly enough to let him go again."

"Yes, yes, of course you're right, but it . . . it's sad, don't you think? No, I see you don't." He started to surface, and she put him under again. "Hunt up something to tie him with. Please?"

Harskari nodded. She got to her feet, hesitated. "Be careful."

Aleytys looked up, smiled. "Yes."

Alert to signs of stirring, she hauled him from the lock and stretched him out on the grass. She knelt at his shoulder looking down at him. After a few moments she bent over him and brushed away the hair straggling across his eyelids. She felt strange, uncertain . . . a lot of anger, but it was diffuse, hanging about her like the dust cloud about Avenar . . . as if all these years what she'd cursed and hated was an idea, not a man, and now she was having trouble fitting that idea onto Kell . . . at least while he was lying there with the tantalizing vulnerability most sleepers have. Not that he was asleep . . . she felt the first stirrings in his brain and put him under again. Again she was tempted to twitch just a little harder, it would be so easy, painless for him and painless for her. She looked away, suddenly afraid. Easy.

Harskari came back with a coil of coated wire, pliers and a pair of shears. Aleytys got up to give her working room and wandered aimlessly about, kicking at the grass, trying not to think about what was coming. Harskari wrapped the wire about ankles, knees and wrists, then rolled him onto his face and wired his elbows together. He wore a soft knitted silk shipsuit, a dark blue-green that made his hands and face an icy white, his hair a shout in the brilliant morning light. Harskari tightened the last twist, rolled him back. "Package all wrapped, Lee, neat and waiting."

Aleytys came back. She felt the stirring in him. "It won't be long now," she said, reluctance and distaste in the slow words. She opened and closed her hands, watching and feel-

ing him swim up out of the darkness she had nearly drowned
him in, hoping that when his eyes opened and she saw and
felt the strong hate there, she could lose this helplessness
before his vulnerability, could lose this image of him as a
beautiful battered boy and see the man who'd done his best to
kill her, who'd killed her mother. She tightened her mouth
into a thin line as the pain of that moment came back to her
and the frustration of it, the uselessness of that gesture. *But
she died of it, my mother died to save my life; yes, one could
look at it that way—one could hope she did. That it wasn't
her version of the Vryhh sun dives. Futile act, stupid, useless.
Useless. What a snake hiss of a word. She tried to help me,
but she died. Tried and died.*

*Stand by Kell's right shoulder. Smile. Harskari stands by
his left shoulder. Twin pillars of vengeance we are. Furies we
are, with retribution written on our brows. Oh yes.*

*How harmless you look, my enemy, flat out on the grass,
trussed up with that silly purple wire. Purple for a king. King
Cobra. Flattened by a pair of quick-foot mongooses. Purple,
what a hideous color. Wonder where Harskari found it? Silly,
silly. King cobra wound in cheap taffy, one of those poisonous colors they use for glop like that. Harskari, Harskari,
it's lonesome in here without you.*

Kell opened his eyes.

Her ambivalence vanished.

Enemy as implacable as time.

She recognized the finality of this encounter. It was rather
a comfort to know she had no choice. Gratitude was an odd
bond between them, but there it was. Hunter and hunted,
bound in a kind of complicity until the end of the hunt.

His eyes on her face, he moved his body in a rapid ripple
that put sufficient pressure on those wires to tell him there
was no way he could break them or break loose from them.
He shifted his gaze to Harskari, wasn't quick enough to hide
the flicker of fear when he met her serene green gaze. There
was already a change in Shareem's body. A new persona
wore it and shone through it. He looked away.

As he turned toward her again, she felt a darkness tightening to a knot, reached into him and tweaked those nerves

again, putting him under. There was no way he could stop that, as long as she acted in time. As long as she didn't let him distract her.

Harskari set her hands on her hips. "Do you think that's going to change?"

Aleytys moved a hand, dropped it back to her side, her eyes fixed on Kell as she waited for him to surface again.

Kell's eyelids flickered, opened.

"I can put you under faster than you can strike," she said quickly, hand lifted again, held as if she meant to push away whatever he threw at her. "Don't think you can fool me, cousin—I'm aware of every twitch in that twisted brain."

"What do you want?"

"Grey."

"Haven't got him."

"He's in your trap. Tell me how to release him."

"You're dreaming. What trap?"

"You're lying. Do you think I can't tell?"

"You want me to think you can."

"Psi-empath, Kell. Among other things. How do I release Grey?"

"Go suck a sun."

"That's your answer?"

"Only one you'll get."

"I see." She sighed and stepped back. "Harskari, another favor. Fetch me a knife from the kitchen. Make sure it's sharp."

"Let me do this for you, Lee." Harskari scowled down at Kell.

"No. Get the knife."

"Why a knife? Wouldn't it be easier . . ."

"I don't want it easier."

Harskari pursed her lips, looked as if she wanted to argue some more, but she finally nodded. "Watch him." She swung around and trotted toward the house.

"Don't try it, Kell."

He relaxed. "Deal?"

"Terms?"

"The answers you want. Peace between us. My life."

"I wish I could believe . . ." She dropped into a squat, frowned at him. After a long silence, she sighed again. "I wish . . . I was never your enemy, Kell. I never went after you. . . . I'm afraid there'll never be peace between us as long as you're alive. That's the truth of it."

"I'll swear peace at the Mesochthon on forfeit of my place."

"Why don't I find that reassuring?" She turned her head, spat on the grass. "Your word is worth that."

His mouth pinched into a hard straight line. She watched him struggle to control himself, a pinpoint hope beginning to burn in her in spite of her skepticism, a hope that he was trying to deal with the madness that drove him. Harskari came from the house, walking slowly, almost hesitantly. The blued-steel blade of the knife caught the sun and gleamed with a dark deadliness that Aleytys knew was mostly in her head, not in the knife. Pressing her hand against her stomach as it lurched, momentarily distracted by the knife and what it meant, she watched that blue-black sheen and forgot about watching Kell.

Fire and dark exploded over her
she fell down down down, shrinking as she fell
tiny twisting whirling fluff caught in a huffing wind
enormous pressure on her, squeezing her smaller and smaller
   squeezing her to a point presence   toward nothing   nothingness
nada.

But the pressure faltered before nada, before the endpoint when the point itself would vanish. It returned an instant later, strong as before, but she'd had a breath to anchor herself, she'd had chance to fling up walls about herself, then time to throw a tap into her black river, time to understand that Harskari had thrown herself into this struggle; as before they would whipsaw him, break his timing, his concentration. She sucked the dark energy into herself and blew it out at him. Another break in the pressure; laughter bubbled in her, and she stabbed out and tweaked those nerves he could not protect from her. Turned him off as easily as she turned out a light when she left a room.

Harskari laid the knife on his chest. "Listen to me next time."

"Thanks." Aleytys pushed up off the grass where she'd curled up under his attack, knelt close to Kell's head. She swallowed as she saw the bloody socket, the eye leaking its fluids, and understood how Harskari had managed the distraction. She brushed the straggles of sweaty hair off his forehead, sighed for what seemed the hundredth time. "I had to ask," she said, very softly, almost tenderly. "There was a chance he'd be reasonable." Her hand started shaking. She held it out, gazed at it a moment, then reached for the knife.

"Lee, if you won't put him down the easy way . . ."

"Easy!"

". . . then let me do it."

"No." She laughed, an ugly sound. "Aversion therapy, old friend." She looked at the knife, then at the unconscious man. "I could do it so gently, you know, a twist and a pull and he'd be dead so fast he wouldn't feel a thing. I wouldn't feel a thing beyond perhaps a tiny absence, a gap where something used to be. And the next time, I wouldn't bother fussing. Bad man, crazy woman, pop! pop! angel of death sitting judgment pop! pop! and where would it end? Old friend, I warned Shadith about the pull of her body and how it would distort her reactions. I think it's time to warn you about that same thing. When you rode along as my resident conscience, you taught me well, my best of teachers; don't back off now."

Harskari passed a hand across her face, looked bewildered for a moment, then grim. She nodded, but said nothing.

Aleytys knelt without moving until she felt consciousness stir in him, waited until he groaned with the pain in his mutilated eye, then she pushed the sleeves of her robe up past her elbows, slashed the knife hard and fast across his neck, hot blood splashing over her hands and wrists.

She felt him die, suddenly and hard. She died with him, but unlike him, she came to life again a few breaths later. Shuddering, her hand shaking so badly she nearly cut her leg, she bent to the side, set the knife on the grass. She hugged her arms across her breasts, leaving bloody handprints on the grass-stained white of her sleeves, and began to cry, gulping tearing sobs that jarred her body but gave her little relief from the ache that seized on her, the cold spreading inside her.

Arms closed about her. Someone who seemed an uneasy amalgam of Shareem and Harskari held her and rocked her and sang softly to her until the shock passed off.

With a last pat Harskari let go of her and moved on her knees to Kell's body. She began prodding at his torso with her fingertips, avoiding for the moment the splotch of drying blood.

Aleytys started to rub her eyes, stopped, grimaced at the sticky, browning stains on her hands. She wiped her nose on her sleeve, avoiding the bloody handprint, sniffed, scrubbed her hands on the grass, then on the skirt of her robe, turned up a part of that skirt, wiped her eyes on it, blew her nose into it. She knelt watching Harskari a moment. "What are you doing?"

"Kell's key strip. His dome and ship should be yours now." Harskari began poking her fingertips into the glutinous mess at the neck, clicked her tongue as she discovered the catch and popped it loose. She pulled the front of the shipsuit open. "I thought so." A wide soft belt about Kell's waist. She used her nails to dig under the overlapping end and pried it loose. "Remember what Loguisse said. Seems to me if you're the first to touch it after he's dead, that transfers some sort of control to you." Wrapping the end around her left hand, she jerked hard. Kell's body flopped about, it groaned as the air in his lungs was expelled, his arms and legs flailed briefly at the grass, then went still as the body settled back. Harskari got to her feet, held out the belt. "Here. Take it."

"I couldn't . . ." Her revulsion faded quickly; there were too many reasons why she must. Kell wasn't her only enemy on Vrithian. She needed a ship. Shareem's wasn't . . . she couldn't use it, not for a long long time. Harskari might as well have that; no doubt she counted on it. *War, Kell, your war, and to the victor the spoils. Oh-ah-Madar! Spoils.* She quelled a rising hysteria and got shakily to her feet. "All right. I agree. I'll claim the things. No. You carry the belt. I don't want to touch it, not yet." She looked down at herself.

"I want a bath." The words came out sounding plaintive, like a child calling for something she wasn't sure she was supposed to have. She closed her eyes. *Madar! I'm falling apart.* Giggles erupted from her throat, surprising her. "All ye all ye out's in free. Game's over. I won. Won. Look at what I won . . ."

Harskari mmphed at her, then led her back to the house. "Bath and breakfast, that'll shut off this nonsense."

LOGUISSE: Take the body to the Mesochthon. Not pretty? Doesn't matter. Dump it in the middle of the floor. Declare the war over and yourself the winner (chuckle), though that would seem rather obvious considering the condition of your opponent. You're supposed to hold yourself ready to answer challenges. I wouldn't worry much about that. There's not a Stayer on Vrithian who'd dare come near you.

The dome and the ship. Dome first. You've got his key strip? good. Shareem tell you . . . not Shareem anymore? That will take some explaining. Right. This isn't the time or method for explanations. Once you've made the announcement, go directly to Kell's dome. Yes, leave the body. Not your responsibility after delivery. Where was I? Go directly to Kell's dome. All kephaloi are linked to the Mesochthon. Kell's will be waiting for you. You could have trouble with it; he was a very complex man. I suggest you tie Kell's kephalos into yours, use it to help you overlay Kell's persona with your own. If you run into something peculiar, give me a call.

The ship. Don't—I repeat do not—try anything with the ship until you've pacified kephalos. A loyal ship won't kill you even inadvertently.

How long will this take? Optimally, three to four days. Probably triple that.

Congratulations. Come see me when you
have a little time. We'll whip up some sort of
celebration. And you can tell me about Kell's
downfall and why Shareem isn't Shareem any
more.

SHAREEM'S DOME

Hastily erected shacks on a dusty rutted flat outside the
ground entrance to the dome. A few children, both kinds,
orpetzh and galaphorze, played together in the dust, watched
over by a galaphorze female and an orpetzh naish, sitting side
by side on low chairs, chatting together as Aleytys flew over,
working on something too small for her to see.

Inside the dome: noise and bustle compounded as Harskari
directed the work, reshaping house and gardens to suit her
tastes. Aleytys landed on a dusty saucer, the dome opening
automatically as she approached to let her through.

She stood in the lock feeling battered by the indescribable
cacophony, the whiny rasp of saws; syncopated hammer raps;
shouts from the galaphorze swarming over the house, the
orpetzh teeming across the land; earthmoving juggernauts
growling, grunting, clattering as they reshaped the surface;
drills biting into the earth; backhoes laying pipe. Energy and
excitement were thick as the noise—as if some huge beast
long dormant had suddenly waked to vigorous life.

Aleytys smiled. *It begins,* she thought. *Vrithian is changing.*
She stepped from the lock and began walking toward the
small section of Shareem's house that Harskari had left intact,
circling around an orpetzh spading a flowerbed, then a squad
planting an irregular line of small bushes with smoky blue-
gray leaves, jumped aside at the squawk of a horn and the
cheerfully obscene shout of the galaphorze driving a lumber
sled toward a knot of carpenters just visible behind three huge

old trees Harskari had exempted from destruction when the rest of the garden was swept away. When she finally reached the door, she flattened her hand on the call plate and smiled with relief as the door slid open. As she had a handful of times before, she said, "Ah, Lampos, how goes the transformation?"

The damascened android bowed, the movement making his tracery shimmer. "With noise and verve, anassa," he answered as he always did.

"Where is she?"

"In the bookroom, anassa. Loguisse also."

"Well . . ." She was both irritated and amused. "That will save me some traipsing."

She stood in the doorway watching them. They were too engrossed in what they were doing to notice her. Loguisse had finally found someone to talk to. Once she'd gotten over her shock and skepticism, she was excited by Harskari's history and fascinated with that ancient science she impatiently refused to call sorcery. Harskari's people had worked more by instinct and intuition than by any rigorous development of theory, and Loguisse was immersed in an attempt to provide what she considered proper mathematical descriptions of the forces and conditions Harskari described and illustrated. The two women argued endlessly and with much passion over things Aleytys acknowledged to herself she'd never comprehend. And Loguisse threw herself into the remodeling of the house and gardens with a ferocity nearly equaling Harskari's.

The closeness between Harskari and Aleytys might never have existed. Aleytys was still uneasy when she saw her mother's body walking about; she found it disturbing, rather like watching a zombie prance on its coffin. Shareem's spirit . . . soul . . . persona . . . whatever . . . was gone. There was nothing of her mother left, yet when she saw her mother's flesh vibrant with life, she could not come to terms with her mother's death. She could not grieve. That loss, that pain, was sealed up inside her until she was bloated with it, about to explode if she couldn't find relief. She drew her hand across her brow, then smiled. "Looks like you've got half of Guldafel working here," she said.

The two women broke off what they were doing, looked around at her, startled. Harskari set her stylus down, wiped her palms with a handkerchief she pulled from the cuff of her sleeve. "Lunchtime already? Or are you early?"

"Lunchtime. And more than time. I see I'll have to tell Lampos to make sure you eat something now and then."

Harskari laughed. "Yes, Mama."

Loguisse gave Aleytys a quick welcoming smile. "Just as well we hire them. There's been an influx of refugees from Agishag the last several years, and Guldafel's economy is showing the strain. Apparently Hyaroll has cancelled all contact with the outside. The uplands of Agishag are reverting to desert."

Change, Aleytys thought. *Ah well, it was never going to be all sweetness and laughing*. "He said don't call him again the last time I saw him."

Loguisse looked austere. "All this interference with Vrithli lives, it's nonsense. Harskari agrees with me. We'll guard our borders and leave the rest."

"I thought you simply weren't interested in your Vrithli."

Loguisse grinned. "That too."

Lampos came to the door. "Archira, lunch is served. In the hall where you wished."

Harskari shoved her chair back and got to her feet. "Now that I think about it, I'm starved. Did we eat breakfast?"

"Not that I remember." Loguisse followed Harskari across the room. "We started to, I think, but we got into the similarity equations and . . ."

"No wonder I've got this hole in my middle. The tribulations of a bo . . ." She glanced at Aleytys, broke off. "Coming, Lee?"

"That's what I'm here for."

"Seems to me you invited yourself."

"So I did."

Aleytys angled the knife across her plate, set the fork beside it. "I had a reason for inviting myself."

"And we're supposed to ask what it is?"

"No need to stir yourselves. I'm off."

"What?"

"This evening. Ship's tested enough and I . . . I can't wait any longer."

"Avosing." Harskari sighed. "Don't hope too much, Lee."

"I don't, but I've got to know." She lifted her glass, tilted and rotated it so the last half inch of the golden wine slid across the bowl, leaving a faint film behind. "I'm taking some of Kell's nastier warbots. Them and me . . ." She managed a brief smile. "We can take on anything."

"And if Grey's dead?"

"I don't know. Yes I do. I'll go back to Wolff for a while no matter what I find on Avosing. I . . . I need it . . . I need the people there. And maybe Canyli can find a really horrendous Hunt for me. Take my mind off."

"Coming back here?"

"In a while. When doesn't matter, does it? The one thing I've got plenty of is time."

ARKADJ ON BREPHOR

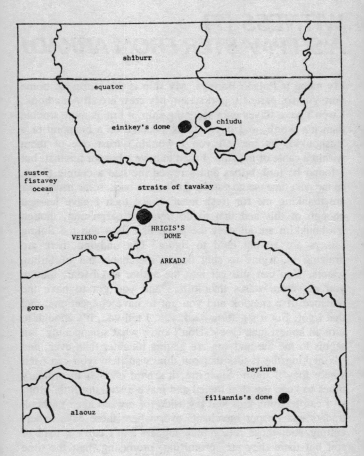

VRITHIAN
WITNESS [7]
A SHIPMASTER FROM ARKADJ

My name is Polado Barrega. My ship is the *Marespa*, home
port Veikro, part sail, part steam. My crew are all Arkadjonk.
I won't have slaves on a seagoing ship; it brings more trouble
than it's worth, and if you think I'd take on a Fosporat or a
Yashoukki, let me tell you I wouldn't trust one of them
within a cable of my ship. I used to have a Fospor linguist, but
I found he took bribes and screwed me bad a couple times,
so the next time we go out, he don't come back; some haddyronk
are thanking me for fresh meat. Since then I have learned
enough of this and that to do my own bargaining, though
Yashoukkim are all over the place like fleas and the Suling
Lallers are getting hard to figure. The undying there are
drawing in, trying to shut honest merchants out of Suling
waters. You can still get into the harbor at Obattar, though
you get more stares than offers and you got to have the
patience of a sneglok and you got to have connections, and
that I got. But it's getting hard, yah, I tell you, it's enough to
turn an honest man crook. Don't know what's happening, but
seems to me the undying are getting touchier than ever, and
it's making the randts that run things so itchy you can't tell
where they'll jump. Slangstra, it's hard enough in ordinary
times to keep my ship fueled and make a stinking little profit
so I can feed my kids and lay aside for my old age. Yashouk
traders and Fospor merchants everywhere these days under-
cutting you; those rotten little luggers can't carry a load of
spit but there they are, promising, promising, half the time
they're pirates on the side, a land-trader's lucky they don't
take his skin and sell that. Then you get home and find some

Fospor naftiko anchored in your own port skimming off the cream while you get tangled up in paperwork until it cost you a fortune in silver to cut through it and he gone before you finish and half the time he kill the market for your best goods. Slanstro-damned Fospor, weren't for the undying, I'd get together with Toricas and Gestang and lay a hard hand on Tropagora and put the fear of Salanggor into those godless squeeze-pennies and sneaking cheats. Days like this, I think I'm going to burn to ash from the inside when I think about Yashoukkim and Fosporain and what they're doing to me. Salanggor curse them, those undying. I know they been here since my granda's granda was a nit, and his granda too, but anytime some hardworking merchant makes a change here and there just to make things a little easier, they stomp him. Hasn't never been a war, no matter how bad things get. Smash an honest man but don't give shit about pirates; they can burn villages and sink ships and who gives one holy damn about it? They just don't want men feeling free, that's all, they don't want men ignoring them, the shitheads; they want to play with us like dolls, that's it, they look down here and watch us and laugh. They don't care what we think. They don't care how much we try. But if we start doing what we want to do, it's foot on the neck, face in the mud and breathe how you can. I could go up to one of them and say I want to kill you, I could go up to haddyr-face Hrigis and say I want to peel your skin off a strip at a time and feed it to you, I want to chop you into bait and catch a hold full of fish with you. And she'd laugh in my face and tell me to lick her feet and I'd be on my belly licking. Yah, I tell you. And the bloodsuckers who run us, they're worse, the Vennor and Vannish and the leeches in the government sucking us dry and eating the meat off our bones. No, I'd never talk this way to their faces, not them, those vipers are too poisonous and too scared, they'd have me dead between one breath and the next. And I can't do one thing about it, no one can, because those parasites are backed by the undying, yah, the undying prop them up and let them go on draining us, stealing the breath out of our throats. But what can a man do? Live by his wits and scrape around the tangle of paperwork. Smuggle

what he can and get what he can for the rest. I think of the
undying and there's a fire in my belly. I think of them
watching, they've come strolling by and betrayed me with a
grin more than once, I think of them watching and I wonder
what it would be like to live where there were no undying, to
go about your days without some demigod peering over your
shoulder. I wonder. Oh yah, I wonder.

VRITHIAN
on the oblique file [4]

KEPHALOS TO SUNCHILD: Kell is dead. Hours, no more, before Hyaroll goes.

SUNCHILD TO WILLOW: Kell is dead. Time is now. Now the bow, now the anointed arrows.

SUNCHILD TO BODRI: Kell is dead. The time is now. Now the herds, the helpers. Fetch them.

Sunchild flitted away to wind in an elaborate gavotte with kephalos, a dance around the strictures that bound it. Kephalos was not to notice what it knew was happening.

Willow watched Sunchild streak down the hillside. For a moment she sat very still, then she got onto her feet with a swift surge of her small body. "Otter hunts," she sang. "Otter hunts in me. Watch, my children, watch, Otter hunts." Still singing, she dropped to her hands and knees and crawled into her hut. The bow and arrows were wrapped in a fine cloth Sunchild had brought her; the stoppered gourd of poosha sat beside the bundle. She gathered these and backed out, clicking her tongue in the rhythm of her song.

Bodri came trundling into the camp. Humming her song, Willow straightened, stared. She hadn't seen ol' beetle for more than half a Minachron. He'd changed. The garden on his back was gone, replaced by a mosaic of mosses. "What what?" she said.

"I will start a new garden when the effort seems worthwhile," he said.

"Your piece part, ol' Bug. You get us in?"

"Had better, hadn't I? Ah Willow, sweet Willow, trust me, I have indeed worked out a way. While Sunchild keeps kephalos occupied, with its consent, of course, we enter through the kitchen."

Willow looked skeptically at him. "You climb wall, bang door down?"

"No, Whisper in my heart, I walk through both doors."

"And what do ironheads be doing?"

"You'll see. It's time we went."

They went quickly down the mountainside, down the footpath they'd used many times to reach the gardens or the lake, left the path and circled to the back of the house where a high stone wall shut in the kitchen garden. Bodri stopped Willow and drew her into the shade of a lod-bush, making a grating, gnashing sound of pure irritation.

"What? what?"

"Lazy skelos, they were supposed to have the herd waiting . . . ah! There. Look."

A small herd of girilk came trickling out of the trees, coaxed along by a pair of six-legs who trotted about them and touched them with stinging feelers if they showed inclination to move in the wrong direction.

Moving at a lumbering gallop, Bodri crossed the grass to the door in the wall. One of the long thin fingers at the end of a fore-right tentacle slipped through the hole he'd bored through the hard tough wood and touched the latch button. He drew it swiftly back as the gate began to swing open. With a high warbling call he went through the opening, shoving the door as far back as it would go. Willow followed him through, looked back. The girilk were trotting toward her, driven into a honking run by the skelos. She grinned. Sneaky ol' beetle.

The kitchen garden was a half acre of cultivated land protected from roaming beasts by a high wall a good three times Willow's height. Bodri settled himself into a crouch between two rows of peach trees, waiting for the herd to pass.

Willow broke away, ran between vine rows and crouched by the trunk of an espaliered pear. She unwrapped the bow and strung it, slipped the strap of the arrow pouch over her shoulder. She thought about nocking an arrow but changed her mind. *Keep the hands free until you get close to what you're tracking,* Otter sang in her. *Be loose and ready to ride the winds of chance.* Bodri and she were creeping up on Hyaroll, down the kephalos wind from him. And kephalos would keep the wind blowing to them as long as they did not harm Hyaroll. When Bodri had finished mixing the right poosha, Willow had proved how benign it was by pricking herself with the point of an anointed arrow, had gone down deep and come swimming out of sleep unhurt. Kephalos would not betray them as long as they were true.

Bodri came rushing through the vines as silent as thought. She grinned at him, excited and nervous and at the back of her mind weaving a song of this hunt.

The girilk were munching briskly at some rows of thrix.

Bodri settled beside her, a mossy hump, head drawn inside his carapace though his antennae curled up and out, quivering in a wind that didn't exist. She waited, Otter's ghost watching over her shoulder, his patience entering her, possessing her who had seldom been able to keep still from one minute to the next. She was warm with his presence and quiet now with a hunter's unending stillness, waiting, waiting, waiting, for the door to open.

The girilk snorted and crunched placidly down the rows, leaving a swath of kicked-up earth behind them. The skelos were nowhere about.

The door hissed into the wall and an ironhead came out, a smaller one, more fragile than most she'd seen. It rushed at the girilk, who snorted and shook their heads, danced away from it and began eating in another section of the garden.

As soon as the door hissed, Bodri's head came out, and he surged onto his six feet, tentacles held in ready loops before him. While the ironhead was busy with the recalcitrant herd, he moved with a swift and powerful silence up the steps and into the house, charging the other one waiting inside. It stopped what it was doing and stared, then three of Bodri's tentacles closed around it and the fourth searched over its torso, slid open a panel and twitched a plug loose, killing it for that moment.

Willow followed him more sedately. While he was struggling with the ironhead, she dipped the needle points of two arrows in the gourd of poosha, nocked one of them and held the second between two fingers of her bowstave hand.

A tiny patch of gold light flitted into the kitchen, bobbed up and down in front of Bodri, then darted away. Bodri rushed after it, Willow ran after him. They went up and up along a lazily spiraling ramp to a small round room domed with colored glass where the sun came in hot and thick and gold.

Hyaroll lay face down on a padded table. The ironhead Megathen was kneading his shoulders and back, talking to him quietly. The room was filled with small sounds, distant running water, the hum of insects from some ancient summer evening, the lazy rustle of leaves.

Willow stepped past Bodri, lifted her bow and loosed the arrow, smiled as it lodged in Old Vryhh's rump, two fingerwidths buried in the mound of muscle.

Megathen cried out and reached for the arrow. Hyaroll yelled and started to swing around. Bodri brushed past Willow, almost knocking her off her feet, charged at Megathen, wrapped his tentacles around the ironhead and pulled it away from the table. Willow set herself again, nocked the second arrow, then put it in Old Vryhh's shoulder, high up in the muscle, taking care to hit a spot where the point wouldn't do serious damage.

A moment of stillness as Hyaroll stared at her, fighting off the poosha longer than she'd thought possible, Old Stone Vryhh. To her astonishment he smiled, began to lift a hand in salute. Before he could finish the gesture, the poosha took him and he collapsed in a heap on the table.

Bodri held Megathen in a strangling grip, though the ironhead stopped struggling the moment Hyaroll lost consciousness. Willow danced across to the table. "Sleep long, no dream,

sleep long, Old Vryhh, no dream, Old Vryhh,'' she sang to
Old Vryhh, and shut his eyes for him. She pulled the arrows
out of him and tossed them aside, dipped into the pouch on
her belt and smeared some styptic paste on the wounds to
stop the bleeding. No need to worry about evil demons
crawling into those wounds, though puncture wounds were
the worst. In the stasis boxes even demons slept.

Sunchild came drifting in, collecting the piece of himself
as he passed it. "Bodri, you can let Megathen go; I need his
arms." He hovered over Hyaroll. "Willow-Willow, kephalos
sends compliments on your aim." He drifted back to the
door. "Megathen, bring Hyaroll down to the Reserve. Willow, you and Bodri better stay here awhile. This next bit's,
um, kind of touchy."

Willow nodded. She had no desire to see that dread array
again, tiers on tiers of boxes marching into the darkness,
meat lockers filled with stopped lives.

Megathen picked up Hyaroll and followed Sunchild from
the room.

Willow unstrung her bow and set it aside, slipped off the
arrow pouch, checked to see if the cork was tight in the
poosha gourd and put that down too. Otter's spirit slipped
away from her, and she felt a sudden grief. She squatted on
the mossy rug. It was too warm and breathless in here for her
tastes, but she set that aside and began hunting among her
song dances. Her people didn't fight wars, but now and then a
feud started up between two clans and went too far for the
pa'tanish to reconcile them; then it lasted until one clan or the
other ran out of folk. *Yes*, she thought, *yes, I the last living
and my enemy he gone*. It was a song that needed nothing but
the singer. It was a song that had no dance, no triumph,
nothing but sadness. She squatted by the padded table and
sang against the small sounds the song of the last alive.

Sunchild returned while she was singing. When she finished, he came and squatted beside her, Otter to the eye.
"Kephalos says thank you for the song."

Bodri's antennae quivered; Willow said nothing.

"It's done. He's tucked away in a stasis box. He won't die
now, so we won't either."

Bodri stirred after a while, shook himself, his carapace swaying like a bell. "I'm hungry." He started for the door. Still saying nothing, even her body subdued, Willow gathered bow, arrows, the poosha gourd and started out after him.

"Wait. The house is ours now. Everything. What do we do with it?"

Bodri stopped at the door, backed around so he could see Sunchild. "Not mine. Don't like walls. If this place belongs to anyone now, I would say kephalos has it. Maybe the two of you. Willow?"

"No."

"You sure?"

She stroked her throat, drew her shoulders up, hugged her arms across her breasts. "Can't breathe this place."

"You see?"

Sunchild quivered. "We see. Yes. Bodri?"

"Yes?"

"Kephalos gets lonesome."

"Let me think." Bodri curled up his antennae, closed his eyes, swayed his big head back and forth. "Ah. Let kephalos make ironheads that are just talkers, it can send them out and talk to everyone, so we're comfortable and it's not lonesome." Bodri chuckled, his carapace swinging side to side in time with his laughter. "Not so different, after all—old Vryhh wasn't doing that much these last years."

Sunchild lost his slightly forlorn look. "Yes yes, let it be as it was, kephalos working everything and us outside. We'll have to think what to do with the sleepers, but there's no hurry now, is there?"

Willow giggled, clapped her hand against her side and went dancing out the door. "No hurry, no hurry, no hurry, none no more."

VRITHIAN
action on the periphery [5]
Bygga Modig

Weary, aching, layered with grime, Amaiki hefted her bag of belongings and joined the dispirited line of refugees filing off the ship. Never enough water, food that would choke a varka, the stench of too many concs in too small a space, day on day on day in a shuddering juddering sickening slide and roll. And beyond the body's suffering there was the raveling of the spirit. Elbow to elbow with alien concs whose lines she didn't know and didn't want to know. Elbow to elbow with galaphorze seamen whose stench nauseated her, on a battered rust-bucket whose owner had the instinctive greed of all Arkadjonk. The *Marespa*. She'd never forget it. Never. Its grime was ground into her skin, its creaks and thumps and squeals and hisses had carved themselves into her brain. Even now Barrega harried his men into prodding the weary line along so he could wash his ship of them and rush back across the Istenger to cram another load on board. The crowds were thinning on the wharves of Shim Shupat. If he dawdled here he might even have to put out with a normal cargo rather than this jammed mass of stinking life.

The wharf they tied to was at the far end of a busy crowded port, the noise, the crowds, the smell, all worse than those on the ship, but there was a different feel here, something freer and bolder that crept inside Amaiki's insulating coat of grime and gloom. Something wild . . . it was hard to say just what it was, but it called to that part of her which had responded so disturbingly to the laughter and shouts and songs of the manai-gone-wild. She breathed in a great lungful of the air, expelled it, sucked in more. She wanted no trace of the

339

Marispa's miasma left in her lungs. She walked off the ship with a straighter back, her ears up and forward.

With a growling impatience she worked her way through the swarm of confused passengers that clotted the wharf, shoved herself to the gate and the U-shaped counter where a bored galaphorze male sat questioning each conc before he or she or na could leave the wharf, punching the answers into a datarec, turning a few back, passing the others on, stamping some hands, leaving the others bare.

NAME:	Amaiki-manetai line Jallis meld Sinyas
PURPOSE IN COMING TO GULDAFEL:	To join the rest of my mate-meld who are already here.
THEIR NAMES:	Keran-manetai line Sinyas meld Sinyas Betaki-tokontai line Yarimm meld Sinyas Muri-tokontai line Sinyas meld Sinyas Kimpri-manetai line Hussou meld Sinyas Se-Passhi naish Sinyas

The galaphorze glanced at the readout, grunted, then waved her through the gate. She walked down the crudely built chute that shuddered and bounced under her feet. At the other end of the chute a tall conc female halted her. ''Hands,'' she said.

Amaiki held out her hands, palm up.

"Over."

Irritated but too weary to argue, feeling like a naughty child hauled before the line mother, she turned her palms down.

With a grunt much like the galaphorze the conc motioned to the left. "That way."

The chute split into two arms beyond the counter where the conc sat. Amaiki started down the left branch, looked over her shoulder. A mate-meld was being directed down the right. A singling like her was the next, hands inspected, waved after the meld. Another singling, hands held out, sent after her. She shrugged and went on. No telling what criteria they were using, and she was too tired to bother speculating.

The chute opened onto a noisy street. She stepped out, moved aside to give those following room to go by while she decided what to do. None of those passing along the street paid much attention to her, a glance or two from the galaphorze and conoch'hi and other orpetzh moving briskly both ways along the street, mixing with sleds piled high with boxes and bales. Horns blatting constantly, shouts, laughter, voice raised in a sudden explosion of anger; the noise was extravagant and bewildering, the colors were as raw and confusing. She blinked; it was impossible to focus on anything; there were no patterns anywhere she could find to give her a place to start as she tried to make some sense out of the chaos around her. It was ugly and loud and strange and she should have hated it—and she did hate it, but there was also something seductive about the vigor and aliveness of the scene, something that energized her.

"Ami-sim. Ami-sim." Muri came running across the street, elbowing his way through the walkers, darting around the sleds, exchanging unserious curses with one of the drivers who came close to running over him. He slammed into Amaiki, nearly broke her in half with the urgency of his hug.

Amaiki laughed and stroked his weedy crest. "Oh it is good good to touch you again, sim-sim, my Muri, my sweeting, my jintii."

He caught her hand and tugged her away from the wall. Frightened and excited, she followed him into the confusion in the street, trying to ignore the nudges and shoves from galaphorze and orpetzh alike. Orpetzh. Not just Conoch'hi from Agishag, but cousins from all over the world, strangers whose manners and smells and voices and languages were almost as alien as those of the galaphorze.

Muri didn't try to talk to her, but led her at a trot through a maze of streets, deeper and deeper into the city, away from the waterfront. Gradually the noise and confusion died to a manageable level. There was still a disturbing strangeness about the place, and the thick lowland air was hard for her to handle even after the months on the ship.

Muri slowed a little and turned into a narrow street with high walls on both sides. Over his shoulder he said, "Not much further, Ami-sim."

She nodded, though he didn't wait for her response. *Muri too-quick.* Laughing inside for the first time in days, she hurried after him.

He stopped before a door set deep in the wall, tapped the caller plate and stood waiting.

In a moment the door hummed into the wall. Muri caught her wrist and pulled her inside with him.

A garden like her own. Not exactly, the plants were strange, but the patterns were as familiar as breathing, so wonderful, so comforting. She tried to linger, but Muri hurried her on. "Pinbo has done well for herself over here, Ami. This is her meld-house. Meld Likut-Dassha runs a trading company and has shops in just about every Dum and galaphorze Garat in Guldafel." He pushed open a gate in an archway, moved into another garden, this one not quite so familiar. "Things are crazy here, Ami-sim. No work, the price of everything, well, you wouldn't believe what folk have to pay for a week-old egg. Hadn't been for Pinbo and her meld, we'd've had a miserable time. She's even found work for us. The undying here is rebuilding everything in her dome; we're going north soon as you've rested a bit. Good thing about that is the undying is paying us in land. We'll have a place for ourselves again, Ami-sim. One year's labor for the undying and that's all."

Amaiki jerked loose, cold and fearing and angry, all pleasure lost. Undying. *I forgot, ay mother, I forgot what I knew coming across the uplands. The undying. Here too. Everywhere.* Back to the same futile dependence. She felt helpless and furious. Muri was staring at her, surprised by the turn in her. "Undying," she whispered, then spat. "Not again. How could you, Muri, how could any of you . . ."

"It's different here," Muri said, speaking slowly for once. "I know, I understand, but you'll see. This undying is hardly ever here, she doesn't want anything from us except what she pays for. It's always been like that, Ami. No one here depends on her for anything; they wouldn't get it if they tried. This is our chance to make a new life, a real life, sim-sim." He patted her arm. "I know, we all know. Come. You're just worn to a nub, that's all. Whew! after that trip we could hardly move an ear."

Struggling to deal with the anger knotting her insides, Amaiki walked silently beside him.

"The one thing you'll really have to get used to," he said as he led her into a court behind the main house, "is all the galaphorze about. But they're not so bad when you get to know them. It's the other orpetzh that, well, the way they act, ahhhgh, Ami . . ." His ears flickered, his hands flailed the air. She was startled into laughter, and after that the tension drained quickly out of her.

Then they were in the guesthouse, touching and hugging, a confusion of talk, everyone at once, no one bothering to listen, no one minding that no one heard what they were saying.

Then Betaki brought in the new hatchling and gave na to Amaiki. She held the small soft body close to her, felt the little mouth sucking at the side of her neck, tasting her flavor, adding it to the other flavors na knew as na's own. She blinked away tears and couldn't speak. Se-Passhi pressed against her, the others made a circle about her, lapping her in their warmth. All the aches and sorrows and the bitterness she brought across the sea with her washed out of her. They'd be back, she knew that well enough, but now there was no room for anything but a joy beyond words.

*   *   *

About midmorning the next day, they carried children and
gear aboard a Fel river barge and started north into their new
life.

CABOZH ON GYNNOR

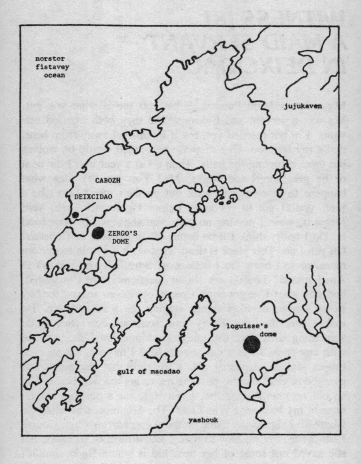

VRITHIAN
WITNESS [8]
A MAID SERVANT
IN DEIXCIDAO

My name is Meni Peraroz. What you see is what you get.
Ma was a servant and Grandma and they both married servants. I'm not married yet, but if I can't get away from here,
that's my fate too. One of those half-assed would-be wolves
out there prowling the halls. Then a kid a year unti I die of it
or he gets bored and walks. Me? You got any idea what
happens to women who walk out on their men? Don't be a
fool, you. I got to get away before I get stuck, yeh, yeh,
forget it, wasn't making no pun, you show where your head
is. Do I really think I'll be better off in Borbhal or Cobarzh?
Oh yeh I do. This place is dead. Frozen. It's a little looser out
there, or so I hear. Do I believe it? Sure. I have to, don't I?
Am I scared? You do ask stupid questions. Sure I'm scared,
but look what I've got here. Creepy old Zergo around the bay
in his dome, he likes things staying the way they are. He
makes sure they do. Every time someone here tries to do
something different, the undying stomps on him. Anyone
with any push, he gets out young. Me? I'm going on for nine
[about sixteen standard]. Ma's all right but my aunts and
everybody else, they're pushing me to get married before I'm
so old no man'll want me. Even Her, she's pushing her fat
nose in my business. Who? Her. The Mistress, who else? So
what? So I signed my name on the Agencharosh's list. Course
I can write, my ma saw to that. I know most of us can't, but
she saved out some of her tips, hid it where Dado couldn't
get to it and drink it up, and she hired a Tempestao half-
priest to teach me and my sister. She left last year, my sister
did. We haven't got word one from her, but I figure maybe

346

where she is it's rough getting the coin to send a message. Where was I, ah yeh, I signed my name on the Agencharosh's list, the bride list. Lot of those men who left want old-country wives. What if I don't like mine? Tell you. I run, that's what. I figure there's probably someone I'm gonna like better. Yeh I'll get married. What else can a girl do? But my kids will have it better. There's always a way. Ma showed me that. But you got to fight hard and you got to fight smart and you got to know you can't do much for yourself, but your kids will have it better'n you, or what's the use of living? Cobarzh. They say it's wild and dangerous, but there's land for the taking. Fight smart and hold hard to what you got. I'm gonna make something of myself. You'll see.

AVOSING
action on the second line [2]

Sucked through a too-small hole. Pain scraping along her body. Disorientation. Terror. Anger. A smashing blow. Something stopped her like slamming against a brick wall, then punted her into a vast nothingness where she lost all sense contact, even the feel of her own body.

More confusion. She never quite lost awareness, but for a while all she had was an assurance that she still lived. Until she came to rest, a quivering shivering nothing.

She couldn't feel her body.

Rush of fear and rage that almost tore her apart. Fear she'd been wrenched loose from her hard-won body, condemned to that tenuous existence she'd known as a prisoner of the diadem.

After the first shock dissipated, she understood what had happened. Attacking the Ajin's body with those claws had triggered Kell's trap. Remembering Grey and Ticutt turning and twisting in the screen, bodies intact, she clutched at hope and calmed herself further. She wasn't as helpless as the others would be, she knew this state (or one too like it for her comfort), had learned to deal with it, circumventing its restrictions. What she'd done before, she could do again.

Using her adopted gift and old experience, she *reached*, probing through the nothing about her.

Linfyar. Screaming with his whole body, terrified, doubly blinded now.

Linfy, Linfy, she sent to him, his name over and over, nothing more, until her mind-voice punctured his panic and quieted him.

Shadow? Voice echoing like a shout in her mind, sense of floundering.

Hang on, Linfy, I'm going to try moving over to you. Keeping her hold tight on him, she willed herself toward him, the ache in her head this brought on paradoxically welcome because at least she was feeling something. Then she was touching something, though she still couldn't feel her own body. Not much. It was a blurred, dull stimulus that crept like a slow fuse along her, slow currents stirring in a body almost turned off, but there, thank whatever gods there be, *there*. Linfyar clung desperately to her, trembling all over in agonizingly slow shudders.

Linfy, Linfy, it's all right, it is. We're in the trap, that's all, but I'm going to get us out. Trust me, Linfy, trust me, haven't I got us loose before? Don't worry, don't fuss, I'll get us out. She rubbed her hand up and down his back, pressing hard so she could feel what she was doing, so he could feel it. Finally he lay quiet against her; some of his heat crossed into her and she began to feel herself somewhat more. She started to pull away, but he butted into her, clutched frantically at her. *Easy, easy, Linfy,* she said. *You're hurting me, imp, ease off or I'll have bruises in places I wouldn't want to explain. Ah, that's better. I know you're sorry, imp. Listen to me. Let me go. Grey's in here too. And Ticutt and Taggert. I've got to find them, Linfy. Umm. There's something you can do. I can't say anything or hear anything through my ears, but your range is way wider than mine. You can help me hunt. Try your top and bottom and see if you get any echoes, huh?* She thought a moment. *If it doesn't work, don't worry, I'll keep touch with you, you won't get lost. All right?*

She felt curiosity and a growing excitement in him, an excitement that swamped his panic; turning his focus off his helplessness and setting him to doing something about it made an immediate difference. He let himself swing away from her, though he did keep one hand closed painfully tight about her arm. She felt him get set, then felt the effort he was putting into throwing out the sound, felt his disappointment when there was no return. Then he started pulsing again, long

slow beats that she didn't actually hear but felt as tickles
across her skin. She stiffened, nearly choked on her excitement. *I'm feeling that.* *I feel that,* she mind-yelled at
Linfyar. *I feel that.* Linfyar radiated glee, then pressed
harder, delighted with the tickling thrum. A sound that was a
physical presence here, as solid as their flesh.

He let go of her, began turning in a slow circle, throwing
out the subsonics. He burned with excitement when he located
another three echo points evenly spaced about him.

I did it, Shadow, he sang to her. *I did it, way way
down, 'bout as far as I can go. Three and you, Shadow.
Three and you.*

This was the final evidence that her body was here with
her, not just a hope and a prayer and self-delusion. *Splendid, Linfy. I'm going to try reaching them. This one on my
left first. Keep track of me, will you, and tell me if I'm going
wrong, huh?*

Sure, Shadow. He was a little trembly at the prospect of
her going away from him, but he had enough information
coming in so he didn't feel wholly lost and could regain that
stubborn independence circumstances had built in him.

She *pushed*, ignoring the ache in her head, knew she was
drifting away from Linfyar because she lost the body-sense of
his presence. *Who?* she thrust at the faint warmth that drew
her. *Who?*

After several repetitions and a slow drift closer, she got a
startled response from the presence ahead. *Who?* came back
at her.

Shadith. Friend of Aleytys. You?

Grey. Shadith?

You've met me.

No. . . .

When I sang through Lee's body.

What?

Shadith the singer. From the diadem.

Lee! More energy in the mindvoice, then pain, then a
sudden fear and anguish. *Another dream.*

No. Lee's nowhere near here, and you're not dreaming.
She willed herself to drift closer to him; she couldn't think

talk and shift positions at the same time, so she gave herself
successive pushes between fragments of speech. *Head . . .
sent me and. . . Taggert . . . after Ticutt dropped . . . out of
. . . no, you wouldn't know . . .* In each of the pauses she
surged closer. *When she didn't . . . hear from you . . . after
four months . . . Head sent Ticutt . . . to see . . . what he
could . . . find out . . . when he stopped . . . reporting . . .
Head waited . . . for Aleytys, but we . . . figured . . . it was
a trap for . . . her, so she went . . . somewhere else . . .
suck Kell off . . . so we wouldn't have to . . . fight him off
. . . while we looked for . . . you! Uh!* She wrapped herself
around him. *Grey?*

Real?

Feel that. She pinched his arm hard, pushing back her
dismay at how wasted it felt.

He shuddered, the contact closer to breaking him than those
eternities of nothingness. She held him and let him sob and
struggle into calm, knowing it was good that she was here
instead of Aleytys to see his weakness and help him deal with
it. For his pride's sake and Lee's place in his life. He'd dealt
with Aleytys taking over his position as premier Hunter.
After all, he'd been expecting that to happen; he was aging
and it was the natural order of things for him to pass on into
other aspects of Hunters as he withdrew from active field
service. That this had come before he was ready to retire and it
was his lover who replaced him, that had been difficult to
swallow, but he was strong enough in himself to accept that,
and her special heritage had in a way eased the transition.
And he'd seen her grieve for her son, he'd comforted her and
helped her through it. This was different. Not something he
wanted between himself and Aleytys. Shadith was a stranger
to him, a name, an acquaintance he could trust enough to fall
apart in front of without shame or a sense he'd have to live
with the memory of his breakdown every time he saw her.
She waited in silence, holding him, saying nothing, letting
him wear through the reaction and come shuddering back into
control.

Where's Lee? he said finally.

Vrithian. Look, if you concentrate and will yourself along, you can move. A minute, I can show you. . . . Linfy?

Uh-huh?

Got us located?

Yah.

Who's closest to us? What direction?

She felt the brushing tickle of his subsonics, then it moved on. A moment later, sounding more confident than before, with more than a touch of cockiness, he said, *Go left and ease back toward me, like you're coming down a lazy hill.*

Gotcha. You hear that, Grey? No? Hmmm. Well, listen. She repeated what Linfyar had said, altering directions to fit his orientation. "I think all of us ought to get together. I'm getting glimmerings of maybe a plan.*

She felt the straining of his body, the hard knots in what muscle he had left as he struggled to do something he didn't know how to do, powered by desire and will. They were moving faster, she was sure of it, she could actually sense the medium, it felt like half-set gelatin. His will blended with hers was more effective than hers alone. Her optimism increased. If they could build up enough momentum in here, maybe she could jump them all out. After all, she was experienced in this sort of leap, popping from the diadem matrix into the body she was wearing now. Of course, she had Aleytys powering that jump and guiding her, but maybe, just maybe . . .

They slammed into another form. Grey grabbed at it; Shadith wrapped herself around them both and did her best to steady their tumble. When they were quieted, she *touched* the other. Ticutt. Cautious Ticutt, who went into nothing without thinking it through three times and then again. *Ticutt,* she said. *Shadith. A friend of Aleytys. Grey's here with me.*

Ticutt went stiff. Even in his mind there was almost no response.

*You got that? I come to get you out of this. (chuckle) I suppose I mean get *us* out now.*

Silence a moment longer, then quiet slow words, no emotion in them, "spoken" with the mild precision of his ordinary speech. *A good trick. If you can do it.* The mindvoice shook a little on the last words, but he wouldn't allow himself to show more of the terrors that haunted him, couldn't allow anyone to know how shattering his relief was. Grey could weep and shiver and purge his self-created demons because Shadith was the only witness. Precise and prideful, jealous of the reputation he had for his calm assessment of possibilities in the most unnerving circumstances—and with Grey there to see him falter—Ticutt could not allow himself to show any of the demons working on him.

Well, she said, *I hadn't planned on being in here with you when I started this. But I've got an idea or two. Come on. Let's go find Taggert.*

He's here too? Grey spoke more slowly than before; he was running on the dregs of his strength, and there was nothing here to replenish it.

A little way off. Point us, Linfy.

Uh-huh. Tickle of subsonics passing over them, moving on. "Left again. Turn. Turn. Turn. Stop! Go on in that direction.*

Got it. And you come over to us, Linfy. Then we start working on busting out of here.

Got it.

Ticutt, if you put your mind to it, you can move yourself. Keep hold of us and shove.

This time she rode a power that woke in her a wild excitement, like the times she'd handled Lee's talent and felt that surge of strength that was only barely within her control. They cannoned into Taggert and went spinning into nowhere, finally steadied, rocked as Linfyar landed on them, steadied again.

Hi, Tag. That old acquaintance again.

Shadow. What the hell.

Me and Grey and Ticutt and Linfyar.

Grey! You all right, man?

He can't hear you, Tag. Looks like I'm the only one who can talk in here. Umm. Maybe not. Maybe I can be a kind of switchboard. Focus on me, Tag. Focus on me, Ticutt. Focus on me, Linfy. Can you all hear me now?

Yes. *Yes.* *Yes.* *Yes.*

Echoes bounced about inside her skull. She waited till the
worst was over, then she said, "Tag, keep the focus on me
and see if you can talk to the others."

Right. Grey, can you hear this?

Coming through. Sorry to hear you, old friend.

Sorrier to be here. What did it to you?

*Got a chance to put my hands on the Ajin. Looked good,
fast snatch and out. No oppos worth mentioning. Got a
handful of Ajin—and here I am."

Uh . . . huh! Ticut, you listening?

*I hear you both. Same with me. I got what looked like a
safe shot. I took it. Here I am.*

Uh . . . huh! Shadow, you still hearing this?

*Yes. Looks like we tripped the trigger when we put the
claws in. Linfy, you listening?*

Uh . . . huh! Shadow.

*Right. (chuckle) Listen, everyone. I said I had had a few
ideas. Grey, did you notice how much faster and easier we
made the move for Taggert when Ticutt was helping with the
push?*

I noticed. Lot more energy.

*Energy increase feels geometric rather than additive. Which
is interesting. Ordinary sounds don't seem to travel in here,
but Linfyar can make sounds and hear them a long way past
both ends of our range. He tried out the top end and didn't
get anywhere. Then he tried the low end. He located you for
me with some very low notes, about as far down as he can
go. Don't bother telling me sound waves that long are lousy
for echo location. It shouldn't work, but it does. Which
means something, but who the hell knows what? I sure don't.
But I don't have to know how it works to use it. What I think
is this: we should link up with Linfy and give him energy to
push his notes way out so he can explore this miserable hole
for us. If he can find some kind of, well, edge, something to
push against, we can try busting through it. I don't know
where we'll be if we break through, but just about anything's
better than this. Even dead. Don't you think? If any of you
has a better idea, say something. No? Right, then, focus
through me. Linfy, I'm going to start feeding you some push;

pinch me if it gets more than you can handle. You start feeling about and see what you can find.*

Got it, Shadow.

Here we go. Start looking, imp.

AVOSING
the lines converge

Stretched out on a grassy knoll that kneaded itself to her shape whenever she shifted position, a pleasant noisy stream running behind her, huge horans rising on three sides of her, invisible kuskus singing in them, their five-fingered leaves whispering just loud enough to be heard over the water, Aleytys watched Avosing grow larger in a viewscreen thirty meters on a side. Ship nudged into an orbit that kept it stationary over a mountain range that ran through a broad continent, part woodlands, part immense prairies, rippling grass that must have reached horizon to horizon for anyone standing on the ground. "Where's the trap?"

"There." A flashing light in the mountains. "We are maintaining position directly over it."

"Any difficulty with probes or visuals?"

"Aleytys." Ship sounded pained. Its voice had startled her the first time she'd heard it. Shareem's voice. For a while it curdled her stomach every time ship spoke to her, but she didn't try to change it. Shareem's voice. After what he'd done to her. Why? What did it mean? He tormented her, he killed her, why did he have to own this small piece of her? Lot of whys. There was an urgency in her to know as much as she could about Kell now that outside urgencies no longer existed for her. He was dead, but she had as yet unshaped plans for digging into him like a zenologist into a city mound.

"And the trigger?"

"There also."

An inert square bloomed on the image of the world, isolating a single mountain, a huge long-dead volcano with a lake in its crumbling center. The square spread out, another square bloomed in the center of it, a schematic showing the pier, the landing field, the outer structures, the confusing web of tunnels running through the mountain's stone. At a confluence of lines near the edge of the stone she saw the flare marking the scaffolding that supported the mechanisms which created and held in place the pocket universe and brought into being the umbilical joining the two when anyone attempted to lay hands on the Ajin with aggressive intent. A short way on, a pinlight flashed. The trigger. So the Ajin was home, waiting for her, though he didn't know that.

Aleytys sat up, the knoll shifting shape to conform to her unexpressed wishes, reading muscles and posture to gain a disconcertingly accurate knowledge of her intentions before she'd formulated them to herself. "What's down there?"

Beside the map, ship listed the number of mercenaries, technicians and support personnel. Shadith, Taggert and Linfyar weren't among those. Either they had been sucked into the trap already or they hadn't gotten this far. Aleytys sighed. "Weapons? Anything to worry us?"

"Nothing the warbots can't handle. I'll watch. If the numbers are too great, I'll thin your weeds for you. Take Abra with you—we're linked; even stone that thick won't break the bond."

Aleytys got to her feet. "I'll do that. Get me to the lander."

The lander swooped down, ignoring fire from the base, shrugging off beams and missiles with a contemptuous ease. It settled onto the landing field and disappeared beneath a hot yellow dome as one side opened out to let Aleytys, Abra and six warbots come sweeping out. The six 'bots moved out in tight circle about Aleytys, walking with the sinuous flickering stride of the scorpions they vaguely resembled.

With the warbots wiping all resistance before and behind, irresistible as a tsunami, she swept through the trees and the mercenaries, burned her way into the main building; she blew the offices and central control to smoking shards, moved farther in, striding along just short of a run, mouth set in a grim line, hair blowing free; nothing could touch her, nothing could stop her, into the lava caves she went, leaving two 'bots to guard the mouth of the main tunnel and two others to search out and destroy anything or anyone that attacked them.

Behind her the mercenaries and technicians and others still alive began gathering whatever they could get their hands on and heading for the boat, the fliers or the few hidden trails leading out of the crater. Some among them stayed behind, those that had bought what the Ajin was selling; they retreated into the rockfalls and sniped at the 'bots or tried to work their way into the tunnels and rescue the Ajin.

Aleytys stopped before the door to the Ajin's quarters, stood back while one of the warbots melted the lock out of it and kicked it in. The 'bot skittered inside on multiple multisegmented legs. Its armored scanners whirled over the six surfaces of the room, its weapons pattered at high speed, taking out the lasers in the walls, the mines in floor and ceiling, shedding everything thrown at it, letting the remaining 'bot shield Aleytys and Abra from the flare-offs. The room was clean in seconds. The 'bot skittered to one side and waited.

Abra beside her, Aleytys strode into the room, looked around. The walls were melted and congealing, splatters of cooling stone were flung across the cratered floor, most of the furniture was torn and leaking its stuffing, smoldering here and there, adding its stench to that of hot stone and charred wood. A slim metal case leaned against a smoking chair, its neat, precisely machined lines like a shout in all that disorder. "What's that?"

Abra crossed the room, picked it up, opened the catches. "Psychprobe. Portable. Suggestion: Taggert?"

Aleytys shook her head. "Impossible to say. Where now?"

Abra pointed, moved ahead of her down the hallway. One warbot followed them, the second stayed to guard the door.

Abra stopped at an open door, shone light into the room.

The Ajin lay unconscious in a mess of bloody sheets and blankets, a tangle-web smeared across his naked body, claws at the end of two extensible rods set in wrist and ankle, blood crusted about the wounds, a little still trickling. An hour since the attack, not more, probably less. Shadith and Taggert;

Abra was right about the probe. She moved closer to the door. A metal arm flashed before her, stopping her. "No," Abra said. "Ship says don't pass the door."

"I hear." As the arm dropped, she said, "Turn the light on that small table by the bed." A heavy silver ring gleamed in the harsh glare of the light. She recognized it immediately. The trigger. She *reached* for her power river, filled herself from it, pleased that it seemed to take little more effort even though she'd taken off the diadem, *reached* for the ring.

She couldn't lift it.

That puzzled her. It wasn't that heavy; couldn't be if the man wore the thing. She tried for a firmer hold, but her mindfingers slipped off as if the metal were greased; she staggered backward as her concentration slipped with her *reach*, landed with a whoosh against a foreleg of the 'bot behind her. She straightened and went back to scowling at the ring. What next? Send one of the 'bots after it? She rubbed at the buttock that had slammed into the 'bot's leg. Send it and lose it, if the ship was right. She began prodding delicately at the ring with the fingertips of her outreach, pit-a-pit-a-pit, throttling back the frustration that made her want to scream, pit-a-pit-a-pit, soapy metallic feel under her mindfingers, couldn't get a grip anywhere.

Abruptly she slapped her side. "Aschla's hells, I'm stupid stupid stupid." With a shaky laugh she *reached* for the bedtable and began sliding it slowly and carefully toward the door. It moved with a touch of reluctance, but came along to her tugging without challenging her hold.

She'd moved the table about a meter when a grayish patch formed in the air above it. She stiffened, stopped the table where it was and waited.

The grayness bulged and throbbed. It split, decanting a clump of bodies clinging together. The clump hit the floor with a whistle, several grunts, and a hissing curse, broke apart into five forms. Shadith scrambled onto her feet, pulling Linfyar up with her. Taggert rolled up into a crouch, scanning for trouble. Ticutt came up more slowly, holding himself in tight control. Grey didn't bother getting up, just lifted his torso, bracing himself on his elbow. He grinned at the doorway. "Lee."

She blinked back the tears that blurred her eyes; it was a minute before she could speak. "Well. Good to see you, Grey. At least I think so. You look like a silvercoat after a hard winter."

"You pop the bubble?"

"Not me." She nodded at the bedtable. "I was giving myself fits trying to get hold of that ring."

Shadith walked over to the table, poked at the ring. "This the trigger?"

"According to Kell's ship."

"Uh. I take it he isn't around anymore."

"No."

"Mmm. You know, I think your moving the table messed things up just enough so we could crash out."

"I doubt it. Coincidence, that's all. That I was here." Aleytys turned to the android. "What's ship say about the door?"

Pause. Abra stood poised, head tilted, light making a grotesquerie from the planes of his nonface. "Ship says don't go in yet. Ships feels a force about the doorway. Ships suggests you get hold of the ring."

"And what happens if Shadith tries to lift it?"

Pause. "Don't know."

"Shadow?"

"I can't see spending the rest of my life in this room." She poked tentatively at the ring; over her shoulder she said, "What's Harskari think?"

"Harskari's a long way from here, getting settled in body and home. She said to say hello."

"Ah." She swung around. "And our common curse?"

"Sitting in a lokbox in the ship till I hand it over."

"Um. That sort of complicates things."

"I wouldn't argue with you on that. You want a guarantee? I'll come after you if it comes to that. Promise."

"You know I don't mean anything like that, Lee. I'm just talking to get my nerve up. Here goes." She switched around again and reached for the ring.

She couldn't lift it. When she tried to tighten her hold, her fingers slipped off. "Shit." She tried again. "Like it's greased or something." She looked at her fingers, wiped them on her sweater.

Taggert touched her shoulder. "Let me see what I can do." His fingers slipped off no matter how hard he pinched. He tried shoving the ring sideways off the table. It wouldn't budge. The table tipped over, the ring stuck firmly in the center of it. He picked the table up and set it on its legs.

"That steems to settle that." Aleytys looked quickly at Grey, turned away; he was stretched out on the rug, his eyes closed, his gaunt face still; he hardly seemed to breathe. "Tag, see if you can find something to push that table through the door to me. Stay as far back as you can." She glanced at Grey, then Ticutt. "Hurry a little, please."

Taggert frowned at the nearest of the claw rods, shook his head; he prowled about the room, found a closet, a wooden rod holding some of the Ajin's clothing; he knocked it loose and brought it back, held it flat in front of him. "Should be long enough." He set the table close to the door, then used the rod to nudge it through.

The table juddered through the doorway, the ring suddenly loose, clunking against its top as it shivered from the rug to the tiles of the hallway. Taggert stepped back and stood leaning on the rod, watching Aleytys as she scooped up the ring. She ran fingertips over the incised design on its square flat top. "I can't read anything in this," she said. "Abra, what about the doorway now?"

A long silence, then the android spoke. "Ship says, still activity around the doorway. Ship does not—repeat, does not—think you should be the one to try crossing. Ship says Kell has certainly set special snares for you." Silence again. "Ship says since all the captives are out, she is going to burn out the scaffolding, let the bubbleverse collapse. That should remove the last danger. Ship says wait, don't do anything yet. Ship is coming in low to make sure of the cut, says she stops talking now because she is busy. Wait."

Aleytys drew her hand across her forehead, down the side of

her face, pressed it against her mouth, her eyes fixed on Grey.

Shadith glanced at her, went to kneel beside him. "He's all right, Lee, just taking it easy."

Grey chuckled suddenly, tried to sit up. Taggert dragged a chair over to him, raised his shoulders so he could lean against it. He looked exhausted but alert. His hands were shaking on his thighs; the cloth of his trousers, bunched about wasted legs, trembled with the trembling of his hands. "Don't fuss, Lee."

"I'll fuss if I want. Look at you."

"I have felt more heroic."

"Well, it's better than dead. I thought . . ." She broke off as Abra touched her arm.

"Ship says scaffolding is gone, archira. No activity detectable about the doorway."

Aleytys looked down. The ring was melting into smoke that curled away from her hand, fading into nothing. Another breath and even the smoke was gone. She flung herself into the bedroom and knelt beside Grey. She caught hold of his hands, lifted them to her face, her eyes on his. He smiled at her, the hurts between them forgotten for the moment, the need back. "Stretch out," she said after a while. "Let me work on you."

Shadith scrambled to her feet, stood watching a moment as Aleytys set her hands on Grey's chest. *Lee's changed,* she thought. *More settled, I think. That's the word. Settled. Yes. She knows who she is now and where she's going.* Linfyar brushed past her, went to poke at the sodden figure of the Ajin, radiating satisfaction. The Ajin had never liked him, a feeling fully reciprocated. Shadith sighed, stretched, then shooed him away. The Ajin was twisted in sprawl that made her back ache as she inspected him. She looked up as Taggert came to stand beside her. "How long does that gas keep them under?"

"Couple hours." He felt about his jacket, pulled out two patch seals. "I'll slip the claws, you paste these on."

Shadith nodded. She pulled the backing off one of the

patches. The claws whipped out of the Ajin's wrist and blood started to pump. She slapped on the patch, smoothed it out, moved along the bed, dealt with the ankle wound as Taggert collapsed the second claw. She stepped back. "I'll get a wet towel so we can clean him up a bit. You pull the tangle off." She felt in her pockets. "I've got cord somewhere."

"Never mind, Shadow, I've got slave wire."

She nodded. "Back in a minute. And hey, you ought to hunt in those things you dumped for something he can wear. Unless you prefer him wrapped like a piece of meat." She looked around. Aleytys was bent over Ticutt. Grey was asleep. "Just had a thought. And you know what you can do with your funny faces. Grey and Ticutt aren't going to want to put those stinking clothes back on once they've had a bath."

Taggert took out a flat tin. "Get the towel, Shadow."

"Yessir, yessir, happy to serve you, yessir." Giggling, she trotted into the fresher. "Hey, Tag, you ought to see this, there's a tub in here big enough to float a harem."

"Get the towel, Shadow." Laughter in his voice.

She pulled a towel off the rack, bunched it in the basin and turned the water on. With a groaning yawn, she stretched, then splashed handful of cold water on her face. She yawned again, dabbled her fingers in the water. *Got to talk to Po' sometime soon; he's probably whirling in his whatever with all that's going on.* She wrung the towel out and went back into the bedroom.

The Ajin was laid out like a corpse, cleaned up, dressed, bound with Taggert's slave wire. Shadith checked him again. He should be waking in a bit; when she *touched* him, she could feel a sluggish stirring. She smiled, thinking about what he'd be going through when he did wake *.You earned every second of it too. Mmm. Harp. And a chat with Po'*. She left the bedroom and tried to leave the apartment, but the warbot at the door wouldn't let her pass.

"Lee."

"What, Shadow?"

"Got some stuff I want to get. Tell that 'bot to let me out."

"Go where? It's quiet in here, but the 'bots outside say thre are still snipers in the rubble. They're clearing them out, but . . ."

"I'm not going outside, just over to the rooms where the Ajin put me. Left my harp there. I want it back. Send the extra 'bot with me if you're nervous."

"I'll do that. You'll probably need it to power the door. We chewed up the control center when we passed through it. Before you go, Shadow, Grey and Ticutt are going to wake starving. And Linfyar's hungry. Any kind of kitchen in here? I don't want to leave until we're all ready to run."

"Linfy's always hungry. God knows how big he's going to get before he stops growing. Kitchen. Uh-huh. The Ajin was pretty paranoid. Has a separate power source and aircon system for these rooms. Kept his food separate too, sealed in an autochef Kell had his androids build for him." Shadith grinned. "Poison tasters and all. Come on. I'll show you."

Lights flaring, the warbot crouched in the sitting room. Shadith looked around, sniffed cautiously. With the door open the air wasn't too bad. The viewscreen was gray glass, a mirror reflecting the 'bot, a figure out of nightmare sketched in light and shadow. The room had a dulled dusty feel, abandoned, though she'd been gone less than one night; it looked like any cheap hotel room after the guests had left. She jerked the velvet curtain to one side and went into the bedroom.

The air smelled staler in the bedroom; it was harder to breathe in there. The harp in its case stood beside the bed where she'd left it. She started to hoist the strap onto her shoulder, then frowned at the screen. The Ajin's stash. He had to have the gold and the sweetamber to pay off whatever runner he dealt with. Those types never heard of credit. Should be in his rooms somewhere. *Now there's a hoard I'd like to get my hands on. I'm not riding free anymore; have to make my own way.* Her reflection floated in the glass, insubstantial as a ghost. *Ghost. Old Po'. This is about the only place I'm going to have privacy enough. Well, Shadow, quit dithering and do something.* She let the strap fall and stretched out on the bed, resting her forearm across her eyes to shut out the lights from the other room. With her tiredness in this the dregs of a very long night, it was hard to quiet mind and body enough without slipping too far and dropping into sleep.

What is happening there, Shadow? Who was that came down like a fire wind? (agitation, suspicion, anger)

Hello, Old Po'. Relax.

Relax!

Sure. It's over. My friends are sprung. The Ajin's in Hunters' hands. And you don't have to worry about that ship. Belongs to a friend of mine. She tends to overreact at times, but she's good to have around if there's problems.

I've got lice in my forest. (indignant grumbling) *Blown there by the big wind your friend made.*

Hey, Old Po', don't you try telling me you don't know what to do with them. Hah! You and your soft sides, you run your forest hard and tight, god help anyone tries to go against you. Which reminds me, let Perolat know I'm all right, huh? Tell her what's happened and why I came here. I'd tell her myself, but that'd just make trouble for her. The closest I'm going to get to Dusta is that islet where I parked my lander. Listen, Po' Annutj, what I'm gonna say is important. There'll be trouble when Hunters hands over the Ajin. I think I can talk Grey into hauling him off to Pajungg itself to turn him over. That'd give you a nineday or so to get ready to handle the homeworlders. Ajin's been making them look stupid and small; when their egos start expanding, they're going to come out stomping. Um. Maybe it'd be a good idea to organize a little guerrilla activity on your own, something to keep them honest without being too serious about it. But that's your problem now. How you deal with it is up to you. 'F you don't mind, I'll come back in a few years to see how things worked out and we could have that chat we talked about but never did.

Ancient child, I'll miss you.

Ahh, no you won't, Old Po', you'll be a lot too busy.

Never too busy. The All keep you, Shadow.

Well, see you, friend.

Shadith shook herself out of the half-doze and sat up. The

air in the bedroom was heavy and dusty, and it smelled. She caught hold of the harp case's strap, slid it over her shoulder, coughed, got to her feet, coughed again, wrinkled her nose in disgust and went out.

Aleytys and the others were sitting at the Ajin's dining table, eating and listening to Linfy tell about their part in the Ajin's campaign. Taggert looked up, saw her, waved her to the empty chair beside him. Sensing the divided interest of his audience, Linfy went back to eating.

Aleytys pushed at her hair, smiled at Shadith. "You've had quite a time here."

"Surprised the hell out of me first time it happened." Shadith began filling her plate. "My sisters used to do that. Not me. I thought the art died with them. Apparently not. Though maybe it's just the pollen."

Grey set his cup down, shook his head. "Hard to believe. It's a good thing I didn't get a look at you in there, Shadow." He passed a hand over shaggy hair. The gray streaks were growing into patches, more of them than she remembered from the last time she'd seen him. He was relaxed and calm now; the drawn look was gone.

She shrugged. "It's a problem I'll grow out of." She touched the belly of the cha pot—still hot—and filled her cup. "Where we going from here?"

"That's up in the air still, Shadow," Aleytys said.

"Me and Linfy, we need lift to my lander. I borrwoed it from a friend and he wants it back."

"That I can do. Come on board with me and tell ship where to go." Aleytys looked around the table. "What about the rest of you?" She chuckled. "Between you all and the smugglers, there must be more ships than rocks in the Belt."

Taggert nodded. "I could use a lift. The Ajin collected me with the other runners, so I've got no way back. Besides, I always wanted to see the inside of a Vryhh ship."

Grey frowned. "Mine's been in orbit about Avosing for the better part of a year. For all I know the Pajunggs could have towed it away."

Ticutt looked up. "Still there when I got here. I used it as a drop station for my reports."

Aleytys looked at her hands. "I didn't see it, but I didn't waste time when I got here, just came charging ahead. Well, I was in a hurry. Ship didn't say anything." She tilted her chair onto its back legs so she could look through the doorway. "Abra. Come here, please."

The android moved with silky grace into the opening. "Archira?"

"Ask ship to locate . . . you tell it, Grey."

As he ran through the characteristics of his ship and what signals she'd respond to, Aleytys sat frowning at the table. She picked up a fork and began drawing lines in a drop of gravy. When Grey finished, she tapped the tines on the table and watched the planes of the android's nonface.

After a moment's silence, Abra said, "Ship says Hunter ship is in the orbit described and appears undamaged."

"Good. Tell ship to be ready to pick us up in about an hour. What's happening with the snipers out front?"

"Warbots report eleven killed, three injured, seventeen fled, two still firing. All other life sources have left the crater. Ah! Now, only one sniper left."

"Something else we'd better get settled." Grey sat up, waited until he had their attention. "The Field Ops' share of the fee. I'm out of it, it's up to you all, but it seems to me the one who's done the most to earn it is young Shadow here. Hunter or not."

Shadith shook her head. "Just make compliations." She grinned. "I figure the Ajin's stash would be pay enough for my trouble."

Taggert gave a shout of laughter. "I'm sure you do. Well, Shadow, you awesome child, far as I'm concerned, you more than earned it."

Ticutt nodded, then sat silent again, removed from all this, locked in his head, fighting shadows he made for himself.

"Right. I'll ask ship to find the stash for you." Aleytys set her fork across her plate. "About the fee. I'm out too. That leaves you, Tag, and Ticutt; the two of you can figure percentages later. Who's taking charge of the body in there?"

"Grey," Taggert said. "You're Hunter of Record, Grey; the rest of this is none of their damn business, those Pajunggs."

Grey sighed. "I was hoping to head straight home."

Taggert's pale eyes laughed at him; his off-center nose seemed to twitch. "Time you stopped lazing around letting the rest of us do all the work."

"Umm. Grey."

"Shadow?"

"I'd kind of appreciate it if you hauled the Ajin to Pajungg itself before you turned him over. There's some good people here who could use the time to get set for what the Grand Doawai and his creeps are going to do to them."

Ticutt looked up. "Perolat?"

"Uh-huh. And a bunch more."

He sucked in a long breath, let it out. "Add my voice to Shadow's."

Shadith waited to see if he'd say more, but he was finished.

Grey hesitated. "Lee . . ."

"I could take your ship in tow?"

He looked down at his hands, a private man who didn't like exposing his feelings to outsiders. "We've got some talking to do," he said finally. "Your ship's as good a place as any."

WOLFF

the diadem cleared off the board goodbye to the RMoahl

Wolff system.

Teegah's Limit.

The Pajungg Hunt was completed. Grey, Ticutt, Taggert were sitting in the Records and Accounting room at Hunters, flaking their file reports. With Aleyty's first ship signed over to her, Shadith had taken off to hunt up Swartheld/Quayle so she could return his lander. She'd be back eventually; the greater part of the Ajin's stash was in Aleytys's lokbox at Wolff's only bank.

The RMoahl ship was a dark blotch filling the screen.

"Call them," Aleytys said.

A square bloomed in the center of the screen, in the screen a face that only another RMoahl could love: dark leathery skin, flat nose, thin horizontal nostrils, long upper lip, mouth a gash filled with omnivore's teeth. Antennae twitched from pompoms of orange fuzz. Great yellow eyes with slit pupils blinked slowly. The RMoahl second, Mok'tekii.

"Show me to them."

Mok-tekii's antennae whipped about, the orange fur of his pompoms stirred as if blown by an erratic wind.

Aleytys sat up, the grassy knoll remolding itself to support her. "Hounds of the RMoahl, how would you like to quit this tedious watch and go home?"

"Don't mock us, Aleytys Hunter."

"I do not mock, Mok-tekii Second. Or if I do, only a little. You've complicated my life quite a lot, you know. Well, that's finished now. I have come into my heritage and rid myself of yours." She opened the box on her lap and lifted out the diadem, held it up, the flexible round draped over her hand. "I hope you take better care of it this time. It's empty now and hungry. If you want it still, come get it."

"Forgive us, despina. We do indeed desire the diadem, but to come aboard that ship . . ."

"I understand. Abra." When the android was in the viewrange, she pointed at it and said, "Abra will wait in the lock for whomever or whatever you choose to send. Meaning no discourtesy, Hound, I'm quite as reluctant to visit as you are."

The diadem passed smoothly into RMoahl claws.

The koeiyi Sensayii appeared in the screen, went through an elaborate salute. "All honor is yours, Aleytys Hunter. The debt is ours. Should you have need, we three will come however far you call."

Aleytys suppressed a chuckle. The koeiyi had shown little sign he possessed anything resembling humor. *All in the best heroic tradition,* she thought. *Ah well, he means well.* She sketched a bow of her own, spread her hands. "No debt at all, koeiyi. Let there be peace between my kin and yours."

To her relief the koeiyi had nothing more to say. The square blanked and the RMoahl globe ship backed away, began to gather speed. In seconds it was beyond the reach of her screens, running toward the speed it needed to slip into the intersplit and dive toward the RMoahl sun.

WOLFF

signing off

Grey came to her. In a way his time inside the pocket universe had been like a wild trek, stripping away confusions and hurt and anger. He wanted her, needed her, yet he knew he could live well enough without her if they couldn't reach some accommodation that would let them share a life. It wasn't going to be easy. She knew that. He knew it. And quietly he came to her, without fuss he came to her, knowing her more intimately, in his way, than those who lived within her head had known her. Understanding that her need for home was far greater than his, he came to her.

He said beside her as they'd sat so many times, watching the sun go down, watching one of the paler more subtle sunsets, a cloudless sky, the glaciers summer-shrunken.

What she'd grasped on Ibex she knew more intimately now. In the first part of her life she'd had a goal that was simple and essentially extrinsic. What lay before her now was more complex. The thing she wanted now lived in words like society, relationship, friend, compromise, patience, involvement, building. And time. Vrithian had altered her outlook on a lot of things. Time to be a part of Wolff in ways she'd never been. She didn't even know the parents of the girl who took care of her horses. Head had produced her when Aleytys asked for someone. Who was she? What was her life like at home? Why did she prefer a small cramped apartment built onto a stable? *Why wonder they suspect me, the Wolfflan, no wonder they don't trust me. What do they know about me? Nothing except rumor.* She smiled to herself. *Turn me into your comfortable neighborhood housewife worrying about*

*paying the bills and what her kids were doing with whom
Kids? I suppose so. Now that I have a past and a future to
give them. My Sharl, my lovely son, you came too soon. I'm
not going to look for you; I've said farewell to you twice now
and that's enough. Well, we've got time. If nothing else, you
and I have time.*

The last embers of the sunset died. The fire was down to
coals and the room was beginning to chill. Grey rose from his
chair, stood waiting for her.

She went to him, leaned against him, enjoying the mingled
odors of hair, flesh and clothing.

Wordless, they walked to the door. Their talking was done.
She touched a sensor, let him draw her into the hall.

Behind them the shutters rolled across the windows. Crawling over the coals, the fire moved slower and slower until it
died completely. The house creaked and sighed into its summer temper and settled into a deepening stillness.